# CONTINENTAL
# CRIMES

# CONTINENTAL CRIMES

*edited and introduced by*
MARTIN EDWARDS

BRITISH LIBRARY

First published 2017 by
The British Library
96 Euston Road
London NW1 2DB

Introduction and notes copyright © 2017 Martin Edwards

Cataloguing in Publication Data
A catalogue record for this book is available from the British Library

ISBN 978 0 7123 5679 4

Typeset by Tetragon, London
Printed and bound by TJ International Ltd

# CONTENTS

# INTRODUCTION

At first sight, a book which collects classic British crime stories set on the continent of Europe may seem an unlikely enterprise. It is often assumed that detective novelists like Agatha Christie, who established their reputations during 'the Golden Age of Murder' between the world wars, tended to be rather narrow and parochial in their outlook. Colin Watson said in his amusing book *Snobbery with Violence* (1971) that their books' central appeal to readers was a 'familiar homeliness'. He argued that the typical setting for their mysteries was 'a cross between a village and a commuters' dormitory in the South of England... It would have a well-attended church, an inn with reasonable accommodation for itinerant detective-inspectors... and shops—including a chemist's where weed-killer and hair-dye might conveniently be bought.'

Although writers did often set their stories against such a background, a great many—and Christie herself was a prominent example—were much more adventurous than Watson suggested. The truth is that crime writers had long understood that foreign settings fascinated their readers. People who had little or no prospect of ever being able to afford to travel extensively took pleasure in experiencing something of the appeal of exotic locales while devouring a good mystery. This was so even in the Victorian and Edwardian eras. For example, B.C. Skottowe's intriguing and unusual mystery *Sudden Death* (1886) is set in part in Homburg, while A.E.W. Mason created a popular French detective, Inspector Hanaud, who first appeared in *At the Villa Rose* (1910), and made his final bow as late as 1946 in *The House in Lordship Lane*, the only book in the series set in England.

The crime writing career of Freeman Wills Crofts got off to a cracking start with the publication in 1920 of his first novel, *The Cask*. The story opens with a startling discovery at a London dock, but Inspector Burnley's investigation soon takes him across the Channel, and much of the book details his collaboration with his French counterpart Lefarge as the police forces of London and Paris strive to bring a ruthless murderer to justice. Christie's debut novel, *The Mysterious Affair at Styles*, appeared in the same year as *The Cask*; it introduced Hercule Poirot, a retired Belgian policeman with a genius for detection. At first the book made less of an impression than Crofts' novel, although eventually it earned a large and devoted readership. Poirot returned in *The Murder on the Links* (1923), in which a millionaire's desperate plea causes the detective to travel to France, where almost the whole of the story is set. Unfortunately, he arrives too late to prevent the man's murder, and the local police officer, Giraud, treats the elderly Belgian with condescension. Crofts' interest lay in describing how meticulous police work enabled justice to be done, whereas Christie's focus was on concocting a baffling whodunit mystery to be solved with the aid of Poirot's genius. Even though neither author specialised in atmospherics, in each book, the French background enhanced the appeal of a cleverly conceived mystery.

Countless Golden Age detective novels and short stories made good use of settings in continental Europe. They included an excellent story by Christopher Bush about a serial killer called 'Marius' who is determined to keep one step ahead of the police. In *The Perfect Murder Case* (1929), the early scenes are set in London, but the action switches to France, and a dramatic confrontation at the climax of the novel takes place on a French island. Sir Basil Thomson, whose varied career included a spell as head of the CID, employed continental settings in several of his books about Richardson, a policeman who starts out as a constable and enjoys an astonishingly rapid rise to the top of Scotland Yard; *The Corpse of the Dead Diplomat* (1935), also known as *Richardson Goes Abroad*, is set almost entirely in France, and the reliable Sergeant Cooper makes good use of his linguistic skills in the course of his investigation.

Sometimes, real life events on the Continent complicated attempts by authors to capture foreign settings authentically. Freeman Wills Crofts, having undertaken a Mediterranean cruise himself, hit on the idea of writing a book which featured a very similar cruise. By the time *Found Floating* (1937) saw the light of day, however, circumstances had changed: the Spanish Civil War had begun. Crofts' ship's itinerary had included a stop at Cadiz, and he had to include a prefatory note explaining that the trip taken in the story by William Carrington and his family also pre-dated the conflict.

Christie, a seasoned traveller, whose second husband, Max Mallowan, was an archaeologist whom she met in the Middle East, continued to make economical yet telling use of overseas locations. They supplied the background for many of her most impressive novels, including *Murder on the Orient Express* (1934) and *Death on the Nile* (1937), as well as one or two of her worst, notably *The Mystery of the Blue Train* (1928) and a thriller written late in her career, *Passenger to Frankfurt* (1970). Even Miss Marple, so closely associated with village life, found herself on the other side of the Atlantic in *A Caribbean Mystery* (1964). It is fair to say that the character types in Christie's books set overseas scarcely vary from those set in England, but it is a mistake to see this solely as a sign of her limitations as a writer; rather, it reflects a key element in the enduring global appeal of her work—she recognised that human nature is much the same all the world over.

After the Second World War, overseas travel became more affordable, and many more people took the opportunity to holiday abroad. This trend was reflected in crime fiction. Writers such as John Bude, whose first four books were set in attractive English locations, namely Cornwall, the Lake District, the Sussex Downs, and Cheltenham, moved with the times by venturing overseas on trips that combined enjoyable holidays with research for his books; his post-war titles included *Murder on Montparnasse* (1949), *Death on the Riviera* (1952), and *A Telegram from Le Touquet* (1956).

In more recent times, many more books by foreign writers have been translated into English, and 'Scandi-Noir' has become especially popular. But British writers have continued to produce notable work set on the continent—examples include the Aurelio Zen books written by the late Michael Dibdin and set in Italy, Martin Walker's series about the French cop Bruno, and Robert Wilson's novels set in Spain and Portugal.

As the world grows smaller, more and more crime fans are seizing the chance to see for themselves the scenes of crime in their favourite continental mysteries, whether written by Britons or local authors. This collection of stories about crime on the Continent, which includes contributions from some of the genre's greatest names as well as several who are much less renowned, may suggest a few more destinations for an enjoyable visit.

MARTIN EDWARDS
www.martinedwardsbooks.com

# THE NEW CATACOMB

## Arthur Conan Doyle

When one reads the wide-ranging fiction of Arthur Conan Doyle (1859–1930), it does not take a Sherlock Holmes to deduce that he saw a great deal of the world. As one of his biographers, Michael Coren, said, travel 'always rejuvenated [him]. He enjoyed the different assumptions and attitudes that he found abroad and the new challenges he encountered.' Sherlock may have felt most at home in foggy, gas-lit London, but even he ventured across the Channel in 'The Final Problem', apparently meeting his death at the Reichenbach Falls. Doyle had visited the scene of Holmes' fateful encounter with Professor Moriarty a few years earlier, after speaking at a conference in Lucerne, and making his way to Lucerne via Meiringen and the Falls.

Doyle visited Italy several times, and the country provided the backdrop for this example of his taste for the macabre. Written at a time when Holmes had not yet returned from the dead, and Doyle was trying his hand at various types of fiction, this dark little story first appeared, improbably enough, in *The 'Sunlight' Year-Book* in 1898, a compendium produced by Lever Brothers, the manufacturers of 'Sunlight' soap, under the title 'Burger's Secret'.

'LOOK HERE, BURGER,' SAID KENNEDY, 'I DO WISH THAT YOU would confide in me.'

The two famous students of Roman remains sat together in Kennedy's comfortable room overlooking the Corso. The night was cold, and they had both pulled up their chairs to the unsatisfactory Italian stove which threw out a zone of stuffiness rather than of warmth. Outside under the bright winter stars lay the modern Rome, the long, double chain of the electric lamps, the brilliantly lighted cafés, the rushing carriages, and the dense throng upon the footpaths. But inside, in the sumptuous chamber of the rich young English archæologist, there was only old Rome to be seen. Cracked and timeworn friezes hung upon the walls, grey old busts of senators and soldiers with their fighting heads and their hard, cruel faces peered out from the corners. On the centre table, amidst a litter of inscriptions, fragments, and ornaments, there stood the famous reconstruction by Kennedy of the Baths of Caracalla, which excited such interest and admiration when it was exhibited in Berlin. Amphoræ hung from the ceiling, and a litter of curiosities strewed the rich red Turkey carpet. And of them all there was not one which was not of the most unimpeachable authenticity, and of the utmost rarity and value; for Kennedy, though little more than thirty, had a European reputation in this particular branch of research, and was, moreover, provided with that long purse which either proves to be a fatal handicap to the student's energies, or, if his mind is still true to its purpose, gives him an enormous advantage in the race for fame. Kennedy had often been seduced by whim and pleasure from his studies, but his mind was an incisive one, capable of long and concentrated efforts which ended in sharp reactions of sensuous languor. His handsome face, with its high, white forehead, its aggressive nose, and its somewhat loose and sensual mouth, was a fair index of the compromise between strength and weakness in his nature.

Of a very different type was his companion, Julius Burger. He came of a curious blend, a German father and an Italian mother, with the robust qualities of the North mingling strangely with the softer graces of the South. Blue Teutonic eyes lightened his sunbrowned face, and above them rose a square, massive forehead, with a fringe of close yellow curls lying round it. His strong, firm jaw was clean-shaven, and his companion had frequently remarked how much it suggested those old Roman busts which peered out from the shadows in the corners of his chamber. Under its bluff German strength there lay always a suggestion of Italian subtlety, but the smile was so honest, and the eyes so frank, that one understood that this was only an indication of his ancestry, with no actual bearing upon his character. In age and in reputation, he was on the same level as his English companion, but his life and his work had both been far more arduous. Twelve years before, he had come as a poor student to Rome, and had lived ever since upon some small endowment for research which had been awarded to him by the University of Bonn. Painfully, slowly, and doggedly, with extraordinary tenacity and single-mindedness, he had climbed from rung to rung of the ladder of fame, until now he was a member of the Berlin Academy, and there was every reason to believe that he would shortly be promoted to the Chair of the greatest of German Universities. But the singleness of purpose which had brought him to the same high level as the rich and brilliant Englishman, had caused him in everything outside their work to stand infinitely below him. He had never found a pause in his studies in which to cultivate the social graces. It was only when he spoke of his own subject that his face was filled with life and soul. At other times he was silent and embarrassed, too conscious of his own limitations in larger subjects, and impatient of that small talk which is the conventional refuge of those who have no thoughts to express.

And yet for some years there had been an acquaintanceship which appeared to be slowly ripening into a friendship between these two very different rivals. The base and origin of this lay in the fact that in their own studies each was the only one of the younger men who had knowledge and enthusiasm enough to properly appreciate the other. Their common interests and pursuits had brought them together, and each had been attracted by the other's knowledge. And then gradually something had been added to this. Kennedy had been amused by the frankness and simplicity of his rival, while Burger in turn had been fascinated by the brilliancy and vivacity which had made Kennedy such a favourite in Roman society. I say 'had,' because just at the moment the young Englishman was somewhat under a cloud. A love-affair, the details of which had never quite come out, had indicated a heartlessness and callousness upon his part which shocked many of his friends. But in the bachelor circles of students and artists in which he preferred to move there is no very rigid code of honour in such matters, and though a head might be shaken or a pair of shoulders shrugged over the flight of two and the return of one, the general sentiment was probably one of curiosity and perhaps of envy rather than of reprobation.

'Look here, Burger,' said Kennedy, looking hard at the placid face of his companion, 'I do wish that you would confide in me.'

As he spoke he waved his hand in the direction of a rug which lay upon the floor. On the rug stood a long, shallow fruit-basket of the light wicker-work which is used in the Campagna, and this was heaped with a litter of objects, inscribed tiles, broken inscriptions, cracked mosaics, torn papyri, rusty metal ornaments, which to the uninitiated might have seemed to have come straight from a dustman's bin, but which a specialist would have speedily recognised as unique of their kind. The pile of odds and ends in the flat wicker-work basket supplied exactly one of those missing links of social development which are of such interest to the student. It was the German who had brought them in, and the Englishman's eyes were hungry as he looked at them.

'I won't interfere with your treasure-trove, but I should very much like to hear about it,' he continued, while Burger very deliberately lit a cigar. 'It is evidently a discovery of the first importance. These inscriptions will make a sensation throughout Europe.'

'For every one here there are a million there!' said the German. 'There are so many that a dozen savants might spend a lifetime over them, and build up a reputation as solid as the Castle of St Angelo.'

Kennedy sat thinking with his fine forehead wrinkled and his fingers playing with his long, fair moustache.

'You have given yourself away, Burger!' said he at last. 'Your words can only apply to one thing. You have discovered a new catacomb.'

'I had no doubt that you had already come to that conclusion from an examination of these objects.'

'Well, they certainly appeared to indicate it, but your last remarks make it certain. There is no place except a catacomb which could contain so vast a store of relics as you describe.'

'Quite so. There is no mystery about that. I *have* discovered a new catacomb.'

'Where?'

'Ah, that is my secret, my dear Kennedy. Suffice it that it is so situated that there is not one chance in a million of anyone else coming upon it. Its date is different from that of any known catacomb, and it has been reserved for the burial of the highest Christians, so that the remains and the relics are quite different from anything which has ever been seen before. If I was not aware of your knowledge and of your energy, my friend, I would not hesitate, under the pledge of secrecy, to tell you everything about it. But as it is I think that I must certainly prepare my own report of the matter before I expose myself to such formidable competition.'

Kennedy loved his subject with a love which was almost a mania—a love which held him true to it, amidst all the distractions which come to a wealthy and dissipated young man. He had ambition, but his ambition was secondary to his mere abstract joy and interest in everything which concerned the old life and history of the city. He yearned to see this new underworld which his companion had discovered.

'Look here, Burger,' said he, earnestly, 'I assure you that you can trust me most implicitly in the matter. Nothing would induce me to put pen to paper about anything which I see until I have your express permission. I quite understand your feeling and I think it is most natural, but you have really nothing whatever to fear from me. On the other hand, if you don't tell me I shall make a systematic search, and I shall most certainly discover it. In that case, of course, I should make what use I liked of it, since I should be under no obligation to you.'

Burger smiled thoughtfully over his cigar.

'I have noticed, friend Kennedy,' said he, 'that when I want information over any point you are not always so ready to supply it.'

'When did you ever ask me anything that I did not tell you? You remember, for example, my giving you the material for your paper about the temple of the Vestals.'

'Ah, well, that was not a matter of much importance. If I were to question you upon some intimate thing would you give me an answer, I wonder! This new catacomb is a very intimate thing to me, and I should certainly expect some sign of confidence in return.'

'What you are driving at I cannot imagine,' said the Englishman, 'but if you mean that you will answer my question about the catacomb if I answer any question which you may put to me I can assure you that I will certainly do so.'

'Well, then,' said Burger, leaning luxuriously back in his settee, and puffing a blue tree of cigar-smoke into the air, 'tell me all about your relations with Miss Mary Saunderson.'

Kennedy sprang up in his chair and glared angrily at his impassive companion.

'What the devil do you mean?' he cried. 'What sort of a question is this? You may mean it as a joke, but you never made a worse one.'

'No, I don't mean it as a joke,' said Burger, simply. 'I am really rather interested in the details of the matter. I don't know much about the world and women and social life and that sort of thing, and such an incident has the fascination of the unknown for me. I know you, and I knew her by sight—I had even spoken to her once or twice. I should very much like to hear from your own lips exactly what it was which occurred between you.'

'I won't tell you a word.'

'That's all right. It was only my whim to see if you would give up a secret as easily as you expected me to give up my secret of the new catacomb. You wouldn't, and I didn't expect you to. But why should you expect otherwise of me? There's Saint John's clock striking ten. It is quite time that I was going home.'

'No; wait a bit, Burger,' said Kennedy; 'this is really a ridiculous caprice of yours to wish to know about an old love-affair which has burned out months ago. You know we look upon a man who kisses and tells as the greatest coward and villain possible.'

'Certainly,' said the German, gathering up his basket of curiosities, 'when he tells anything about a girl which is previously unknown he must be so. But in this case, as you must be aware, it was a public matter which was the common talk of Rome, so that you are not really doing Miss Mary Saunderson any injury by discussing her case with me. But still, I respect your scruples, and so good night!'

'Wait a bit, Burger,' said Kennedy, laying his hand upon the other's arm; 'I am very keen upon this catacomb business, and I can't let it drop quite so easily. Would you mind asking me something else in return—something not quite so eccentric this time?'

'No, no; you have refused, and there is an end of it,' said Burger, with his basket on his arm. 'No doubt you are quite right not to answer, and no doubt I am quite right also—and so again, my dear Kennedy, good night!'

The Englishman watched Burger cross the room, and he had his hand on the handle of the door before his host sprang up with the air of a man who is making the best of that which cannot be helped.

'Hold on, old fellow,' said he; 'I think you are behaving in a most ridiculous fashion; but still, if this is your condition, I suppose that I must submit to it. I hate saying anything about a girl, but, as you say, it is all over Rome, and I don't suppose I can tell you anything which you do not know already. What was it you wanted to know?'

The German came back to the stove, and, laying down his basket, he sank into his chair once more.

'May I have another cigar?' said he. 'Thank you very much! I never smoke when I work, but I enjoy a chat much more when I am under the influence of tobacco. Now, as regards this young lady, with whom you had this little adventure. What in the world has become of her?'

'She is at home with her own people.'

'Oh, really—in England?'

'Yes.'

'What part of England—London?'

'No, Twickenham.'

'You must excuse my curiosity, my dear Kennedy, and you must put it down to my ignorance of the world. No doubt it is quite a simple thing to persuade a young lady to go off with you for three weeks or so, and then to hand her over to her own family at—what did you call the place?'

'Twickenham.'

'Quite so—at Twickenham. But it is something so entirely outside my own experience that I cannot even imagine how you set about it. For example, if you had loved this girl your love could hardly disappear in three weeks, so I presume that you could not have loved her at all. But if you did not love her why should you make this great scandal which has damaged you and ruined her?'

Kennedy looked moodily into the red eye of the stove.

'That's a logical way of looking at it, certainly,' said he. 'Love is a big word, and it represents a good many different shades of feeling. I liked her, and—well, you say you've seen her—you know how charming she could look. But still I am willing to admit, looking back, that I could never have really loved her.'

'Then, my dear Kennedy, why did you do it?'

'The adventure of the thing had a great deal to do with it.'

'What! You are so fond of adventures!'

'Where would the variety of life be without them? It was for an adventure that I first began to pay my attentions to her. I've chased a good deal of game in my time, but there's no chase like that of a pretty woman. There was the piquant difficulty of it also, for, as she was the companion of Lady Emily Rood, it was almost impossible to see her alone. On the top of all the other obstacles which attracted me, I learned from her own lips very early in the proceedings that she was engaged.'

'Mein Gott! To whom?'

'She mentioned no names.'

'I do not think that anyone knows that. So that made the adventure more alluring, did it?'

'Well, it did certainly give a spice to it. Don't you think so?'

'I tell you that I am very ignorant about these things.'

'My dear fellow, you can remember that the apple you stole from your neighbour's tree was always sweeter than that which fell from your own. And then I found that she cared for me.'

'What—at once?'

'Oh, no, it took about three months of sapping and mining. But at last I won her over. She understood that my judicial separation from my wife made it impossible for me to do the right thing by her—but she came all the same, and we had a delightful time, as long as it lasted.'

'But how about the other man?'

Kennedy shrugged his shoulders.

'I suppose it is the survival of the fittest,' said he. 'If he had been the better man she would not have deserted him. Let's drop the subject, for I have had enough of it!'

'Only one other thing. How did you get rid of her in three weeks?'

'Well, we had both cooled down a bit, you understand. She absolutely refused, under any circumstances, to come back to face the people she had known in Rome. Now, of course, Rome is necessary to me, and I was already pining to be back at my work—so there was one obvious cause of separation. Then, again, her old father turned up at the hotel in London, and there was a scene, and the whole thing became so unpleasant that really—though I missed her dreadfully at first—I was very glad to slip out of it. Now, I rely upon you not to repeat anything of what I have said.'

'My dear Kennedy, I should not dream of repeating it. But all that you say interests me very much, for it gives me an insight into your way of looking at things, which is entirely different from mine, for I have seen so little of life. And now you want to know about my new catacomb. There's no use my trying to describe it, for you would never find it by that. There is only one thing, and that is for me to take you there.'

'That would be splendid.'

'When would you like to come?'

'The sooner the better. I am all impatience to see it.'

'Well, it is a beautiful night—though a trifle cold. Suppose we start in an hour. We must be very careful to keep the matter to ourselves. If anyone saw us hunting in couples they would suspect that there was something going on.'

'We can't be too cautious,' said Kennedy. 'Is it far?'

'Some miles.'

'Not too far to walk?'

'Oh, no, we could walk there easily.'

'We had better do so, then. A cabman's suspicions would be aroused if he dropped us both at some lonely spot in the dead of the night.'

'Quite so. I think it would be best for us to meet at the Gate of the Appian Way at midnight. I must go back to my lodgings for the matches and candles and things.'

'All right, Burger! I think it is very kind of you to let me into this secret, and I promise you that I will write nothing about it until you have published your report. Good-bye for the present! You will find me at the Gate at twelve.'

The cold, clear air was filled with the musical chimes from that city of clocks as Burger, wrapped in an Italian overcoat, with a lantern hanging from his hand, walked up to the rendezvous. Kennedy stepped out of the shadow to meet him.

'You are ardent in work as well as in love!' said the German, laughing.

'Yes; I have been waiting here for nearly half an hour.'

'I hope you left no clue as to where we were going.'

'Not such a fool! By Jove, I am chilled to the bone! Come on, Burger, let us warm ourselves by a spurt of hard walking.'

Their footsteps sounded loud and crisp upon the rough stone paving of the disappointing road which is all that is left of the most famous highway of the world. A peasant or two going home from the wine-shop, and a few carts of country produce coming up to Rome, were the only things which they met. They swung along, with the huge tombs looming up through the darkness upon each side of them, until they had come as far as the Catacombs of St Calixtus, and saw against a rising moon the great circular bastion of Cecilia Metella in front of them. Then Burger stopped with his hand to his side.

'Your legs are longer than mine, and you are more accustomed to walking,' said he, laughing. 'I think that the place where we turn off is somewhere here. Yes, this is it, round the corner of the trattoria. Now, it is a very narrow path, so perhaps I had better go in front and you can follow.'

He had lit his lantern, and by its light they were enabled to follow a narrow and devious track which wound across the marshes of the Campagna. The great Aqueduct of old Rome lay like a monstrous caterpillar across the moonlit landscape, and their road led them under one of its huge arches, and past the circle of crumbling bricks which marks the old arena. At last Burger stopped at a solitary wooden cow-house, and he drew a key from his pocket.

'Surely your catacomb is not inside a house!' cried Kennedy.

'The entrance to it is. That is just the safeguard which we have against anyone else discovering it.'

'Does the proprietor know of it?'

'Not he. He had found one or two objects which made me almost certain that his house was built on the entrance to such a place. So I rented it from him, and did my excavations for myself. Come in, and shut the door behind you.'

It was a long, empty building, with the mangers of the cows along one wall. Burger put his lantern down on the ground, and shaded its light in all directions save one by draping his overcoat round it.

'It might excite remark if anyone saw a light in this lonely place,' said he. 'Just help me to move this boarding.'

The flooring was loose in the corner, and plank by plank the two savants raised it and leaned it against the wall. Below there was a square aperture and a stair of old stone steps which led away down into the bowels of the earth.

'Be careful!' cried Burger, as Kennedy, in his impatience, hurried down them. 'It is a perfect rabbits'-warren below, and if you were once to lose your way there the chances would be a hundred to one against your ever coming out again. Wait until I bring the light.'

'How do you find your own way if it is so complicated?'

'I had some very narrow escapes at first, but I have gradually learned to go about. There is a certain system to it, but it is one which a lost man, if he were in the dark, could not possibly find out. Even now I always spin out a ball of string behind me when I am going far into the catacomb. You can see for yourself that it is difficult, but every one of these passages divides and subdivides a dozen times before you go a hundred yards.'

They had descended some twenty feet from the level of the byre, and they were standing now in a square chamber cut out of the soft tufa. The lantern cast a flickering light, bright below and dim above, over the cracked brown walls. In every direction were the black openings of passages which radiated from this common centre.

'I want you to follow me closely, my friend,' said Burger. 'Do not loiter to look at anything upon the way, for the place to which I will take you contains all that you can see, and more. It will save time for us to go there direct.'

He led the way down one of the corridors, and the Englishman followed closely at his heels. Every now and then the passage bifurcated, but Burger was evidently following some secret marks of his own, for he neither stopped nor hesitated. Everywhere along the walls, packed like the berths upon an emigrant ship, lay the Christians of old Rome. The yellow light flickered over the shrivelled features of the mummies, and gleamed upon rounded skulls and long, white armbones crossed over fleshless chests. And everywhere as he passed Kennedy looked with wistful eyes upon inscriptions, funeral vessels, pictures, vestments, utensils, all lying as pious hands had placed them so many centuries ago. It was apparent to him, even in those hurried, passing glances, that this was the earliest and finest of the catacombs, containing such a storehouse of Roman remains as had never before come at one time under the observation of the student.

'What would happen if the light went out?' he asked, as they hurried onwards.

'I have a spare candle and a box of matches in my pocket. By the way, Kennedy, have you any matches?'

'No; you had better give me some.'

'Oh, that is all right. There is no chance of our separating.'

'How far are we going? It seems to me that we have walked at least a quarter of a mile.'

'More than that, I think. There is really no limit to the tombs—at least, I have never been able to find any. This is a very difficult place, so I think that I will use our ball of string.'

He fastened one end of it to a projecting stone and he carried the coil in the breast of his coat, paying it out as he advanced. Kennedy saw that it was no unnecessary precaution, for the passages had become more complex and tortuous than ever, with a perfect network of intersecting corridors. But these all ended in one large circular hall with a square pedestal of tufa topped with a slab of marble at one end of it.

'By Jove!' cried Kennedy in an ecstasy, as Burger swung his lantern over the marble. 'It is a Christian altar—probably the first one in existence. Here is the little consecration cross cut upon the corner of it. No doubt this circular space was used as a church.'

'Precisely,' said Burger. 'If I had more time I should like to show you all the bodies which are buried in these niches upon the walls, for they are the early popes and bishops of the Church, with their mitres, their croziers, and full canonicals. Go over to that one and look at it!'

Kennedy went across, and stared at the ghastly head which lay loosely on the shredded and mouldering mitre.

'This is most interesting,' said he, and his voice seemed to boom against the concave vault. 'As far as my experience goes, it is unique. Bring the lantern over, Burger, for I want to see them all.'

But the German had strolled away, and was standing in the middle of a yellow circle of light at the other side of the hall.

'Do you know how many wrong turnings there are between this and the stairs?' he asked. 'There are over two thousand. No doubt it was one of the means of protection which the Christians adopted. The odds are two thousand to one against a man getting out, even if he had a light; but if he were in the dark it would, of course, be far more difficult.'

'So I should think.'

'And the darkness is something dreadful. I tried it once for an experiment. Let us try it again!' He stooped to the lantern, and in an instant it was as if an invisible hand was squeezed tightly over each of Kennedy's eyes. Never had he known what such darkness was. It seemed to press upon him and to smother him. It was a solid obstacle against which the body shrank from advancing. He put his hands out to push it back from him.

'That will do, Burger,' said he, 'let's have the light again.'

But his companion began to laugh, and in that circular room the sound seemed to come from every side at once.

'You seem uneasy, friend Kennedy,' said he.

'Go on, man, light the candle!' said Kennedy impatiently.

'It's very strange, Kennedy, but I could not in the least tell by the sound in which direction you stand. Could you tell where I am?'

'No; you seem to be on every side of me.'

'If it were not for this string which I hold in my hand I should not have a notion which way to go.'

'I dare say not. Strike a light, man, and have an end of this nonsense.'

'Well, Kennedy, there are two things which I understand that you are very fond of. The one is an adventure, and the other is an obstacle to surmount. The adventure must be the finding of your way out of this catacomb. The obstacle will be the darkness and the two thousand wrong turns which make the way a little difficult to find. But you need not hurry, for you have plenty of time, and when you halt for a rest now and then, I should like you just to think of Miss Mary Saunderson, and whether you treated her quite fairly.'

'You devil, what do you mean?' roared Kennedy. He was running about in little circles and clasping at the solid blackness with both hands.

'Good-bye,' said the mocking voice, and it was already at some distance. 'I really do not think, Kennedy, even by your own showing that you did the right thing by that girl. There was only one little thing which you appeared not to know, and I can supply it. Miss Saunderson was engaged to a poor ungainly devil of a student, and his name was Julius Burger.'

There was a rustle somewhere, the vague sound of a foot striking a stone, and then there fell silence upon that old Christian church—a stagnant, heavy silence which closed round Kennedy and shut him in like water round a drowning man.

\*

Some two months afterwards the following paragraph made the round of the European Press:

One of the most interesting discoveries of recent years is that of the new catacomb in Rome, which lies some distance to the east of the well-known vaults of St Calixtus. The finding of this important burial-place, which is exceeding rich in most interesting early Christian remains, is due to the energy and sagacity of Dr Julius Burger, the young German specialist, who is rapidly taking the first place as an authority upon ancient Rome. Although the first to publish his discovery, it appears that a less fortunate adventurer had anticipated Dr Burger. Some months ago Mr Kennedy, the well-known English student, disappeared suddenly from his rooms in the Corso, and it was conjectured that his association with a recent scandal had driven him to leave Rome. It appears now that he had in reality fallen a victim to that fervid love of archæology which had raised him to a distinguished place among living scholars. His body was discovered in the heart of the new catacomb, and it was evident from the condition of his feet and boots that he had tramped for days through the tortuous corridors which make these subterranean tombs so dangerous to explorers. The deceased gentleman had, with inexplicable rashness, made his way into this labyrinth without, as far as can be discovered, taking with him either candles or matches, so that his sad fate was the natural result of his own temerity. What makes the matter more painful is that Dr Julius Burger was an intimate friend of the deceased. His joy at the extraordinary find which he has been so fortunate as to make has been greatly marred by the terrible fate of his comrade and fellow-worker.

# A BRACELET AT BRUGES

## *Arnold Bennett*

Enoch Arnold Bennett (1867–1931) was, in his heyday, an author as popular as he was versatile and prolific. He was born in Hanley, Staffordshire, and his books set in his native Potteries, including *Anna of the Five Towns* (1902) and *The Card* (1911), enjoyed much success, but his outlook was far from parochial. After working as a journalist in London, he moved to Paris in 1903. He married a French actress in 1907, spending eight years in France before returning to Britain. His literary influences included Guy de Maupassant and Flaubert, and during the First World War he served as Director of Propaganda for France at the Ministry of Information. His work earned the disfavour of Virginia Woolf, and for much of the twentieth century his literary reputation slipped into an undeserved decline, but in recent years his storytelling gifts have been increasingly appreciated.

Bennett was not primarily a crime writer, but he enjoyed the genre, and his occasional reviews of detective novels displayed insight and enthusiasm. 'A Bracelet in Bruges', originally published in the *Windsor* magazine in 1905, was collected in *The Loot of the Cities* in the same year; the book earned the accolade of inclusion by Ellery Queen in *Queen's Quorum*, a list of the most important books of short stories in the genre.

## I

T HE BRACELET HAD FALLEN INTO THE CANAL.
And the fact that the canal was the most picturesque canal in the old Flemish city of Bruges, and that the ripples caused by the splash of the bracelet had disturbed reflections of wondrous belfries, towers, steeples, and other unique examples of Gothic architecture, did nothing whatever to assuage the sudden agony of that disappearance. For the bracelet had been given to Kitty Sartorius by her grateful and lordly manager, Lionel Belmont (U.S.A.), upon the completion of the unexampled run of *The Delminico Doll*, at the Regency Theatre, London. And its diamonds were worth five hundred pounds, to say nothing of the gold.

The beautiful Kitty, and her friend Eve Fincastle, the journalist, having exhausted Ostend, had duly arrived at Bruges in the course of their holiday tour. The question of Kitty's jewellery had arisen at the start. Kitty had insisted that she must travel with all her jewels, according to the custom of theatrical stars of great magnitude. Eve had equally insisted that Kitty must travel without jewels, and had exhorted her to remember the days of her simplicity. They compromised. Kitty was allowed to bring the bracelet, but nothing else save the usual half-dozen rings. The ravishing creature could not have persuaded herself to leave the bracelet behind, because it was so recent a gift and still new and strange and heavenly to her. But, since prudence forbade even Kitty to let the trifle lie about in hotel bedrooms, she was obliged always to wear it. And she had been wearing it this bright afternoon in early October, when the girls, during a stroll, had met one of their new friends, Madame Lawrence, on the world-famous Quai du Rosaire, just at the back of the Hotel de Ville and the Halles.

Madame Lawrence resided permanently in Bruges. She was between twenty-five and forty-five, dark, with the air of continually subduing a natural instinct to dash, and well dressed in black. Equally interested in the peerage and in the poor, she had made the acquaintance of Eve and Kitty at the Hotel de la Grande Place, where she called from time to time to induce English travellers to buy genuine Bruges lace, wrought under her own supervision by her own paupers. She was Belgian by birth, and when complimented on her fluent and correct English, she gave all the praise to her deceased husband, an English barrister. She had settled in Bruges like many people settle there, because Bruges is inexpensive, picturesque, and inordinately respectable. Besides an English church and chaplain, it has two cathedrals and an episcopal palace, with a real bishop in it.

'What an exquisite bracelet! May I look at it?'

It was these simple but ecstatic words, spoken with Madame Lawrence's charming foreign accent, which had begun the tragedy. The three women had stopped to admire the always admirable view from the little quay, and they were leaning over the rails when Kitty unclasped the bracelet for the inspection of the widow. The next instant there was a *plop*, an affrighted exclamation from Madame Lawrence in her native tongue, and the bracelet was engulfed before the very eyes of all three.

The three looked at each other non-plussed. Then they looked around, but not a single person was in sight. Then, for some reason which, doubtless, psychology can explain, they stared hard at the water, though the water there was just as black and foul as it is everywhere else in the canal system of Bruges.

'Surely you've not dropped it!' Eve Fincastle exclaimed in a voice of horror. Yet she knew positively that Madame Lawrence had.

The delinquent took a handkerchief from her muff and sobbed into it. And between her sobs she murmured, 'We must inform the police.'

'Yes, of course,' said Kitty, with the lightness of one to whom a five-hundred-pound bracelet is a bagatelle. 'They'll fish it up in no time.'

'Well,' Eve decided, 'you go to the police at once, Kitty; and Madame Lawrence will go with you, because she speaks French, and I'll stay here to mark the exact spot.'

The other two started, but Madame Lawrence, after a few steps, put her hand to her side. 'I can't' she sighed, pale. 'I am too upset. I cannot walk. You go with Miss Sartorius,' she said to Eve, 'and I will stay,' and she leaned heavily against the railings.

Eve and Kitty ran off, just as if it was an affair of seconds, and the bracelet had to be saved from drowning. But they had scarcely turned the corner, thirty yards away, when they reappeared in company with a high official of police, whom, by the most lucky chance in the world, they had encountered in the covered passage leading to the Place du Borg. This official, instantly enslaved by Kitty's beauty, proved to be the very mirror of politeness and optimism. He took their names and addresses, and a full description of the bracelet, and informed them that at that place the canal was nine feet deep. He said that the bracelet should undoubtedly be recovered on the morrow, but that, as dusk was imminent, it would be futile to commence angling that night. In the meantime the loss should be kept secret; and to make all sure, a succession of gendarmes should guard the spot during the night.

Kitty grew radiant, and rewarded the gallant officer with smiles; Eve was satisfied, and the face of Madame Lawrence wore a less mournful hue.

'And now,' said Kitty to Madame, when everything had been arranged, and the first of the gendarmes was duly installed at the exact spot against the railings, 'you must come and take tea with us in our winter-garden; and be gay! Smile: I insist. And I insist that you don't worry.'

Madame Lawrence tried feebly to smile.

'You are very good-natured,' she stammered.

Which was decidedly true.

II

The winter-garden of the Hotel de la Grande Place, referred to in all the hotel's advertisements, was merely the inner court of the hotel, roofed in by glass at the height of the first storey. Cane flourished there, in the shape of lounge-chairs, but no other plant. One of the lounge-chairs was occupied when, just as the carillon in the belfry at the other end of the Place began to play Gounod's 'Nazareth', indicating the hour of five o'clock, the three ladies entered the winter-garden. Apparently the toilettes of two of them had been adjusted and embellished as for a somewhat ceremonious occasion.

'Lo!' cried Kitty Sartorius, when she perceived the occupant of the chair, 'the millionaire! Mr Thorold, how charming of you to reappear like this! I invite you to tea.'

Cecil Thorold rose with appropriate eagerness.

'Delighted!' he said, smiling, and then explained that he had arrived from Ostend about two hours before and had taken rooms in the hotel.

'You knew we were staying here?' Eve asked as he shook hands with her.

'No,' he replied; 'but I am glad to find you again.'

'Are you?' She spoke languidly, but her colour heightened and those eyes of hers sparkled.

'Madame Lawrence,' Kitty chirruped, 'let me present Mr Cecil Thorold. He is appallingly rich, but we mustn't let that frighten us.'

From a mouth less adorable than the mouth of Miss Sartorius such an introduction might have been judged lacking in the elements of good form, but for more than two years now Kitty had known that whatever she did or said was perfectly correct because she did or said it. The new acquaintances laughed amiably and a certain intimacy was at once established.

'Shall I order tea, dear?' Eve suggested.

'No, dear,' said Kitty quietly. 'We will wait for the Count.'

'The Count?' demanded Cecil Thorold.

'The Comte d'Avrec,' Kitty explained. 'He is staying here.'

'A French nobleman, doubtless?'

'Yes,' said Kitty; and she added, 'you will like him. He is an archaeologist, and a musician—oh, and lots of things!'

'If I am one minute late, I entreat pardon,' said a fine tenor voice at the door.

It was the Count. After he had been introduced to Madame Lawrence, and Cecil Thorold had been introduced to him, tea was served.

Now, the Comte d'Avrec was everything that a French count ought to be. As dark as Cecil Thorold, and even handsomer, he was a little older and a little taller than the millionaire, and a short, pointed, black beard, exquisitely trimmed, gave him an appearance of staid reliability which Cecil lacked. His bow was a vertebrate poem, his smile a consolation for all misfortunes, and he managed his hat, stick, gloves, and cup with the dazzling assurance of a conjurer. To observe him at afternoon tea was to be convinced that he had been specially created to shine gloriously in drawing-rooms, winter-gardens, and *tables d'hôte*. He was one of those men who always do the right thing at the right moment, who are capable of speaking an indefinite number of languages with absolute purity of accent (he spoke English much better than Madame Lawrence), and who can and do discourse with *verve* and accuracy on all sciences, arts, sports, and religions. In short, he was a phoenix of a count; and this was certainly the opinion of Miss Kitty Sartorius and of Miss Eve Fincastle, both of whom reckoned that what they did not know about men might be ignored. Kitty and the Count, it soon became evident, were mutually attracted; their souls were approaching each other with a velocity which increased inversely as the square of the lessening distance between them. And Eve was watching this approximation with undisguised interest and relish.

Nothing of the least importance occurred, save the Count's marvellous exhibition of how to behave at afternoon tea, until the refection was nearly over; and then, during a brief pause in the talk, Cecil, who was sitting to the left of Madame Lawrence, looked sharply round at the right shoulder of his tweed coat; he repeated the gesture a second and yet a third time.

'What is the matter with the man?' asked Eve Fincastle. Both she and Kitty were extremely bright, animated, and even excited.

'Nothing. I thought I saw something on my shoulder, that's all,' said Cecil. 'Ah! It's only a bit of thread.' And he picked off the thread with his left hand and held it before Madame Lawrence. 'See! It's a piece of thin black silk, knotted. At first I took it for an insect—you know how queer things look out of the corner of your eye. Pardon!' He had dropped the fragment on to Madame Lawrence's black silk dress. 'Now it's lost.'

'If you will excuse me, kind friends,' said Madame Lawrence, 'I will go.' She spoke hurriedly, and as though in mental distress.

'Poor thing!' Kitty Sartorius exclaimed when the widow had gone. 'She's still dreadfully upset'; and Kitty and Eve proceeded jointly to relate the story of the diamond bracelet, upon which hitherto they had kept silence (though with difficulty), out of regard for Madame Lawrence's feelings.

Cecil made almost no comment.

The Count, with the sympathetic excitability of his race, walked up and down the winter-garden, asseverating earnestly that such clumsiness amounted to a crime; then he grew calm and confessed that he shared the optimism of the police as to the recovery of the bracelet; lastly he complimented Kitty on her equable demeanour under this affliction.

'Do you know, Count,' said Cecil Thorold, later, after they had all four ascended to the drawing-room overlooking the Grande Place, 'I was quite surprised when I saw at tea that you had to be introduced to Madame Lawrence.'

'Why so, my dear Mr Thorold?' the Count inquired suavely.

'I thought I had seen you together in Ostend a few days ago.'

The Count shook his wonderful head.

'Perhaps you have a brother—?' Cecil paused.

'No,' said the Count. 'But it is a favourite theory of mine that everyone has his double somewhere in the world.' Previously the Count had been discussing Planchette—he was a great authority on the supernatural, the sub-conscious, and the subliminal. He now deviated gracefully to the discussion of the theory of doubles.

'I suppose you aren't going out for a walk, dear, before dinner?' said Eve to Kitty.

'No, dear,' said Kitty, positively.

'I think I shall,' said Eve.

And her glance at Cecil Thorold intimated in the plainest possible manner that she wished not only to have a companion for a stroll, but to leave Kitty and the Count in dual solitude.

'I shouldn't, if I were you, Miss Fincastle,' Cecil remarked, with calm and studied blindness. 'It's risky here in the evenings—with these canals exhaling miasma and mosquitoes and bracelets and all sorts of things.'

'I will take the risk, thank you,' said Eve, in an icy tone, and she haughtily departed; she would not cower before Cecil's millions. As for Cecil, he joined in the discussion of the theory of doubles.

III

On the next afternoon but one, policemen were still fishing, without success, for the bracelet, and raising from the ancient duct long-buried odours which threatened to destroy the inhabitants of the quay. (When Kitty Sartorius had hinted that perhaps the authorities might see their way to drawing off the water from the canal, the authorities had intimated that the death-rate of Bruges was already as high as convenient.) Nevertheless, though nothing had happened, the situation had somehow developed, and in such a manner that the bracelet itself was in danger of being partially forgotten; and of all places in Bruges, the situation had developed on the top of the renowned Belfry which dominates the Grande Place in particular and the city in general.

The summit of the Belfry is three hundred and fifty feet high, and it is reached by four hundred and two winding stone steps, each a separate menace to life and limb. Eve Fincastle had climbed those steps alone, perhaps in quest of the view at the top, perhaps in quest of spiritual calm. She had not been leaning over the parapet more than a minute before Cecil Thorold had appeared, his field-glasses slung over his shoulder. They had begun to talk a little, but nervously and only in snatches. The wind blew free up there among the forty-eight bells, but the social atmosphere was oppressive.

'The Count is a most charming man,' Eve was saying, as if in defence of the Count.

'He is,' said Cecil; 'I agree with you.'

'Oh, no, you don't, Mr Thorold! Oh, no, you don't!'

Then there was a pause, and the twain looked down upon Bruges, with its venerable streets, its grass-grown squares, its waterways, and its innumerable monuments, spread out maplike beneath them in the mellow October sunshine. Citizens passed along the thoroughfare in the semblance of tiny dwarfs.

'If you didn't hate him,' said Eve, 'you wouldn't behave as you do.'

'How do I behave, then?'

Eve schooled her voice to an imitation of jocularity—

'All Tuesday evening, and all day yesterday, you couldn't leave them alone. You know you couldn't.'

Five minutes later the conversation had shifted.

'You actually saw the bracelet fall into the canal?' said Cecil.

'I actually saw the bracelet fall into the canal. And no one could have got it out while Kitty and I were away, because we weren't away half a minute.'

But they could not dismiss the subject of the Count, and presently he was again the topic.

'Naturally it would be a good match for the Count—for *any* man,' said Eve; 'but then it would also be a good match for Kitty. Of course, he is not so rich as some people, but he is rich.'

Cecil examined the horizon with his glasses, and then the streets near the Grande Place.

'Rich, is he? I'm glad of it. By the by, he's gone to Ghent for the day, hasn't he?'

'Yes, he went by the 9.27, and returns by the 4.38.'

Another pause.

'Well,' said Cecil at length, handing the glasses to Eve Fincastle, 'kindly glance down there. Follow the line of the Rue St Nicholas. You see the cream-coloured house with the enclosed courtyard? Now, do you see two figures standing together near a door—a man and a woman, the woman on the steps? Who are they?'

'I can't see very well,' said Eve.

'Oh, yes, my dear lady, you can,' said Cecil. 'These glasses are the very best. Try again.'

'They look like the Comte d'Avrec and Madame Lawrence,' Eve murmured.

'But the Count is on his way from Ghent! I see the steam of the 4.38 over there. The curious thing is that the Count entered the house of Madame Lawrence, to whom he was introduced for the first time the day before yesterday, at ten o'clock this morning. Yes, it would be a very good match for the Count. When one comes to think of it, it usually is that sort of man that contrives to marry a brilliant and successful actress. There! He's just leaving, isn't he? Now let us descend and listen to the recital of his day's doings in Ghent—shall we?'

'You mean to insinuate,' Eve burst out in sudden wrath, 'that the Count is an—an *adventurer*, and that Madame Lawrence... Oh! Mr Thorold!' She laughed condescendingly. 'This jealousy is too absurd. Do you suppose I haven't noticed how impressed you were with Kitty at the Devonshire Mansion that night, and again at Ostend, and again here? You're simply carried away by jealousy; and you think because you are a millionaire you must have all you want. I haven't the slightest doubt that the Count...'

'Anyhow,' said Cecil, 'let us go down and hear about Ghent.'

His eyes made a number of remarks (indulgent, angry, amused, protective, admiring, perspicacious, puzzled), too subtle for the medium of words.

They groped their way down to earth in silence, and it was in silence that they crossed the Grande Place. The Count was seated on the *terrasse* in front of the hotel, with a liqueur glass before him, and he was making graceful and expressive signs to Kitty Sartorius, who leaned her marvellous beauty out of a first-storey window. He greeted Cecil Thorold and Eve with an equal grace.

'And how is Ghent?' Cecil inquired.

'Did you go to Ghent, after all, Count?' Eve put in.

The Comte d'Avrec looked from one to another, and then, instead of replying, he sipped at his glass. 'No,' he said, 'I didn't go. The rather curious fact is that I happened to meet Madame Lawrence, who offered to show me her collection of lace. I have been an amateur of lace for some years, and really Madame Lawrence's collection is amazing. You have seen it? No? You should do so. I'm afraid I have spent most of the day there.'

When the Count had gone to join Kitty in the drawing-room, Eve Fincastle looked victoriously at Cecil, as if to demand of him 'Will you apologise?'

'My dear journalist,' Cecil remarked simply, 'you gave the show away.'

That evening the continued obstinacy of the bracelet, which still refused to be caught, began at last to disturb the birdlike mind of Kitty Sartorius. Moreover, the secret was out, and the whole town of Bruges was discussing the episode and the chances of success.

'Let us consult Planchette,' said the Count. The proposal was received with enthusiasm by Kitty. Eve had disappeared.

Planchette was produced; and when asked if the bracelet would be recovered, it wrote, under the hands of Kitty and the Count, a trembling 'Yes'. When asked 'By whom?' it wrote a word that faintly resembled 'Avrec.'

The Count stated that he should personally commence dragging operations at sunrise. 'You will see,' he said, 'I shall succeed.'

'Let me try this toy, may I?' Cecil asked blandly, and, upon Kitty agreeing, he addressed Planchette in a clear voice 'Now, Planchette, who will restore the bracelet to its owner?'

And Planchette wrote 'Thorold,' but in characters as firm and regular as those of a copy-book.

'Mr Thorold is laughing at us,' observed the Count, imperturbably bland.

'How horrid you are, Mr Thorold!' Kitty exclaimed.

IV

Of the four persons more or less interested in the affair, three were secretly active that night, in and out of the hotel. Only Kitty Sartorius, chief mourner for the bracelet, slept placidly in her bed. It was towards three o'clock in the morning that a sort of preliminary crisis was reached.

From the multiplicity of doors which ventilate its rooms, one would imagine that the average foreign hotel must have been designed immediately after its architect had been to see a Palais Royal farce, in which every room opens into every other room in every act. The Hotel de la Grande Place was not peculiar in this respect; it abounded in doors. All the chambers on the second storey, over the public rooms, fronting the Place, communicated one with the next, but naturally most of the communicating doors were locked. Cecil Thorold and the Comte d'Avrec had each a bedroom and a sitting-room on that floor. The Count's sitting-room adjoined Cecil's; and the door between was locked, and the key in the possession of the landlord.

Nevertheless, at three a.m. this particular door opened noiselessly from Cecil's side, and Cecil entered the domain of the Count. The moon shone, and Cecil could plainly see not only the silhouette of the Belfry across the Place, but also the principal objects within the room. He noticed the table in the middle, the large easy-chair turned towards the hearth, the old-fashioned sofa; but not a single article did he perceive which might have been the personal property of the Count. He cautiously passed across the room through the moonlight to the door of the Count's bedroom, which apparently, to his immense surprise, was not only shut, but locked, and the key in the lock on the sitting-room side. Silently unlocking it, he entered the bedroom and disappeared...

In less than five minutes he crept back into the Count's sitting-room, closed the door and locked it.

'Odd!' he murmured reflectively; but he seemed quite happy.

There was a sudden movement in the region of the hearth, and a form rose from the armchair. Cecil rushed to the switch and turned on the electric light. Eve Fincastle stood before him. They faced each other.

'What are you doing here at this time, Miss Fincastle?' he asked, sternly. 'You can talk freely; the Count will not waken.'

'I may ask you the same question,' Eve replied, with cold bitterness.

'Excuse me. You may not. You are a woman. This is the Count's room—'

'You are in error,' she interrupted him. 'It is not the Count's room. It is mine. Last night I told the Count I had some important writing to do, and I asked him as a favour to relinquish this room to me for twenty-four hours. He very kindly consented. He removed his belongings, handed me the key of that door, and the transfer was made in the hotel books. And now,' she added, 'may I inquire, Mr Thorold, what you are doing in my room?'

'I—I thought it was the Count's,' Cecil faltered, decidedly at a loss for a moment. 'In offering my humblest apologies, permit me to say that I admire you, Miss Fincastle.'

'I wish I could return the compliment,' Eve exclaimed, and she repeated with almost plaintive sincerity: 'I do wish I could.'

Cecil raised his arms and let them fall to his side.

'You meant to catch me,' he said. 'You suspected something, then? The "important writing" was an invention.' And he added, with a faint smile: 'You really ought not to have fallen asleep. Suppose I had not wakened you?'

'Please don't laugh, Mr Thorold. Yes, I did suspect. There was something in the demeanour of your servant Lecky that gave me the idea… I did mean to catch you. Why you, a millionaire, should be a burglar, I cannot understand. I never understood that incident at the Devonshire Mansion; it was beyond me. I am by no means sure that you didn't have a great deal to do with the Rainshore affair at Ostend. But that you should have stooped to slander is the worst. I confess you are a mystery. I confess that I can make no guess at the nature of your present scheme. And what I shall do, now that I have caught you, I don't know. I can't decide; I must think. If, however, anything is missing to-morrow morning, I shall be bound in any case to denounce you. You grasp that?'

'I grasp it perfectly, my dear journalist,' Cecil replied. 'And something will not improbably be missing. But take the advice of a burglar and a mystery, and go to bed, it is half past three.'

And Eve went. And Cecil bowed her out and then retired to his own rooms. And the Count's apartment was left to the moonlight.

v

'Planchette is a very safe prophet,' said Cecil to Kitty Sartorius the next morning, 'provided it has firm guidance.'

They were at breakfast.

'What do you mean?'

'I mean that Planchette prophesied last night that I should restore to you your bracelet. I do.'

He took the lovely gewgaw from his pocket and handed it to Kitty.

'Ho-ow did you find it, you dear thing?' Kitty stammered, trembling under the shock of joy.

'I fished it up out—out of the mire by a contrivance of my own.'

'But when?'

'Oh! Very early. At three o'clock a.m. You see, I was determined to be first.'

'In the dark, then?'

'I had a light. Don't you think I'm rather clever?'

Kitty's scene of ecstatic gratitude does not come into the story. Suffice it to say that not until the moment of its restoration did she realise how precious the bracelet was to her.

It was ten o'clock before Eve descended. She had breakfasted in her room, and Kitty had already exhibited to her the prodigal bracelet.

'I particularly want you to go up the Belfry with me, Miss Fincastle,' Cecil greeted her; and his tone was so serious and so urgent that she consented. They left Kitty playing waltzes on the piano in the drawing-room.

'And now, O man of mystery?' Eve questioned, when they had toiled to the summit, and saw the city and its dwarfs beneath them.

'We are in no danger of being disturbed here,' Cecil began; 'but I will make my explanation—the explanation which I certainly owe you—as brief as possible. Your Comte d'Avrec is an adventurer (please don't be angry), and your Madame Lawrence is an adventuress. I knew that I had seen them together. They work in concert, and for the most part make a living on the gaming-tables of Europe. Madame Lawrence was expelled from Monte Carlo last year for being too intimate with a croupier. You may be aware that at a roulette-table one can do a great deal with the aid of the croupier. Madame Lawrence appropriated the bracelet 'on her own', as it were. The Count (he may be a real Count, for anything I know) heard first of that enterprise from the lips of Miss Sartorius. He was annoyed, angry—because he was really a little in love with your friend, and he saw golden prospects. It is just this fact—the Count's genuine passion for Miss Sartorius—that renders the case psychologically interesting. To proceed, Madame Lawrence became jealous. The Count spent six hours yesterday in trying to get the bracelet from her, and failed. He tried again last night, and succeeded, but not too easily, for he did not re-enter the hotel till after one o'clock. At first I thought he had succeeded in the daytime, and I had arranged accordingly, for I did not see why he should have the honour and glory of restoring the bracelet to its owner. Lecky and I fixed up a sleeping-draught for him. The minor details were simple. When you caught me this morning, the bracelet was in my pocket, and in its stead I had left a brief note for the perusal of the Count, which has had the singular effect of inducing him to decamp; probably he has not gone alone. But isn't it amusing that, since you so elaborately took his sitting-room, he will be convinced that you are a party to his undoing—you, his staunchest defender?'

Eve's face gradually broke into an embarrassed smile.

'You haven't explained,' she said, 'how Madame Lawrence got the bracelet.'

'Come over here,' Cecil answered. 'Take these glasses and look down at the Quai du Rosaire. You see everything plainly?' Eve could, in fact, see on the quay the little mounds of mud which had been extracted from the canal in the quest of the bracelet. Cecil continued: 'On my arrival in Bruges on Monday, I had a fancy to climb the Belfry at once. I witnessed the whole scene between you and Miss Sartorius and Madame Lawrence, through my glasses. Immediately your backs were turned, Madame Lawrence, her hands behind her, and her back against the railing, began to make a sort of rapid, drawing up motion with her forearms. Then I saw a momentary glitter... Considerably mystified, I visited the spot after you had left it, chatted with the gendarme on duty and got round him, and then it dawned on me that a robbery had been planned, prepared, and executed with extraordinary originality and ingenuity. A long, thin thread of black silk must have been ready tied to the railing, with perhaps a hook at the other end. As soon as Madame Lawrence held the bracelet, she attached the hook to it and dropped it. The silk, especially as it was the last thing in the world you would look for, would be as good as invisible. When you went for the police, Madame retrieved the bracelet, hid it in her muff, and broke off the silk. Only, in her haste, she left a bit of silk tied to the railing. That fragment I carried to the hotel. All along she must have been a little uneasy about me... And that's all. Except that I wonder you thought I was jealous of the Count's attentions to your friend.' He gazed at her admiringly.

'I'm glad you are not a thief, Mr Thorold,' said Eve.

'Well,' Cecil smiled, 'as for that, I left him a couple of louis for fares, and I shall pay his hotel bill.'

'Why?'

'There were notes for nearly ten thousand francs with the bracelet. Ill-gotten gains, I am sure. A trifle, but the only reward I shall have for my trouble. I shall put them to good use.' He laughed, serenely gay.

# THE SECRET GARDEN

## G.K. Chesterton

'The traveller sees what he sees,' mused Gilbert Keith Chesterton (1870–1936); 'the tourist sees what he has come to see.' This was a characteristic piece of phrase-making from one of the most renowned wordsmiths of his day. Chesterton picked up the travel bug after accompanying his father to France for a long holiday that was a reward for his success at St Paul's School, and never lost it. Shortly before his death, his secretary drove his wife and himself to Europe, and they visited France, Spain, Italy, Switzerland and Belgium. Despite deteriorating health, Chesterton still found time to write, in particular about Italian imperialism in Abyssinia.

Chesterton was an exceptionally versatile writer, with a remarkably wide range of interests, but today he is best remembered for his detective stories, and in particular for the creation of Father Brown, who has recently been reincarnated for daytime television with considerable success. Unexpectedly, even the little priest with a flair for solving mysterious puzzles shared Chesterton's love of travel, and ventured as far afield as South America and the United States. Here, in one of his most celebrated cases, he becomes embroiled in an 'impossible crime' committed in France. The story was originally published in *The Storyteller* in 1910, and was included in *The Innocence of Father Brown* the following year.

ARISTIDE VALENTIN, CHIEF OF THE PARIS POLICE, WAS LATE for his dinner, and some of his guests began to arrive before him. These were, however, reassured by his confidential servant, Ivan, the old man with a scar and a face almost as grey as his moustaches, who always sat at a table in the entrance hall—a hall hung with weapons. Valentin's house was perhaps as peculiar and celebrated as its master. It was an old house, with high walls and tall poplars almost overhanging the Seine; but the oddity—and perhaps the police value—of its architecture was this: that there was no ultimate exit at all except through this front door, which was guarded by Ivan and the armoury. The garden was large and elaborate, and there were many exits from the house into the garden. But there was no exit from the garden into the world outside; all round it ran a tall, smooth unscalable wall with special spikes at the top; no bad garden, perhaps, for a man to reflect in whom some hundred criminals had sworn to kill.

As Ivan explained to the guests, their host had telephoned that he was detained for ten minutes. He was, in truth, making some last arrangements about executions and such ugly things; and though these duties were rootedly repulsive to him, he always performed them with precision. Ruthless in the pursuit of criminals, he was very mild about their punishment. Since he had been supreme over French—and largely over European—police methods, his great influence had been honourably used for the mitigation of sentences and the purification of prisons. He was one of the great humanitarian French freethinkers; and the only thing wrong with them is that they make mercy even colder than justice.

When Valentin arrived he was already dressed in black clothes and the red rosette—an elegant figure, his dark beard already streaked with grey. He went straight through his house to his study, which opened on the grounds behind. The garden door of it was open, and after he had carefully locked his box in its official place, he stood for a few seconds at the open door looking out upon the garden. A sharp moon was fighting with the flying rags and tatters of a storm, and Valentin regarded it with a wistfulness unusual in such scientific natures as his. Perhaps such scientific natures have some psychic prevision of the most tremendous problem of their lives. From any such occult mood, at least, he quickly recovered, for he knew he was late and that his guests had already begun to arrive. A glance at his drawing-room when he entered it was enough to make certain that his principal guest was not there, at any rate. He saw all the other pillars of the little party: he saw Lord Galloway, the English Ambassador—a choleric old man with a russet face like an apple, wearing the blue ribbon of the Garter. He saw Lady Galloway, slim and thread-like, with silver hair and a face sensitive and superior. He saw her daughter, Lady Margaret Graham, a pale and pretty girl with an elfish face and copper-coloured hair. He saw the Duchess of Mont St Michel, black-eyed and opulent, and with her her two daughters, black-eyed and opulent also. He saw Dr Simon, a typical French scientist, with glasses, a pointed brown beard, and a forehead barred with those parallel wrinkles which are the penalty of superciliousness, since they come through constantly elevating the eyebrows. He saw Father Brown of Cobhole, in Essex, whom he had recently met in England. He saw—perhaps with more interest than any of those—a tall man in uniform, who had bowed to the Galloways without receiving any very hearty acknowledgment, and who now advanced alone to pay his respects to his host. This was Commandant O'Brien, of the French Foreign Legion. He was a slim yet somewhat swaggering figure, clean-shaven, dark-haired, and blue-eyed, and as seemed natural in an officer of that famous regiment of victorious failures and successful suicides, he had an air at once dashing and melancholy. He was by birth an Irish gentleman, and in boyhood had known the Galloways—especially Margaret Graham. He had left his country after some crash of debts, and now expressed his complete freedom from British etiquette by swinging about in uniform, sabre and spurs. When he bowed to the Ambassador's family, Lord and Lady Galloway bent stiffly, and Lady Margaret looked away.

But for whatever old causes such people might be interested in each other, their distinguished host was not specially interested in them. No one of them at least was in his eyes the guest of the evening. Valentin was expecting, for special reasons, a man of world-wide fame, whose friendship he had secured during some of his great detective tours and triumphs in the United States. He was expecting Julius K. Brayne, that multimillionaire whose colossal and even crushing endowments of small religions have occasioned so much easy sport and easier solemnity for the American and English papers. Nobody could quite make out whether Mr Brayne was an atheist or a Mormon, or a Christian Scientist; but he was ready to pour money into any intellectual vessel, so long as it was an untried vessel. One of his hobbies was to wait for the American Shakespeare—a hobby more patient than angling. He admired Walt Whitman, but thought that Luke P. Tanner, of Paris, Pa., was more 'progressive' than Whitman any day. He liked anything that he thought 'progressive.' He thought Valentin 'progressive,' thereby doing him a grave injustice.

The solid appearance of Julius K. Brayne in the room was as decisive as a dinner bell. He had this great quality, which very few of us can claim, that his presence was as big as his absence. He was a huge fellow, as fat as he was tall, clad in complete evening black, without so much relief as a watch-chain or a ring. His hair was white and well brushed back like a German's; his face was red, fierce and cherubic, with one dark tuft under the lower lip that threw up that otherwise infantile visage with an effect theatrical and even Mephistophelean. Not long, however, did that *salon* merely stare at the celebrated American; his lateness had already become a domestic problem, and he was sent with all speed into the dining-room with Lady Galloway upon his arm.

Except on one point the Galloways were genial and casual enough. So long as Lady Margaret did not take the arm of that adventurer O'Brien her father was quite satisfied; and she had not done so; she had decorously gone in with Dr Simon. Nevertheless, old Lord Galloway was restless and almost rude. He was diplomatic enough during dinner, but when, over the cigars, three of the younger men—Simon the doctor, Brown the priest, and the detrimental O'Brien, the exile in a foreign uniform—all melted away to mix with the ladies or smoke in the conservatory, then the English diplomatist grew very undiplomatic indeed. He was stung every sixty seconds with the thought that the scamp O'Brien might be signalling to Margaret somehow; he did not attempt to imagine how. He was left over the coffee with Brayne, the hoary Yankee who believed in all religions, and Valentin, the grizzled Frenchman who believed in none. They could argue with each other, but neither could appeal to him. After a time this 'progressive' logomachy had reached a crisis of tedium; Lord Galloway got up also and sought the drawing-room. He lost his way in long passages for some six or eight minutes: till he heard the high-pitched, didactic voice of the doctor, and then the dull voice of the priest, followed by general laughter. They also, he thought with a curse, were probably arguing about 'science and religion.' But the instant he opened the *salon* door he saw only one thing—he saw what was not there. He saw that Commandant O'Brien was absent, and that Lady Margaret was absent, too.

Rising impatiently from the drawing-room, as he had from the dining-room, he stamped along the passage once more. His notion of protecting his daughter from the Irish-Algerian ne'er-do-weel had become something central and even mad in his mind. As he went towards the back of the house, where was Valentin's study, he was surprised to meet his daughter, who swept past with a white, scornful face, which was a second enigma. If she had been with O'Brien, where was O'Brien? If she had not been with O'Brien, where had she been? With a sort of senile and passionate suspicion he groped his way to the dark back parts of the mansion, and eventually found a servants' entrance that opened on to the garden. The moon with her scimitar had now ripped up and rolled away all the storm-wrack. The argent light lit up all four corners of the garden. A tall figure in blue was striding across the lawn towards the study door; a glint of moonlit silver on his facings picked him out as Commandant O'Brien.

He vanished through the french windows into the house, leaving Lord Galloway in an indescribable temper, at once virulent and vague. The blue-and-silver garden, like a scene in a theatre, seemed to taunt him with all that tyrannic tenderness against which his worldly authority was at war. The length and grace of the Irishman's stride enraged him as if he were a rival instead of a father; the moonlight maddened him. He was trapped as if by magic into a garden of troubadours, a Watteau fairyland; and, willing to shake off such amorous imbecilities by speech, he stepped briskly after his enemy. As he did so he tripped over some tree or stone in the grass; looked down at it first with irritation and then a second time with curiosity. The next instant the moon and the tall poplars looked at an unusual sight—an elderly English diplomatist running hard and crying or bellowing as he ran.

His hoarse shouts brought a pale face to the study door, the beaming glasses and worried brow of Dr Simon, who heard the nobleman's first clear words. Lord Galloway was crying: 'A corpse in the grass—a bloodstained corpse.' O'Brien at least had gone utterly from his mind.

'We must tell Valentin at once,' said the doctor, when the other had brokenly described all that he had dared to examine. 'It is fortunate that he is here'; and even as he spoke the great detective entered the study, attracted by the cry. It was almost amusing to note his typical transformation; he had come with the common concern of a host and a gentleman, fearing that some guest or serv-ant was ill. When he was told the gory fact, he turned with all his gravity instantly bright and business-like; for this, however abrupt and awful, was his business.

'Strange, gentlemen,' he said, as they hurried out into the garden, 'that I should have hunted mysteries all over the earth, and now one comes and settles in my own backyard. But where is the place?' They crossed the lawn less easily, as a slight mist had begun to rise from the river; but under the guidance of the shaken Galloway they found the body sunken in deep grass—the body of a very tall and broad-shouldered man. He lay face downwards, so they could only see that his big shoulders were clad in black cloth, and that his big head was bald, except for a wisp or two of brown hair that clung to his skull like wet seaweed. A scarlet serpent of blood crawled from under his fallen face.

'At least,' said Simon, with a deep and singular intonation, 'he is none of our party.'

'Examine him, doctor,' cried Valentin rather sharply. 'He may not be dead.'

The doctor bent down. 'He is not quite cold, but I am afraid he is dead enough,' he answered. 'Just help me to lift him up.'

They lifted him carefully an inch from the ground, and all doubts as to his being really dead were settled at once and frightfully. The head fell away. It had been entirely sundered from the body; whoever had cut his throat had managed to sever the neck as well. Even Valentin was slightly shocked. 'He must have been as strong as a gorilla,' he muttered.

Not without a shiver, though he was used to anatomical abortions, Dr Simon lifted the head. It was slightly slashed about the neck and jaw, but the face was substantially unhurt. It was a ponderous, yellow face, at once sunken and swollen, with a hawk-like nose and heavy lids—the face of a wicked Roman emperor, with, perhaps, a distant touch of a Chinese emperor. All present seemed to look at it with the coldest eye of ignorance. Nothing else could be noted about the man except that, as they had lifted his body, they had seen underneath it the white gleam of a shirtfront defaced with a red gleam of blood. As Dr Simon said, the man had never been of their party. But he might very well have been trying to join it, for he had come dressed for such an occasion.

Valentin went down on his hands and knees and examined with his closest professional attention the grass and ground for some

twenty yards round the body, in which he was assisted less skil-
fully by the doctor, and quite vaguely by the English lord. Nothing
rewarded their grovellings except a few twigs, snapped or chopped
into very small lengths, which Valentin lifted for an instant's examination, and then tossed away.

'Twigs,' he said gravely; 'twigs, and a total stranger with his
head cut off; that is all there is on this lawn.'

There was an almost creepy stillness, and then the unnerved
Galloway called out sharply:

'Who's that? Who's that over there by the garden wall?'

A small figure with a foolishly large head drew waveringly near
them in the moonlit haze; looked for an instant like a goblin, but
turned out to be the harmless little priest whom they had left in
the drawing-room.

'I say,' he said meekly, 'there are no gates to this garden, do
you know.'

Valentin's black brows had come together somewhat crossly, as
they did on principle at the sight of the cassock. But he was far too
just a man to deny the relevance of the remark. 'You are right,' he
said. 'Before we find out how he came to be killed, we may have to
find out how he came to be here. Now listen to me, gentlemen. If
it can be done without prejudice to my position and duty, we shall
all agree that certain distinguished names might well be kept out of
this. There are ladies, gentlemen, and there is a foreign ambassador.
If we must mark it down as a crime, then it must be followed up
as a crime. But till then I can use my own discretion. I am the head
of the police; I am so public that I can afford to be private. Please
Heaven, I will clear every one of my own guests before I call in my
men to look for anybody else. Gentlemen, upon your honour, you
will none of you leave the house till to-morrow at noon; there are

bedrooms for all. Simon, I think you know where to find my man, Ivan, in the front hall; he is a confidential man. Tell him to leave another servant on guard and come to me at once. Lord Galloway, you are certainly the best person to tell the ladies what has happened, and prevent a panic. They also must stay. Father Brown and I will remain with the body.'

When this spirit of the captain spoke in Valentin he was obeyed like a bugle. Dr Simon went through to the armoury and routed out Ivan, the public detective's private detective. Galloway went to the drawing-room and told the terrible news tactfully enough, so that by the time the company assembled there the ladies were already startled and already soothed. Meanwhile the good priest and the good atheist stood at the head and foot of the dead man motionless in the moonlight, like symbolic statues of their two philosophies of death.

Ivan, the confidential man with the scar and the moustaches, came out of the house like a cannon ball, and came racing across the lawn to Valentin like a dog to his master. His livid face was quite lively with the glow of this domestic detective story, and it was with almost unpleasant eagerness that he asked his master's permission to examine the remains.

'Yes; look, if you like, Ivan,' said Valentin, 'but don't be long. We must go in and thrash this out in the house.'

Ivan lifted his head, and then almost let it drop.

'Why,' he gasped, 'it's—no, it isn't; it can't be. Do you know this man, sir?'

'No,' said Valentin indifferently; 'we had better go inside.'

Between them they carried the corpse to a sofa in the study, and then all made their way to the drawing-room.

The detective sat down at a desk quietly, and even with hesitation;

but his eye was the iron eye of a judge at assize. He made a few rapid notes upon paper in front of him, and then said shortly: 'Is everybody here?'

'Not Mr Brayne,' said the Duchess of Mont St Michel, looking round.

'No,' said Lord Galloway, in a hoarse, harsh voice. 'And not Mr Neil O'Brien, I fancy. I saw that gentleman walking in the garden when the corpse was still warm.'

'Ivan,' said the detective, 'go and fetch Commandant O'Brien and Mr Brayne. Mr Brayne, I know, is finishing a cigar in the dining-room; Commandant O'Brien, I think, is walking up and down the conservatory. I am not sure.'

The faithful attendant flashed from the room, and before anyone could stir or speak Valentin went on with the same soldierly swift-ness of exposition.

'Everyone here knows that a dead man has been found in the garden, his head cut clean from his body. Dr Simon, you have examined it. Do you think that to cut a man's throat like that would need great force? Or, perhaps, only a very sharp knife?'

'I should say that it could not be done with a knife at all,' said the pale doctor.

'Have you any thought,' resumed Valentin, 'of a tool with which it could be done?'

'Speaking within modern probabilities, I really haven't,' said the doctor, arching his painful brows. 'It's not easy to hack a neck through even clumsily, and this was a very clean cut. It could be done with a battle-axe or an old headsman's axe, or an old two-handed sword.'

'But, good heavens!' cried the Duchess, almost in hysterics; 'there aren't any two-handed swords and battle-axes round here.'

Valentin was still busy with the paper in front of him. 'Tell me,' he said, still writing rapidly, 'could it have been done with a long French cavalry sabre?'

A low knocking came at the door, which for some unreasonable reason, curdled everyone's blood like the knocking in *Macbeth*. Amid that frozen silence Dr Simon managed to say: 'A sabre—yes, I suppose it could.'

'Thank you,' said Valentin. 'Come in, Ivan.'

The confidential Ivan opened the door and ushered in Commandant Neil O'Brien, whom he had found at last pacing the garden again.

The Irish officer stood disordered and defiant on the threshold. 'What do you want with me?' he cried.

'Please sit down,' said Valentin in pleasant, level tones. 'Why, you aren't wearing your sword! Where is it?'

'I left it on the library table,' said O'Brien, his brogue deepening in his disturbed mood. 'It was a nuisance, it was getting—'

'Ivan,' said Valentin: 'please go and get the Commandant's sword from the library.' Then, as the servant vanished: 'Lord Galloway says he saw you leaving the garden just before he found the corpse. What were you doing in the garden?'

The Commandant flung himself recklessly into a chair. 'Oh,' he cried in pure Irish; 'admirin' the moon. Communing with Nature, me boy.'

A heavy silence sank and endured, and at the end of it came again that trivial and terrible knocking. Ivan reappeared, carrying an empty steel scabbard. 'This is all I can find,' he said.

'Put it on the table,' said Valentin, without looking up.

There was an inhuman silence in the room, like that sea of inhuman silence round the dock of the condemned murderer.

The Duchess's weak exclamations had long ago died away. Lord Galloway's swollen hatred was satisfied and even sobered. The voice that came was quite unexpected.

'I think I can tell you,' cried Lady Margaret, in that clear, quivering voice with which a courageous woman speaks publicly. 'I can tell you what Mr O'Brien was doing in the garden, since he is bound to silence. He was asking me to marry him. I refused; I said in my family circumstances I could give him nothing but my respect. He was a little angry at that; he did not seem to think much of my respect. I wonder,' she added, with rather a wan smile, 'if he will care at all for it now. For I offer it him now. I will swear anywhere that he never did a thing like this.'

Lord Galloway had edged up to his daughter, and was intimidating her in what he imagined to be an undertone. 'Hold your tongue, Maggie,' he said in a thunderous whisper. 'Why should you shield the fellow? Where's his sword? Where's his confounded cavalry—'

He stopped because of the singular stare with which his daughter was regarding him, a look that was indeed a lurid magnet for the whole group.

'You old fool!' she said, in a low voice without pretence of piety; 'what do you suppose you are trying to prove? I tell you this man was innocent while with me. But if he wasn't innocent, he was still with me. If he murdered a man in the garden, who was it who must have seen—who must at least have known? Do you hate Neil so much as to put your own daughter—'

Lady Galloway screamed. Everyone else sat tingling at the touch of those satanic tragedies that have been between lovers before now. They saw the proud, white face of the Scotch aristocrat and her lover, the Irish adventurer, like old portraits in a dark house. The long silence was full of formless historical memories of murdered husbands and poisonous paramours.

In the centre of this morbid silence an innocent voice said: 'Was it a very long cigar?'

The change of thought was so sharp that they had to look round to see who had spoken.

'I mean,' said little Father Brown, from the corner of the room. 'I mean that cigar Mr Brayne is finishing. It seems nearly as long as a walking-stick.'

Despite the irrelevance there was assent as well as irritation in Valentin's face as he lifted his head.

'Quite right,' he remarked sharply. 'Ivan, go and see about Mr Brayne again, and bring him here at once.'

The instant the factotum had closed the door, Valentin addressed the girl with an entirely new earnestness.

'Lady Margaret,' he said, 'we all feel, I am sure, both gratitude and admiration for your act in rising above your lower dignity and explaining the Commandant's conduct. But there is a hiatus still. Lord Galloway, I understand, met you passing from the study to the drawing-room, and it was only some minutes afterwards that he found the garden and the Commandant still walking there.'

'You have to remember,' replied Margaret, with a faint irony in her voice, 'that I had just refused him, so we should scarcely have come back arm in arm. He is a gentleman, anyhow; and he loitered behind—and so got charged with murder.'

'In those few moments,' said Valentin gravely, 'he might really—'

The knock came again, and Ivan put in his scarred face.

'Beg pardon, sir,' he said, 'but Mr Brayne has left the house.'

'Left!' cried Valentin, and rose for the first time to his feet.

'Gone. Scooted. Evaporated,' replied Ivan, in humorous French. 'His hat and coat are gone, too; and I'll tell you something to cap it all. I ran outside the house to find any traces of him, and I found one, and a big trace, too.'

'What do you mean?' asked Valentin.

'I'll show you,' said his servant, and reappeared with a flashing naked cavalry sabre, streaked with blood about the point and edge. Everyone in the room eyed it as if it were a thunderbolt; but the experienced Ivan went on quite quietly:

'I found this,' he said, 'flung among the bushes fifty yards up the road to Paris. In other words, I found it just where your respectable Mr Brayne threw it when he ran away.'

There was again a silence, but of a new sort. Valentin took the sabre, examined it, reflected with unaffected concentration of thought, and then turned a respectful face to O'Brien. 'Commandant,' he said, 'we trust you will always produce this weapon if it is wanted for police examination. Meanwhile,' he added, slapping the steel back in the ringing scabbard, 'let me return you your sword.'

At the military symbolism of the action the audience could hardly refrain from applause.

For Neil O'Brien, indeed, that gesture was the turning-point of existence. By the time he was wandering in the mysterious garden again in the colours of the morning the tragic futility of his ordinary mien had fallen from him; he was a man with many reasons for happiness. Lord Galloway was a gentleman, and had offered him an apology. Lady Margaret was something better than a lady, a woman at least, and had perhaps given him something better than an apology, as they drifted among the old flower-beds before breakfast. The whole company was more light-hearted and humane, for though the riddle of the death remained, the load of suspicion was lifted off them all, and sent flying off to Paris with the strange millionaire—a man they hardly knew. The devil was cast out of the house—he had cast himself out.

Still, the riddle remained; and when O'Brien threw himself on a garden seat beside Dr Simon, that keenly scientific person at once resumed it. He did not get much talk out of O'Brien, whose thoughts were on pleasanter things.

'I can't say it interests me much,' said the Irishman frankly, 'especially as it seems pretty plain now. Apparently Brayne hated this stranger for some reason; lured him into the garden, and killed him with my sword. Then he fled to the city, tossing the sword away as he went. By the way, Ivan tells me the dead man had a Yankee dollar in his pocket. So he was a countryman of Brayne's, and that seems to clinch it. I don't see any difficulties about the business.'

'There are five colossal difficulties,' said the doctor quietly; 'like high walls within walls. Don't mistake me. I don't doubt that Brayne did it; his flight, I fancy, proves that. But as to how he did it. First difficulty: Why should a man kill another man with a great hulking sabre, when he can almost kill him with a pocket knife and put it back in his pocket? Second difficulty: Why was there no noise or outcry? Does a man commonly see another come up waving a scimitar and offer no remarks? Third difficulty: A servant watched the front door all the evening; and a rat cannot get into Valentin's garden anywhere. How did the dead man get into the garden? Fourth difficulty: Given the same conditions, how did Brayne get out of the garden?'

'And the fifth,' said Neil, with eyes fixed on the English priest, who was coming slowly up the path.

'Is a trifle, I suppose,' said the doctor, 'but I think an odd one. When I first saw how the head had been slashed, I supposed the assassin had struck more than once. But on examination I found many cuts across the truncated section; in other words, they were struck *after* the head was off. Did Brayne hate his foe so fiendishly that he stood sabring his body in the moonlight?'

'Horrible!' said O'Brien, and shuddered.

The little priest, Brown, had arrived while they were talking, and had waited, with characteristic shyness, till they had finished. Then he said awkwardly:

'I say, I'm sorry to interrupt. But I was sent to tell you the news!'

'News?' repeated Simon, and stared at him rather painfully through his glasses.

'Yes, I'm sorry,' said Father Brown mildly. 'There's been another murder, you know.'

Both men on the seat sprang up, leaving it rocking.

'And, what's stranger still,' continued the priest, with his dull eyes on the rhododendrons, 'it's the same disgusting sort; it's another beheading. They found the second head actually bleeding in the river, a few yards along Brayne's road to Paris; so they suppose that he—'

'Great Heaven!' cried O'Brien. 'Is Brayne a monomaniac?'

'There are American vendettas,' said the priest impassively. Then he added: 'They want you to come to the library and see it.'

Commandant O'Brien followed the others towards the inquest, feeling decidedly sick. As a soldier, he loathed all this secretive carnage; where were these extravagant amputations going to stop? First one head was hacked off, and then another; in this case (he told himself bitterly) it was not true that two heads were better than one. As he crossed the study he almost staggered at a shocking coincidence. Upon Valentin's table lay the coloured picture of yet a third bleeding head; and it was the head of Valentin himself. A second glance showed him it was only a Nationalist paper, called *The Guillotine*, which every week showed one of its political opponents with rolling eyes and writhing features just after execution; for Valentin was an anti-clerical of some note. But O'Brien was an Irishman, with a kind of chastity even in his sins; and his gorge rose against that great brutality of the intellect which belongs only to France. He felt Paris as a whole, from the grotesques on the Gothic churches to the gross caricatures in the newspapers. He remembered the gigantic jests of the Revolution. He saw the whole city as one ugly energy, from the sanguinary sketch lying on Valentin's table up to where, above a mountain and forest of gargoyles, the great devil grins on Notre Dame.

The library was long, low, and dark; what light entered it shot from under low blinds and had still some of the ruddy tinge of morning. Valentin and his servant Ivan were waiting for them at the upper end of a long, slightly-sloping desk, on which lay the mortal remains, looking enormous in the twilight. The big black figure and yellow face of the man found in the garden confronted them essentially unchanged. The second head, which had been fished from among the river reeds that morning, lay streaming and dripping beside it; Valentin's men were still seeking to recover the rest of this second corpse, which was supposed to be afloat. Father Brown, who did not seem to share O'Brien's sensibilities in the least, went up to the second head and examined it with his blinking care. It was little more than a mop of wet, white hair, fringed with silver fire in the red and level morning light; the face, which seemed of an ugly, empurpled and perhaps criminal type, had been much battered against trees or stones as it tossed in the water.

'Good morning, Commandant O'Brien,' said Valentin, with quiet cordiality. 'You have heard of Brayne's last experiment in butchery, I suppose?'

Father Brown was still bending over the head with white hair, and he said, without looking up:

'I suppose it is quite certain that Brayne cut off this head, too.'

'Well, it seems common sense,' said Valentin, with his hands in his pockets. 'Killed in the same way as the other. Found within a few yards of the other. And sliced by the same weapon which we know he carried away.'

'Yes, yes; I know,' replied Father Brown, submissively. 'Yet, you know, I doubt whether Brayne could have cut off this head.'

'Why not?' inquired Dr Simon, with a rational stare.

'Well, doctor,' said the priest, looking up blinking, 'can a man cut off his own head? I don't know.'

O'Brien felt an insane universe crashing about his ears; but the doctor sprang forward with impetuous practicality and pushed back the wet, white hair.

'Oh, there's no doubt it's Brayne,' said the priest quietly. 'He had exactly that chip in the left ear.'

The detective, who had been regarding the priest with steady and glittering eyes, opened his clenched mouth and said sharply: 'You seem to know a lot about him, Father Brown.'

'I do,' said the little man simply. 'I've been about with him for some weeks. He was thinking of joining our church.'

The star of the fanatic sprang into Valentin's eyes; he strode towards the priest with clenched hands. 'And, perhaps,' he cried, with a blasting sneer: 'perhaps he was also thinking of leaving all his money to your church.'

'Perhaps he was,' said Brown stolidly; 'it is possible.'

'In that case,' cried Valentin, with a dreadful smile: 'you may indeed know a great deal about him. About his life and about his—'

Commandant O'Brien laid a hand on Valentin's arm. 'Drop that slanderous rubbish, Valentin,' he said: 'or there may be more swords yet.'

But Valentin (under the steady, humble gaze of the priest) had already recovered himself. 'Well,' he said shortly: 'people's private opinions can wait. You gentlemen are still bound by your promise to stay; you must enforce it on yourselves—and on each other. Ivan here will tell you anything more you want to know; I must get to business and write to the authorities. We can't keep this quiet any longer. I shall be writing in my study if there is any more news.'

'Is there any more news, Ivan?' asked Dr Simon, as the chief of police strode out of the room.

'Only one more thing, I think, sir,' said Ivan, wrinkling up his grey old face; 'but that's important, too, in its way. There's that old buffer you found on the lawn,' and he pointed without pretence of reverence at the big black body with the yellow head. 'We've found out who he is, anyhow.'

'Indeed!' cried the astonished doctor; 'and who is he?'

'His name was Arnold Becker,' said the under-detective, 'though he went by many aliases. He was a wandering sort of scamp, and is known to have been in America; so that was where Brayne got his knife into him. We didn't have much to do with him ourselves, for he worked mostly in Germany. We've communicated, of course, with the German police. But, oddly enough, there was a twin brother of his, named Louis Becker, whom we had a great deal to do with. In fact, we found it necessary to guillotine him only yesterday. Well, it's a rum thing, gentlemen, but when I saw that fellow flat on the lawn I had the greatest jump of my life. If I hadn't seen Louis Becker guillotined with my own eyes, I'd have sworn it was Louis Becker lying there in the grass. Then, of course, I remembered his twin brother in Germany, and following up the clue—'

The explanatory Ivan stopped, for the excellent reason that nobody was listening to him. The Commandant and the doctor were both staring at Father Brown, who had sprung stiffly to his feet, and was holding his temples tight like a man in sudden and violent pain.

'Stop, stop, stop!' he cried; 'stop talking a minute, for I see half. Will God give me strength? Will my brain make the one jump and see all? Heaven help me! I used to be fairly good at thinking. I could paraphrase any page in Aquinas once. Will my head split—or will it see? I see half—I only see half.'

He buried his head in his hands, and stood in a sort of rigid torture of thought or prayer, while the other three could only go on staring at this last prodigy of their wild twelve hours.

When Father Brown's hands fell they showed a face quite fresh and serious, like a child's. He heaved a huge sigh, and said: 'Let us get this said and done with as quickly as possible. Look here, this will be the quickest way to convince you all of the truth.' He turned to the doctor. 'Dr Simon,' he said, 'you have a strong head-piece, and I heard you this morning asking the five hardest questions about this business. Well, if you will now ask them again, I will answer them.'

Simon's pince-nez dropped from his nose in his doubt and wonder, but he answered at once. 'Well, the first question, you know, is why a man should kill another with a clumsy sabre at all when a man can kill with a bodkin?'

'A man cannot behead with a bodkin,' said Brown, calmly, 'and for *this* murder beheading was absolutely necessary.'

'Why?' asked O'Brien, with interest.

'And the next question?' asked Father Brown.

'Well, why didn't the man cry out or anything?' asked the doctor; 'sabres in gardens are certainly unusual.'

'Twigs,' said the priest gloomily, and turned to the window which looked on the scene of death. 'No one saw the point of the twigs. Why should they lie on that lawn (look at it) so far from any tree? They were not snapped off; they were chopped off. The murderer occupied his enemy with some tricks with the sabre, showing how he could cut a branch in mid air, or what not. Then, while his enemy bent down to see the result, a silent slash, and the head fell.'

'Well,' said the doctor slowly, 'that seems plausible enough. But my next two questions will stump anyone.'

The priest still stood looking critically out of the window and waited.

'You know how all the garden was sealed up like an air-tight chamber,' went on the doctor. 'Well, how did the strange man get into the garden?'

Without turning round, the little priest answered: 'There never was any strange man in the garden.'

There was a silence, and then a sudden cackle of almost childish laughter relieved the strain. The absurdity of Brown's remark moved Ivan to open taunts.

'Oh!' he cried; 'then we didn't lug a great fat corpse on to a sofa last night? He hadn't got into the garden, I suppose?'

'Got into the garden?' repeated Brown reflectively. 'No, not entirely.'

'Hang it all,' cried Simon, 'a man gets into a garden, or he doesn't.'

'Not necessarily,' said the priest, with a faint smile. 'What is the next question, doctor?'

'I fancy you're ill,' exclaimed Dr Simon sharply; 'but I'll ask the next question if you like. How did Brayne get out of the garden?'

'He didn't get out of the garden,' said the priest, still looking out of the window.

'Didn't get out of the garden?' exploded Simon.

'Not completely,' said Father Brown.

Simon shook his fists in a frenzy of French logic. 'A man gets out of a garden, or he doesn't,' he cried.

'Not always,' said Father Brown.

Dr Simon sprang to his feet impatiently. 'I have no time to spare on such senseless talk,' he cried angrily. 'If you can't understand a man being on one side of the wall or the other, I won't trouble you further.'

'Doctor,' said the cleric very gently, 'we have always got on very pleasantly together. If only for the sake of old friendship, stop and tell me your fifth question.'

The impatient Simon sank into a chair by the door and said briefly: 'The head and shoulders were cut about in a queer way. It seemed to be done after death.'

'Yes,' said the motionless priest, 'it was done so as to make you assume exactly the one simple falsehood that you did assume. It was done to make you take for granted that the head belonged to the body.'

The borderland of the brain, where all the monsters are made, moved horribly in the Gaelic O'Brien. He felt the chaotic presence of all the horse-men and fish-women that man's unnatural fancy has begotten. A voice older than his first fathers seemed saying in his ear: 'Keep out of the monstrous garden where grows the tree with double fruit. Avoid the evil garden where died the man with two heads.' Yet, while these shameful symbolic shapes passed across the ancient mirror of his Irish soul, his Frenchified intellect was quite alert, and was watching the odd priest as closely and incredulously as all the rest.

Father Brown had turned round at last, and stood against the window with his face in dense shadow; but even in that shadow they could see it was pale as ashes. Nevertheless, he spoke quite sensibly, as if there were no Gaelic souls on earth.

'Gentlemen,' he said; 'you did not find the strange body of Becker in the garden. You did not find any strange body in the garden. In face of Dr Simon's rationalism, I still affirm that Becker was only partly present. Look here!' (pointing to the black bulk of the mysterious corpse); 'you never saw that man in your lives. Did you ever see this man?'

He rapidly rolled away the bald-yellow head of the unknown, and put in its place the white-maned head beside it. And there, complete, unified, unmistakable, lay Julius K. Brayne.

'The murderer,' went on Brown quietly, 'hacked off his enemy's head and flung the sword far over the wall. But he was too clever to fling the sword only. He flung the *head* over the wall also. Then he had only to clap on another head to the corpse, and (as he insisted on a private inquest) you all imagined a totally new man.'

'Clap on another head!' said O'Brien, staring. 'What other head? Heads don't grow on garden bushes, do they?'

'No,' said Father Brown huskily, and looking at his boots; 'there is only one place where they grow. They grow in the basket of the guillotine, beside which the Chief of Police, Aristide Valentin, was standing not an hour before the murder. Oh, my friends, hear me a minute more before you tear me in pieces. Valentin is an honest man, if being mad for an arguable cause is honesty. But did you ever see in that cold, grey eye of his that he is mad? He would do anything, *anything,* to break what he calls the superstition of the Cross. He has fought for it and starved for it, and now he has murdered for it. Brayne's crazy millions had hitherto been scattered among so many sects that they did little to alter the balance of things. But Valentin heard a whisper that Brayne, like so many scatter-brained sceptics, was drifting to us; and that was quite a different thing. Brayne would pour supplies into the impoverished and pugnacious Church of France; he would support six Nationalist newspapers like *The Guillotine.* The battle was already balanced on a point, and the fanatic took flame at the risk. He resolved to destroy the millionaire, and he did it as one would expect the greatest of detectives to commit his only crime. He abstracted the severed head of Becker on some criminological excuse, and took it home in his official box. He had that last argument with Brayne, that Lord Galloway did not hear the end of; that failing, he led him out into the sealed garden, talked about swordsmanship, used twigs and a sabre for illustration, and—'

Ivan of the Scar sprang up. 'You lunatic,' he yelled; 'you'll go to my master now, if I take you by—'

'Why, I was going there,' said Brown heavily; 'I must ask him to confess, and all that.'

Driving the unhappy Brown before them like a hostage or sacrifice, they rushed together into the sudden stillness of Valentin's study.

The great detective sat at his desk apparently too occupied to hear their turbulent entrance. They paused a moment, and then something in the look of that upright and elegant back made the doctor run forward suddenly. A touch and a glance showed him that there was a small box of pills at Valentin's elbow, and that Valentin was dead in his chair; and on the blind face of the suicide was more than the pride of Cato.

# THE SECRET OF THE *MAGNIFIQUE*

## *E. Phillips Oppenheim*

Edward Phillips Oppenheim (1886–1946), famed in his lifetime as 'the Prince of Storytellers', was, according to Colin Watson's *Snobbery With Violence* (1971), 'the son of a Leicester leather manufacturer, who first tasted the delights of the Cote d'Azur when he was travelling in France on behalf of his father's firm... His output in the long life that ended in 1946 was enormous... a total of 150 novels. Into these and countless short stories and articles he poured some thirteen million words. Crime was an important but not the dominant ingredient of an Oppenheim story. His preoccupation always was the elegance and luxury of high life.'

He benefited from having first-hand knowledge of that high life. Exotic foreign locations formed the background to many of his stories, and contributed to their appeal to readers who never came closer to the Riviera than devouring stories set there. Oppenheim's fellow spy novelist Valentine Williams said: 'Anyone more thoroughly steeped in the Cote d'Azur atmosphere it is impossible to conceive... he has the sweetest and gentlest of natures... yet... lives in a world of his own imagining, peopled with potential assassins, with mystery behind every lighted window and violent death behind every bush'. This story, a good example of his work, first appeared in *The Popular Magazine* in 1912 and was collected a year later in *Mr Laxworthy's Adventures*; it was adapted for television as an episode in *The Rivals of Sherlock Holmes*, in 1973.

THE MAN WAS AWAITING THE SERVICE OF HIS DINNER IN THE magnificent buffet of the Gare de Lyons. He sat at a table laid for three, on the right-hand side of the entrance and close to the window. From below came the turmoil of the trains. Every few minutes the swing doors opened to admit little parties of travellers. The solitary occupant of the table scarcely ever moved his head. Yet he had always the air of one who watches.

In appearance he was both unremarkable and undistinguished. He was of somewhat less than medium height, of unathletic, almost frail physique. His head was thrust a little forward, as though he were afflicted with a chronic stoop. He wore steel-rimmed spectacles with the air of one who has taken to them too late in life to have escaped the constant habit of peering, which had given to his neck an almost stork-like appearance. His hair and thin moustache were iron-grey, his fingers long and delicate. The labels upon his luggage were addressed in a trim, scholarly hand:

MR JOHN T. LAXWORTHY,
Passenger to —— ,
Via Paris.

A maître d'hôtel, who was passing, paused and looked at the two as yet unoccupied places.

'Monsieur desires the service of his dinner?' he inquired.

Mr John T. Laxworthy glanced up at the clock and carefully compared the time with his own watch. He answered the man's inquiry in French which betrayed no sign of any accent.

'In five minutes,' he declared, 'my friends will have arrived. The service of dinner can then proceed.'

The man bowed and withdrew, a little impressed by his customer's trim precision of speech. Almost as he left the table, the swing doors opened once more to admit another traveller. The new-comer stood on the threshold for a moment, looking around him. He carried a much-labelled dressing-case in his hand, and an umbrella under his arm. He stood firmly upon his feet, and a more thoroughly British, self-satisfied, and obvious person had, to all appearance, never climbed those stairs. He wore a travelling-suit of dark grey, a check ulster, broad-toed boots, and a Homburg hat. His complexion was sandy, and his figure distinctly inclined towards corpulence. He wore scarcely noticeable side-whiskers, and his chin and upper lip were clean-shaven. His eyes were bright and his mouth had an upward and humorous turn. The initials upon his bag were W.F.A., and a printed label upon the same indicated his full name as:

MR W. FORREST ANDERSON,
Passenger to —— ,
Via Paris.

His brief contemplation of the room was soon over. His eyes fell upon the solitary figure, now deep in a book, seated at the table on his right. He set down his dressing-case by the side of the wall, yielded his coat and hat to the attendant vestiaire, and, with the pleased smile of one who greets an old friend approached the table at which Mr John T. Laxworthy sat waiting.

The idiosyncrasies of great men are always worth noting, and Mr John T. Laxworthy was, without a doubt, foredoomed from the cradle to a certain measure of celebrity. His method of receiving the new-comer was in some respects curious. From the moment when the swing doors had been pushed open and the portly figure of Mr Forrest Anderson had crossed the threshold, his eyes had not once quitted the heavy-looking volume, the contents of which appeared so completely to absorb his attention. Even now, when his friend stood by his side, he did not at once look up. Slowly, and with his eyes still riveted upon the pages he was studying, he held out his left hand.

'I am glad to see you, Anderson,' he said. 'Sit down by my side here. You are nearly ten minutes late. I have delayed ordering the wine until your arrival. Shall it be white or red?'

Mr Anderson shook with much heartiness the limp fingers which had been offered to him, and took the seat indicated. His friend's eccentricity of manner appeared to be familiar to him, and he offered no comment upon it.

'White, if you please—Chablis of a dry brand, for choice. Sorry if I'm late. Beastly crossing, beastly crowded train. Glad to be here, anyhow.'

Mr John T. Laxworthy closed his book with a little sigh of regret, and placed a marker within it. He then carefully adjusted his spectacles and made a deliberate survey of his companion. Finally he nodded, slowly and approvingly.

'How about the partridges?' he inquired.

'Bad,' Mr Anderson declared, with a sigh. 'It was one storm in June that did it. We went light last season, though, and I'm putting down forty brace of Hungarians. You see—'

Mr Laxworthy touched the table with his forefinger, and his companion almost automatically stopped.

'Quite excellent,' the former pronounced dryly. 'Don't overdo it. I should think that this must be Sydney.'

Mr Anderson glanced towards the entrance. Then he looked back at his companion a little curiously. Mr Laxworthy had not raised his head.

'How the dickens did you know that it was Sydney?' he demanded.

Mr Laxworthy smiled at the tablecloth.

'I have a special sense for that sort of thing,' he remarked. 'I like to use my eyes as seldom as possible.'

A young man who had just completed a leisurely survey of the room dropped his monocle and came towards them. From the tips of his shiny tan shoes to his smoothly brushed hair, he was unmistakable. He was young, he was English, he was well-bred, he was an athlete. He had a pleasant, unintelligent face, a natural and prepossessing ease of manner. He handed his ulster to the attendant vestiaire and beamed upon the two men.

'How are you, Forrest? How do you do, Laxworthy?' he exclaimed. 'Looking jolly fit, both of you.'

Mr Laxworthy raised his glass. He looked thoughtfully at the wine for a moment, to be sure that it was free from any atom of cork. Then he inclined his head in turn to each of his companions.

'I am glad to see you both,' he said. 'On the whole, I think that I may congratulate you. You have done well. I drink to our success.'

The toast was drunk in silence. Mr Forrest Anderson set down his glass—empty—with a little murmur of content.

'It is something,' he remarked, vigorously attacking a new course, 'to have satisfied our chief.'

The young man opposite to him subjected the dish which was being offered to a long and deliberate survey through his eyeglass, and finally refused it.

'Give me everything in France except the beef,' he declared. 'Must be the way they cut it, I think. Quite right, Andy,' he went on, glancing across the table. 'To have satisfied such a critic as the chief here is an achievement indeed. Having done it, let us hear what he proposes to do with us.'

'In other words,' Mr Anderson put in, 'what is the game to be?'

There was a short pause. Mr John T. Laxworthy was continuing his repast—which was, by the by, of a much more frugal character than that offered to his guests—without any sign of having even heard the inquiry addressed to him by his companions. They knew him, however, and they were content to wait. Presently he commenced to peel an apple and simultaneously to unburden himself.

'A great portion of this last year,' he said, 'which you two have spent apparently with profit in carrying out my instructions, I myself have devoted to the perfection of a certain scholarly tone which I feel convinced is my proper environment. Incidentally, I have devoted myself to the study of various schools of philosophy.'

'I will take a liqueur,' decided the young man, whose name was Sydney—'something brain-stimulating. A Grand Marnier, waiter, if you please.'

'The same for me,' Mr Forrest Anderson put in hastily. 'Also, in a few moments, some black coffee.'

Mr Laxworthy did not by the flicker of an eyelid betray the slightest annoyance at these interruptions. He waited, indeed, until the liqueurs had been brought before he spoke again, continuing the while in a leisurely fashion the peeling and preparing of his apple. Even for some time after his friends had again offered him their undivided attention, he continued his task of extracting from it, with precise care, every fragment of core.

'In one very interesting treatise,' he recommenced at last, 'I found several obvious truths ingeniously put. A certain decadence in the material prosperity of an imaginary state is clearly proved to be due to a too blind following of the tenets of what is known as the hysterical morality, as against the decrees of what we might call expediency. A little sentiment, like garlic in cookery, is a good thing; too much is fatal. A little—sufficient—morality is excellent; a superabundance disastrous. Society is divided into two classes, those who have and those who desire to have. The one must always prey upon the other. They are, therefore, always changing places. It is this continued movement which lends energy to the human race. As soon as it is suspended, degeneration must follow as a matter of course. It is for those who recognise this great truth to follow and obey its tenets.'

'May we not hear more definitely what it is that you propose?' Anderson asked, a little anxiously.

'We stand,' Mr Laxworthy replied, 'always upon the threshold of the land of adventure. At no place are we nearer to it than in this room. It is our duty to use our energies to assist in the great principles of movement to which I have referred. We must take our part in the struggle. On which side? you naturally ask. Are we to be amongst those who have, and who, through weakness or desire, must yield to others? or shall we take our place amongst the more intellectual, the more highly gifted minority, those who assist the progress of the world by helping towards the redistribution of its wealth? Sydney, how much money have you?'

'Three hundred and ninety-five francs and a few coppers,' the young man answered promptly. 'It sounds more in French.'

'And you, Anderson?'

Mr Forrest Anderson coughed.

'With the exception of a five-franc piece,' he admitted, 'I am worth exactly as much as I shall be able to borrow from you presently.'

'In that case,' Mr Laxworthy said dryly, 'our position is preordained. We take our place amongst the aggressors.'

The young man whose name was Sydney dropped his eyeglass.

'One moment,' he said. 'Andy here and I have exposed our financial impecuniosity at your request. It can scarcely be a surprise to you, considering that we have practically lived upon your bounty for the last year. It seems only fair that you should imitate our candour. There were rumours, a short time ago, of a considerable sum of money to which you had become entitled. To tell you the truth,' the young man went on, leaning a little across the table, 'we were almost afraid, or rather I was, that you might abandon this shadowy enterprise of ours.'

Mr John T. Laxworthy, without being discomposed, which was almost too much to expect of a man with such perfect poise, seemed nevertheless somewhat taken aback. He opened his lips as though to make some reply, and closed them again. When he did speak, it was grudgingly.

'No successful enterprise, or series of enterprises, can be conducted without capital,' he said. 'I am free to admit that I am in possession of a certain amount of that indispensable commodity. I do not feel myself called upon to state the exact amount, but such money as is required for our journeyings, or for any enterprise in which we become engaged will be forthcoming.'

Mr Anderson stroked his chin meditatively.

'I am sure,' he said, 'that that sounds quite satisfactory.'

'I call it jolly fine business,' the young man declared. 'There is just one thing more upon which I think we ought to have an understanding. You say that we are to take our place amongst the aggressors. Exactly what does that mean?'

Mr Laxworthy looked at him coldly.

'It means precisely what I choose that it shall mean,' he replied. 'Any enterprise or adventure in which we may become engaged will be selected by me, and by me only. My chief aim—I have no objection to telling you this—is to make life tolerable for ourselves, to escape the dull monotony of idleness, and, incidentally, to embrace any opportunity which may present itself to enrich our exchequer. Have you any objection to that?'

'None,' Mr Forrest Anderson declared.

'None at all,' Sydney echoed.

'There are three of us,' Mr Laxworthy went on. 'We each have our use. Mine is the chief of all. I supply the brains. My position must be unquestioned.'

'For my part, I am willing enough,' Sydney remarked. 'It's been your show from the first.'

Mr Forrest Anderson, who had dined well and forgotten his empty pockets, laughed a genial laugh.

'I agree,' he declared. 'Tell us, when and where do we start, and shall our first enterprise be Pickwickian, or am I to play the Sancho Panza to your Don Quixote and Sydney's donkey?'

Mr Laxworthy regarded his associates coldly. There was a silence, a silence which became somehow an ominous thing. Around them reigned a babel of tongues, a clatter of crockery. Below, the turmoil of the busy station, the shrieking of departing trains. But at the table presided over by Mr Laxworthy no word was spoken. Mr Anderson's geniality faded away. His young companion's amiable nonchalance entirely deserted him. Either of them would have given worlds to have been able to dispel the strange effect of this silence with some casual remark. But upon them lay the spell of the conqueror. The little man at the head of the table held them in the hollow of his hand.

'It may be,' he said, breaking at last that curious silence, 'that no other occasion will ever arise when it will be necessary to speak to you in this fashion. So now listen. You are right to indulge in the urbanities of existence. Keep always the smile upon your lips, if you can, but underneath let the real consciousness of life be ever present. I do not claim for myself the genius of a Pickwick or the valour of a Don Quixote. On the other hand, we are not paltry aggressors against Society, failing in one enterprise, successful in the next, a mark for ridicule and contempt one moment, and for good-humoured sufferance the next. I do not ask you to embark with me as farceurs upon a series of enterprises carried out upon the principle of "Let us do our best and chance the rest." It is just possible that the fates may be against us, and that we may live together for many months the lives of ordinary and moderately commonplace human beings. I ask you to remember that no sense of danger would ever deter me from embarking upon any adventure which I deemed likely to afford us either diversion, wealth, or satisfaction of any sort whatsoever. We are not pleasure-seekers. We are men whose one end and aim is to escape from the chains of everyday existence, to avoid the humdrum life of our fellows. Therein may lie for us many and peculiar dangers. Adopt, if you will, the motto of the pagans—"Let us eat and drink, for to-morrow we die!" So long as you remember. Will you drink with me to that remembrance?'

Mr Laxworthy, as he grew less enigmatic in his speech, became, if possible, more whimsical in his mannerisms. He ordered the best Cognac, at which he himself scarcely glanced, and turned with a little sigh of relief to his book. In the midst of this hubbub of sounds and bustle of diners he continued to read with every appearance of studious enjoyment. His two companions were content enough, apparently, to relax after their journey and enjoy their cigars. Nevertheless, they once or twice glanced curiously at their chief. One of these glances he seemed, although he never raised his head, to have intercepted, for, carefully marking the place in his book, he pushed it away and addressed them.

'Our plans,' he announced abruptly, 'are not yet wholly made. We wait here for—shall we call it an inspiration? Perhaps, even at this moment, it is not far from us.'

Mr Forrest Anderson and his vis-à-vis turned as though instinctively towards the door. At that moment two men who had just passed through were standing upon the threshold. One was rather past middle-age, corpulent, with red features of a coarse type. His companion, who was leaning upon his arm, was much younger, and a very different sort of person. He was tall and exceedingly thin. His features were wasted almost to emaciation, his complexion was ghastly. He seemed to have barely strength enough to move.

'They are coming to the table next us,' Laxworthy said, in a very low tone. 'The address upon their luggage will be interesting.'

Slowly the two men came down the room. As Laxworthy had expected, they took possession of an empty table close at hand. The young man sank into his chair with a little sigh of exhaustion.

'A liqueur brandy, quick,' the older man ordered, as he accepted the menu from a waiter. 'My friend is fatigued.'

Sydney took the bottle which stood upon their own table poured out a wineglassful, and, rising to his feet, stepped across and accosted the young man.

'Do me the favour of drinking this, sir,' he begged. 'The service here is slow and the brandy excellent. I can see that you are in need of it. It may serve, too, as an aperitif.'

The young man accepted it with a smile of gratitude. His companion echoed his thanks.

'Very much obliged to you, sir,' he declared. 'My friend here is a little run down and finds travelling fatiguing.'

'A passing malady, I trust?' Sydney remarked, preparing to return to his seat.

'A legacy from that cursed graveyard—South Africa,' the older man growled.

Sydney stepped back and resumed his seat. In a few minutes he leaned across the table.

'The Paradise Hotel, Hyères,' he said under his breath.

Mr Laxworthy looked thoughtful.

'You surprise me,' he admitted.

'What do you know of them?' Anderson inquired.

Mr Laxworthy shrugged his shoulders.

'Not much beyond the obvious facts,' he admitted. 'Even you, my friends, are not wholly deceived, I presume, by the young man's appearance?'

They evidently were. Their faces expressed their non-comprehension.

Mr Laxworthy sighed.

'You must both of you seek to develop the minor senses,' he enjoined reprovingly. 'Your powers of observation, for instance, are, without doubt, exceedingly stunted. Let me assure you, for example, that your sympathy for that young man is entirely wasted.'

'You mean that he is not really ill?' Sydney asked incredulously.

'Most certainly he is not as ill as he pretends,' Mr Laxworthy declared dryly. 'If you look at him more closely you will discover a certain theatricality in his pose which of itself should undeceive you.'

'You know who he is?' Sydney asked.

'I believe so,' Laxworthy admitted. 'I can hazard a guess even to his companion's identity. But—the Paradise Hotel, Hyères! Order some fresh coffee. We are not ready to leave yet. Anderson, watch the door. Sydney, don't let them notice it, but watch our friends there. Something may happen.'

A tall, broad-shouldered man with a fair moustache and wearing a long travelling-coat had entered the buffet. He stood there for a moment looking around, as though in search of a table. The majority of those present suffered his scrutiny, unnoticing, indifferent, naturally absorbed in themselves and their own affairs. Not so these two men who had last entered. Every nerve of the young man's body seemed to have become tense. His hand had stolen into the pocket of his travelling-coat, and with a little thrill Sydney saw the glitter of steel half shown for a moment between his interlocked fingers. No longer was this young man's countenance the countenance of an invalid. It had become instead like the face of a wolf. His front teeth were showing—he had moved slightly so as to give his arm full play. It seemed as though a tragedy were at hand.

The man who had been standing on the threshold deposited his handbag upon the floor near the wall, and came down the room. Laxworthy and his two associates watched. Their two neighbours at the next table sat in well simulated indifference, only once more Sydney saw the gleam of hidden steel flash for a moment from the depths of that ulster pocket. The new-comer made no secret of his destination. He advanced straight to their table and came to a standstill immediately in front of them. Both the stout man and his invalid companion looked up at him as one might regard a stranger.

To all appearance Laxworthy was engrossed in his book. Sydney and Anderson watched and listened, but of all the words which passed between those three men, not one was audible. No change of countenance on the part of any one of the three indicated even the nature of that swift and fluent interchange of words. Only at the last, the elder man touched the label attached to his dressing-bag, and they heard his words:

'The Paradise Hotel, Hyères. We shall be there for at least a month.'

The new-comer stood perfectly still for several moments, as though deliberating. The young man's hand came an inch or two from his pocket. Chance and tragedy trifled together in the midst of that crowded room, unnoticed save by those three at the adjoining table. Then, as though inspired with a sudden resolution, this stranger, whose coming had seemed so unwelcome, raised his hat slightly to the two men with whom he had been talking, and turned away.

'The Paradise Hotel at Hyères,' he repeated. 'I shall know, then, where to find you.'

The little scene was over. Nothing had happened. Nevertheless, the fingers of the young man, as his hand emerged from his pocket, were moist and damp, and his appearance was now veritably ghastly. His companion watched, with a deep purple flush upon his face, the passing of this stranger who had accosted him. He had the appearance of one threatened with apoplexy.

'One might be interested to know the meaning of these things,' Sydney murmured softly.

Their chief looked up from his book.

'Then one must follow—to the Paradise Hotel,' he remarked.

'I begin to believe,' Anderson declared, 'that it is our destination.'

'There is no hurry,' Laxworthy replied. 'Grimes once told me that this room in which we are now sitting was perhaps the most interesting rendezvous in Europe. Grimes was at the head of the Foreign Department at Scotland Yard in those days, and he knew what he was talking about.'

A woman, wrapped in magnificent furs, who was passing their table, was run into by a clumsy waiter and dropped a satchel from her finger. Sydney hastened to restore it to her, and was rewarded by a gracious smile in which was mingled a certain amount of recognition.

'You seem fated to be my Good Samaritan to-day,' she remarked.

'It is my good fortune,' the young man replied. 'Can I help you to get a table or anything? This place is always overcrowded.'

She motioned with her head to where a maître d'hôtel was holding a chair for her.

'It is already arranged,' she said. 'Perhaps we shall meet in the Luxe afterwards, if you are going south.'

'You are travelling far?' Sydney ventured to inquire.

'Only to the outskirts of the Riviera,' she answered. 'I am going to Hyères—to the Paradise Hotel. Why do you smile?'

'My friends and I,' he explained, 'have met here to decide upon the whereabouts of a little holiday we mean to spend together. We were at that moment discussing a suggestion to proceed to the same place.'

She gave him a little farewell nod as she passed on.

'If you decide to do so,' she declared, 'it will give me great pleasure to meet you again.'

'I congratulate you,' Laxworthy remarked dryly, as Sydney resumed his seat. 'A most interesting acquaintance, yours.'

'Do you know who she is?' the young man asked. 'I only met her on the train.'

His chief nodded gravely.

'She is Madame Bertrand,' he replied. 'Her husband at one time held a post in the Foreign Office, under Fauré. For some reason or other he was discredited, and since then he has died. There was some scandal about Madame Bertrand herself, and some papers which were missing from her husband's portfolio, but nothing definite ever came to light.'

'Madame seems to survive the loss of her husband,' Mr Forrest Anderson remarked, looking across at her admiringly.

Laxworthy held up his hand. Almost for the first time he was sitting upright in his chair, his head still thrust forward in his usual attitude, his eyes fixed upon the door. The thin fingers of his right hand were spread flat upon the tablecloth.

'We have finished, for the moment, with the Madame Bertrands of the world,' he announced. 'After all, they are for the pigmies. Here comes food for giants.'

The light of battle was in Laxworthy's eyes. The greatest of men have their moments of weakness, and even Laxworthy, for that brief space of time, forgot himself and his pose toward the world. His thin lips were a little parted, the veins at the sides of his forehead stood out like blue cords. His lips moved slowly.

'You can both look,' he said. 'They are probably used to it. You will see the two greatest personages on earth.'

His companions gazed eagerly toward the door. Two men were standing there, being relieved of their wraps and directed toward a table. One was middle-aged, grey-headed, with a somewhat worn but keen face. The other was taller, with black hair streaked with grey, a face half Jewish, half romantic, a skin like ivory.

'The greatest men in the world?' Sydney repeated, under his breath. 'You are joking, chief. I never saw even a photograph of either of them before in my life.'

'The one nearest you,' Laxworthy announced, 'is Mr Freeling Poignton. The newspapers will tell you that his fortune exceeds the national debt of any country in the world. He is, without doubt, the richest man who was ever born. There has never yet breathed an emperor whose upraised finger could provoke or stop a war, whose careless word could check the prosperity of the proudest nation that ever breathed. These things Mr Freeling Poignton can do.'

'And the other?' Anderson whispered.

'It is chance,' Mr Laxworthy said softly, 'which placed a sceptre of unlimited power in the hands of Richard Freeling Poignton. It is his own genius which has made the Marquis Lefant the greatest power in the diplomatic world. It was his decision which brought about war between Russia and Japan. It was he who stopped the declaration of war against Germany by our own Prime Minister at the time of the Algeciras difficulty. It was he who offered a million pounds to bring the Tsar of Russia to Germany—and he did it. There is little that he cannot do.'

'Is he a German?' Anderson asked.

'No one knows of what race he comes,' Mr Laxworthy replied. 'No one knows what country is really nearest to his heart. It is his custom to accept commissions or refuse them, according to his own belief as to their influence upon international peace. They say that he has English blood in his veins. If so, he has been a sorry friend to his native land.'

'We seem,' Sydney remarked, 'to have chosen a very fortunate evening for our little dinner here. The place is full of interesting people. I wonder where those two are going.'

A maître d'hôtel, whose respect had been gained by the lavish orders from their table, paused and whispered confidentially in Mr Laxworthy's ear.

'The gentleman down there, sir,' he announced. 'The grey gentleman with his own servant waiting upon him, is Mr Freeling Poignton, the great American multi-millionaire.'

Laxworthy nodded slowly.

'I thought I recognised him by his photographs,' he said. 'Is he going to Monte Carlo?'

The attendant shook his head.

'I was speaking to them a moment ago, sir,' he declared. 'Mr Poignton has been here a good many times. He and his friend are going for a fortnight's quiet to the Paradise Hotel at Hyères.'

The maître d'hôtel passed on with another bow. The three men looked at one another. Mr Laxworthy glanced at the clock.

'Sydney,' he said, 'will you step down into the bureau and find out whether it is possible to get three seats in the train de luxe?'

'For Hyères?' Sydney asked.

Mr Laxworthy assented gravely.

'Certainly,' he said. 'You might at the same time telegraph to the hotel.'

'To the Paradise Hotel?'

Mr Laxworthy inclined his head.


A black cloud, long and with jagged edges, passed away from the face of the moon. The plain of Hyères was gradually revealed—the cypress trees, tall and straight, the shimmering olive trees with their ghostly foliage, the fields of violets, the level vineyards. And beyond, the phalanx of lights on the warships lying in the bay. The hotel on the hill-side, freshly painted and spotlessly white, stood sharply out against the dark background. The whole world was becoming visible.

Upon the balcony of one of the rooms upon the second floor a man was standing with his back to the wall. He looked around at the flooding moonlight and swore softly to himself. Decidedly, things were turning out ill with him. From the adjoining balcony a thin rope was hanging, swaying very slightly in the night breeze. The young man gazed helplessly at the end, which had slipped from his fingers, and which was hanging just now over some flowerbeds. He was face to face with the almost insoluble problem of how to regain the shelter of his own room.

From the gardens below came the melancholy cry of a passing owl. From the white, barnlike farmhouse, perched on the mountain-side in the distance, came the bark of a dog. Then again there was silence. The man looked back into the room from which he had escaped, and down at the end of that swinging rope. He was indeed on the horns of a dilemma. To return into the room was insanity. To stay where he was was to risk being seen by the earliest passer-by or the first person who chanced to look out from a window. To try to pass to his own veranda without the aid of that rope which he had lost was an impossibility.

It was already five minutes since he had crept out from the room and had let the rope slip from his fingers. The owl had finished his mournful serenade, the watch-dog on the mountain-side slept. The deep silence of the hours before dawn brooded over the land. The man, fiercely impatient though he was to escape, was constrained to wait. There seemed to be nothing which he could do.

Then again the silence of the night was strangely, almost harshly broken, this time from the interior of the hotel. An alarm bell, harsh and discordant, rang out a brazen note of terror. Lights suddenly flashed in the windows, footsteps hurried along the corridor. The man outside upon the balcony set his teeth and cursed. Detection now seemed unavoidable.

The room behind him was speedily invaded. Madame Bertrand, in a dressing-gown whose transparent simplicity had been the triumph of a celebrated establishment in the Rue de la Paix, her beautiful hair tied up only with pink ribbon, her eyes kindling with excitement, received a stream of agitated callers. The floor waiter, three guests in various states of déshabillé, and finally the manager, breathless with haste, all claimed her attention at the same time.

'It was I who rang the danger-bell,' madame declared indignantly. 'In an hotel where such things are possible, it is well, indeed, that one should be able to sound the alarm. There has been a man in my rooms.'

'But it is unheard of, madame!' the manager replied.

'It is nevertheless true,' madame insisted. 'Not two minutes since, I opened my eyes and he disappeared into my sitting-room. I saw him distinctly. I could not recognise him, for he kept his face turned away. Either he has escaped through the sitting-room door and down the corridor, or he is still there, or he is hiding in this room.'

'The jewels of madame!' the manager gasped.

'I tremble in every limb. How can I know whether or not I have been robbed?'

'The pearls of madame,' he persisted—'the string of pearls?'

'That is safe,' madame admitted. 'My diamond collar, too, is in its place.'

The manager and two of the guests searched the sitting-room, which opened to the left from the bedroom. Others spread themselves over the hotel to calm fears of the startled guests, and to assure everybody that there was no fire and that nothing particular had happened. The search was, of necessity, not a long one; there was no one in the sitting-room. The manager and his helpers returned.

'The room is empty, madame,' the former declared.

'Then the burglar has escaped!' she cried.

Monsieur Helder went down on his knees and peered in vain under the bed.

'Madame is sure,' he inquired, raising his head with some temerity but remaining upon his knees—'madame is absolutely convinced that it was not an illusion—the fragment of a dream, perhaps? It is strange that there should have been time for anyone to have escaped.'

'A dream, indeed!' madame declared indignantly. 'I do not dream such things, Monsieur Helder.'

Monsieur Helder dived again under the valance. It was just at that moment that Madame Bertrand, gazing into the plate-glass mirror of the wardrobe, received a shock. Distinctly she saw a man's face reflected there. With the predominant instinct of her sex aroused, she opened her lips to scream—and just as suddenly closed them again. She stood for a moment quite still, her hand pressed to her side. Then she turned her head and looked out of the French windows which led on to the balcony. There was nothing to be seen. She looked across at Monsieur Helder, whose head had disappeared inside the wardrobe. Then she stole up to the window and glanced once more on to the balcony.

'Madame,' Monsieur Helder declared, 'the room is empty. Your sitting-room also is empty. There remains,' he added, with a sudden thought, 'only the balcony.'

He advanced a step. Madame Bertrand, however, remained motionless. She was standing in front of the window.

'The balcony I have examined myself,' she said quietly. 'There is no one there. Besides, I am not one of the English cranks who sleep always with the damp night air filling their rooms. My windows are bolted.'

'In that case, madame,' Monsieur Helder declared, with a little shrug of the shoulders, 'we must conclude that the intruder escaped through your sitting-room door into the corridor. Madame can at least assure me that nothing of great value is missing from her belongings?'

Madame Bertrand, though pale, was graciously pleased to reassure the inquirer.

'You have reason, my friend,' she admitted. 'Nothing of great value is missing. The shock, however, I shall not get over for days. After this, Monsieur Helder, you will not banish my maid again to that horrible annexe. Whoever occupies the next room to mine here must give it up. Not another night will I sleep here alone and unprotected.'

Monsieur Helder bowed.

'Madame,' he said, 'the adjoining room is occupied by Mr Sydney Wing, an Englishman, whom madame will perhaps recollect. He is, I am sure, a man of gallantry. After the adventure of to-night he will doubtless offer to vacate his room for the convenience of madame's maid.'

'It must be arranged,' madame insisted.

Monsieur Helder backed toward the door.

'If madame would like her maid for the rest of the night—' he suggested.

Madame Bertrand shook her head.

'Not now,' she replied. 'I will not have the poor girl disturbed. After what has passed, she would lie here in terror. As for me, I shall lock all my doors, and perhaps, after all, I shall sleep.'

Monsieur Helder drew himself up upon the threshold. He was not a very imposing-looking object in his trousers and a crumpled shirt, but he permitted himself a bow.

'Madame,' he said, 'will accept this expression of my infinite regret that her slumbers should have been so disturbed.'

'I thank you very much, Monsieur Helder,' she answered graciously. 'Good night!'

Monsieur Helder executed his bow and disappeared. Madame paused for a moment to listen to his footsteps down the corridor. Then she moved forward to the door and locked it. For a few seconds longer she hesitated. Then she walked deliberately to the French windows, threw them open, and stepped on to the balcony.

'Good evening, Monsieur Sydney Wing—or rather good morning!'

The young man gripped for a moment the frail balustrade. It must be confessed that he had lost entirely his savoir-faire.

'Madame!' he faltered.

She pointed to the open doors.

'Inside!' she whispered imperatively—'inside at once!'

She pointed to the swinging cord. The young man stepped only too willingly inside the room. She followed him and closed the windows.

'You will gather, Monsieur Sydney Wing,' she said, 'that I am disposed to spare you. I knew that you were outside, even while my room was being searched. I preferred first to hear your explanation, before I gave you up to be treated as a common burglar.'

The young man's courage was returning fast. He lifted his head. His eyes were full of gratitude—or what, at any rate, gleamed like gratitude.

'Oh, madame,' he murmured, 'you are too gracious!'

He raised her hand to his lips and kissed it. She looked at him not unkindly.

'You will come this way,' she said, leading him into the sitting-room and turning on the electric light. 'Now, tell me, monsieur, and tell me the truth if you would leave this room a free man and without scandal. When I saw you first you were bending over that table. Upon it was my necklace, my earrings, a lace scarf, my chatelaine and vanity box, a few of my rings, perhaps a jewelled pin or two. Now tell me exactly what you came for, what you have taken, and why?'

The young man held himself upright. He drew a little breath. Fate was certainly dealing leniently with him.

'Madame,' he said, 'think. Was there nothing else upon that table?'

She shook her head.

'I can think of nothing,' she acknowledged.

'To-night,' he continued, 'you were scarcely so kind to me. We danced together, it is true, but there were many others. There was the Admiral—the French Admiral, for instance. Madame was favourably disposed towards him.'

She was a coquette, and she shrugged her shoulders as she smiled.

'Why not? Admiral Christodor is a very charming man. He dances well, he entertains upon his wonderful battleship most lavishly, he is a very desirable and delightful acquaintance. And you, Monsieur Sydney Wing, what have you to say that I should not dance and be friendly with this gentleman?'

The young man was feeling his feet upon the ground. Nevertheless, he continued to look serious.

'Alas!' he said, 'I have no right to find fault. Yet two nights ago madame gave me the rose I asked for. To-night—you remember?'

She looked at him softly yet steadily. Then she glanced at the table and back again into his face.

'You told me,' he continued, 'that the rose belonged to him who dared to pluck it.'

'It is a saying,' she murmured. 'I was not in earnest.'

Mr Sydney Wing sighed deeply.

'Madame,' he declared, 'I come of a literal nation. When we love, the word of a woman means much to us. To-night there seemed nothing dearer to me in life than the possession of that rose. I told myself that your challenge was accepted. I told myself that to-night I would sleep with that rose on the pillow by my side.'

Slowly he unbuttoned his coat. From the breast pocket he drew out a handkerchief and unfolded it. In the centre, crushed, and devoid of many of its petals, but still retaining its shape and perfume, lay a dark red rose.

Madame Bertrand moved a step towards him.

'Monsieur,' she cried incredulously, yet with some tenderness in her tone—'monsieur, you mean to tell me that for the sake of that rose you climbed from your balcony to mine, you ran these risks?'

'For the sake of this rose, madame, and all that it means to me,' he answered.

She drew a long sigh. Then she held out her hand. Again he raised it to his lips.

'Monsieur Sydney,' she said, 'I have done your countrymen an injustice all my life. I had not thought such sentiment was possible in any one of them. I am very glad indeed that when I saw your face reflected in the mirror of my wardrobe, something urged me to send Monsieur Helder away. I am very glad.'

'Madame.'

She held up her finger. Already the faint beginning of dawn was stealing into the sky. From the farmhouse away on the hill-side a cock commenced to crow.

'Monsieur,' she whispered, 'not another word. I have risked my reputation to save you. See, the door is before you. Unlock it softly. Be sure there is no one in the corridor when you leave. Do not attempt to close it. I myself in a few minutes' time will return and do that.'

'But Madame—' he begged.

She pointed imploringly towards the door, but there was tenderness in her farewell glance.

'To-morrow we will talk,' she promised. 'To-morrow night, if you should fancy my roses, perhaps I may be more kind. Good night!'

She stole back to her room and sat on the edge of her bed. Very noiselessly the young man opened the door of the sitting-room, glanced up and down, and with swift, silent footsteps made his way to his own apartment. Madame, some few minutes later, closed the door behind him, slowly slipped off her dressing-gown, and curled herself once more in her bed. Mr Sydney Wing, in the adjoining room, lit a cigarette and mixed himself a whisky-and-soda. There were drops of perspiration still upon his forehead as he stepped out on to the balcony and wound up his rope.

It was the most cheerful hour of the day at the Paradise Hotel—the hour before luncheon. A swarthy Italian was singing love-songs on the gravel sweep to the music of a guitar. The very air was filled with sunshine. A soft south wind was laden with perfumes from the violet farm below. Everyone seemed to be out of doors, promenading, or sitting about in little groups. Mr Laxworthy and Mr Forrest Anderson had just passed along the front and were threading their way up the winding path which led through the pine woods at the back of the hotel. Mr Lenfield, the invalid young man, was lying in a sheltered corner, taking a sunbath; his companion by his side smoking a large cigar and occasionally reading extracts from a newspaper. The pretty American girl, who was one of the features of the place, and Madame Bertrand, were missing, the former because she was playing golf with Sydney Wing, the latter because she never rose until luncheon-time. Mr Freeling Poignton and the Marquis Lefant were sitting a little way up amongst the pine trees. Mr Freeling Poignton was smoking his morning cigar. Lefant was leaning forward, his eyes fixed steadily upon that streak of blue Mediterranean. In his hand he held his watch.

'I am quite sure,' he said softly, 'that I can rely upon my information. At a quarter past twelve precisely the torpedo is to be fired.'

'Which is the *Magnifique*, anyway?' Mr Freeling Poignton inquired.

Lefant pointed to the largest of the grey battleships which were riding at anchor. Then his fingers slowly traversed the blue space until it paused at a black object, like a derelict barge, set out very near the island of Hyères. He glanced at his watch.

'A quarter past,' he muttered. 'Look! My God!'

The black object had disappeared. A column of white water rose gracefully into the air and descended. It was finished. Lefant leaned towards his companion.

'You and I,' he said, 'have seen a thing which is going to change the naval history of the future. You and I alone can understand why the French Admiralty have given up building battleships, why even their target practice here and at Cherbourg continues as a matter of form only.'

Mr Freeling Poignton withdrew his cigar from his mouth.

'I can't say,' he admitted, 'that I have ever given any particular attention to these implements of warfare, because I hate them all; but there's nothing new, anyway, in a torpedo. What's the difference between this one and the ordinary sort?'

'I will tell you in a very few words,' Lefant answered. 'This one can be fired at a range of five miles, and relied upon to hit a mark little larger than the plate of a battleship with absolutely scientific accuracy. There is no question of aim at all. Just as you work out an exact spot in a surveying expedition by scientific instruments, so you can decide precisely the spot which that torpedo shall hit. It travels at the pace of ten miles a minute, and it has a charge which has never been equalled.'

Mr Freeling Poignton shivered a little, as he dropped the ash of his cigar.

'I'd like to electrocute the man who invented it,' he declared tersely.

Lefant shook his head.

'You are wrong,' he replied. 'The man who invented that torpedo is the friend of your scheme and not the enemy. Listen. It is your desire—is it not—the great ambition of your life, to secure for the world universal peace?'

Mr Freeling Poignton thrust his hands into his trousers pockets.

'Marquis,' he said, 'there is no man breathing who could say how much I am worth. Capitalise my present income, and you might call it five hundred million pounds. Put a quarter of a million somewhere in the bank for me, and I'd give the rest to see every army in Europe disbanded, every warship turned into a trading vessel, and every soldier and sailor turned into the factories or upon the land to become honest, productive units.'

'Just so,' Lefant assented. 'It may sound a little Utopian, but it is magnificent. Now listen. You will never induce the rulers of the world to look upon this question reasonably, because every nation is jealous of some other, and no one is great enough to take the lead. The surest of all ways to prevent war is to reduce the art of killing to such a certainty that it becomes an absurdity even to take the field. What nation will build battleships which can be destroyed with the touch of a finger at any time, from practically any distance? I tell you that this invention, which only one or two people in the world outside of that battleship yonder know of at present, is the beginning of the end of all naval warfare. There is only one thing to be done—to drive this home. No nation must be allowed to keep the secret for her own. It must belong to all.'

Mr Freeling Poignton nodded thoughtfully.

'I begin to understand,' he remarked. 'Guess that's where you come in, isn't it?'

'I hope so,' Lefant assented. 'I have already spent a hundred thousand dollars of your money, but I think I have had value for it.'

'Say, why don't you treat this matter as we should on the other side?' Mr Freeling Poignton demanded. 'It's all very well to bribe these petty officers and such-like, but the admiral's your man. Remember that the money-bags of the world are behind you.'

Lefant smiled faintly.

'Alas!' he exclaimed, 'the admiral belongs to a race little known in the world of commerce. Money-bags which reached to the sky would never buy him. There are others on the ship who are mine, and with the information I have the rest should be possible.'

Mr Freeling Poignton frowned. He disliked very much to hear of a man who denied the omnipotence of money. He felt like the king of some foreign country to whom a stranger had refused obeisance.

'Well, you've got to run this thing,' he remarked, 'and I suppose you know what kind of lunatics you've got to deal with. Seems to me the most difficult job is for you to get on the battleship at all without the admiral's consent.'

Lefant kicked a pebble away from beneath his feet.

'That is the chief difficulty,' he admitted. 'I was rather hoping that Madame Bertrand might have been of use to me there. She has been devoting herself to the admiral for some days, and last night she got a pass from him, allowing the bearer to visit the ship at any time, with access to any part of it. This morning, however, she declares that she must have torn it up with her bridge scores.'

'I suppose she can get it replaced?' Mr Freeling Poignton suggested.

Lefant hesitated for a moment.

'To tell you the truth,' he declared, 'my own belief is that the admiral declined to give it to her. Julie hates to admit defeat, however. Hence her little story. That does not trouble me very much, though. My plans are all made in another direction. To-night is the night of the fancy-dress ball here, and the admiral is coming. When he returns to the *Magnifique*, the drawings of the torpedo will be in my possession.'

Mr Freeling Poignton laid his hand for a moment on Lefant's shoulder.

'Marquis,' he said, 'I've been a little led into this affair by you. Remember, these aren't my methods, and it's only because I see just how difficult it is to make a move that I'm standing in. But let this be understood between you and me. The moment those plans are in your possession, a copy of them is to be handed simultaneously to the Government of every civilised Power in the world, so that everyone can build the darned things if they want to.'

'Naturally,' Lefant assented. 'It is already agreed.'

'No favouritism,' Mr Freeling Poignton declared vigorously, 'no priority. We steal those plans, not to give any one nation an advantage over any other, but to put every country on the same footing.'

'It is already agreed,' Lefant repeated.

Mr Laxworthy and Mr Forrest Anderson passed along, on their way back to the hotel. Courteous greetings were exchanged between the four men. Lefant watched them with a faint smile: Mr Laxworthy with a grey shawl around his shoulders, his queer little stoop, his steel-rimmed spectacles; Anderson in his well-cut tweeds, brightly polished tan shoes, and neat Homburg hat.

'That,' Lefant remarked, inclining his head towards Mr Laxworthy, 'is exactly the type of English person whom one meets in a place like Hyères, at an hotel like this. One could swear that he lives somewhere near the British Museum, writes heavily upon some dull subject, belongs to a learned society, and has never had to make his own way in the world. He probably hates draughts, has a pet ailment, and talks about his nerves. He makes a friend of that red-faced fellow-countryman of his because he is attracted by his robust health and his sheer lack of intelligence.'

'I dare say you're right,' Mr Freeling Poignton remarked carelessly. 'What about luncheon?'

It was the night of the great fancy-dress ball at the Paradise Hotel.

Down in the lounge the tumult became more boisterous every minute. Automobiles and carriages were all the time discharging their bevy of visitors from the neighbouring hotels and villas. A large contingent of naval officers arrived from Toulon. The ball-room was already crowded. Admiral Christodor, looking very handsome, led the promenade with Madame Bertrand, concealed under the identity of an Eastern princess. There were many who wondered what it was that he whispered in her ear as he conducted her into the ball-room.

'It was careless of me,' she admitted softly, 'but I am really quite, quite sure that it was destroyed. It was with my bridge scores, and I tore them all up without thinking. You will give me another, perhaps?'

'Whenever you will,' he promised.

'Listen,' she continued. 'To-night you must not leave me. There is a young Englishman—you understand?'

'To-night shall be mine,' the admiral answered gallantly. 'I will not quit your side for a second for all the Englishmen who ever left their sad island.'

It was a gallant speech, but if Fritz, the concierge, could have heard it he would have been puzzled, for, barely half an hour later, a gust of wind blew back the cloak of a man who was stepping into a motor-car, and his uniform was certainly the uniform of an admiral in the French navy. Through the windy darkness the motor-car rushed on its way to La Plage. The men who waited in the pinnace rose to the salute. The admiral took his place in silence, and the little petrol-driven boat tore through the water.

'The admiral takes his pleasure sadly,' one of them muttered, as their passenger climbed on to the deck.

'He has returned most devilish early,' another of them, whose thoughts were in the café at La Plage, grumbled.

The admiral turned his head sharply.

'I shall return,' he announced. 'Await me.'

Most of the officers of the *Magnifique* were in the ball-room of the Paradise Hotel. The admiral received the salute of the lieutenant on duty, and passed at once to his cabin. Arrived there, he shut the door and listened. There was no sound save the gentle splashing of the water near the porthole. Like lightning he turned to a cabinet set in the wall. He pulled out a drawer and touched a spring. Everything was as he had been told. A roll of papers was pushed back into a corner of this compartment. He drew the sheets out one by one, shut the cabinet quickly, and swung round. Then he stood as though turned to stone. The inner door of the cabin, which led into the sleeping apartment, was open. Seated at the table before him was Mr Laxworthy.

Lefant was a man who had passed through many crises in life. Sheer astonishment, however, on this occasion overmastered him. His savoir-faire had gone. He simply stood still and stared. It was surely a vision, this. It could not be that little old-fashioned man who went about with a grey shawl on his shoulders who was sitting there watching him.

'What in the devil's name are you doing there?' he demanded.

'I might ask you the same question,' Mr Laxworthy replied. 'I imagine we are both—intruders.'

Lefant recovered himself a little. He came nearer to the table.

'Tell me exactly what you want,' he insisted.

'First, let us have an understanding,' Mr Laxworthy answered, 'and as quickly as possible. For obvious reasons, the less time we spend here the better. The pinnace which brought you is waiting, I presume, to take you back. In this light you might still pass as an Admiral, but every moment you spend here adds to the risk—for both of us. My foot is on the electric bell, which I presume would bring the admiral's steward. You perceive, too, that I have a revolver in my hand, to the use of which I am accustomed. Am I in command, or you?'

'It appears that you are,' Lefant admitted grimly. 'Go on.'

'You hold in your hand,' Mr Laxworthy continued, 'the plans of the Macharin torpedo, the torpedo which is to make warfare in the future impossible.'

Then Lefant waited no longer. He flung himself almost bodily upon the little old man, who to all appearance presented such small powers of resistance. His first calculation was correct enough. Mr Laxworthy made no attempt to discharge the revolver which he held in his hand. In other respects, however, a surprise was in store for Lefant. His right hand was suddenly held in a grip of amazing strength. The fingers of Mr Laxworthy's other hand were upon his throat.

'If you utter a sound, remember we are both lost,' the latter whispered.

Lefant set himself grimly to the struggle, but it lasted only a few seconds! Before he realised what had happened, his shoulders and the back of his head were upon the table and Mr Laxworthy's fingers were like bars of steel upon his throat. He felt his consciousness going.

'You are content to discuss this matter?' his assailant asked calmly.

Lefant could only gasp out his answer. Mr Laxworthy released his grasp. Lefant breathed heavily for a minute or two. He was half dazed. The thing seemed impossible, yet it had happened. The breath had very nearly left his body in the grip of this insignificant-looking old man.

'Now, if you are willing to be reasonable,' Mr Laxworthy said, 'remember that for both our sakes it is well we do not waste a single second.'

Lefant's fingers stiffened upon the roll of papers, which he was still clutching. Mr Laxworthy read his thoughts unerringly.

'I do not ask you for the plans,' he continued grimly. 'You want them for your country. I am not a patriot. My country shall fight her own battles as long as they are fought fairly. These are my terms: put back those papers, or destroy them, and pay me for my silence.'

'You do not ask, then, for the plans for yourself?' Lefant demanded.

'I do not,' Laxworthy replied. 'They belong to France. Let France keep them. You have corrupted half the ship with Poignton's dollars, but it was never in your mind to keep your faith with him. The plans were for Germany. Germany shall not have them. If I forced you to hand them over to me, I dare say I could dispose of them for—what shall we say?—a hundred thousand pounds. You shall put them back in their place and pay me ten thousand for my silence.'

'So you are an adventurer?' Lefant muttered.

'I am one who seeks adventures,' Laxworthy replied. 'We will let it go at that, if you please. Remember that you are in my power. The pressure of my foot upon this bell, or my finger upon the trigger of this revolver, and your career is over. Will you restore the plans and pay me ten thousand pounds?'

Lefant sighed.

'It is agreed,' he declared.

He turned back to the cabinet, and Laxworthy half rose in his seat to watch him restore the plans. In a few seconds the affair was finished.

'Monsieur the Admiral returns to the ball?' Mr Laxworthy remarked smoothly. 'I will avail myself of his kind offer to accept a seat in the pinnace.'

They left the cabin and made their way to the side of the ship where the pinnace was waiting, and the lieutenant stood with his hand to the salute. Secretly, the latter was a little relieved to see the two together. Once more the pinnace rushed towards the land. The two men walked down the wooden quay, side by side.

'You will permit me to offer you a lift to the hotel?' Lefant asked.

'With much pleasure,' Laxworthy replied, drawing his grey shawl around him. 'I find the nights chilly in these open cars, though.'

Smoothly, but at a great pace, they tore along the scented road, through a grove of eucalyptus trees, and into the grounds of the hotel whose lights were twinkling far and wide. Lefant for the first time broke the silence.

'Mr Laxworthy,' he said, 'the honours of this evening rest with you. I do not wish to ask questions that you are not likely to answer, but there is one matter on which if you would enlighten me—'

Mr Laxworthy waved his hand.

'Proceed,' he begged.

'My little enterprise of this evening,' Lefant continued slowly, 'was known of and spoken of only between Mr Freeling Poignton and myself. We discussed it in the grounds of the hotel, where we were certainly free from eavesdroppers. I am willing to believe that you are a very remarkable person, but this is not the age of miracles.'

Mr Laxworthy smiled.

'Nor is it the age,' he murmured, 'wherein we have attained sufficient wisdom to be able to define exactly what a miracle is. Ten years ago, what would men have said of flying? Fifty years ago even the telephone was considered incredible. Has it never occurred to you, my dear Lefant, that there may be natural gifts of which one or two of us are possessed, almost as strange?'

Lefant turned in his seat.

'You mean—' he began.

Mr Laxworthy held up his hand. 'I have given you a hint,' he said; 'the rest is for you.'

Lefant was silent for a moment.

'Tell me at least this,' he begged. 'How the devil did you get on the *Magnifique*?'

They were passing along the front by the ball-room. Admiral Christodor and Madame Bertrand were sitting near the window. Laxworthy sighed.

'The greatest men in the world,' he said, 'make fools of themselves when they put pencil to paper for the sake of a woman... Take my advice, Marquis. Destroy that uniform and arrange for an alibi. In a few hours' time there will be trouble on the *Magnifique*!'

Lefant nodded. His cocked hat was thrust into the pocket of his overcoat—he was wearing a motor cap and goggles.

'There will be trouble,' he remarked dryly, 'but it will not touch you or me. As regards Madame Bertrand—'

'She is innocent,' Laxworthy assured him. 'Nevertheless, a pass on to the *Magnifique* is a little too valuable a thing to be left in a lady's chatelaine bag.'

Lefant sighed.

'One makes mistakes,' he remarked.

'And one pays!' Laxworthy agreed.

# Ian Hay

Ian Hay was the pen-name under which schoolteacher and soldier Major General John Hay Beith (1876–1952) became well known as an author of novels, short stories, plays, essays and works of history. His first novel appeared in 1907, and five years later he was able to give up teaching to write full-time. When war broke out, he served as an officer in France, and wrote articles about life as a soldier which were put together to form a best-seller, *The First Hundred Thousand* (1915; the title refers to Kitchener's army).

Hay fought in the Battle of Loos, earning the Military Cross, before being sent to Washington D.C. to join the information bureau of the British War Mission. After the war, he became a prolific playwright; in addition to his solo work for the theatre, he collaborated with such notable writers as A.E.W. Mason, Edgar Wallace, and P.G. Wodehouse. He seldom ventured into the crime genre, but wrote this story during the war and chose it for inclusion in an anthology published in 1931 and called *My Best Detective Story*.

U PON THE BELGIAN LARGE-SCALE MAP THE PLACE IS described as *Fme. du Gde Etang*, which being expanded and interpreted means, 'The Farm by the Big Pond'. But after the War had been in progress for some few months the British Army Ordnance Department took the map in hand and issued a revised version, in which the original imposing title was converted into 'Cow Corpse Farm'. The cow in question had expired suddenly and rather inconsiderately right outside the door of the outhouse which did duty as Company Headquarters and Officers' Mess. Unfortunately the current occupants of the billet, being on the eve of departure into other regions, contented themselves with holding an inquest—the verdict was Death by Misadventure, an injudicious repast of jettisoned quartermaster-sergeant's stores, including a nose-bag and a machine-gun belt, being ascribed as the contributing cause—and left the funeral arrangements to their successors. When these arrived the cow had already lain in state for more than a week, and it became immediately obvious that the obsequies had been all too long delayed. The interment took place the same afternoon, a warm afternoon in May, and was attended by a half-platoon of B Company and about half a million bluebottles. The returning mourners unanimously decided to follow up the funeral with a christening. The baptismal ceremony took place in the *estaminet* at the cross-roads close by, and the name stuck.

Within the precincts of Cow Corpse Farm resided, at the moment of our story, first, Mme la Fermière, variously referred to as 'Madame' by the company commander, 'the old gel' by the officers' mess cook, and 'the lady of the'ouse' by the courteous rank and file.

Secondly, Mlles Hélène and Marguérite, Madame's daughters. The two girls worked unceasingly about the farm or fields. They were a cheerful and friendly pair, and Hélène was pretty, especially upon a Sunday morning, when she donned her best dress and discarded sabots in favour of quite smart boots.

Thirdly, the officer commanding B Company, with four subalterns. Their united ages amounted to about a hundred years.

Fourthly, B Company, two hundred strong.

Fifthly, Henri, of whom more anon.

*And*, as they say on theatrical posters, sixthly, Petit-Jean.

Truly, Madame's hands were full. Her husband was almost certainly dead. He and Liège had fallen together, and no news of him had since been obtainable. Her eldest son, Jacques, was somewhere near Dixmude, serving with what was left of the Belgian Artillery. Madame's sole male prop in the upkeep of the farm, always excepting Petit-Jean, was a shambling, shifty-eyed hobbledehoy of twenty-five or so—one ''Nrri', as Madame called him.'Nrri was saved from military service by a mysterious disorder connected with *'ma poitrine, M'sieur le Capitaine'* (a hollow cough).'Nrri, one learned, was not a member of the family. He was a *réfugié*. He had arrived one day in the early autumn of nineteen fourteen, hastening with other breathless persons before a tide of Prussian bayonets. Almost immediately afterwards the tide turned, owing to the intervention of French and British bayonets, and Madame and Cow Corpse Farm were left safely above high-water mark, some three miles back from the trench-line.

'Nrri remained on the farm like a piece of particularly unattractive flotsam. Labour was scarce in Belgium in those days, and Madame was glad to keep him. He ploughed, delved, and splashed about from dawn till dusk, and slept in the loft over the cow-house with Petit-Jean.

As for Petit-Jean himself, he was a sturdy youth of uncertain age. In his workaday clothes, as he ordered the cows about or enjoyed himself in the unspeakable morass of manure which filled the yard, he looked a grimy fifteen. On Sundays, when, as a preliminary to attending Mass, he was washed and attired in a tight blue knickerbocker suit with brass buttons, black stockings, buttoned boots, and a species of yachting cap, he looked an angelic twelve.

B Company, who have only been introduced to you, so far, *en bloc*, were commanded by a veteran of twenty-three, one Crombie. Promotion came quickly upon the Western Front. A year previously Crombie had been leading a platoon round a barrack square at Aldershot. Since then he had seen as much active service as would have sufficed a soldier of the previous generation for a lifetime. This year's service had enabled him, in the elegant phraseology of the moment, 'to put up two more pips'—in other words, to achieve the three stars of a captain. He was assisted in the task of ruling, feeding, housing, and leading some two hundred men by his four youthful subalterns and one seasoned warrior of enormous antiquity, Company Sergeant-Major Goffin.

B Company were 'back at rest'. They had handed over their trenches to D Company last Wednesday, and did not propose to return thither for seven days. For the moment they were at peace. It is true that a pair of British six-inch guns (named respectively Ferdinand and Isabella), artfully concealed in a meadow a hundred yards distant, roared forth their message of destruction at uncertain periods both by day and night, shaking Cow Corpse Farm to its foundations; but they hardly disturbed the well-earned slumber of B Company.

About three o'clock each afternoon the methodical Boche gunners would begin their daily exercise of 'searching' for Ferdinand and Isabella. Sometimes their shells came sufficiently near to make it necessary for B Company to congregate for half an hour or so in a sandbag retiring-room, specially constructed for the purpose in rear of the barn.

On this particular Saturday morning Captain Crombie, having concluded his orderly room and having dealt out admonition, reproof, and in one case Field Punishment Number One, with an even hand, continued to sit in the seat of judgment at the head of the kitchen table, frowning gloomily at a heap of parcels from home, which lay upon the stone floor in the corner by the grandfather's clock.

He turned to his second-in-command—one Rumbelow.

'Any more gone this morning, Rum?' he asked.

'Two.'

'Curse the fellow, whoever he is!' exclaimed Crombie.

The parcels in question contained such comforts as go to mitigate the discomforts of the soldier on active service, and were addressed to members of the company to which 'B' acted as relief. On Tuesday this company would come out of trenches and take over Cow Corpse Farm and all that appertained to it, including the heap of parcels which had been accumulating for them in their absence. But the heap would not be a complete heap.

'We shall have to do something,' said Rumbelow.

'Did you speak to the sergeant-major about it?' asked Crombie.

'Yes. He wants to see you.'

Presently Sergeant-Major Goffin arrived, and saluted with the stately thoroughness of a generation which learned its drill in days when time was no object.

'Sergeant-Major,' began Crombie, 'I want to consult you about this parcel business. Do you suspect anybody?'

'In a manner of speaking, sir—yes.'

'Well, let's get down to it. Who?'

The sergeant-major pointed an accusing finger—about the size and shape of a banana—towards the door which led from the kitchen to the inner room, an apartment which served as kitchen and dining-room for the whole of Madame's *ménage*, and as a bedroom for all the ladies of the establishment.

'Not Madame?' exclaimed Crombie.

'No, sir,' conceded the sergeant-major; 'nor one of the young women.'

'Well—who?' repeated Crombie, impatiently.

'I *think*, sir,' said the sergeant-major, 'that we ought to look for the accused in that loft above the cow-house.'

'Who lives there?'

'The odd man, sir—Henry, I think his name is—and the young boy.'

'Jean?'

'The boy John, sir.' (The sergeant-major declined to recognise Gallic affectations.)

'Why?'

The sergeant-major cleared his throat and swung into his main theme.

'In my opinion, sir, these thefts are committed during the night. This room is fully occupied by day. There's the officers and the officers' servants, and the cooking and so forth. It would be difficult for anybody to come in here and pin—extract anything, sir, by day.'

Here Rumbelow, who seldom spoke except to the point, intervened.

'What about the night?' he said. 'I sleep here myself.'

'That, sir,' resumed the sergeant-major, a little reproachfully, 'is what I was coming to. That is the reason why I suspect the boy. A full-grown man couldn't come groping about in here without making a noise. But a boy might creep in; and you, sir, if you will pardon the liberty, being perhaps a heavy sleeper, he might be able to help himself without disturbing you.'

Sergeant-Major Goffin ran down and stood at ease. Crombie pondered.

'There is only one thing to do,' he said at last—'search the loft. I don't like the idea. Neither will Madame. But—'

'I have a plan, sir,' announced the sergeant-major modestly.

'What is it?'

'I was thinking, sir, that we might invite John and Henry into the N.C.O.'s quarters this evening on some excuse.'

'M'yes. But the excuse? However, I have no doubt you have one manufactured already, sergeant-major.'

'Yes, sir,' admitted the sergeant-major, with humble pride. 'Will you inspect the loft yourself, sir?'

'I am going out to dine with A Company this evening,' said Crombie. 'Mr Rumbelow will take on the job. Is that settled, Rum?'

Mr Rumbelow nodded assent.

'It's got to be done, I suppose,' concluded the tender-hearted Crombie, 'but I don't like it. This is a friendly country, and Madame is a good sort. Jean's a decent little beggar, too. Personally, I hope it turns out to be Henri; he's a shifty-looking tripe-hound: I should like to catch him bending. That will do, sergeant-major. You can report to me in the morning.'

II

Crombie, on returning home to Cow Corpse Farm, found that overcrowded establishment still rocking from an upheaval of capital dimensions.

*Imprimis*, Jean and 'Nrri were both under close arrest.

*Item*, most of the stolen property had been discovered under 'Nrri's bed. This fact seemed to designate 'Nrri as the criminal, but the sergeant-major, who, like other great specialists in crime, disliked seeing his theories falsified, had confined Petit-Jean as well.

Finally, Madame, Hélène, Marguérite, and Sergeant-Major Goffin were all in the kitchen, waiting to exert undue influence upon the returning company commander. This, despite the fact that the phlegmatic Rumbelow had gone to bed, and was now sleeping soundly in their very presence.

The sensitive Crombie smiled feebly upon the tearful ladies, told the sergeant-major to bring up the prisoners in the morning, and withdrew, in bad order, to his Armstrong hut behind the hay rick.

Meanwhile, Petit-Jean and 'Nrri sat in the straw in the screened-off corner of the barn which served as a guard-room, talking. Most of the guard were sleeping heavily, but in no circumstances would they have been able to understand the *patois* employed by the prisoners. The President of the French Academy would not have been able to understand it.

Petit-Jean had wept copiously when arrested. 'Nrri had merely glowered, though as a matter of fact he was by far the more badly frightened of the two. Jean was now comparatively cheerful. He had partaken of bully beef and ration tea—much more luxurious fare than he would have received as a free man—and a friendly corporal had cried, 'Hey, Johnny!' and tossed him a Woodbine. Petit-Jean was now feeling something of a dare-devil.

'Hear me!' said 'Nrri, in a low, snarling voice. 'To-morrow, when the pig of a *sergent* brings us before the camel of a *capitaine*, you will say that *you* stole the packets—you only.'

'But,'Nrri,' argued Petit-Jean, 'you know that I only entered myself into the kitchen, and passed the little packets out to you through the window.'

'Nevertheless,' replied 'Nrri grimly, 'you will say that you alone were the thief.'

'Why?'

'Because they will not punish a little one like you. Me they might punish severely.'

'But no,' Petit-Jean pointed out eagerly; 'you are a *réfugié*, 'Nrri. You know he is kind, that English. You will tell him who you are— that the Boches have taken all you have.'

'To-morrow,' announced 'Nrri, with unpleasant finality, 'you will say that you alone are the thief. If you do not, I shall kill you.'

'How?' asked Petit-Jean, not because he wished to know, but in order to give himself time to think the matter over. He had always been more than a little afraid of 'Nrri, and now there was a look in the man's crafty little eyes which gave him a cold crawly feeling right up his spine.

'I shall wait', explained 'Nrri, with relish, 'until you are asleep one night in the loft. Then I will kill you with the bayonet of the Scotch whom we found dead in the ditch last winter. Your body I will slide into the cess-pit below the cow-house. There will be a *tohu-bohu*, but they will not find you. And no one will suspect 'Nrri. Is it not so?'

Petit-Jean, tingling now in the pit of his stomach as well as up his spine, agreed that it was so, and, further, promised to shoulder the entire responsibility in the morning.

III

Next morning Captain Crombie, returning with B Company from church parade at battalion headquarters about half-past nine, found that the *affaire* Petit-Jean had entered another phase. 'Nrri was a free man, and Petit-Jean was out on bail.

Rumbelow explained.

'Just after you moved off with the company this morning Petit-Jean owned up to the sergeant-major that he was the desperate criminal, and that Henri was as pure as driven snow.'

Crombie frowned.

'I'm sorry to hear that,' he said. 'Are you sure Petit-Jean didn't say that Henri was the criminal? I would back the sergeant-major to get hold of the sticky end of the wand when conversing in the language of this country every time.'

'No; apparently all was in order. Goffin was corroborated by the cook, who was called in as assistant interpreter. So Henri left the court without a stain on his character.'

'What have you done with Petit-Jean?'

Rumbelow grinned.

'I thought you would prefer to deal with the case yourself,' he said, 'so I remanded him.'

'Curse you!' replied the company commander cordially. 'What am I to do with the little beast?'

'There is a *gendarmerie* in that village near Brigade Headquarters,' said Cradock, who was reading by the window.

Crombie shook his head.

'If we hand him over to the local rozzer,' he said, 'it will mean a civil action, and all sorts of complications.'

'Let the sergeant-major bend him over and give him six of the best,' suggested the practical Rumbelow.

The harassed Crombie shook his head again.

'It would mean a devil of a lot of unpleasantness with Madame,' he observed ruefully, 'not to mention the young ladies.'

'Then why not give the youth a good telling off, and dismiss the case?'

'And a pretty fair Juggins I should look,' retorted Crombie, with justifiable heat, 'sitting here and *strafing* Petit-Jean in a language which I can't speak, and which he can't understand!' He puffed savagely at his pipe. 'However, the longer we look at it the less we shall like it. Where is the little swine? Still in the guard-room?'

'No. Madame has bailed him out for an hour or two. I am not a French scholar myself; but I gathered from her that there would be the father and mother of a row with the *curé* if I didn't let Petit-Jean off for Sunday Mass.'

'The *curé*?' Over the troubled features of Captain Crombie stole a flicker of relief—almost of inspiration. 'The *curé* here is a friend of mine,' he continued, 'I gave him a lift in the mess-cart only the day before yesterday. Ha-*ha*! Tell the sergeant-major I want him, Cradock, like a good chap.'

When Cradock returned with the sergeant-major, five minutes later, Crombie was sitting in the judgment-seat behind the kitchen table, furtively scribbling certain sentences upon a sheet of official paper. Rumbelow, in the chimney-corner, was regarding his superior officer with an air of whimsical solemnity. Mr Rumbelow possessed a keen sense of humour, but, unlike most humorists, preferred to consume his own smoke.

'Sergeant-major,' commanded Crombie, in his orderly-room voice, 'bring in the prisoner.'

The great man saluted.

'Shall I fetch an escort, sir?' he inquired.

Crombie, immersed in the labours of composition, nodded absently. Straightway the sergeant-major withdrew to the yard outside, where his voice was heard uplifted in command:

'Escort—*tchu-urn*! Left *turn*! Quick—*march*?'

*Clump! clump! clump!* The sergeant-major entered the kitchen, followed by an enormous private. The pair tramped across the stone-floored kitchen, in solemn majesty, to the door of the inner room, where the escort, in response to an ear-splitting order, halted.

The sergeant-major, advancing one pace, knocked three times upon the door, and exclaimed in a terrible voice: 'Garsong!'.

There was a flutter within; the door was opened by a person unseen, and the procession disappeared. Mr Rumbelow turned his face to the brickwork of the chimney-corner, and held it there. Cradock hastily buried his features in an obsolete copy of *The Tatler*. Crombie, oblivious to his surroundings, still scribbled nervously.

'Prisoner and escort—*tchu-urn*! Into file, left turn! *Quick—march!*'

*Clump! clump! clump!*

Presently Captain Crombie, conscious of the near presence of several warm human beings, looked up. Before him, in a rigid row, stood the large private, Petit-Jean, and the sergeant-major. Petit-Jean was wearing his Sunday suit, already described, with the exception of his yachting cap, which, in accordance with King's Regulations, had been plucked from his head.

'The boy John, sir!' announced the sergeant-major, in a voice of thunder, and handed Crombie a yellow Army form, containing Petit-Jean's 'crime'.

Crombie took the paper, and from sheer force of habit began to read:

*'John, charged with stealing the following articles upon various dates, namely—'*

Then, realising for the first time the imbecility of the present procedure, he thrust the document away from him, and glanced stealthily at the first sentence on his scribbled sheet. After this he cleared his throat in a distressing manner, looked Petit-Jean straight in the face, and began:

'Er—h'm—*vous êtes voleur?'*

Petit-Jean promptly burst into tears. This gave Crombie an opportunity of studying the next sentence.

*'Voulez-vous,'* he continued when Petit-Jean had regained a measure of composure, *'que je vous donnerai'* (I'm not sure that oughtn't to be in the subjunctive) *'aux gendarmes?'*

Petit-Jean responded with a further outburst, supplemented by a violent attack of hiccups. Cradock rose unsteadily to his feet, and groped his way out of the kitchen. The conscientious Crombie proceeded to his next conundrum:

*'Voulez-vous que je vous*—er—*donne au sergent, pour être battu*—*n'est-ce pas?'* The last phrase was thrown in on the spur of the moment, and Crombie felt rather proud of it.

The prisoner, however, made no attempt to reply to these engaging propositions. Instead, he sobbed out a long and incomprehensible rigmarole, the only intelligible item of which was the word 'pardon'. Crombie, again utilising his opportunity, made a further study of his brief. Then he launched his master-thrust:

'*Est-ce que vous avez fait*—no, *fit*—no—never mind—I mean *ça ne fait rien.*' He took a good breath and started again.

'*Est-ce que vous avez fait confession à Monsieur le Curé*—eh?'

There was a dramatic silence, broken by a rending hiccup from the accused. Crombie continued hastily:

'*Demain, vous irez chez Monsieur le Curé, et vous ferez confession, tout de suite—complet—absolument*'—he was gagging wildly now—'*entièrement, et sans doute—que vous êtes voleur. Comprenez?* Anyhow, I'll tell the *Curé* myself, my son, so you'll get it put across you either way. Now, then, clear out! *Allez vous en!* Sergeant-major, for heaven's sake, take this hiccuping little blighter away!'

Whether Petit-Jean was duly appreciative of the linguistic effort made on his behalf by Captain Crombie will never be known. But the fact remains that on the following Tuesday afternoon Madame appeared at the kitchen doorway, and summoned Petit-Jean, who was engaged upon some professional duty in the pigsty, to the family living-room. He emerged half an hour later, uncannily clean and dressed in his Sunday suit, supplemented by a large umbrella, and set off with dragging feet across the fields which led to the *curé's* house. What happened there I cannot tell, but it is probable that Petit-Jean duly 'had it put across him', as predetermined by that wise and merciful young judge, Captain Crombie.

IV

For the next ten days life pressed very heavily upon Petit-Jean. He was in disgrace. The *officiers* no longer gave him a smile on passing, or made observations to him in a language which they imagined to be French and which Petit-Jean judged to be English.

It was an uncomfortable time for more important persons than

Petit-Jean. The two six-inch guns, Ferdinand and Isabella, were receiving attentions from the Boche artillery which grew daily more tiresome and accurate. It was obvious that they had been 'spotted'. One day a big howitzer shell swung lazily out of the blue and landed ten yards from the abiding place of Isabella. Fortunately it was a 'dud', but the battery commander, realising the undesirability of tempting Providence too far, telephoned for his traction engine, and within a few hours the two big guns had been towed to a fresh anchorage some distance to a flank. The next morning was devoted to 'registering', with the aid of an aeroplane, upon a convenient château behind the Boche lines. This formality completed, regular business was resumed.

Exactly twenty-four hours later a salvo of hostile 'crumps' descended upon the new emplacements. The guns escaped damage, but the bursts of shrapnel which followed the 'crumps' accounted for the battery sergeant-major and two gunners. Once more transport was hurriedly summoned and the royal pair removed to another portion of their realm.

The artillery captain, Maple, who lived in a wooden hut half a mile from the farm, rode over that evening to confide his woes to B Company, who had just returned from another turn in the trenches.

'That Boche battery didn't open fire on my positions by accident,' he observed darkly.

'Well, it wasn't any of us who gave him the tip,' said Rumbelow. 'We have been in trenches all week.'

The captain, disregarding the pleasantry, put down his bowl of tea, and continued:

'We haven't been in those positions a couple of days, and there hasn't been a Boche aeroplane over since Monday. And yet they have us stiff. There's only one explanation.'

Crombie nodded.

'Spies, of course,' he said.

'Of course,' grunted the gunner savagely. 'But it's hopeless to run them to earth in Belgium. There are lots of inhabited farms quite close up to the line, yet we aren't allowed to bung anybody out. If I had my way I'd deport the whole bunch five miles back. The place must be full of refugees whom the *Maire* can't account for. However, I suppose we must put up with it. That's the worst of fighting in a friendly country; you have to consider everybody's feelings so infernally. I bet the Boche has everybody on his side of the line trotting around with a number-plate on like a taxi. Well, I must wander off.'

'Stop and help us to struggle with our Maconochie,' urged the mess.

'Sorry,' replied the gunner, 'but the present situation is too tricky.'

Crombie accompanied his visitor to the farm gate, where an orderly was dispatched for the battery commander's horse.

'If I see any suspicious-looking stranger lounging about,' said Crombie, 'I'll run him in.'

'Thanks, old man,' replied the harried gunner, and trotted away into the dusty sunset. Crombie turned to go back to the kitchen, and found himself face to face with Petit-Jean. Petit-Jean, with hanging head, promptly sidled towards a pigsty. His demeanour was so dejected that Crombie, suddenly reminded of last week's episode, and mindful of the acute sorrows of his own sinful youth, laid a hand upon Petit-Jean's shoulder, and exclaimed affably:

'Halloa, Petit-Jean! *Comment vous portez-vous*—what?'

Petit-Jean, not sure what these incomprehensible words might mean, wriggled nervously.

'*Il fait beau temps,*' continued Crombie, warming to his work. '*Il sera joli chaud demain, n'est-ce pas?*'

He concluded with a smile so jolly that Petit-Jean realised with a joyous thrill that this *was* a friendly conversation, and that his period of ostracism was accomplished. He grinned gratefully, from ear to ear.

'*Et maintenant,*' concluded Crombie, soaring to fresh heights, '*venez avec moi dans la cuisine, et avez—avez*—what I mean is, *je vous donnerai une pièce de gâteau. Mouvons!*'

V

Petit-Jean lay awake under the red tiles of his loft, listening to the endless *plop-plop* of the Verey Lights, punctuated by occasional bursts of machine-gun fire along the distant line. Sleep had forsaken him to-night; but the cause was elation rather than depression of spirits. His youthful palate was still cloyed with Huntley and Palmer cake, but his heart, to quote the Psalmist, indited of a good matter.

It was a dark and cloudy night, and Petit-Jean was thereby deprived of one of his favourite sedative exercises—namely, counting the stars in those patches of sky which were visible through holes in the roof.

Suddenly his sharp senses told him that in some way the peace of the loft had been disturbed. The regular breathing of 'Nrri, who slept at the other end of the loft, had ceased, and had given place to a series of stertorous puffs, accompanied by a creaking sound. 'Nrri was awake and pulling on his boots. 'Nrri was going out.

All good civilians in the war zone are supposed to be safely tucked up and in bed by nine o'clock. Yet here was 'Nrri about to snap his fingers at martial law at two o'clock in the morning. But at first Petit-Jean experienced no surprise. To be quite frank, 'Nrri was an invariable night-bird. He was in the habit of committing the military crime of 'breaking out of billets' at least once a week. Whenever the accumulation of parcels from the kitchen made it worth while, 'Nrri was accustomed to pay a nocturnal visit to the establishment of a venerable female, who supported life, externally, by the sale of small beer, cigarettes, and picture postcards. The lady was known among the light-hearted soldiery of the district—possibly in reference to a figure which bore unmistakable testimony to some sixty years of generous diet and insufficient exercise—as Madame Zeppelin. To Madame 'Nrri bartered the cigarettes, cigars, condensed milk, chocolate, and other comforts stolen from the parcels; and Madame disposed of the same, at cent per cent profit, to the light-hearted soldiery aforesaid.

Presently 'Nrri's sketchy toilet was completed, and he began to move steadily down the ladder. Petit-Jean, silent, but wide awake, was overtaken by a fresh thought. Why should 'Nrri be going to Madame Zeppelin's now? He had no wares to offer; recent legal proceedings had knocked that traffic on the head. A further thought. Was 'Nrri bound for Madame Zeppelin's at all? If not—whither?

After that, Petit-Jean began to think very hard indeed. He had always been afraid of 'Nrri, and since their conversation in the guard-room he had hated him as well. On the other hand, he loved *Monsieur le Capitaine* and his officers like brothers—especially since this afternoon. Petit-Jean felt instinctively that these stealthy movements in the dark were directed in some wise against the safety and wellbeing of the present house-party at Cow Corpse Farm in particular, and of the British Army in general.

Five minutes later 'Nrri had effected an unostentatious departure from the back premises of the farm—thus avoiding the sentry out on the road in front—and was picking his way cautiously across country towards the trenches. The night was black as ink—so black that no object in the landscape cast a shadow. Yet a shadow followed 'Nrri—a small human shadow—inexorably, all the way to his destination; which, by the way, was not the establishment of Madame Zeppelin.

VI

Petit-Jean stepped out of the cow-house, took a deep breath, planted himself full in the path of Captain Crombie, and exclaimed feverishly:

'*M'sieur le Capitaine!*'

'*Bonjour*, Petit-Jean!' replied Crombie, who was in a hurry; and attempted to pass. But Petit-Jean repeated:

'*M'sieur le Capitaine!*'

Crombie paused.

'Well, what about it, old son?' he inquired.

In answer, Petit-Jean embarked upon a hurried recitation, casting anxious glances all the while in the direction of the beetroot-stack, where 'Nrri was selecting the cows' luncheon.

Finally the recitation ceased, and Petit-Jean eyed the captain eagerly. But all the reply he got was:

'*C'est dommage*, my lad, but no compree!'

Then upon Petit-Jean descended the inspiration of a lifetime.

'*M'sieur le Curé?*' he suggested eagerly. The *curé* could speak English of a sort.

'The *curé?*' said Crombie. 'I thought that incident was closed.'

But Petit-Jean was urgent.

'*Le curé, m'sieur, ce soir à six heures!*'

'Oh!' replied Crombie, beginning to see light. 'Er—*ici?*' Petit-Jean nodded his head vigorously.

'Right-o! Carry on with your mysterious project, and I'll be here. But I wonder what the old man wants to see me for?'

As a matter of fact, the *curé* was quite unaware of the approaching symposium. For one thing it was Friday and his busy day. Consequently, when Petit-Jean's bullet head peeped shyly round his kitchen door, and Petit-Jean's voice proffered the modest request that he would present himself at B Company's billet, over a mile away, that evening at six o'clock, the old gentleman's reply was a little testy. But when he had heard the tale which his small parishioner had to unfold, his eyes gleamed through his spectacles, and he said, quite simply:

'I come, my little! But meanwhile, silence thyself.'

As a matter of fact, the last arrival at the meeting was Captain Crombie. That afternoon Ferdinand and Isabella had been shelled out of a third position, and Crombie had ridden over to offer condolences. Finding Maple almost at his wits' end, he bethought him suddenly of the *curé*.

'Look here,' he said, 'I have a kind of notion that it might pay you to come over to my quarters. The *curé* will be there at'—he looked at his watch—'well, he's there now. He's a patriotic old cove. He may be able to suggest a possible renegade among his flock. Come and pump him dry.'

Ten minutes later the pair trotted in at the farm gate, to encounter the *curé*, a little ruffled, on the point of departure. But he was shepherded with fair words into the only armchair. The kitchen doors were shut—fortunately the rest of the household were out in the fields—and Petit-Jean told his tale.

Briefly it amounted to this.

He had tracked 'Nrri to an empty house, some three hundred yards behind the reserve line. The house, which had been badly knocked about by shell-fire, was called Five-Point-Nine Villa. 'Nrri had disappeared within. Jean, with some acumen, had crept round to the east end, facing the German lines, in order to detect suspicious flashes or other signals.

'What did you see?' asked Crombie eagerly.

The *curé* passed the question on. Petit-Jean, with a doleful grimace, shook his head.

'Nothing, eh?' said Maple.

'That doesn't signify anything,' said Crombie. ''Nrri probably stood well back from the window, and Petit-Jean, being on the ground, couldn't spot the flashes. Anything else, Petit-Jean?'

Yes, there was something else. Petit-Jean produced his trump card. Failing to extract any satisfaction from the house, he had turned his attention to the German lines.

'And what is it, my son,' inquired the old *curé*, eagerly, 'that you have seen there?'

'My father,' replied Petit-Jean, with breathless solemnity, 'I have seen a red light which made itself to appear three times.'

'And this light? It proceeded from—'

'From behind the trenches of the Boche.'

'*Ca suffit!*' said the old man briskly, and turned to the two officers.

Next afternoon the trap was laid. Fresh gun-pits were dug, and Ferdinand and Isabella were ostentatiously installed therein. By ten o'clock the same evening Crombie and Maple were inmates of Five-Point-Nine Villa.

The villa possessed two storeys, with the inevitable *grenier*, or loft, running from end to end under the tiles. At the eastern end of this loft, in the apex of the gable, glimmered a circular, unglazed window. Through this drifted the never-ceasing, uneasy sounds of trench warfare. The wood at this point thinned to a mere belt, through which it was possible to see right to the trench-lines. Crombie cautiously turned on his electric torch. The only visible furniture of the loft was a pile of lumber in one corner, and a curious edifice, comprised of British Army ration boxes, standing up like a pulpit in the middle of the floor. The torch went out.

'What is that erection for?' asked Crombie.

'I think I know,' said Maple.

He felt his way in the dark, and presently could be heard climbing.

'I thought so,' remarked his voice, proceeding apparently from just under the low roof. 'Come up here; you'll find a sort of staircase of boxes at the back.'

In a few moments the two officers were standing side by side on the top step of the staircase, looking over the summit of the pulpit at the circular window in the gable end. Through this could be seen the tossing branches of trees, silhouetted against the flares of the trench-line.

'You see?' said Maple. 'This is the signalling stand. It is exactly level with that little round window. Impossible to spot a flash sent from here, unless you were right in the line of the window and the lamp. I should say that the line of sight from this platform to the lower edge of the window just clears our front-line trenches. Pretty neat! Cunning fellow!'

'I wonder where he keeps his lamp?' mused Crombie.

'*Messieurs!*'

'I expect he brings it with him. Too risky to—. Halloa, what's that?'

'*Messieu-u-urs!*' a sibilant panting whisper shot up the rickety staircase. It emanated from Petit-Jean, who had run all the way from Cow Corpse Farm, making a *détour* into the bargain. Crombie descended from the pulpit and went to the stairhead.

'*Il s'approche!*' hissed Petit-Jean, and vanished.

'Nrri's first proceeding upon arrival was to mount the pulpit, apparently with the view to inspecting as much of the landscape as was visible through the circular window.

Next, breathing heavily in the darkness, he betook himself to the eastern end of the room. This was fortunate for Crombie and Maple, who were among the lumber at the other end. A creaking sound was heard.

'He's prising up a plank!' whispered Maple.

Crombie nodded his head in the darkness. Evidently 'Nrri was digging out his lamp.

Presently the shuffling footsteps returned, and to an accompaniment of groaning ration boxes 'Nrri reascended his rostrum. Followed a click, and a dazzling spot of light struck the wall opposite, just under the window. Another click, and the light disappeared.

'Elevation too low, old son!' muttered Maple.

Next time the signaller made no mistake.

The spot of light could not be seen now, for it was impinging upon a Boche retina many hundreds of yards away. But the shutter of the signal lamp could be heard working clear enough.

*Click-click-clickety-click!* 'Nrri was calling up some invisible 'exchange'. He paused, waited, and began again. Then again. So immersed was he in the interesting occupation of getting into touch with his friends beyond the lines that he quite failed to note the somewhat surprising fact that his feet, which stood upon the top-most step of the pulpit, about a yard from the floor, had suddenly become luminous—or, at least, that they were being illuminated at close range by an electric torch. Three seconds later the torch, having served its purpose in locating the exact position of the feet, was switched off; four willing and muscular hands grabbed the ankles of the preoccupied 'Nrri; Captains Crombie and Maple, each planting a foot squarely against his side of the pulpit, gave a gigantic heave; 'Nrri precipitately abandoned the occupation of telegraph operator in favour of that of contortionist; there was a dull thud, followed by a rattle of cascading ration boxes. Then silence.

Crombie's torch shone out again. 'Nrri, having just performed 'the splits' in mid-air and subsequently fallen downstairs on the back of his head, lay quite still.

'Golly, he took a toss and a half!' observed Crombie. 'Have we done him in, do you think?'

'No,' said Maple. 'He's breathing all right. Put the handcuffs on him and I'll whistle up your sergeant-major and escort.'

Ten minutes later 'Nrri, in full possession of his faculties, and perspiring icily, was on his way back to Cow Corpse Farm, escorted by two large British privates, preceded by Petit-Jean, and supervised from the rear by Sergeant-Major Goffin.

Crombie and Maple remained in the loft.

'That chap was a Boche all right,' said Maple. 'He gave himself away when he came to.'

'Was that German? I haven't the pleasure of knowing it.'

'It was; and fairly profane German, too.'

'No idea you were such a linguist.'

'I had a German governess in my youth,' exclaimed Maple modestly. 'Up to this moment I have always wished that she had been

French. This lamp is a good instrument.' He clicked the shutter. 'Not damaged either.'

'It will be useful as evidence,' said Crombie.

Maple chuckled.

'I have another use for it first!' he said, and began to rebuild the platform.

Presently the two captains stood level again with the round window. Maple began to manipulate the shutter of the lamp.

'I'm giving the Morse call-up signal,' he explained. 'I have a notion to jape with the Boche. Let us see if we can draw him. My word, look!'

Far away in the darkness, beyond the fretful, spluttering trench-lines, there suddenly glowed out a red point of light—then again—then again.

'Three red dashes!' said Maple. 'I presume that is the answering signal. Now, let me think. What is the German for—?'

He relapsed into silence, and clicked his shutter vigorously. Then he switched off, and abruptly descended to the floor.

'I have a feeling', he said, 'that we may have a few shells over here shortly. Let us hence!'

'What did you say to the blighters?' inquired Crombie, as the pair stepped out briskly along the muddy track which ran back to Cow Corpse Farm.

'I said: *"Number engaged! Sorry you've been troubled! Gott strafe England!"'*

# THE LOVER OF ST LYS

## F. Tennyson Jesse

Fryniwyd Tennyson Jesse (1888–1958) made a distinctive contribution to the crime genre. She edited the UK edition of *The Baffle Book: A Parlour Game of Mystery and Detection* (1930), originally compiled by Lassiter Wren and Randle McKay, a collection of puzzles in the form of crime stories; she was also a noted criminologist, editing books of trials, and publishing a notable study of homicidal motivation, *Murder and its Motives* (1924). Among her novels, *A Pin to See the Peep-Show* (1934) is outstanding as a poignant fictionalisation of the enduringly controversial Thompson-Bywaters case. In 1939, she co-founded the Black Maria Club, with fellow writers including Marie Belloc Lowndes and the locked-room maestro John Dickson Carr, but the Club met only once before war intervened.

In her youth, Jesse travelled extensively with her parents—her father, a member of the clergy, was a nephew of Alfred, Lord Tennyson—and during the First World War she reported from Belgium for the *Daily Mail*. After her marriage to a playwright, the couple divided their time between Britain and their house in Provence. The south of France supplied a setting for several of her stories about Solange Fontaine, who had an English mother, a French father, and an uncanny gift for sensing evil. This tale first appeared in *The Premier Magazine* in 1919.

I T WAS IN A LITTLE GREY TOWN SET HIGH IN THE MOUNTAINOUS country behind the Riviera that Solange and her father decided to spend their summer holiday. St Lys, seen once on a motor-tour, had enraptured them both—a town of mellow, fluted tiles, of grey walls, of steep streets that were shadowed ways of coolness even at noon-day, and ramparts that circled round the mountain crest as though hacked out of the living rock, so sheer and straight they were. It was a restful place, the very townspeople, with their clear, dark eyes and rough-hewn faces, strong of jaw and cheekbone, tender with pure skins and creamy colours, seemed redolent of peace. Here was a town for tired workers, especially for workers in such dark and dragging ways as those which the Fontaines explored— the ways of crime, not taken as detectives or allies of the law, but studied as scientists, with the end always in view of throwing light on causes rather than on actual deeds. The next generation—it was to save this by greater knowledge that Dr Fontaine laboured, assisted by Solange, and here at least they could hope to continue their new book on the detection of poisons undisturbed by those sudden irruptions of the actual, such as the affair of the negro girl at Marseilles, which so violently tore the tissues of their ordered life.

'Besides,' as Solange said, 'Terence and Raymond will be able to come up from Nice and see us, and that will be ever so much nicer than always being alone.'

Her father glanced at her sharply, to see whether there were any change of her quiet, clear pallor, but eye and cheek were as calm as ever. Terence Corkery—the Consul from Nice—he was an old friend, and as such Solange was wont to treat him, in that affectionate yet aloof way of hers, but young Raymond Ker, with the alertness of a newer civilisation in his confident jaw and bright eyes—he was a comparatively new acquaintance, and though it was true he had been with Solange through much—the tragic affair of the 'Green Parrakeet', and the more grotesque happening at the draper's shop in Marseilles—yet it was unlike Solange to admit any man to quite that degree of intimacy so swiftly. Therefore, Dr Fontaine had wondered, but the clear oval of his daughter's face gave him no clue. He resigned himself to the fact that he could read the countenance of a homicidal maniac with greater ease and accuracy than the familiar features of his daughter.

Corkery was unable to leave Nice while the Fontaines were at St Lys that year, but, true to his promise, Raymond, protesting that he was merely on the look-out for 'copy', arrived at the grey town in the mountains one heavenly evening in June. Solange objected.

'How can you expect copy here, Raymond? This is the abode of innocence and peace. Nothing ever happens, except births and deaths, and the few there are of the latter are invariably from old age!'

'You forget you are a stormy petrel, Solange,' replied Raymond, only half-jesting. 'I always have hopes of something happening where you are.'

But as Solange looked annoyed, and he remembered her distaste for crime encountered in individuals, he changed the conversation. And just at first it looked as though Raymond were out in his theory, and as though peace must always be absolute at St Lys. Never was there a place that seemed so as though the *bon Dieu* kept it in His pocket, as the Fontaines' old servant, Marie, expressed it. There were not many people to know, socially speaking, and the only family with whom the Fontaines visited on at all a society footing—though both Solange and her father cared little for that sort of thing and made friends with every butcher and baker—was that of the De Tourvilles. M. De Tourville was the lord of the manor, a moth-eaten old castle, beautiful from sheer age and fitness for its surroundings, picturesque enough to set all Raymond's American enthusiasms alight, but shabby to an extent that made Madame De Tourville's conversation one perpetual wail. She was a thin, feverish-looking woman, not without a burnt-out air of handsomeness in her straight features and large eyes, but looking older than her husband, though she was a year or so the younger. He was a very picturesque figure, as he went about the windy town in the long blue cloak he affected, his head, where the dark hair was only beginning to be faintly silvered, bare, and his thin, hawklike face held high. A queer man, perhaps, said the townspeople, with his sudden tempers, his deep angers, his impulsive kindnesses, but a man of whom they were all proud. They felt the beauty of his presence in the town, though they could not have expressed it. Madame they liked less; she came from the hard Norman country, and was reported to be more than a little miserly, more so than was necessary even on the meagre income of the De Tourville family.

It was for his sake that everyone had been glad, and not a little curious, when a very rich lady, a young lady, who was a cousin and ward of the De Tourvilles, had come to live with them at the castle. That money should come into the old place, even if only temporarily, was felt to be right, and deep in the minds of the women was the unspoken wonder as to how thin, feverish madame would fare with a young girl in the household. For though he was forty-five,

M. De Tourville had the romantic air which, to some young girls, is more attractive than youth.

So much detail about the De Tourvilles was common gossip, and had filtered from the notary's wife, via the hotel-keeper's wife, to Marie, and thence to Solange. She herself had visited the château several times, for mutual friends in Paris had supplied letters of introduction, and she knew enough of the De Tourville household to have interested Raymond in them before she and her father took him to call at the château.

Raymond was of opinion that Solange had not exaggerated in depicting the household as interesting. There was something about the bleak château, with its faded tapestries and ill-kept terraces, which would have stirred romance in the dullest, but when added to it was a family that to nerves at all sensitive gave a curious impression of under-currents, then interest was bound to follow. Several times during that call Raymond wondered whether Solange had got her 'feeling' about this household, whether that was what interested her, or whether for once he were being more sensitive, perhaps unduly so. For Solange talked gaily, seemed her usual self.

The De Tourville couple were as she had pictured them. The chief interest lay in the personality of Mademoiselle Monique Levasseur, the young ward. She was not, strictly speaking, pretty, but she had a force born of her intense vitality, her evident joy in life. Her dark eyes, large and soft, with none of the beadiness of most brown eyes, glowed in the healthy pallor of her face, her rather large, mobile mouth was deeply red, and her whole girlish form—too thin, with that exquisite appealing meagreness which means extreme youth—seemed vibrant with life. Yet she had her softnesses too—for her cousin, Edmund De Tourville. Her schoolgirl worship was evident in the direction of her limpid gaze, her childish eagerness to wait on him, which he was too much *galant homme* to allow. How much of it all did the wife see, wondered Raymond? He watched the quiet, repressed woman as she dispensed tea, and could gather little from her impassivity. Once he caught a gleam, not between man and girl, but between man and wife—a gleam that surely spoke of the intimacy that needs no words—and felt oddly reassured. The couple understood each other, probably smiled, not heartlessly, tenderly even, with the benignant pity of knowledge, at the schoolgirl enthusiasm. Doubtless that was the under-current that he had felt in the relations between the three. Yet, only a few minutes later, he doubted whether that impression were the true one. For, as they were about to leave, M. De Tourville spoke a few words low to the girl, and she got up and left the room, to reappear a moment later with a little tray, on which was a medicine-bottle and a glass. Everyone looked as they felt, a little surprised, and Edmund De Tourville, measuring out a dose of the medicine carefully, said, smiling:

'You must pardon these domesticities, but the wife has not been well for some time, and the doctor lays great stress on the importance of her taking her drops regularly. Is it not so, Thérèse?'

And Madame De Tourville, obediently draining the little glass, replied that it was. Nothing much in that little incident, but as the girl bore the tray away again her guardian opened the door for her, and slipped out after her; and Raymond, who was by the door, was made the unwilling, but inevitably curious, spectator of an odd little scene. The door did not quite close, and swung a little way open again after De Tourville had pulled it after him, and Raymond saw the girl put the tray down on the buffet which stood in the passage, saw De Tourville catch her as she turned to come back, and saw the hurried kiss that he pressed on her upturned brow. It was not at all a passionate kiss, though. But the girl glowed beneath it like the rose, and Raymond, with a sudden compunction, moved across the room, so that he was away from the door when his host came in. He was not surprised that Monique Levasseur did not return.

That evening Raymond said to Solange, as they were smoking their after-dinner cigarettes in the hotel garden, which hung on the mountain side, the one word:

'Well?'

And Solange, looking up at him, laughed.

'Well? You mean about this afternoon? You're getting very elliptic, my friend.'

'One can, with you.'

'And—"well" meant do I think there is anything—anything odd?' He nodded.

'Yes,' said Solange, 'I do. But I can't for the life of me say what.'

'The girl is obviously in love with him.'

'Oh, that—yes. That doesn't matter. She is of the age. But a schoolgirl's rave on a man much older than herself wouldn't make me feel there was anything odd, not if he were married ten deep. No, it was something—something more sinister than that.'

'What do you make of the girl?' asked Raymond.

'A personality, evidently. But of the passive kind.'

'Passive?' ejaculated Raymond, in surprise; 'she struck me as being most amazingly vital, and vital people aren't passive.'

'Vital women can be. For the height of femininity is an acutely enhanced passivity. The women who made history, the Helens and Cleopatras, didn't go out and do things, they just lay about and things happened. In the annals of crime, also, you will find frequently that women who are as wax have not only inspired crimes, but helped to commit them, or even committed them alone, acting under the orders of their lovers, as Jeanne Weiss did when she tried to poison her husband. It is a definite type. There are, of course, women who are the dominating force, such as Lady Macbeth; but the other kind is quite as forceful in its effects.'

'You are not suggesting, I suppose, that little Monique Levasseur—'

'No, indeed. I got nothing but what was sweet and rather pathetic and feminine with her. But the fact remains that passionate passivity may turn to anything.'

And Solange drifted off to discussion of actual cases, such as those of the two sinister Gabrielles—she who was wife of Fenayrou, and she who was accomplice of Eyraud, and from them to that most pathetic of all the examples of feminine docility, Mary Blandy, who poisoned her father for the sake of her lover. And after that, secret poisoning, that abominable and most enthralling of all forms of murder, held them talking about its manifestations till Dr Fontaine came out to smoke a last pipe.

A month flew past in that enchanted city of towers, and though the Fontaines met the family from the château now and then, no greater degree of intimacy was arrived at between them; indeed, since the arrival of Raymond, the De Tourvilles seemed to withdraw themselves and Monique much more than they had before. Then one day, M. De Tourville arrived at the hotel, only a day before the Fontaines were leaving it, with a request that only intimacy or a great necessity justified. He soon proved that he had the latter to urge him. He told them that his wife, who had been ailing for a long time, as they were aware, had been ordered away, and had left the day before for Switzerland, for a sanatorium, and he asked them whether they would be so good as to take charge of Mademoiselle Levasseur, and escort her to Paris to the house of her former *gouvernante*, at whose school she had been before coming to St Lys? He could not as a man alone—despite his grey hairs, he added with a smile—continue to look after Monique. But if Monsieur and Mademoiselle Fontaine would accord him this favour, he could himself come to Paris later, and make sure that all was well with his ward. What he said was very reasonable, and Solange and her father agreed willingly.

But Raymond saw the long look that the girl turned on her guardian from the window of the train as they were starting, saw the meaning glance with which he replied, and somehow that little scene in the passage flashed up against his memory, clear and vivid. Solange said nothing much, but she was kindness itself to the girl, who was plainly depressed at leaving the god of her adoration, and not till the Fontaines had themselves arrived in Switzerland, whither they were bound—a fact she had not thought needful to mention to M. De Tourville—did Solange say anything to her father. And then it was only to express a little wonder that at the place where M. De Tourville, when she had asked him, had said his wife was staying, there was no trace of any lady of that name to be found.

Raymond had gone over to New York by then, and this little discovery, which would so have interested him, he was not destined to know till the following spring. For in February of the next year—which is when spring begins in the gracious country of southern France, Solange somehow made her father feel that another little stay in St Lys—which, as a matter of fact, had rather bored him—was just what he wanted, and there Raymond, once again on his travels, joined them for a fleeting week. It was less than a year since they had first met the De Tourvilles at St Lys, yet in that time two things had happened which vitally altered life at the château. Madame De Tourville had died in Switzerland, without ever having returned to her home, and M. De Tourville was married to the ward who had so plainly adored him in the days gone by.

Solange had enjoyed those months which had elapsed between the two visits to St Lys. Her work had been purely theoretical during the whole of that time; any problems which the continued presence of Raymond might have evoked had been in abeyance owing to his protracted absence on business for his paper, and her father's book had been a success in the only way that appealed to him and his daughter—a success among the *savants* of their particular line of work. Yet, when she heard of the new marriage of De Tourville, she went back to St Lys, though she knew it meant for her work of the kind she liked least.

When Raymond heard of the changes at the château his mouth and eyes fell open, and he stared at Solange, marvelling that she could tell him so tranquilly. True, she had not seen what he had, that furtive kiss, but yet, where was her gift, what had happened to her famous power of feeling evil, of being aware of dangers to society in her fellowmen, dangers even only contemplated? She had told him calmly, in answer to his questions, that the death of Madame De Tourville seemed certainly mysterious. She had never returned to the home from which she had been so secretively hurried away, no one but her husband, who had joined her in Switzerland, had seen her die—that is to say, no one who knew her in the little world of St Lys, and as for anyone else, they had only her husband's word to take. She had simply ceased to be, as quietly and unobtrusively as she had lived, and the graceful, passionate young girl, who, however unconsciously, had been her rival, had taken her place.

Yet, or so thought Raymond, when first he met him on this second visit, De Tourville did not look a happy man. There was a haunted expression in his deep-set eyes, a queer watchfulness about his manner, a brooding there had never been before about his eagle face. Perhaps, as Solange suggested, this was because his young bride—as adoring and far more charming than before, as the new-opened rose surpasses the tightly folded bud—was ailing in health. The air of the mountains seemed too keen for her, or the fates envied her her transparent happiness—no cloud upon that! If she, too, were involved in that which Raymond could hardly bear even in his thoughts to bring against the man, then was she the most perfect example of the man-moulded woman of whom Solange had spoken, who had ever existed.

There were days on which she seemed almost her old self, though her husband always watched to see she did not tire herself, but again there were other days, increasing in number, when it seemed that she lost strength with every breath she drew, and then nothing but her husband's ministrations would satisfy her, no hand but his was allowed so much as to alter her cushions or give her a glass of water. And, watching the man as he waited on her, and detecting that haunted something in his face, Raymond thought what a bitter irony it was, if indeed he had unlawfully hurried his wife out of this world, that now this more dearly loved woman for whom he had sinned should also be drawing nearer to the brink, and, most poignant irony of all, if his hand had indeed given, in the much-paraded medicine, poison to the first wife, how every time the second refused to accept anything save at that same hand it must seem to him, in his conscience-ridden mind, as though nothing which his hand poured out could bring anything but death.

Yet all that was sheer trickery of the mind, and a man strong enough to carry through a crime would perhaps be beyond such promptings of the nerves? But De Tourville did not seem so immune, Raymond thought, and Solange was forced to agree with him. She, too, was beginning to look worried, to his practised eyes, and he could not but feel a shade of triumph. What if it were he, after all, who had detected what those acute senses of hers had passed over? Yet when he examined himself, Raymond was not sure what he wanted. If De Tourville had indeed hurried his wife away—as he had undeniably hurried with indecent haste into his second marriage—did he still want him to be found out and tried for the crime? What then of the fragile Monique, with her big eyes where happiness fought with physical discomfort, and won every time they rested on her husband? A murderer was a dreadful thing, a secret poisoner the basest of murderers, yet what had the first Madame De Tourville to recommend her, to put it with brutal frankness? Nothing compared with this ardent, gracious girl. And, as though the gods themselves were of Raymond's mind, Monique De Tourville's health began to mend, and with that mending the shadow seemed to pass from the face of her husband. He seemed as a man who has taken a new lease of life, as though in his veins also the blood flowed more strongly, and in his heart resurgent life beat higher. On one thing he was determined—to remove his young wife from the place that had seemed to agree with her so ill. Never again, so he declared, should her life be risked in the châ-teau, even though it had been in his family for a thousand years, and, to the horror of the town, the historical old place was put up for sale, and bought by an American millionaire. Raymond's good offices were called in over the deal; indeed it was he, triumphing over scruples, who had first led the wealthy personage down to St Lys to see the castle. The sale had been concluded, all was ready for the departure of Monique and her husband for South America—a climate M. De Tourville had persuaded himself was just what she needed—when the most terrible yet most thrilling day St Lys had ever known was upon it.

Solange had announced that she was going up to the château to see if she could help the still delicate Monique with her final arrangements—the De Tourvilles were leaving in an automobile to catch the Paris express at midday. Solange had seemed to Raymond's observant eyes oddly watchful of late; he marked well-known symptoms in her, but could not fathom their cause.

Did she, like himself, suspect the picturesque Edmund De Tourville, and even if so, had she, after her individualistic fashion, which often made her take the law into her own hands when she judged fit, decided that Monique's happiness was the important thing, and that Edmund must be allowed to go free for the sake of the girl who hung upon him? It would not be unlike Solange. If, according to her classification of criminals into the congenital and the occasional, De Tourville merely came into the latter, and had only committed the one crime that almost any of us may, if hard enough pressed, and would be safe never to commit another, then it was more than possible she would think he should be allowed to work out his own salvation. If, on the other hand, she had cause to consider him one of those born killers to whom their own desires are sufficient warrant to prey upon society, then, he knew, she would not sacrifice the community to one girl—even apart from the fact that the girl herself might be the next victim. Human tigers, such as are the born killers, are creatures who tire quickly, and who have violent reactions.

Or was he, Raymond, perhaps conjuring up out of a few unfortunately suspicious circumstances a crime that had never been committed, and had the death of Thérèse De Tourville, after all, been merely a convenient but purely natural happening? But against that hope was his knowledge that Solange was aware of something odd in the *affaire* De Tourville, though she had never admitted so much to him.

He walked by her side up to the château on this May morning with a strange quickening of the heart. There seemed a hush as of expectation in the crisp, still air; on the quiet lips of Solange; above all, in the watchful look of De Tourville, whose eyes bore the look of one who is calculating time as though every minute were precious.

Monique alone was radiant, stronger than she had been for some time past, fired with excitement at the thought of the new life in the new world. Raymond had long persuaded himself that, whatever sinister meaning lay behind the drama of the château, she had had no hand in it. Wax as she was in her husband's hands, Raymond told himself her glance was too frank and clear for a guilt to lie behind those eyes.

The big *salon* at the château was dismantled, the pictures were gone from the walls, and packing-cases, already labelled, stood about the bare floor. Edmund had had to sell his family place, but he was taking the most loved of his possessions with him.

'*Cherie*, how sweet of you to come!' cried Monique, springing up from the crate on which she was sitting, already attired in her little close-fitting motor-bonnet that framed her face like a nun's coif, the soft, white chiffon veil streaming behind her, only her full, passionate lips giving the lie to the conventual aspect of her. She kissed Solange, then held out both hands eagerly to Raymond.

'Oh, I'm so excited! And I believe Edmund is, too, though he pretends he isn't. I think he is afraid of something happening to prevent us going!'

'What should happen?' asked Edmund, more harshly than was his wont in addressing her.

'Exactly! That's what I say. What should or could? But I do feel you're anxious all the same, Edmund.'

And Monique nodded with an air of womanly wisdom that was new to her.

At that moment a knocking was heard at the great door—an old wooden structure with a heavy iron knocker. The rapping was insistent, even violent, and to each person there came the sudden feeling that something beyond the usual stood there and made that urgent summons. Of all the people there none seemed so disturbed as Edmund De Tourville. His dark face became very pale, but he did not move.

They heard old Henri, the butler, shuffle to the door, and the next moment came the sound of confused protests, asseverations, then over all rose a voice they knew, but which seemed to two of the people in the *salon* to be a voice out of a dream.

Quick, sharp footsteps came near, the door was flung wide open, and Thérèse De Tourville stood upon the threshold, her head flung back, her eyes blazing in her white face, surveying them all as they stared at her. Then Solange moved swiftly forward to Monique's side, as though to protect her. The girl had fallen back and was staring at this ghost from the dead year, and Raymond's face was like hers. Only De Tourville and Solange did not look amazed; for his part he seemed as a man stricken by a blow he has long dreaded.

'Thérèse—Thérèse,' the unfortunate man stammered, 'have you no pity?'

'Pity!' said Madame De Tourville—the only Madame De Tourville—in a harsh voice. 'No, I do not pity. I leave that to you, who cannot even carry out what you begin, who weaken in every-thing. Pity!'

Raymond interposed. He never knew—did nor dare ask him-self—whether his first feeling had not been regret that Thérèse De Tourville still lived, that her husband had not, as she taunted him, finished what he had begun; but he did know that the immediate thing was to try and shield Monique from greater pain than she must inevitably be made to feel.

'There can be no need for Madame De—for Monique to be here,' he said. 'Solange, take her away.'

'Yes,' said De Tourville, with a groan, 'take her away quickly!'

'Not till she has heard!' cried Thérèse; and planted her tall, thin form against the door.

Behind her the frightened faces of the servants could be seen peering.

Then De Tourville broke down.

'Thérèse, I beg of you—anything but that! I will give you any-thing you like—the money, all of it; we both will! But do not say anything, I implore you! Thérèse—'

Then Monique astonished them all. She gently shook off Solange's detaining hand and went and stood by Edmund, look-ing at the other woman fiercely.

'Go on!' she said. 'What have you to say that can hurt me? You are here, and I am not his wife! What can anything else matter?'

'You don't understand,' said Raymond urgently. 'Come away.'

'What don't I understand?'

'Your Edmund,' began Madame De Tourville, 'is not only a bigamist! He is a murderer, an assassin, or would be if he had had the heart to finish what he began! What do you say to that, you white-faced bit of sentiment?'

'Edmund, it isn't true?' stammered Monique, her eyes fixed on him.

He could only bow his head in reply; all the fight seemed to have gone out of him.

Again Monique surprised them. She flung her arms round Edmund and held him fiercely.

'Edmund—and you were willing to do that for me?'

Wonder, sorrow, and—yes—triumph rang in her voice. In that moment Raymond Ker learnt more about women than in the whole of his thirty years previously.

'Take her away quickly, before she learns the truth!' said Solange urgently to Edmund above the girl's head.

His eyes met hers with desperation in their haggard depths. He swung Monique's frail figure up in his arms and made to carry her from the room, but Thérèse only laughed and still barred the way.

'For you!' she said. 'For you! You little fool! Did you think he had tried to poison *me*? It was all arranged between us! I was to disappear and be given out for dead, and he was to marry you and kill you for the money! It is you he has been poisoning, not me!'

And she laughed again.

'It isn't possible!' cried Raymond. 'De Tourville, why don't you say something? Don't you see it's killing Monique?'

'Tell her—I can't!' muttered De Tourville to Solange.

Monique had dropped her hands from him and had taken a step back; in her white, stricken face her eyes looked suddenly dim, like those of a dying bird. Solange took her gently by the arm.

'Monique, it's true,' she said. 'I'm afraid you've got to know it's true. But he repented, Monique; he hadn't the heart to go on with it. He grew to love you too dearly. Monique—'

'What does all that matter!' said Monique. 'He tried to kill me—to kill me! Oh, it's a joke! You're making it up, all of you! Say it's a joke, say it isn't true! Say it—say it!'

No one stirred; and her voice, which had sharpened to the wild scream of a child, fell into monotony again.

'So it's true? All that time I was ill—that I was so thirsty, that my throat hurt so, and I was so sick—you were doing it, Edmund? When no one but you looked after me, you were doing it all the time?'

'Not all the time. He could not go on with it,' said Solange. 'You remember when you began to get better? That was when he found he cared for you too much.'

'It doesn't matter,' repeated Monique.

'Well, it's brought me back, anyway,' said Madame De Tourville coarsely. 'I wasn't going to be cheated because a weak fool had succumbed to your pretty face and soft ways. Where did I come in, I should like to know? At first when I wrote and said what a long time it was taking, he always replied that he had to go cautiously, that Dr Fontaine and this so-clever *demoiselle* were here, and would suspect if anything happened too soon. And I went on believing him. Then I got suspicious. I kept on picturing them together—my husband and this girl he ought to have killed long ago—and I knew if he wasn't killing her he must be kissing her. So I made inquiries, and found out they were going to do a flit, with the money that should have been mine by now, mine and his. And here I am.'

She finished her extraordinary speech, with its astounding egotism, its brutal claims on what could not conceivably be considered hers, and folded her strong arms across her meagre chest, shooting out her hard jaw contemptuously. There could be little doubt which was the stronger willed of the two—she or her husband.

'The question is,' remarked Solange, in what she purposely made a very matter-of-fact tone, 'what is going to be done about it all now? I suppose everyone in the town saw you come here, madame?'

'Certainly. I am sick of hiding myself.'

'You do not mind going to prison with your husband, then?'

'I care for nothing except to get him from that girl. The money is lost, of course. Well and good, but at least he sha'n't have the girl, either.'

Solange turned to Monique.

'Monique, it rests with you,' she said gently. 'Are you going to prosecute? To give information against these people? They trapped you into a marriage that was a sham, because it was their only way of making sure of the money, and then they tried to kill you. Are you going to let them go free?'

Monique had followed the speech carefully, her lips sometimes moving soundlessly as though she were repeating the words that Solange used to herself the better to impress them upon her dazed brain. Slowly she turned her eyes, as with a strong effort of will, from the face of Solange to that of Edmund De Tourville. He had not spoken since his outburst to Solange, but he had not taken his eyes from Monique. Now he made no appeal, he only moistened his lips with his tongue and waited.

'I won't hurt you,' said Monique slowly.

'Oh, the hussy, the wretch!' cried Madame De Tourville. 'She is not going to prosecute because she still wants him. She couldn't be with him if he went to prison, and she still wants him. Shameful hussy, that's what I call you!'

And the odd thing was that Madame De Tourville was perfectly genuine in her indignation.

'Monique, I can't thank you,' said De Tourville slowly. 'Thanks from me to you would be an insult. I can only tell you—'

'Ah, la la, they will pay each other compliments in a minute!' broke in Madame De Tourville. 'It's as well I made up my mind to what I did before I came here.'

'What do you mean?' asked Monique quickly.

'I mean that I called in on monsieur the magistrate on my way, and he and his gendarmes are waiting at the door now for me and my husband. Oh, I wasn't going to run the risk of your forgiving him!'

And Thérèse turned, walked across the hall, where the pale-faced servants fell back from her in fear, and opened the door to the police.

'Well,' said Raymond to Solange late that evening—'well, what do you know about that? They'll get twenty years with hard labour if they get a day, and that woman gave the whole thing away deliberately when she could have got off scot free. Monique would never have brought the charge. It's jolly hard on her, the whole story'll have to come out now.'

'Exactly,' said Solange, 'that's why Thérèse has done it. That woman has two passions—money and her husband. She thought the former was the stronger when she planned to let him marry the girl as a preliminary to poisoning her, and so it might have been if De Tourville had not played her false. Then she could keep quiet no longer, and she thinks a lifetime in prison cheap so long as she is avenged on him. It is all a question of values. After all, murder is the action behind which lies more distortion of value than behind any other in the world, so you must not be surprised that, when you have found someone who can think it worth while to murder, they are abnormal in their other values also.'

'Perhaps not—but it isn't only Madame De Tourville who needs explaining. What of him? A weak man who repented, who couldn't be true even to an infamous contract?'

'More or less, though in a man of his type there would always be a thousand complications and subtleties that make any sweeping statement rather crude. He is a potential criminal, but in happier circumstances no one—including himself—would have ever found it out. If he could have made his get-away, I don't believe he would ever have done a criminal act again. In time he would doubtless have persuaded himself that the whole thing was a nightmare, and had never taken place; have believed that he had always been devoted to Monique, and that his only sin was a bigamous marriage, which his great love almost excused. If Thérèse had never turned up to trouble them, he would probably have forgotten even that.'

'And Monique?'

'Ah, she is a true type of the *femme aux hommes*. She only lives and breathes in the loved man. You see, even as a young girl fresh from school she started an affair with Edmund, the wife did not exist for her in the strength of her passion, and it was that passion, so innocently undisguised, that first put the whole foul scheme into their heads. For you turned up, a young, eligible man, and they got panicky as they realised that she had only to marry for them to lose her money. If it were not you, it was only a question of time before it was someone else.'

'Solange, when did you guess? Did you not at one time think as I did, that De Tourville had got rid of his wife by foul means so as to marry Monique?'

'I certainly should have thought so if I had gone on the facts alone, but I went on two other things as well—my knowledge of types and my "feeling".

'I got my "feeling" about that household. I couldn't hide it from you, who knew me, and the person I got it with most was Thérèse. That he was of the type to fit in with her I knew—she is of the race of strong women, of the Mrs Mannings and the Brinvilliers of the criminal world; he is one of the Macbeths. But the odd thing is this—if it had been he who was of the dominating criminal type instead of his wife, then he and Monique would have in all probability done as you suspected. She is no criminal as things are, but she is so completely the type of waxen woman that it would only have rested with the man to make her another Marie Vitalis or Jeanne Weiss. At first I thought as you did, and when I did not find Madame De Tourville in Switzerland, I thought it all the more, though I still couldn't fit it in with their characters as I thought they were. Then I heard of the marriage with Monique, and I came back here determined to find out what was wrong. Monique's failing health struck me as very suspicious, and gradually from one little thing and another I put the crime together.'

'What would you have done if Monique had gone on being ill? Given him away, or gone to him privately?' asked Raymond.

'The former, I think, always depending on what Monique wished. For if he could have gone on with it, it would have meant he was impossible to save. But I had hardly got all my facts, hardly tabulated her symptoms and watched them together, when his heart began to fail him, or to prompt him, whichever way you like to put it. I shall always be glad that it was so before I told him that I knew.'

'Then you did?'

'Yes, I should have told him earlier, of course, if I had seen no signs of relenting on his part, but I held out to the last minute, even at the cost of a little more physical suffering for poor little Monique, so as to give him the chance of saving his own soul alive. I knew that if ever it did come out, the knowledge that he had done so would be the only thing to save them both from madness.'

'And in his new intention—taking her away—you would have helped—you did help—knowing she was not his wife?'

'My dear, who was hurt by it?' said Solange. 'When you have seen as many people hurt as I have, that will be your chief consideration, too. I have told you Monique is a *grande amoureuse*. Her life is bound up in him, and that was what I was out to save, not merely from his poison, but from the poison of his wife's tongue. They would have lived very happily in South America, both have been virtuous, and the chief criminal—his wife—would have had the severest punishment possible in the loss of husband and money. As it is, Monique may die of her hurt.'

'Actually die of a broken heart? And in the twentieth century?'

'She may indeed, for she is not a twentieth century type—she is eternal. At present she is very ill of it with papa and a hospital nurse in attendance, as you know. There is only one hope for her which may materialise, as she has at least the balm of knowing that Edmund relented of his own free will.'

'And what's that?'

'That her need of love is greater than her need of any one particular lover. That sometimes happens, you know.'

'She'll never love again,' asserted Raymond with conviction.

'I shall be more surprised if she can live without,' said Solange.

And the conversation wandered away from Monique Levasseur, and plunged—always in theoretic fashion—into the ways of love. Here Raymond refused to follow Solange, as he did in the psychology of matters criminal, and they parted company after an hour of arguing over the route.

Raymond was certain he was far more nearly right than Solange; she was only sure she was right for herself, though very probably wrong for the rest of the world. Yet a few months later it was proved that she had been right in her hope for Monique. A romantic Englishman, who attended the trial of the De Tourvilles, and 'wrote up' Monique as the heroine, was one of the many men who proposed to her on that occasion, and he succeeded in persuading her into what was to be a very happy love-marriage.

## Marie Belloc Lowndes

Marie Belloc Lowndes (1868–1947) was the only daughter of a French barrister and an English feminist. She was born in London, but brought up in La Celle-Saint-Cloud in France, and in later years, she retained a slight French accent. Her fiction reflected her cosmopolitan background, and her daughter Susan, introducing a collection of her diaries and letters, said that she was 'a brilliant interpreter of the French mind and character. She was fascinated by the differences of outlook of Britain and France and considered the French to be far more realistic, and noted with amusement that there is no French equivalent to the term "wishful thinking"'.

Today, she is best remembered for *The Lodger* (1913), which was filmed by Alfred Hitchcock, although she wryly noted that on its original publication 'I did not receive a single favourable review'. The novel was later recommended to Ernest Hemingway by Gertrude Stein (herself a keen fan of detective fiction), together with *The Chink in the Armour* (1912), set in France, and boasting a plot inspired by a murder in Monte Carlo in 1907. Hemingway found them 'both splendid after-work books, the people credible and the action and the terror never false'. She also created Hercules Popeau before Agatha Christie achieved fame with the Hercule Poirot mysteries; Lowndes was not impressed by the resemblances between the characters. Poirot became one of fiction's greatest detectives, while Popeau soon slipped out of sight, but this story offers a reminder of him, and of a writer with a flair for invention.

'THIS IS DEAR, DELIGHTFUL PARIS! PARIS, WHICH I LOVE; Paris, where I have always been so happy with Bob. It's foolish of me to feel depressed. I've nothing to be depressed about—'

Such were the voiceless thoughts which filled the mind of Lady Waverton as she walked down one of the platforms of the vast grey Gare du Nord on a hot, airless, July night. She formed one of a party of three; the other two being her husband, Lord Waverton, and a beautiful Russian émigrée, Countess Filenska, with whom they had become friends. It was the lovely Russian who had persuaded the Wavertons to take a little jaunt to Paris 'on the cheap,' that is without maids and valet. The Countess had drawn a delightful picture of an old hostelry on the left bank of the Seine called the Hotel Paragon, where they would find pleasant quiet rooms.

Perhaps the journey had tired the charming, over-refined woman her friends called Gracie Waverton. Yet this morning she had looked as well and happy as she ever did look, for she was not strong, and for some time past she had felt that she and her husband, whom in her gentle, reserved way, she loved deeply, were drifting apart. Like all very rich men, Lord Waverton had a dozen ways of killing time in which his wife could play no part. Still, according to modern ideas, they were a happy couple.

It did not take long for the autobus to glide across Paris at this time of the night, and when they turned into the quiet *cul de sac*, across the end of which rose the superb eighteenth-century mansion which had been the town palace of one of Marie Antoinette's platonic adorers, Monsieur le Duc de Paragon, Lady Waverton lost her vague feeling of despondency. There was something so cheery, as well as truly welcoming, about Monsieur and Madame Bonchamp, mine host and his wife; and she was enchanted with the high ceilinged, panelled rooms, which had been reserved for their party, and which overlooked a spacious leafy garden.

As Lady Waverton and her Russian friend kissed each other good-night, the Englishwoman exclaimed, 'You didn't say a word too much, Olga. This is a delightful place!'

I

'Robert? This is *too* exquisite! You are the most generous man in the world!'

Olga Filenska was gazing, with greedy eyes, at an open blue velvet-lined jewel-case containing a superb emerald pendant.

'I'm glad you like it, darling—'

Lord Waverton seized the white hand, and made its owner put what it held on a table near which they both stood. Then he clasped her in his arms, and their lips met and clung together.

The secret lovers were standing in the centre of the large, barely-furnished *salon*, which belonged to the private suite of rooms which had been reserved for the party; and they felt secure from sudden surprise by a high screen which masked the door giving into the corridor.

At last, releasing her, he moodily exclaimed, 'Why did you make me bring my wife to Paris? It spoils everything, and makes me feel, too, such a cad!'

'Remember my reputation, Robert. It is all I have left of my vanished treasures.'

He caught her to him again, and once more kissed her long and thirstily.

'My God, how I love you!' he said in a strangled whisper. 'There's nothing, nothing, *nothing* I wouldn't do, to have you for ever as my own!'

'Is that really true?' she asked with a searching look.

'Haven't I offered to give up everything, and make a bolt? It's you who refuse to do the straight thing.'

'Your wife,' she murmured, in a low bitter tone, 'would never divorce you. She thinks divorce wicked.'

'If I'm willing to give up my country, and everything I care for—for love of you, why shouldn't you do as much for me?'

To that she made no answer, only sighed, and looked at him appealingly.

What would each of them have felt had it suddenly been revealed that their every word had been overheard, and each passionate gesture of love witnessed, by an invisible listener and watcher? Yet such was the strange, and the almost incredible, fact. Hercules Popeau, but lately retired on a pension from the Criminal Investigation Branch of the Préfecture de Police, had long made the Hotel Paragon his home, and his comfortable study lay to the right of the stately octagon *salon* which terminated Lord and Lady Waverton's suite of rooms.

Popeau had lived in the splendid seventeenth-century house for quite a long time, before he had discovered—with annoyance rather than satisfaction—that just behind the arm-chair in which he usually sat, and cleverly concealed in the wainscoting, was a slanting sliding panel which enabled him both to hear and see everything that went on in the next room. This sinister 'Judas,' as it was well called, dated from the days of Louis the Fifteenth, when a diseased inquisitiveness was the outstanding peculiarity of both the great and the humble; even the King would spend his leisure in reading copies of the love letters intercepted in the post, of those of his faithful subjects who were known to him.

Hercules Popeau had been closely connected with the British army during the Great War, and he remembered that Lord Waverton, then little more than a boy, had performed an act of signal valour at Beaumont Hamel. That fact had so far interested him in the three tourists, as to have caused him to watch the party while they had sat at dinner in their private sitting-room the evening following their arrival in Paris. The famous secret agent was very human and he had taken a liking to fragile-looking Lady Waverton, and a dislike to her lovely Russian friend. The scene he was now witnessing confirmed his first judgment of the Countess Filenska.

'I wish Gracie were not here!' exclaimed Lord Waverton.

'She is—how do you call it?—too much thinking of herself to think of us,' was the confident answer of Lady Waverton's false friend.

There came a look of discomfort and shame over the man's face. 'You women are such damn good actresses! Then you think Gracie is really ill this morning?'

'"Ill" is a big word. Still, she is willing to see a doctor. It is fortunate that I know a very good Paris physician. He will be here very soon; but she wants us to start for Versailles now, before he comes.'

'All right! I'll go and get ready.'

When she believed herself to be absolutely alone, Countess Filenska walked across to the long mirror between the two windows and stood there, looking at herself in the bright light with a close dispassionate scrutiny.

Hercules Popeau, as he gazed at her through his hidden 'Judas,' told himself that though in his time he had been brought in contact with many beautiful women, rarely had he seen so exquisite a creature as was Olga Filenska. While very dark, she had no touch of swarthiness, and her oval face had the luminosity of a white camellia petal. She had had the courage to remain unshingled, and the Frenchman, faithful to far away memories of youth, visioned the glorious mantle her tightly coiled hair must form when unbound. Her figure, at once slender and rounded, was completely revealed, as is the fashion to-day, by a plain black dress.

Was she really Russian? Hercules Popeau shook his head. That southern type of beauty is unmistakable. He had known a Georgian princess who might have been the twin sister of the woman he saw before him now.

The hidden watcher's lifelong business had been to guess the innermost thoughts of men and women. But he felt he had no clue as to what was making this dark lady smile, as she was doing now in so inscrutable a way, at herself.

At last she turned round and left the room, and at once her unseen admirer, and, yes, judge, closed the tiny slit in the panelled wall.

What a curious, romantic, and yes, sinister page, he had just turned in the great Book of Life! A page of a not uncommon story; that of a beautiful, unscrupulous woman, playing the part of serpent in a modern Garden of Eden.

It was clear that Lord Waverton was infatuated with this lovely creature, but there had been no touch of genuine passion in her seductive voice, or even in her apparently eager response to his ardour.

Hercules Popeau had a copy of the latest *Who's Who?* on his writing table, and he opened the section containing the letter W.

The entry he sought for began: 'Waverton, Robert Hichfield, of Hichfield, York. Second Baron.'

And then there came back to him the knowledge that this man's father had been one of the greatest of Victorian millionaires. No wonder he had been able to present the woman he loved in secret with that magnificent jewel!

There came the sounds of a motor drawing up under the huge *porte-cochère* of the Hotel Paragon; and, rising, the Frenchman went quickly over to the open window on his right.

Yes, there was a big car, the best money could hire, with his lordship standing by the bonnet. Waverton looked the ideal 'Milord' of French fancy, for he was a tall, broad man, with fair hair having in it a touch of red.

Just now he was obviously impatient and ill at ease. But he had not long to wait, for in a very few moments Countess Filenska stepped out of the great house into the courtyard. Even in her plain motor bonnet she looked entrancingly lovely.

Popeau took a step backwards from his window, as there floated upwards the voices of the two people whose secret he now shared.

'Did you see Gracie?' asked Lord Waverton abruptly.

'Yes, and she was so sweet and kind! She begs us not to hurry back; and she is quite looking forward to the visit of my old friend, Dr Scorpion.'

*Scorpion?* A curious name—not a happy name—for a medical man. Hercules Popeau remembered that he had once known a doctor of that name.

'Are you ready, Olga?'

'Quite ready, *mon ami*,' and she smiled up into his face.

A moment later they were side by side, and Lord Waverton took the wheel.

As the motor rolled out on to the boulevard, the Frenchman went back to his desk, and, taking up the speaking-tube, he whistled down it.

'Madame Bonchamp? I have something important to say to you.' He heard the quick answer: 'At your service always, Monsieur.'

'Listen to me!'

'I am listening.'

'A doctor is coming to see Lady Waverton this morning. *Before he sees Miladi, show him yourself into my bedroom.*'

There came a surprised, 'Do you feel ill, Monsieur?'

'I am not very well; and I have reason to think this doctor is an old friend of mine. *But I do not wish him to know that he is not being shown straight into the bedroom of his English lady patient.* Have I made myself clear?'

He heard her eager word of assent. Madame Bonchamp was as sharp as a needle, and she had once had reason to be profoundly grateful to Hercules Popeau. He knew he could trust her absolutely; sometimes he called her, by way of a joke, 'Madame Discretion.'

II

Hercules Popeau always did everything in what he called to himself an artistic—an Englishman would have said a thorough—way. Before getting into bed, he entirely undressed, and then drew together the curtains of his bedroom window. Thus anyone coming into the room from the corridor would feel as if in complete darkness, while to one whose eyes were already accustomed to the dim light, everything would be perfectly clear.

The time went by slowly, and he had already been in bed half an hour, when at last the door of the room opened, and he heard Madame Bonchamp exclaim: '*Entrez, Monsieur le Docteur!*' And then his heart gave a leap, for the slight elderly individual who had just been shown into the darkened room, was undoubtedly the man he had known twenty years ago.

Quickly the ex-secret agent told himself that as the doctor had been about thirty years of age when he had got into the very serious trouble which had brought him into touch with the then Chief of the French Criminal Investigation Department, he must now be fifty.

With a sardonic look on his powerful face Hercules Popeau watched his visitor grope his way forward into the darkened room.

'Miladi,' he said at last, in an ill-assured tone, 'I will ask your permission to draw the curtains a little? Otherwise, I cannot see you.' He put his hat on a chair as he spoke, and then he went towards the nearest window, and pulled apart the curtains.

Letting in a stream of light, he turned towards the bed. When he saw that it was a man, and not a woman who was sitting up there, he gave a slight gasp of astonishment.

'It is a long time since we have met, is it not, my good Doctor Scorpion?'

For a moment Popeau thought that the man who stood stock still, staring at him as if petrified, was about to fall down in a faint. And a feeling of regret, almost of shame, came over him—for he was a kindly man—at having played the other such a trick.

But the visitor made a great effort to regain his composure, and at last with a certain show of valour, he exclaimed: 'I have been shown into the wrong room. I came here to see an English lady, who is ill.'

'That is so,' said Popeau quietly. 'But I, too, feel ill, and hearing that you had been called to this hotel, I thought I would like to see you first, and ask your advice. I confess I rather hoped you were the Dr Scorpion I had once known.'

To the unfortunate man who stood in the middle of the large room there was a terrible edge of irony in the voice that uttered those quiet words.

'Of course, I know, that is in the old days, you were more accustomed to diagnose the condition of an ailing woman than that of a man,' went on the ex-police chief pitilessly.

And then he changed his tone. 'Come, come!' he exclaimed. 'I have no right to go back to the past. Draw a chair close up to my bed, and tell me how you have got on all these years?'

With obvious reluctance the doctor complied with this almost command. 'I have now been in very respectable practice for some time,' he said in a low voice.

He waited a moment, then he added bitterly: 'Can you wonder that seeing you gave me a moment of great discomfort and pain, reminding me, as this meeting must do, of certain errors of my youth of which I have repented.'

'I am glad to hear you have repented,' said Popeau heartily.

In a clearer, calmer tone, Scorpion went on: 'I made a good marriage; I have a sweet wife, and two excellent children.'

'Good! Good!'

Hercules Popeau's manner altered. He felt convinced that this man's account of himself was substantially true. And yet? And yet a doubt remained.

'Are you always called in to the clients of this hotel?' he asked suddenly.

The other hesitated, and the ex-police chief again felt a touch of misgiving.

'No, I am not the regular medical attendant of the Hotel

Paragon,' answered Scorpion at last. 'But I've been here before, and oddly enough,' he concluded jauntily, 'to see another foreign lady.'

'Then who sent for you now, to-day?'

Again the doctor did not answer at once; but when he did speak it was to say, with a forced smile: 'A lady whom I attended for a quinsy, the last time she was in this hotel. It is to see a friend of hers that I am here.'

The doctor's statement fitted in with what he, Hercules Popeau, knew to be true. Yet something—a kind of sixth sense which sometimes came to his aid—made Popeau tell his visitor a lie of which he was ashamed.

'Although I know seeing me again must have revived sore memories, I am glad to have seen you, Scorpion, and to have heard that the past is dead. Now tell me if I can safely go off to-night to Niort, where I am to spend the rest of this hot summer?'

The doctor at once assumed a professional manner. He peered into his new patient's throat, he felt his new patient's pulse, and at last he said gravely: 'Yes, you can leave Paris to-night, though it might be more prudent to stay till to-morrow morning.'

'Now that you have reassured me, I shall go to-night.'

Then Dr Scorpion asked, almost in spite of himself, a question: 'Are you still connected with the police, Monsieur Popeau?'

'No, I took my pension at the end of the war, and I am now a rolling stone, for I have not the good fortune, like you, to be married to a woman I love. Also, alas! I am not a father.' He waited a moment. 'And now for what the British call a good hand-shake.'

He held out his hand, and then felt a sensation of violent recoil, for it was as if the hand he held was a dead hand. Though to-day was a very hot day, that hand was icy cold—an infallible sign of shock.

The ex-member of the dreaded Sûreté felt a touch of sharp remorse. He had nothing in him of the feline human being who likes to play with a man or a woman as a cat plays with a mouse.

As soon as he had dressed himself Hercules Popeau spoke down his speaking-tube. 'Has the doctor left?' he asked casually.

'Yes, some minutes ago.'

He went down to the office, and drew a bow at a venture: 'You knew Dr Scorpion before, eh?'

Madame Bonchamp said in a singular tone: 'The Countess Filenska and that little doctor have been great friends for a long time. Beauty sometimes likes Ugly, and Ugly always likes Beauty.'

Popeau had meant to go upstairs again, but after that casual word or two, instead of going upstairs, he walked out of the hotel.

Sauntering along, he crossed a bridge, and came at last to the big building, the very name of which fills every Parisian's heart with awe.

Now there is a small, almost hidden, door in the Préfecture of Police which is only used by the various heads of departments. It was through this door that Popeau went up to his former quarters, being warmly greeted on the way by various ex-colleagues with whom he had been popular.

Soon he was in the familiar room where are kept the secret *dossiers*, or records which play so important a part in the lives of certain people, and very soon there was laid before him an envelope with the name of *Victor Alger Scorpion* inscribed on it. Glancing over the big sheet of copy paper he saw at once the entry concerning the serious affair in which Scorpion had been concerned some twenty years before. And then came *General Remarks*:

Victor Alger Scorpion has made a great effort to become respectable. He is living a quiet, moral life with his wife and two children, and to the latter he is passionately devoted. But it is more than suspected that now and again he will take a serious risk in order to make a big sum of money to add to his meagre savings. *Such risks are always associated with—*

Then followed three capital letters with whose meaning Hercules Popeau was acquainted, though he had never been directly in touch with that side of the police force which concerns itself specially with morals.

He read on:

Just after the end of the war, Scorpion was concerned with the mysterious death of a young Spanish lady. But though he was under grave suspicion, it was impossible actually to prove anything against him; also the fact that he had done even more than his duty as a surgeon in the war, benefited him in the circumstances. He was, however, warned that he would be kept under observation. Since then there has been nothing to report.

### III

Lord and Lady Waverton and their friend had arrived on a Saturday night, and Dr Scorpion's first visit to the hotel had been paid on the Monday morning. As the days went on, Lady Waverton, while still keeping to her room, became convalescent, though the doctor recommended that her ladyship should go on being careful till she was to leave Paris, on the following Saturday.

Hercules Popeau, who had constituted himself a voluntary prisoner, cursed himself for a suspicious fool. Cynically he told himself that though marital infidelity is extremely common, murder is comparatively rare.

On the Friday morning Madame Bonchamp herself brought up his *petit déjeuner*. She looked anxious and worried. 'Miladi is worse,' she said abruptly. 'I have already telephoned for the doctor. The Countess Filenska is greatly distressed! I must hurry, now, as I have to serve an English breakfast for two in the next room at once.'

A few minutes later Popeau, peeping through the slanting 'Judas,' sat watching Lord Waverton and his beautiful companion. After having exchanged a long passionate embrace, they sat down, but the excellent omelette provided by Madame Bonchamp remained untasted for a while.

'I don't see why you should be going to England to-day!' exclaimed Lord Waverton.

She said firmly: 'It is imperative that I should see the picture dealer who will start for Russia to-morrow.'

'Well then, if you must go'—he had the grace to look ashamed— 'I don't see why I shouldn't go, too, darling? Gracie hates to have me about when she's ill, and I can't help thinking that the sensible thing to do would be to get a trained nurse over from England. I've only got to telephone to my mother to have a nurse here by to-morrow morning.'

The Countess looked violently disturbed. 'I know Gracie would not like that!' she exclaimed.

She was pouring some black coffee into her cup, and Popeau saw that the lovely hand shook. 'You cannot do better than leave Gracie in my French doctor's hands,' she went on. 'I was seriously ill here last year, and he was wonderful!'

There came a knock at the door, and the man to whom his ex-patient had just given such a good character, came into the sitting-room.

Dr Scorpion was pale, but composed: 'I am indeed sorry,' he began, 'to hear that my patient is worse—'

The Countess cut him short, almost rudely. 'Let us go to her,' she cried, and together they left the room. But in a few moments she came back, alone.

'Gracie is much better,' she observed. 'She will probably be able to go home Friday.'

She put her hand caressingly through Lord Waverton's arm. 'I will go over to England to-day at four o'clock, and I will be back here by to-morrow night. What do you say to *that* for devotion?'

Her lover's face cleared. 'Does that mean—'

'—that I'm a foolish woman? That I do not like being away from you even for quite a little while? Yes, it does mean that!'

She submitted—the unseen watcher thought with a touch of impatience—to his ardent caresses.

Suddenly the door behind the screen opened. The two sprang apart, and, as the doctor edged his way in again, Lord Waverton left the room.

'What have you come back to tell me?' said the Countess sharply.

Scorpion looked at her fixedly. 'Is it true that Madame la Comtesse is going away to England to-day?'

'I am returning to Paris at once,' she said evasively.

'I have thought matters over, and I refuse to go on with the treatment before payment, or part payment, is made,' he said firmly.

'Come! Don't be unreasonable!' she exclaimed.

He answered at once, in a fierce, surly tone: 'I refuse to risk my head unless it is made worth my while. I did not think it possible that you meant to leave me to face a terrible danger alone.'

'I tell you that I am coming back to-morrow night! Also it is absolutely true that I have no money—as yet.'

'Surely the Milord would give you some money? Cannot you invent something which requires at once an advance of say—' he hesitated, then slowly uttered the words, 'fifty thousand francs.'

Popeau expected to hear a cry of protest, but the beautiful woman who now stood close to the ugly, clever-looking little doctor, opened her handbag and said coldly: 'I have something here which is worth a great deal more than fifty thousand francs,' and she handed him the jewel-case which contained the emerald pendant.

Scorpion opened the case. 'Is the stone real?' he asked suspiciously.

'Fool!' she said angrily, 'walk into the first jeweller's shop you pass by, offer it for sale, and see.'

He was looking at the gorgeous stone with glistening, avid eyes. Slowly he shut the jewel-case and put it in his pocket. 'I know where I can dispose of it, should it become necessary that I should do so.'

'Then you will keep your promise?'

There was a long pause. Then the doctor produced a loose-leaved prescription block.

'I will fulfil my promise,' he said firmly, 'if you will write on this sheet of paper what I dictate.'

He handed her a fountain pen:

'My dear friend and doctor: I beg you to accept the jewel I am sending you, a square-cut emerald, which is my own property to dispose of, in consideration of the great care and kindness you showed me when I was so extremely ill last year.—Your ever grateful, Olga Filenska.'

She hesitated for what seemed both to the invisible watcher, and to her accomplice, a long time. But at last she wrote out the words he again dictated, and he put the piece of paper in the pocket where already reposed the small jewel-case.

'*C'est entendu*,' he exclaimed, and turned towards the door.

A moment later Hercules Popeau took off his telephone receiver. 'Invent a pretext to keep the doctor till I come down!' he exclaimed.

Then, taking out of a drawer a large sheet of notepaper headed *Préfecture de Police, Paris*, he wrote on it:

Madame la Comtesse,

You are in grave danger. The man you are employing to rid you of your rival is affiliated to the French Police. He has revealed your plot. An affidavit sworn by him will reach Scotland Yard in the course of to-morrow. A copy of the sworn statement of Dr Scorpion will also be laid before Lord Waverton, who will be summoned to appear as a witness at the extradition proceedings. An admirer of your beauty thinks it kind to warn you that you will be well advised to break your journey to-day, and proceed to some other destination than England. The value of the jewel which I enclose is eight hundred pounds sterling. Lord Waverton paid for it close on two thousand pounds.

He put this letter in a drawer, and then went down to the hall of the hotel.

Dr Scorpion was chatting to Madame Bonchamp, and looked startled and disturbed when he saw Hercules Popeau coming towards him.

'I found Niort dull, so I came back to Paris,' said the latter genially. 'How is your patient, my good Scorpion?'

'Going on fairly,' said the other hesitatingly. 'Though not well enough to leave the hotel this week, as she had hoped to do. Well! Now I must be off—'

'I have a further word to say to you, Scorpion.'

Popeau's voice had become cold and very grave. 'Come upstairs to my rooms.'

Scorpion stumbled up the staircase of the grand old house, too frightened, now, to know what he was doing, or where he was going.

When they reached the corridor, the other man took hold of his shoulder, and pushed him through into his study. Then he locked the door, and turning, faced his abject visitor.

'The first thing I ask you to do is to put on the table the emerald which has just been given you as the price of blood.'

'The emerald?'

Scorpion was shaking, now, as if he had the ague. 'What do you mean?' he faltered, 'I know nothing of any emerald.'

'Come—come! Don't be a fool.'

A look of rage came over the livid face. 'Does that woman dare to call me a thief?' he exclaimed. 'See what she herself wrote when she gave me this jewel!'

With a shaking hand he drew a folded sheet of paper from his pocket.

'I want that, too, of course.'

Scorpion sank down on to a chair. He asked himself seriously if Hercules Popeau was in league with the Devil?

The ex-police chief came and stood over him. 'Listen carefully to what I am going to say. It is important.'

The wretched man looked up, his eyes full of terror, while Popeau went on, tonelessly.

'Once more I am going to allow you to escape the fate which is your due. Last time it was for the sake of your mother. This time it will be for the sake of two women—your good wife, and the unfortunate lady whom you, or perhaps I ought to say, your temptress and accomplice, had doomed to a hideous death by poison.'

Scorpion stared at Hercules Popeau. His face had gone the colour of chalk.

'Get up!'

The unhappy man stood up on his trembling legs.

'Just now you dictated a letter to your accomplice, and I now dictate to you the following confession.'

He placed a piece of notepaper on his writing-table, and forced the other man to go and sit down in his own arm-chair. Then, slowly, he dictated the following!

'I, Victor Scorpion, confess to having entered into a conspiracy with a woman I know under the name of the Countess Filenska, to bring about the death of Lady Waverton on—'

Popeau stopped his dictation and looked fixedly at Scorpion.

'What day was she to die?' he asked.

Scorpion stared woefully at his tormentor. He did not, he felt he could not, answer.

'Must I repeat my question?'

In a whimpering voice he said: 'I did not mean that she should die.'

'What was the exact proposal made to you?'

Twice the man moistened his lips, then at last he answered: 'Five hundred pounds sterling within a fortnight of—of the accident, and ten thousand pounds sterling within six months of the Countess's marriage to Lord Waverton.'

'To your mind I suppose the emerald represented the five hundred pounds?'

'She was going away,' murmured Scorpion. 'I might not have got anything, the more so that I did not mean the poor Miladi to die.'

'On what day did the Countess expect her victim to die?'

Popeau had to bend down to hear the two words. 'Next Friday.'

'I see. Write down the following:

'I was to receive five hundred pounds sterling on the day of her death, and within six months of the Countess's marriage to Lord Waverton ten thousand pounds sterling, whatever the rate of exchange might be at the time. (Signed) Victor Alger Scorpion.'

'Do allow me to put down that I did not intend to carry out this infamous plan?' asked the unhappy wretch pleadingly.

Popeau hesitated a moment. 'No,' he said firmly, 'I will not allow you to do that. But this I will promise. Within a few hours from now, you yourself shall do what you wish with that piece of paper.'

'And the emerald?' said Scorpion in a faltering voice.

'The emerald,' said Popeau thoughtfully, 'will be returned to its owner. I regret that necessity almost as much as you do. But it is to your interest, Scorpion, as to that of others concerned, that the Countess Filenska should have enough to live on till she has found another lover.'

'Perhaps you are right,' muttered Scorpion sadly.

'Of course I am right! And now,' went on Popeau, 'you can make yourself at home in these two rooms for a while, and you can have the use of my bathroom also, should you care to take a bath.'

He smiled genially. 'You may telephone home to your wife, saying you will not be home till late.'

'Can I trust you?' asked his prisoner. 'Remember that I am a father. It was for the sake of my dear children that I placed myself in this dangerous position!'

'I have never yet betrayed any human being,' said Hercules Popeau seriously. 'I am not likely to begin by you, who are such an old—' he hesitated, and then he said 'acquaintance.'

## EPILOGUE

The beautiful cosmopolitan woman, who had made so many warm friends in English society, had just settled herself comfortably in a first-class compartment of the Paris-Calais express. She was quite alone, for in July there are few travellers to England. So she was rather taken aback when a big man, dressed in a pale grey alpaca suit, suddenly thrust his body and head through the aperture leading into the corridor.

'Have I the honour of speaking to Countess Filenska?' he asked.

She hesitated a moment. Then she saw that he held in his hand a bulky envelope, and involuntarily she smiled. From dear foolish Waverton, of course! A *billet doux*, accompanied no doubt by some delightful gift. So, 'I am the Countess Filenska,' she answered.

'I have been told to give you this little parcel, Madame la Comtesse. I am glad I had the good fortune to arrive before your train started.'

The Frenchman had a cultivated voice, and a good manner. No doubt he was a jeweller. She was pleased, being the kind of woman she was, that there need be no question of a gratuity.

'I thank you, monsieur,' she said graciously.

He lifted his hat, and went off. She thought, but she may have been mistaken, that she heard a chuckle in the corridor.

The train started; slowly the traveller broke the seal of the big envelope. Yes! As she had half expected, there was a jewel-case wrapped up in a piece of notepaper. Eagerly she opened the case, and then came mingled disappointment and surprise, for it only contained the emerald which she had given that morning to Scorpion.

With a feeling of sudden apprehension she quickly unfolded the piece of notepaper and then, slowly, with eyes dilated with terror, she read the terrible words written there. The warning sent her, maybe, from some old ex-lover, from the Préfecture de Police.

Could she leap now, out of the train? No, it was now gathering speed, and she could not afford to risk an accident.

Feverishly she counted over her money. Yes, she had enough, amply enough to break her journey at Calais, and go on to—?

After a moment's deep thought she uttered aloud the word 'Berlin.'

Late that same afternoon Madame Bonchamp opened the door of Hercules Popeau's study. 'Milord Waverton,' she murmured nervously, and the Englishman walked into the room.

He looked uncomfortable, even a little suspicious. He had not been able to understand exactly what was wanted of him, only that a Frenchman, whose name he did not know, desired his presence—at once.

He felt anxious. Was his wife worse, and was the man who had asked to see him so urgently a specialist called in by the Countess's French doctor?

'I have a painful, as well as a serious, communication to make to your lordship,' began Hercules Popeau in slow, deliberate tones. He spoke with a strong French accent, but otherwise his English was perfect.

'I belong to the French branch of what in England is called the Criminal Investigation Department, and a most sinister fact has just been brought to our notice.'

He looked fixedly—it was a long, searching glance—into the other man's bewildered face. And then he felt a thrill of genuine relief. His instinct had been right! Lord Waverton, so much was clear, was quite unconscious of the horrible plot which had had for object that of ridding him of his wife.

'The fact brought to our notice,' went on Popeau quietly, 'does not concern your lordship; it concerns Lady Waverton.'

'My wife? Impossible!'

Lord Waverton drew himself up to his full height. He looked angry, as well as incredulous.

'Lady Waverton,' went on the other, 'possesses a terrible enemy.'

'I assure you,' said Lord Waverton coldly, 'that the French police have made some absurd mistake. My wife is the best of women, kindness itself to all those with whom she comes in contact. I may have enemies; she has none.'

'Lady Waverton has an enemy,' said Popeau positively. 'And what is more, that enemy intended to compass her death, and indeed nearly succeeded in doing so.'

The Englishman stared at the Frenchman. He felt as if he was confronting a lunatic.

'This enemy of Lady Waverton's laid her plans—for it is a woman—very cleverly,' said Popeau gravely. 'She discovered in this city of Paris a man who will do anything for money. That man is a doctor, and for what appeared to him a sufficient consideration, he undertook to poison her ladyship.'

He waited a moment, then added in an almost casual tone, 'Lady Waverton's death was to have occurred next Friday.'

'What!' exclaimed Lord Waverton, in a horror-stricken voice, 'do you mean that the little French doctor who has been attending my wife is—'

'—a would-be murderer? Yes,' said Hercules Popeau stolidly. 'Dr Scorpion had undertaken to bring about what would have appeared to everybody here, in the Hotel Paragon, a natural death.'

Lord Waverton covered his face with his hands. Yet even now no suspicion of the woman who had been behind Scorpion had reached his brain. He was trying to remember the name of a French maid his wife had had for a short time soon after their marriage, and who had been dismissed without a character.

'Most fortunately for you, Lord Waverton, this infamous fellow-countryman of mine had already had trouble with the police. So he grew suddenly afraid, and made a full confession of the hideous plot. He brought with him a written proof, as well *as a valuable emerald*, which was part of the price his infamous temptress was willing to pay the man she intended should be the actual murderer.'

The speaker turned away, for he desired to spare the unhappy man, whose sudden quick, deep breathing, showed the awful effect those last words had had on him.

'The rest of the blood money—ten thousand pounds sterling—was to be paid when Scorpion's temptress became the second wife of a wealthy English peer.'

Lord Waverton gave a strangled cry.

'I should now like to show you the proof of the story I have told you. I take it you do not desire to see the emerald?'

The other shook his head violently.

'That is as well,' said Popeau calmly, 'for it is once more in the possession of the woman who calls herself the Countess Filenska.'

He took out of his pocket the two documents, the deed of gift written out by the Countess, and the confession signed by Scorpion himself.

'I will ask you to read these through,' he said, 'and then I must beg you to put a firm restraint upon yourself. I have kept the man here so that he may confirm the fact that the whole of this statement is in his handwriting.'

Popeau waited till Lord Waverton had read Scorpion's confession. Then he opened the door of his bedroom.

'Come here for a moment,' he called out in a quick, business-like tone. 'I have done with that paper I asked you to sign, and I am ready to give you it back the moment you have informed this gentleman that you wrote it.'

Scorpion sidled into the room.

'Now then,' said Popeau sharply, 'say in English, "I, Scorpion, swear that all I wrote down here is true, and that this is my signature."'

The man repeated the words in a faltering voice.

Popeau handed him back the confession.

'Take this piece of paper,' he observed, 'down into the court-yard; there set a light to it, and watch it burn; then go home and thank the good God, and your good wife, that you have not begun the long road which leads to the Devil's Island.'

After Scorpion had left the room, Hercules Popeau turned to the Englishman. 'I trust,' he said, 'that your lordship will not think it impertinent if I ask you to listen to me for yet another two or three minutes?'

Lord Waverton bent his head. His face had gone grey under its tan.

'I am old enough to be your father, and this I would say to you, and I trust that you will take it in good part. There was a time when a man in your position was guarded by high invisible barriers from many terrible dangers. Those barriers, Milord, are no longer there, and—'

There came a knock at the door. A telegram was handed to Lord Waverton. He tore open the envelope.

An unexpected chance has come my way of getting back to Russia, and of recovering some of my lost property. Good-bye, dear friends. Thank you both for your goodness to an unhappy woman. Dear love to Gracie.

As Lord Waverton handed the two slips of paper to his new friend, Hercules Popeau looked much relieved.

'All you have to do,' he exclaimed, 'is to show Miladi this telegram, and then to give her—how do you say it in English?—a good kiss on her sweet face!'

# THE PERFECT MURDER

## *Stacy Aumonier*

The short stories of Stacy Aumonier (1877–1928) have long been relished by connoisseurs. James Hilton, author of *Lost Horizon* and *Goodbye, Mr Chips*, and also an occasional writer of crime fiction, reckoned that Aumonier's best work ranked with the finest short stories ever written, while the present-day crime novelist Christopher Fowler, writing in *The Independent*, said his stories 'should rightly be regarded as classics—but aren't. Worse, his work has vanished completely... Yet John Galsworthy and Alfred Hitchcock were admirers of his style, his way with suspense, his wit, humanity and lightness of touch. He was described as "never heavy, never boring, never really trivial".'

Aumonier was born in London, his surname giving a clue to Huguenot ancestry. His father was a sculptor, and his uncle a well-regarded artist. Aumonier himself was a capable painter, exhibiting in the Royal Academy, and he wrote and performed in sketches for the stage with some success before earning widespread acclaim for his short fiction. Gifted and personable, he seemed to lead a charmed life until he contracted tuberculosis. He sought treatment for the disease in Switzerland, but died there at the age of 51. This story, which appeared in *The Strand* magazine in 1926, was singled out for praise by Julian Symons in his influential study of the genre, *Bloody Murder*.

ONE EVENING IN NOVEMBER TWO BROTHERS WERE SEATED in a little *café* in the Rue de la Roquette discussing murders. The evening papers lay in front of them, and they all contained a lurid account of a shocking affair in the Landes district, where a charcoal-burner had killed his wife and two children with a hatchet. From discussing this murder in particular they went on to discussing murder in general.

'I've never yet read a murder case without being impressed by the extraordinary clumsiness of it,' remarked Paul, the younger brother. 'Here's this fellow murders his victims with his own hatchet, leaves his hat behind in the shed, and arrives at a village hard by with blood on his boots.'

'They lose their heads,' said Henri, the elder. 'In cases like that they are mentally unbalanced, hardly responsible for their actions.'

'Yes,' replied Paul, 'but what impresses me is—what a lot of murders must be done by people who take trouble, who leave not a trace behind.'

Henri shrugged his shoulders. 'I shouldn't think it was so easy, old boy; there's always something that crops up.'

'Nonsense! I'll guarantee there are thousands done every year. If you are living with anyone, for instance, it must be the easiest thing in the world to murder them.'

'How?'

'Oh, some kind of accident—and then you go screaming into the street, "Oh, my poor wife! Help!" You burst into tears, and

everyone consoles you. I read of a woman somewhere who murdered her husband by leaving the window near the bed open at
night when he was suffering from pneumonia. Who's going to
suspect a case like that? Instead of that, people must always select
revolvers, or knives, or go and buy poison at the chemist's across
the way.'

'It sounds as though you were contemplating a murder yourself,'
laughed Henri.

'Well, you never know,' answered Paul; 'circumstances might
arise when a murder would be the only way out of a difficulty. If
ever my time comes I shall take a lot of trouble about it. I promise
you I shall leave no trace behind.'

As Henri glanced at his brother making this remark he was
struck by the fact that there was indeed nothing irreconcilable
between the idea of a murder and the idea of Paul doing it. He was
a big, saturnine-looking gentleman with a sallow, dissolute face,
framed in a black square beard and swathes of untidy grey hair. His
profession was that of a traveller in cheap jewellery, and his business dealings were not always of the straightest. Henri shuddered.
With his own puny physique, bad health, and vacillating will, he
was always dominated by his younger brother. He himself was a
clerk in a drapery store, and he had a wife and three children. Paul
was unmarried.

The brothers saw a good deal of each other, and were very
intimate. But the word friendship would be an extravagant term
to apply to their relationship. They were both always hard up,
and they borrowed money from each other when every other
source failed.

They had no other relatives except a very old uncle and aunt
who lived at Chantilly. This uncle and aunt, whose name was

Taillandier, were fairly well off, but they would have little to do with the two nephews. They were occasionally invited there to dinner, but neither Paul nor Henri ever succeeded in extracting a franc out of Uncle Robert. He was a very religious man, hard-fisted, cantankerous, and intolerant. His wife was a little more pliable. She was in effect an eccentric. She had spasms of generosity, during which periods both the brothers had at times managed to get money out of her. But these were rare occasions. Moreover, the old man kept her so short of cash that she found it difficult to help her nephews even if she desired to.

As stated, the discussion between the two brothers occurred in November. It was presumably forgotten by both of them immediately afterwards. And indeed there is no reason to believe that it would ever have recurred, except for certain events which followed the sudden death of Uncle Robert in the February of the following year.

In the meantime the affairs of both Paul and Henri had gone disastrously. Paul had been detected in a dishonest transaction over a paste trinket, and had just been released from a period of imprisonment. The knowledge of this had not reached his uncle before his death. Henri's wife had had another baby, and had been very ill. He was more in debt than ever.

The news of the uncle's death came as a gleam of hope in the darkness of despair. What kind of will had he left? Knowing their uncle, each was convinced that, however it was framed, there was likely to be little or nothing for them. However, the old villain might have left them a thousand or two. And in any case, if the money was all left to the wife, here was a possible field of plunder. It need hardly be said that they repaired with all haste to the funeral, and even with greater alacrity to the lawyer's reading of the will.

The will contained surprises both encouraging and discouraging. In the first place the old man left a considerably larger fortune than anyone could have anticipated. In the second place all the money and securities were carefully tied up, and placed under the control of trustees. There were large bequests to religious charities, whilst the residue was held in trust for his wife. But so far as the brothers were concerned the surprise came at the end. On her death this residue was still to be held in trust, but a portion of the interest was to be divided between Henri and Paul, and on their death to go to the Church. The old man had recognised a certain call of the blood after all!

They both behaved with tact and discretion at the funeral, and were extremely sympathetic and solicitous towards Aunt Rosalie, who was too absorbed with her own trouble to take much notice of them. It was only when it came to the reading of the will that their avidity and interest outraged perhaps the strict canons of good taste. It was Paul who managed to get it clear from the notary what the exact amount would probably be. Making allowances for fluctuations, accidents, and acts of God, on the death of Mme Taillandier the two brothers would inherit something between eight and ten thousand francs a year each. She was now eighty-two and very frail.

The brothers celebrated the good news with a carouse up in Montmartre. Naturally their chief topic of conversation was how long the old bird would keep on her perch. In any case, it could not be many years. With any luck it might be only a few weeks. The fortune seemed blinding. It would mean comfort and security to the end of their days. The rejoicings were mixed with recriminations against the old man for his stinginess. Why couldn't he have left them a lump sum down now? Why did he want to waste all this good gold on the Church? Why all this trustee business?

There was little they could do but await developments. Except that in the meantime—after a decent interval—they might try and touch the old lady for a bit. They parted, and the next day set about their business in cheerier spirits.

For a time they were extremely tactful. They made formal calls on Aunt Rosalie, inquiring after her health, and offering their services in any capacity whatsoever. But at the end of a month Henri called hurriedly one morning, and after the usual professions of solicitude asked his aunt if she could possibly lend him one hundred and twenty francs to pay the doctor who had attended his wife and baby. She lent him forty, grumbling at his foolishness at having children he could not afford to keep. A week later came Paul with a story about being robbed by a client. He wanted a hundred. She lent him ten.

When these appeals had been repeated three or four times, and received similar treatment—and sometimes no treatment at all—the old lady began to get annoyed. She was becoming more and more eccentric. She now had a companion, an angular, middle-aged woman named Mme Chavanne, who appeared like a protecting goddess. Sometimes when the brothers called Mme Chavanne would say that Mme Taillandier was too unwell to see anyone. If this news had been true it would have been good news indeed, but the brothers suspected that it was all prearranged. Two years went by, and they both began to despair.

'She may live to a hundred,' said Paul.

'We shall die of old age first,' grumbled Henri.

It was difficult to borrow money on the strength of the will. In the first place their friends were more of the borrowing than the lending class. And anyone who had a little was suspicious of the story, and wanted all kinds of securities. It was Paul who first thought of going to an insurance company to try to raise money on the reversionary interest. They did succeed in the end in getting an insurance company to advance them two thousand francs each, but the negotiations took five months to complete, and by the time they had insured their lives, paid the lawyer's fees and paid for the various deeds and stamps, and signed some thirty or forty forms, each man only received a little over a thousand francs, which was quickly lost in paying accrued debts and squandering the remainder. Their hopes were raised by the dismissal of Mme Chavanne, only to be lowered again by the arrival of an even more aggressive companion. The companions came and went with startling rapidity. None of them could stand for any time the old lady's eccentricity and ill-temper. The whole of the staff was always being changed. The only one who remained loyal all through was the portly cook, Ernestine. Even this may have been due to the fact that she never came in touch with her mistress. She was an excellent cook, and she never moved from the kitchen. Moreover, the cooking required by Mme Taillandier was of the simplest nature, and she seldom entertained. And she hardly ever left her apartment. Any complaints that were made were made through the housekeeper, and the complaints and their retaliations became mellowed in the process; for Ernestine also had a temper of her own.

Nearly another year passed before what appeared to Paul to be a mild stroke of good fortune came his way. Things had been going from bad to worse. Neither of the brothers was in a position to lend a sou to the other. Henri's family was becoming a greater drag, and people were not buying Paul's trinkets.

One day, during an interview with his aunt—he had been trying to borrow more money—he fainted in her presence. It is difficult to know what it was about this act which affected the old lady, but she ordered him to be put to bed in one of the rooms of the villa. Possibly she jumped to the conclusion that he had fainted from lack of food—which was not true—Paul never went without food and drink—and she suddenly realised that after all he was her husband's sister's son. He must certainly have looked pathetic, this white-faced man, well past middle age, and broken in life. Whatever it was, she showed a broad streak of compassion for him. She ordered her servants to look after him, and to allow him to remain until she countermanded the order.

Paul, who had certainly felt faint, but quickly seized the occasion to make it as dramatic as possible, saw in this an opportunity to wheedle his way into his aunt's favours. His behaviour was exemplary. The next morning, looking very white and shaky, he visited her, and asked her to allow him to go, as he had no idea of abusing her hospitality. If he had taken up the opposite attitude she would probably have turned him out, but because he suggested going she ordered him to stop. During the daytime he went about his dubious business, but he continued to return there at night to sleep, and to enjoy a good dinner cooked by the admirable Ernestine. He was in clover.

Henri was naturally envious when he heard of his brother's good fortune. And Paul was fearful that Henri would spoil the whole game by going and throwing a fit himself in the presence of the aunt. But this, of course, would have been too obvious and foolish for even Henri to consider seriously. And he racked his brains for some means of inveigling the old lady. Every plan he put forth, however, Paul sat upon. He was quite comfortable himself, and he didn't see the point of his brother butting in.

'Besides,' he said, 'she may turn me out any day. Then you can have your shot.'

They quarrelled about this, and did not see each other for some time. One would have thought that Henri's appeal to Mme Taillandier would have been stronger than Paul's. He was a struggling individual, with a wife and four children. Paul was a notorious ne'er-do-well, and he had no attachments. Nevertheless the old lady continued to support Paul. Perhaps it was because he was a big man, and she liked big men. Her husband had been a man of fine physique. Henri was puny, and she despised him. She had never had children of her own, and she disliked children. She was always upbraiding Henri and his wife for their fecundity. Any attempt to pander to her emotions through the sentiment of childhood failed. She would not have the children in her house. And any small acts of charity which she bestowed upon them seemed to be done more with the idea of giving her an opportunity to inflict her sarcasm and venom upon them than out of kindness of heart.

In Paul, on the other hand, she seemed to find something slightly attractive. She sometimes sent for him, and he, all agog—expecting to get his notice to quit—would be agreeably surprised to find that, on the contrary, she had some little commission she wished him to execute. And you may rest assured that he never failed to make a few francs out of all these occasions. The notice to quit did not come. It may be—poor deluded woman!—that she regarded him as some kind of protection. He was in any case the only 'man' who slept under her roof.

At first she seldom spoke to him, but as time went on she would sometimes send for him to relieve her loneliness. Nothing could have been more ingratiating than Paul's manners in these circumstances. He talked expansively about politics, knowing beforehand his aunt's views, and just what she would like him to say. Her eyesight was very bad, and he would read her the news of the day, and tell her what was happening in Paris. He humoured her every whim. He was astute enough to see that it would be foolish and dangerous to attempt to borrow money for the moment. He was biding his time, and trying to think out the most profitable plan of campaign. There was no immediate hurry. His bed was comfortable, and Ernestine's cooking was excellent.

In another year's time he had established himself as quite one of the permanent household. He was consulted about the servants, and the doctors, and the management of the house, everything except the control of money, which was jealously guarded by a firm of lawyers. Many a time he would curse his uncle's foresight. The old man's spirit seemed to be hovering in the dim recesses of the over-crowded rooms, mocking him. For the old lady, eccentric and foolish in many ways, kept a strict check upon her dividends. It was her absorbing interest in life, that and an old grey perroquet, which she treated like a child. Its name was Anna, and it used to walk up and down her table at meal-times and feed off her own plate. Finding himself so firmly entrenched Paul's assurance gradually increased. He began to treat his aunt as an equal, and sometimes even to contradict her, and she did not seem to resent it.

In the meantime Henri was eating his heart out with jealousy and sullen rage. The whole thing was unfair. He occasionally saw Paul, who boasted openly of his strong position in the Taillandier household, and he would not believe that Paul was not getting money out of the old lady as well as board and lodging. With no additional expenses Paul was better dressed than he used to be, and he looked fatter and better in health. All—or nearly all—of Henri's appeals, although pitched in a most pathetic key, were rebuffed. He felt a bitter hatred against his aunt, his brother, and life in general.

If only she would die! What was the good of life to a woman at eighty-five or six? And there was he—four young children, clamouring for food, and clothes, and the ordinary decent comforts. And there was Paul, idling his days away at *cafés* and his nights at cabarets—nothing to do, and no responsibilities.

Meeting Paul one day he said:

'I say, old boy, couldn't you spring me a hundred francs? I haven't the money to pay my rent next week.'

'She gives me nothing,' replied Paul.

Henri did not believe this, but it would be undiplomatic to quarrel. He said:

'Aren't there—isn't there some little thing lying about the villa you could slip in your pocket? We could sell it, see? Go shares. I'm desperately pushed.'

Paul looked down his nose. Name of a pig! did Henri think he had never thought of that? Many and many a time the temptation had come to him. But no; every few months people came from the lawyer's office, and the inventory of the whole household was checked. The servants could not be suspected. They were not selected without irreproachable characters. If he were suspected—well, all kinds of unpleasant things might crop up. Oh, no, he was too well off where he was. The game was to lie in wait. The old lady simply must die soon. She had even been complaining of her chest that morning. She was always playing with the perroquet. Somehow this bird got on Paul's nerves. He wanted to wring its neck. He imitated the way she would say: 'There's a pretty lady! Oh, my sweet! Another nice grape for my little one. There's a pretty lady!' He told Henri all about this, and the elder brother went on his way with a grunt that only conveyed doubt and suspicion.

In view of this position it seemed strange that in the end it was Paul who was directly responsible for the *dénouement* in the Taillandier household. His success went to his rather weak head like wine. He began to swagger and bluster and abuse his aunt's hospitality. And, curiously enough, the more he advanced the further she withdrew. The eccentric old lady seemed to be losing her powers of resistance so far as he was concerned. And he began to borrow small sums of money from her, and, as she acquiesced so readily, to increase his demands. He let his travelling business go, and sometimes he would get lost for days at a time. He would spend his time at the races, and drinking with doubtful acquaintances in obscure *cafés*. Sometimes he won, but in the majority of cases he lost. He ran up bills and got into debt. By cajoling small sums out of his aunt he kept his debtors at bay for nearly nine months.

But one evening he came to see Henri in a great state of distress. His face, which had taken on a healthier glow when he first went to live with his aunt, had become puffy and livid. His eyes were bloodshot.

'Old boy,' he said, 'I'm at my wits' end. I've got to find seven thousand francs by the twenty-first of the month, or they're going to foreclose. How do you stand? I'll pay you back.'

To try to borrow money from Henri was like appealing to the desert for a cooling draught. He also had to find money by the twenty-first, and he was overdrawn at the bank. They exchanged confidences, and in their mutual distress they felt sorry for each other and for themselves. It was a November evening, and the rain was driving along the boulevards in fitful gusts. After trudging a long way they turned into a little *café* in the Rue de la Roquette, and sat down and ordered two cognacs. The *café* was almost deserted. A few men in mackintoshes were scattered around reading the evening papers. They sat at a marble table in the corner and tried to think of ways and means. But after a time a silence fell between them. There seemed nothing more to suggest. They could hear the rain beating on the skylight. An old man four tables away was poring over *La Patrie*.

Suddenly Henri looked furtively around the room and clutched his brother's arm.

'Paul!' he whispered.

'What is it?'

'Do you remember—it has all come back to me—suddenly—one night, a night something like this—it must be five or six years ago—we were seated here in this same *café*—do you remember?'

'No. I don't remember. What was it?'

'It was the night of that murder in the Landes district. We got talking about—don't you remember?'

Paul scratched his temple and sipped the cognac. Henri leant closer to him.

'You said—you said that if you lived with anyone, it was the easiest thing in the world to murder them. An accident, you know. And you go screaming into the street—'

Paul started, and stared at his brother, who continued:

'You said that if ever you—you had to do it, you would guarantee that you would take every trouble. You wouldn't leave a trace behind.'

Paul was acting. He pretended to half remember, to half understand. But his eyes narrowed. Imbecile! Hadn't he been through it all in imagination a hundred times? Hadn't he already been planning and scheming an act for which his brother would reap half the benefit? Nevertheless he was staggered. He never imagined that the suggestion would come from Henri. He was secretly relieved. If Henri was to receive half the benefit, let him also share half the responsibilities. The risk in any case would be wholly his. He grinned enigmatically, and they put their heads together. And so in that dim corner of the *café* was planned the perfect murder.

Coming up against the actual proposition, Paul had long since realised that the affair was not so easy of accomplishment as he had so airily suggested. For the thing must be done without violence, without clues, without trace. Such ideas as leaving the window open at night were out of the question, as the companion slept in the same room. Moreover, the old lady was quite capable of getting out of bed and shutting it herself if she felt a draught. Some kind of accident? Yes, but what? Suppose she slipped and broke her neck when Paul was in the room. It would be altogether too suspicious. Besides, she would probably only partially break her neck. She would regain sufficient consciousness to tell. To drown her in her bath? The door was always locked or the companion hovering around.

'You've always got to remember,' whispered Paul, 'if any suspicion falls on me, there's the motive. There's a strong motive why I should—it's got to be absolutely untraceable. I don't care if some people do suspect afterwards—when we've got the money.'

'What about her food?'

'The food is cooked by Ernestine, and the companion serves it. Besides, suppose I got a chance to tamper with the food, how am I going to get hold of—you know?'

'Weed-killer?'

'Yes, I should be in a pretty position if they traced the fact that I had bought weed-killer. *You* might buy some and let me have a little on the quiet.'

Henri turned pale. 'No, no; the motive applies to me too. They'd get us both.'

When the two pleasant gentlemen parted at midnight their plans were still very immature, but they arranged to meet the following evening. It was the thirteenth of the month. To save the situation the deed must be accomplished within eight days. Of course they wouldn't get the money at once, but, knowing the circumstances, creditors would be willing to wait. When they met the following evening in the Café des Sentiers, Paul appeared flushed and excited, and Henri was pale and on edge. He hadn't slept. He wanted to wash the whole thing out.

'And sell up your home, I suppose?' sneered Paul. 'Listen, my little cabbage. I've got it. Don't distress yourself. You proposed this last night. I've been thinking about it and watching for months. Ernestine is a good cook, and very methodical. Oh, very methodical! She does everything every day in the same way exactly to schedule. My apartment is on the same floor, so I am able to appreciate her punctuality and exactness. The old woman eats sparingly and according to routine. One night she has fish. The next night she has a soufflé made with two eggs. Fish, soufflé, fish, soufflé, regular as the beat of a clock. Now listen. After lunch every day Ernestine washes up the plates and pans. After that she prepares roughly the evening meal. If it is a fish night, she prepares the fish ready to pop into the pan. If it is a soufflé night, she beats up two eggs and puts them ready in a basin. Having done that, she changes her frock, powders her nose, and goes over to the convent to see her sister who is working there. She is away an hour and a half. She returns punctually at four o'clock. You could set your watch by her movements.'

'Yes, but—'

'It is difficult to insert what I propose in fish, but I don't see any difficulty in dropping it into two beaten-up eggs, and giving an extra twist to the egg-whisk, or whatever they call it.'

Henri's face was quite grey.

'But—but—Paul, how are you going to get hold of the—poison?'

'Who said anything about poison?'

'Well, but what?'

'That's where *you* come in.'

'I!'

'Yes, you're in it too, aren't you? You get half the spoils, don't you? Why shouldn't you—some time to-morrow when your wife's out—'

'What?'

'Just grind up a piece of glass.'

'Glass!'

'Yes, you've heard of glass, haven't you? An ordinary piece of broken wineglass will do. Grind it up as fine as a powder, the finer the better, the finer the more—effective.'

Henri gasped. No, no, he couldn't do this thing. Very well, then; if he was such a coward Paul would have to do it himself. And perhaps when the time came Henri would also be too frightened to draw his dividends. Perhaps he would like to make them over to his dear brother Paul? Come, it was only a little thing to do. Eight days to the twenty-first. To-morrow, fish day, but Wednesday would be soufflé. So easy, so untraceable, so safe.

'But you,' whined Henri, 'they will suspect you.'

'Even if they do they can prove nothing. But in order to avoid this unpleasantness I propose to leave home soon after breakfast. I shall return at a quarter-past three, letting myself in through the stable yard. The stables, as you know, are not used. There is no one else on that floor. Ernestine is upstairs. She only comes down to answer the front-door bell. I shall be in and out of the house within five minutes, and I shan't return till late at night, when perhaps—I may be too late to render assistance.'

Henri was terribly agitated. On one hand was—just murder, a thing he had never connected himself with in his life. On the other hand was comfort for himself and his family, an experience he had given up hoping for. It was in any case not exactly murder on his part. It was Paul's murder. At the same time, knowing all about it, being an accessory before the fact, it would seem contemptible to a degree to put the whole onus on Paul. Grinding up a piece of glass was such a little thing. It couldn't possibly incriminate him. Nobody could ever prove that he'd done it. But it was a terrible step to take.

'Have another cognac, my little cabbage.'

It was Paul's voice that jerked him back to actuality. He said: 'All right, yes, yes,' but whether this referred to the cognac or to the act of grinding up a piece of glass he hardly knew himself.

From that moment to twenty-four hours later, when he handed over a white packet to his brother across the same table at the Café des Sentiers, Henri seemed to be in a nightmarish dream. He had no recollection of how he had passed the time. He seemed to pass from that last cognac to this one, and the interval was a blank.

'Fish to-day, soufflé to-morrow,' he heard Paul chuckling. 'Brother, you have done your work well.'

When Paul went he wanted to call after him to come back, but he was frightened of the sound of his own voice. He was terribly frightened. He went to bed very late and could not sleep. The next morning he awoke with a headache, and he got his wife to telegraph to the office to say that he was too ill to come. He lay in bed all day, visualising over and over and over again the possible events of the evening.

Paul would be caught. Someone would catch him actually putting the powder into the eggs. He would be arrested. Paul would give *him* away. Why did Paul say it was so easy to murder anyone if you lived with them? It wasn't easy at all. The whole thing was chock-a-block with dangers and pitfalls. Pitfalls! At half-past three he started up in bed. He had a vision of himself and Paul being guillotined side by side! He must stop it at any cost. He began to get up. Then he realised that it was already too late. The deed had been done. Paul had said that he would be in and out of the house within five minutes at three-fifteen—a quarter of an hour ago! Where was Paul? Would he be coming to see him? He was going to spend the evening out somewhere, 'returning late at night.'

He dressed feverishly. There was still time. He could call at his aunt's. Rush down to the kitchen, seize the basin of beaten-up eggs, and throw them away. But where? how? By the time he got there Ernestine would have returned. She would want to know all about it. The egg mixture would be examined, analysed. God in Heaven! it was too late! The thing would have to go on, and he suffer and wait.

Having dressed, he went out after saying to his wife:

'It's all right. It's going to be all right,' not exactly knowing what he meant. He walked rapidly along the streets, with no fixed destination in his mind. He found himself in the *café* in the Rue de la Roquette, where the idea was first conceived, where he had reminded his brother.

He sat there drinking, waiting for the hours to pass.

Soufflé day, and the old lady dined at seven! It was now not quite five. He hoped Paul would turn up. A stranger tried to engage him in conversation. The stranger apparently had some grievance against a railway company. He wanted to tell him all the details about a contract for rivets, over which he had been disappointed. Henri didn't understand a word he was talking about. He didn't listen. He wanted the stranger to drop down dead, or vanish into thin air. At last he called the waiter and paid for his reckoning, indicated by a small pile of saucers. From there he walked rapidly to the Café des Sentiers, looking for Paul. He was not there. Six o'clock. One hour more. He could not keep still. He paid and went on again, calling at *café* after *café*. A quarter to seven. Pray God that she threw it away. Had he ground it fine enough?

Five minutes to seven. Seven o'clock. Now. He picked up his hat and went again. The brandy had gone to his head. At half-past seven he laughed recklessly. After all, what was the good of life to this old woman of eighty-six? He tried to convince himself that he had done it for the sake of his wife and children. He tried to concentrate on the future, how he could manage on eight or ten thousand francs a year. He would give notice at the office, be rude to people who had been bullying him for years—that old blackguard Mocquin!

At ten o'clock he was drunk, torpid, and indifferent. The whole thing was over for good or ill. What did it matter? He terribly wanted to see Paul, but he was too tired to care very much. The irrevocable step had been taken. He went home to bed and fell into a heavy drunken sleep.

'Henri! Henri! Wake up! What is the matter with you?'

His wife was shaking him. He blinked his way into a partial condition of consciousness. November sunlight was pouring into the room.

'It's late, isn't it?' he said, involuntarily.

'It's past eight. You'll be late at the office. You didn't go yesterday. If you go on like this you'll get the sack, and then what shall we do?'

Slowly the recollection of last night's events came back to him.

'There's nothing to worry about,' he said. 'I'm too ill to go to-day. Send them another telegram. It'll be all right.'

His wife looked at him searchingly. 'You've been drinking,' she said. 'Oh, you men! God knows what will become of us.'

She appeared to be weeping in her apron. It struck him forcibly at that instant how provoking and small women are. Here was Jeannette crying over her petty troubles. Whereas he—

The whole thing was becoming vivid again. Where was Paul? What had happened? Was it at all likely that he could go down to an office on a day like this, a day that was to decide his fate?

He groaned, and elaborated rather pathetically his imaginary ailments, anything to keep this woman quiet. She left him at last, and he lay there waiting for something to happen. The hours passed. What would be the first intimation? Paul or the gendarmes? Thoughts of the latter stirred him to a state of fevered activity. About midday he arose, dressed, and went out. He told his wife he was going to the office, but he had no intention of doing so. He went and drank coffee at a place up in the Marais. He was terrified of his old haunts. He wandered from place to place, uncertain how to act. Late in the afternoon he entered a *café* in the Rue Alibert. At a kiosk outside he bought a late edition of an afternoon newspaper. He sat down, ordered a drink and opened the newspaper. He glanced at the central news page, and as his eye absorbed one paragraph he unconsciously uttered a low scream. The paragraph was as follows:

*A mysterious affair occurred at Chantilly this morning. A middle-aged man, named Paul Denoyel, complained of pains in the stomach after eating an omelette. He died soon after in great agony. He was staying with his aunt, Mme Taillandier. No other members of the household were affected. The matter is to be inquired into.*

The rest was a dream. He was only vaguely conscious of the events which followed. He wandered through it all, the instinct of self-preservation bidding him hold his tongue in all circumstances. He knew nothing. He had seen nothing. He had a visionary recollection of a plump, weeping Ernestine, at the inquest, enlarging upon the eccentricities of her mistress. A queer woman, who would brook no contradiction. He heard a lot about the fish day and the soufflé day, and how the old lady insisted that this was a fish day, and that she had had a soufflé the day before. You could not argue with her when she was like that. And Ernestine had beaten up the eggs all ready for the soufflé—most provoking! But Ernestine was a good cook, of method and economy. She wasted nothing. What should she do with the eggs? Why, of course, Mr Paul, who since he had come to live there was never content with a *café complet*. He must have a breakfast, like these English and other foreigners do. She made him an omelette, which he ate heartily.

Then the beaten-up eggs with their deadly mixture were intended for Mme Taillandier? But who was responsible for this? Ernestine? But there was no motive here. Ernestine gained nothing by her mistress's death. Indeed she only stood to lose her situation. Motive? Was it possible that the deceased— The inquiry went on a long while. Henri himself was conscious of being in the witness-box. He knew nothing. He couldn't understand it. His brother would not be likely to do that. He himself was prostrate with grief. He loved his brother.

There was nothing to do but return an open verdict. Shadowy figures passed before his mind's eye—shadowy figures and shadowy realisations. He had perfectly murdered his brother. The whole of the dividends of the estate would one day be his, and his wife's and children's. Eighteen thousand francs a year! One day—

One vision more vivid than the rest—the old lady on the day following the inquest, seated bolt upright at her table, like a figure of perpetuity, playing with the old grey perroquet, stroking its mangy neck.

'There's a pretty lady! Oh, my sweet! Another nice grape for my little one. There's a pretty lady!'

# THE ROOM IN THE TOWER

## J. Jefferson Farjeon

Joseph Jefferson Farjeon (1883–1955) was the grandson of an American actor, Joseph Jefferson, son of a popular novelist, Benjamin Farjeon, and brother of a well-regarded children's author, Eleanor Farjeon. With such a pedigree, it is hardly surprising that he tried his hand at both acting and—with much greater success—at writing. He became a journalist, but did not always find it easy to support his wife and child, and decided to supplement his income by producing short stories, novels, and plays. A turning point in his fortunes came when his stage thriller *No. 17* began a tour of Northern theatres at the Winter Gardens, New Brighton on 6 July 1925, and received enthusiastic reviews. Hitchcock directed a film version, and the central character, Ben, featured in several of Farjeon's later novels.

Farjeon was an industrious writer whose entertaining way with words appealed to a large readership in the decades before his death from liver cancer. After he died, as is so often the case with purveyors of popular fiction, his books went out of print, and were neglected for many years until the British Library's reissue of his Christmas crime story *Mystery in White* (1937) introduced him to a new generation of readers. His books and stories benefited from a wide range of settings, ranging from English villages to the Pyrenees; this little tale illustrates his penchant for melodrama.

I T WAS ONE OF THOSE RIDICULOUS RHINE CASTLES YOU CANNOT quite believe. You've seen the sort of thing often enough in pictures—perched high up on a wooded mountain shelf, with a pointed red-roofed tower rising heavenwards and oblong slit-windows looking down sheerly on the winding river hundreds of feet below—and for a moment it has wrenched you from jazz and wireless back to medieval days. 'How picturesque—how quaint!' you have said. But it has probably never occurred to you to live in one.

Nor would it have occurred to me if I had not one day bought a copy of *The Times* to read a bad notice a kind friend had told me of, and if my eye had not been caught by the following advertisement on the front page: 'Castle on the Rhine. Owner, occupying few rooms, willing to let the remainder for summer months. Terms very moderate. Service provided. Apply—'

The name was Steinbaum.

My natural tendency is to spend the summer months in Gleneagles or Frinton or Le Touquet, and no German castle, however picturesque and quaint, would lure me. The picturesqueness may include damp and draughts, and the quaintness may spread to the sanitary arrangements. But the advertisement chanced to fit my mood and my necessity, for I had begun a novel with a romantic German setting, and all I really knew about Germany was the language.

Moreover, the notice when I turned to it was very bad indeed! The reviewer advised me to confine myself to environments with which I was familiar.

So I cast myself adrift from my friends and my relatives, and—
to cut a long journey short—I arrived one gloomy evening at the
ridiculous Rhine castle I had never quite believed. I had caught a
preliminary glimpse of it, when it had still been three miles away,
as the station car had wound round a ghastly hairpin bend, and I
had thought, 'Oh, nonsense!' Now here the nonsense was, sitting
on its mountainous green perch with a kind of mellow coldness
like a bit of crumbling history; and Herr Steinbaum proved to be
as crumbling as his residence.

I confess I endured a few moments of uncomfortable doubt
as I saw the grim old man standing under the entrance arch; and
subsequent events proved, you will agree, that there was something definite about the place, quite apart from its external aspect,
to account for the chill that suddenly ran up and down my spine.
But the chill evaporated at my first sight of Gretchen, Steinbaum's
daughter, a flaxen-haired girl whose smile was an instant welcome.
'I'll put you in my novel,' I decided, as she insisted very unreason-
ably on carrying my suitcase into the castle, 'and you shall marry
a jolly nice chap and be happy for ever after!'

The station car turned—perilously—and went away. Its departure severed my last link with the outer world. It seemed also to
sever my link with the twentieth century. The old man belonged
to a Holbein canvas, and Gretchen would have looked perfectly
appropriate in a costume four hundred years behind the fashion.

They led me to the rooms which it was suggested I should
occupy. Actually, as I discovered later, I had my choice of over forty.
The living-room was enormous, and most of the furniture had
been assembled near a great log-fire. I welcomed the fire, for the
evening was cool. The rest of the furniture seemed very distant
and cold. A narrow, dark passage, lit by a candle in a high niche,

led to my bedroom, almost equally large. The bed itself would have held a family.

'I hope this is satisfactory?' said Herr Steinbaum, while we stood in the bedroom.

They had both been watching me closely and anxiously. I felt their anxiety pressing upon me. I assured them that it was thoroughly satisfactory, and asked if there were a bathroom. I prayed silently while I put the question.

'Oh, yes!' cried Gretchen, her voice alive with joyous relief. My approval had sounded convincing. 'And newly painted. But quite dry—shall I show it to you?'

'Perhaps you will excuse me while she does so?' added Herr Steinbaum. 'Your supper—it will be ready when you are.'

He withdrew, and Gretchen conducted me through another ill-lit passage to a bathroom that was hardly more than a passage itself. It was L-shaped, with the bath round the bend. The ceiling was a mile off. The one narrow window could be reached if one stood on the rim of the bath. But the whiteness of the bath provided illumination. It dazzled through the dimness.

Again I felt Gretchen's eyes upon me.

'You've painted it beautifully,' I said.

'But how did you know?' she exclaimed, as though I had performed a conjuring trick.

Simple Gretchen! I knew because, although I had only been inside the castle a few minutes, I already knew many things. The Steinbaums, like the castle walls themselves, were a conflict of obvious truths and inscrutable secrets. I knew without being told that Gretchen had painted the bath and had washed the spotless towel that hung from a heavy iron hook. I knew that Herr Steinbaum was preparing the supper. I knew that the castle had once contained much more furniture, and that the advertisement in *The Times* had been a desperate remedy. I knew—and the reason for this knowledge was less obvious—that there were only three living souls within the castle walls—Gretchen, Herr Steinbaum, and myself. But I did not know how many dead ones there might be! The latter were included among the inscrutable secrets.

'Just a guess,' I answered Gretchen, lightly. 'I'm good at guessing.'

An odd look came into her eyes. The secrets stirred uneasily. Then she made a sudden excuse, and left me.

I lingered in the impossible bathroom for a few moments. What pages it would fill in my novel! It would write itself. I drank its atmosphere greedily, and wondered whether to have a murder in it, though that would stain Gretchen's beautiful white paint. And as I walked back to my bedroom, my footsteps made hollow echoes behind me on the stone floor of the passage, and the bed shouted voicelessly of centuries of life and death, each ignorant of the other...

But this is not my novel. It is just a short, swift incident, a single chapter of reality that prefaced my thirty imaginative ones, providing them—for me, at any rate—with a strange, underlying vividness. So there is no time here to linger.

Gretchen served my supper in the vast living-room. It was a simple, efficient meal, and every time she came she added human warmth to the chemical heat of the log-fire, and every time she went the chemical heat seemed inadequate. Fortunately for me—I make no bones about my mood—she showed a desire to linger, but I fed this disposition as much for her sake as for my own. Gretchen needed company, though my own was not the kind she needed. A rather elderly author has one foot already in the grave of imagination. Youth requires both feet out.

But even though I was obviously friendly, her lingering was rather furtive—as though she felt she really had no right to stay—and it was only at her last visit that I succeeded in engaging her in conversation that was more than casual.

'Will you want anything more to-night?' she asked.

'Nothing more,' I answered. 'Everything has been perfect. I had no idea a castle could be so comfortable.'

'I am glad you like it,' she said.

'To-morrow I shall want to explore,' I went on. 'What part do you and your father live in? I'd better know, or I shall be walking in on you!'

'Oh, we are down below,' she replied.

'And I can go everywhere else?'

'Yes, of course.'

'That's splendid. I particularly want to go up into the tower. The view from there must be wonderful.'

Again that odd look came into her eyes. I was jerked back to the moment in the bathroom, just before she had left me. But she smiled very quickly, as though to cover a secret that was slipping from its shroud and might betray its nakedness.

'It's not very safe, the stairs are rickety,' she exclaimed. 'But the views are wonderful everywhere.'

The secret slipped back, but Gretchen's simple mind, if it had attempted subtlety, misjudged that of a rather elderly author. I was not too elderly to negotiate a rickety staircase or to be intrigued by so thinly veiled a warning.

'Do you ever get lonely here?' I asked, changing the subject.

'Sometimes, a little,' she admitted. 'But then we have always been here. One grows used to it.'

'And, of course, you have to look after your father?'

'Yes.'

'He likes it here?'

'Oh, he would never leave it! You see, it has been in our family for many generations. I don't know how far back!'

I wondered whether it would belong to the family for many more generations. Would Gretchen herself be the next? Or would some mortgagee step in one day and claim it? And then I found myself wondering about Gretchen's mother. After a moment's hesitation, I put my wonder into words.

'Your mother—is she alive?' I asked.

She shook her head.

'My mother died when I was little,' she told me. 'Too little to remember her.' She paused, then said, with that quaint abruptness that slayed her most interesting moments, 'I must go.'

I deduced that Gretchen's mother had been considerably younger than her father. Herr Steinbaum looked nearly seventy, though, as I was destined soon to learn, the castle had prematurely aged his appearance. I began to learn, indeed, before I saw Gretchen again.

When she had left me, I sat for awhile and smoked. By all the rules I should have gone to bed, for I had had a long day of travelling and had earned my sleep. But I felt restless. Through the great quietude, invisible life tingled all around me. It flowed under my feet, ran along the stone walls, whispered behind a faded tapestry. I had an itch to interpret it, or to convert it into something concrete.

'Why, of course!' I exclaimed, suddenly. 'I must write!'

For here was Atmosphere, first-hand!

I spent a luxurious period in preparation. The sleepiness that had been fighting the restlessness, induced by my fatigue and the warmth of the fire, slipped away as I busied myself with my typewriter and my papers. I thought of the critic whose bad notice had played its part in sending me here, and I smiled at the odd tricks of Fate. His next notice of my work would be very different. I began to compose it for him in my mind.

Then, for over an hour, my typewriter clicked. It clicked with an entirely new voice, a voice not sympathetic to the surroundings, and as I wrote I became conscious of a gradual change. The secret life was slowing up. Pausing. Stopping. Before the incongruous music of my machine I had been listening to it. Now it was listening to me... sullenly... antagonistically...

I began making mistakes. I began taking pages out and starting them again. I began jumping at my errors. When I struck an 'm' on the keyboard instead of a comma, a pang of nervous irritation shot through me.

'This is ridiculous!' I exclaimed aloud.

I read through all I had written, and threw the pages on the dying fire. There they performed their last service of making a temporary blaze.

Again, I should have gone to bed. But again, the atmosphere of the silent castle confounded normality. Now that I had stopped clicking my typewriter, the secret life was starting up again. I felt impotent. The critic laughed at me, and advised me to take up farming.

'I shall never write here,' I murmured, with the clouded vision of the over-fatigued.

And it was then that I thought of the tower.

I usually write in a small room, my imagination functioning best through walls that are close. Of course, *that* was the trouble this room was too large! Instead of remaining near at hand my imagination was wandering all over the place, and refused to come back when it was wanted. It was like a wild dog off the leash. But in the tower, where the rooms were probably very much smaller, my mind would be less nomadic, and I myself would feel less like an ant in space.

Yes, undoubtedly, here lay the solution. The tower might be draughty, and would almost surely be unfurnished, but a few pounds spent on it would be a good investment... As the idea worked into me, my impatience to prove its practicability rose, and I decided to investigate the tower at once—and then to sleep soundly.

Where was it? I tried to locate it by visualising the outside of the castle. It rose distinctly in my memory, a grim sentinel against a background of scudding evening clouds, too far above the winding water to be reflected in it. But though I recalled the tower, I could not locate my own portion of the castle, and I crossed to an oblong, Gothic window, opened it with a loud creak, and looked out. It gave me a bit of a shock. The river below was a dizzy distance down. I twisted my head upwards, and stared at angles of stone, some of them gleaming at the edges in the pale moonlight. I saw nothing that looked like a tower.

Twisting my head back to normal, I was about to withdraw it when I noticed a small movement on the ribbon of road that wound round the mountain to the final lap to the castle. It looked like a tiny insect crawling along a large bird's-eye photograph. A bit late for a traveller, wasn't it?... Now the insect had stopped. I lost it in the shadows, and couldn't find it again. Perhaps I had been mistaken. I closed the window, with another disconcerting creak.

I crossed the vast floor and opened the door to the outer passage. It did not look inviting, but after taking a candle I went out into it, closing the door behind me. I felt guilty at my foolishness. It was nearly midnight. But the castle-itch had got me, Gretchen's thinly-veiled warning had got me, my own stubborn mood had got me. I had to find that tower.

I paid for my stubbornness. I wandered through passages that twisted, and up and down stairs that wound, and I lost myself. I lost myself among shadows and echoes. The echoes seemed to be of footsteps behind me. I opened doors into spaces too big for a single candle's illumination. I walked into a cupboard. Twice I nearly took headers. The second time my candle went out, and I had to light it again. It annoyed me enormously to discover that my fingers were not steady.

I would have given my soul at that moment for a sight of pleasant Gretchen!

'This is just silly!' I told myself. 'I'm going back!'

That was just sillier. I didn't know my way back. I didn't even know what floor I was on.

Presently I stood still and thought. Or, rather, I stood still and thoughts came. I wondered whether the footsteps behind me had really been echoes? I wondered whether the shadow ahead of me really was a shadow? I wondered whether the insect were still on the ribbon of road? I wondered whether to scrap my novel about Germany, and to write one about Brighton? I wondered how I had ever found the maze at Hampton Court difficult?

And then I wondered why I was standing still, and I discovered that it was the shadow ahead—long and upright, like a flat black slab pasted against a wall ahead of me. 'Ha!' I cried, and thrust my candle towards it.

The block slab vanished, to become a narrow passage, with stone steps winding upwards.

I sat on the bottom step and laughed. If Gretchen had come upon me then—I thought more and more about Gretchen, and with more and more gratitude for her existence—she would have taken me for a maniac. My laughter, however, prevented me from becoming one. I floated back to sanity on the tide of the ridiculous.

The outer walls that enclosed the staircase were curved, and so was the central structure round which the ascending steps wound. This, without doubt, was the tower. There was no turning back now, unless I wished to face a future of everlasting shame!

I got up from my cold seat and began to mount the steps. Round and round and round they went. They seemed endless. Was I mounting spirally to heaven? Every now and again little slits in the wall admitted silver glints of moonlight. I gave up counting the steps at 180 as they commenced to develop cracks and holes and looseness. Towards the end of the journey the crumbling stone changed to decaying wood. Then, suddenly, my head emerged through a gap and I found myself gazing along the floor of the tower-room.

Two-thirds of the floor was in deep shadow, but the part in which I had emerged was illuminated by an elongated oval of moonlight that came slanting in through the largest window. No, aperture. Windows have glass. The bottom of the aperture was low and wide, and as I stared across at it I was suddenly seized by a terrible fascination. It was so strong that it frightened me, and I tried to explain it to myself in simple terms.

'You want to see the view,' I thought. 'That's all!'

Of course that was all! And, equally of course, an impression that something stirred in the shadowed portion of the room was imagination. Still—there was no object in prolonging my visit. The idea that this lofty insecure chamber could be used as a study was laughable. I would just take a peep through the window, see the view, and go down again.

That tiny journey to the aperture took only a few seconds, but I have never lived through seconds more packed. I fought dizziness, and also indignation at my dizziness. I am not ordinarily subject to vertigo. I fought other things, as well. It was as though all the forces that had been pressing on me in my room, and the echoing steps and uncanny fancies that had followed me out of it, had suddenly seized me to impel me forward. I was surrounded by the invisible, secret life of the castle.

You may interpret this in your own fashion. You may say that it was the outcome of my own unbalanced mood. For myself, I assert nothing beyond the facts, and one more fact must be added—the impression of an agonised woman hovering near the window. Actually, no living woman was there at all.

Well, I reached the window, and I looked out. Below me was a view of terrible magnificence. The wall of the tower went sheerly down to the rock on which it stood, and the rock went sheerly down to the water. I believe I did go through a miniature brain-storm. I wanted to tear myself away, but something held me there—till all at once I felt rings round my ankles, and found myself being drawn back into the room.

'Do not be alarmed,' said a quiet voice behind me. 'But it is better in here than out there.'

The grip on my ankles relaxed. I scrambled round, and stared into the eyes of Herr Steinbaum.

'I regret this very deeply,' he murmured. 'We should have warned you.'

'Gretchen—your daughter—did warn me,' I answered, my mind in a whirl. Then added, protestingly, 'Yes—but of what?'

His eyes probed mine, seeking their knowledge.

'Of the danger,' he replied, with a little shrug.

'The danger of a high window?' I challenged. 'Just that?'

Again he paused before speaking. Then he said, very slowly,

'But the danger is great. Once—many years ago—a man fell out.' I started, but not merely at his words. Above me, harsh and metallic, clanged a clock. It clanged twelve times. 'At about this hour,' said Herr Steinbaum.

I stared at him. His quiet voice was in conflict with the odd light in his eyes. I steadied myself before asking,

'Were you here, Herr Steinbaum, when I arrived?' He nodded. 'Only you?'

'Who else?' he exclaimed, sharply.

Before I could shape my reply I caught a sound on the stairs below us. Herr Steinbaum's ears were as quick as mine, and we turned simultaneously. My heart thumped as rapid footsteps wound towards us. A moment later Gretchen appeared, agitated and breathless.

Her appearance gave me a double shock. For one instant I thought she was the woman of my fancy, by the window...

She came to a sudden halt when she saw us. She looked as though she were going to faint. 'An old man—I let him in—he frightened me—' she blurted out.

And then she did faint.

I caught her in my arms. Her distressed condition made me forget my own. For a few seconds I held her. The poor child was in her dressing-gown, and I hesitated to lower her to the cold ground.

'She'll be all right in a moment,' I said. 'Is there any water?'

Herr Steinbaum did not reply.

'I'll look after her,' I went on. 'If you want to go?'

Still Herr Steinbaum did not reply. I lowered her carefully to the ground. She seemed to disappear into the shadows. Then I looked up at Herr Steinbaum. He was standing rigid, his eyes fixed on the top of the stairs.

It did not seem possible that the castle could produce any experience more eerie than I had already encountered within its grim walls, but when fresh footsteps sounded on the stairs, I realised that the trump card was yet to be played. But I listened to the sounds, I remember, with a strange sense of detachment. My own story had ended when I had been dragged back from the window. The story that was reaching its culmination up these stairs was Herr Steinbaum's and Gretchen's. I was a mere spectator.

Gretchen's steps had been swift, like the wind. The new steps were slow, like a whisper. Not a clear whisper—a husky whisper, that scraped. And as it scraped upwards it grew slower and slower. I wondered what would happen if it stopped…

Then the top of a white head appeared in the space of moonlight that touched the well of the stairs. The white head paused—as my own head had paused a little earlier—and two old, tired eyes fixed themselves on the window across the room. The eyes did not move, yet I was conscious of something like a tiny flicker of fading light… Then two old, tired legs resumed their whispering progress…

A ghost? Herr Steinbaum's expression suggested it. And as the bent form completed its journey and turned slowly towards us, silvered in the moonlight, it seemed not to belong to this earth.

I knew it was not a ghost, while I also knew it soon would be. I was totally unprepared, however, for the startling suddenness of the transition.

'I came back to bring you peace,' it quavered, 'and for one more glimpse—'

It slipped to the floor. An arm slid forward along the ground, and came to rest within a few inches of Gretchen. The journey was over.

Then Herr Steinbaum came out of his trance. He came out of it with a quietness which drew my admiration and my gratitude. Composure was needed at that moment.

'Can you carry Gretchen down?' he asked, simply. 'I will follow you.'

I stooped and picked her up. Luckily, she was light. I carried her down the countless stairs, and had hardly reached the bottom before I heard Herr Steinbaum behind me. After that, he preceded me to her bedroom, and then directed me to my own.

'Will you wait for me there?' he asked.

'But isn't there anything I can do?' I answered.

'If there is, I will let you know.'

I returned to my rooms. I waited. The walls no longer whispered. They were silent. I felt as though they had lost a fourth dimension.

In ten minutes, Herr Steinbaum joined me.

'She is asleep—and everything else is done,' he said. 'So now, please, ask your questions.'

'I may?' I replied.

'It is your right—and my desire.'

Three questions were racing through my mind. Each one was obvious, but I asked them diffidently.

'Who was he?'

'My brother, who owned this castle before me. The man who—fell out of the window.'

'Who was—the woman?'

'You saw her, then? She was my wife. She used to meet my brother in the tower-room, but had an accident before their last appointment. She told me a minute before she died. So I kept the last appointment for her.'

The third question came after a long pause.

'And Gretchen?'

'Their daughter, sir.' There was a longer pause. 'I learned that, also, in the last minute.' Then Herr Steinbaum added, very quietly, 'But murder is murder. And love is love. And Gretchen, the child of love, is very beautiful.'

'But you did not murder him!' I interposed, quickly.

'We live by our intentions, not by our acts,' he answered. 'But, to-night, my brother has brought peace between us.' Then he asked, abruptly, 'You will not now wish to stay?'

'I wish it more than ever,' I replied.

He took a deep breath.

'That pleases me,' he said. 'It will please Gretchen more. And now, if you will excuse me, I will go up once more to my brother.'

I jumped up and seized his arm.

'You will come down again?' I exclaimed.

'Would I desert Gretchen?' he answered.

A few seconds later, his footsteps died away in the passage.

You have had my story. And Herr Steinbaum's and Gretchen's. But the story of Herr Steinbaum's brother, who fell from a tower and returned to it, is only known to the tide.

# THE TEN-FRANC COUNTER

## H. de Vere Stacpoole

Henry de Vere Stacpoole (1863–1951) was born in Ireland, but his chronic bronchitis led to his family moving to Nice in the hope that his health might improve. He studied medicine in London before working as a ship's doctor during the course of extensive travels overseas. Later he became a GP in Somerset, and drew on his time in the South Pacific when writing *The Blue Lagoon* (1905). This was his most successful novel, spawning several film adaptations, one of which, screened in 1980, starred Brooke Shields and Christopher Atkins.

Stacpoole's tales of intrigue and adventure often benefit from exotic settings. His work has occasionally drawn comparison with that of W. Somerset Maugham, and although Stacpoole's prose was not quite as compelling as Maugham's, he was a capable storyteller; Arthur Conan Doyle was among those who rated his fiction highly. Stacpoole was not primarily a crime writer, but he enjoyed making occasional forays into the genre, and this is probably his best mystery story; it first appeared in *Munsey's Magazine* in 1926.

O F ALL PLACES IN THE MODERN EUROPEAN WORLD MONTE Carlo is the most fascinating. It is most beautiful when seen from a distance as I see it now from my window in Bordighera with the sun full upon it; as I will see it this evening after dark, a spray of coloured lights, winked at by the far revolving light of Cap Ferrat.

Monte Carlo, as I sit smoking at night, sometimes reminds me of a beautiful woman—perhaps because of the necklace effect of the lights—and Cap Ferrat of the attitude of the world to her. The world winks at Monte Carlo and her doings; she is beautiful, she is fascinating, she makes men lose their heads; like all the great loved women of the past she has her private graveyard; she is detestable, which is part of her charm, and she ought long ago to have come under the hands of Monsieur Diebler, or whoever it is that has taken his place.

But there is no Diebler who deals with cities or towns; a town may be a murderer, like Monte Carlo, and a State a confederate, like Monaco, but there is no law to bring them to book, no punishment as yet, not even the mild punishment of reform.

Of course you will understand that I am writing of the tables, that conglomeration of roulette basins—little whirlpools that are yet capable of sucking a man's soul down into the drain-pipes of perdition.

To show you the power exercised by this suction I am going to tell you the story of Madame Bertaux, and that the powder of instruction may be properly balanced by the jam of amusement I am going to give it to you in its full detective dress as it was told to me by one of the international detectives who are always hunting this coast for international crooks. He was an elderly man with a Kalmuck type of face, yellow as old ivory from cigarette smoking, and he told me the yarn to exhibit the powers of M. Henri, of the Paris Sûreté—and for another reason.

Have you ever heard of the case of Madame Bertaux? he asked. Ah, well, she was an old lady who lived in the house of a M. Jacob in the Rue Paradis at Monte Carlo. The house was too large for M. Jacob, so he let the upper part as a flat to Madame Bertaux, a wealthy woman who had kept the old Phocée, a restaurant on the Rue de la Cannebière, of Marseilles. The lady never went out; she was afflicted with some malady of the back that prevented her from walking, and also an eczema that was most disfiguring; she had neither the power nor the desire to go into society, and yet she had the woman's craving for dress and adornment quite unimpaired.

She was very proud of her jewels, which were, in fact, very fine and worth a considerable sum of money. She was never happier than when dressing herself in them—rings, bracelets, brooches, ear-rings and so on—and when she was not wearing them she had the box containing them by her bed or couch so that she could touch them and see them. She also kept in her possession a good deal of loose cash.

All this exercised the mind of M. Jacob, and several times he pointed out to her the danger of valuables kept in a house in such a manner.

'Oh, nobody knows,' said she, 'only Rosalie, and she is safe. Who would bother coming to rob an old woman like me? Besides, I'd be able to defend myself against them if only by screeching for help.

And,' she said, 'they amuse me, which they wouldn't if they were locked up in the bank; and I don't want to be told my business, not even by you, M. Jacob.' In fact, they might have fought, only that he knew her queer ways and that she was an invalid, and refused to get angry with her.

Well, one evening Madame Bertaux was found with her head battered in and her jewels gone. The case was left.

The window was open. There were marks on a drain-pipe close to the window showing where a man had evidently crawled up; otherwise there were very few marks at all, and the room was not disturbed, though from a drawer in an escritoire by the door ten louis in gold had been taken, pre-war money treasured by the old lady and tied in a handkerchief. She had in her possession a roll of notes of the value of ten thousand francs; they had not been touched.

There were no finger-marks anywhere. I was at *déjeuner* in the Hotel de Paris with M. Henri that morning when the Chief of Police of Monaco was shown in to us. He came about a certain person who has no connection with this story, and when he had done his business he mentioned the murder in the Rue Paradis. You know the police mind thinks in the form of reports, and this good gentleman, once he had set his speech machine going, gave us a complete précis of the details of the business, everything but the exhibits, in fact.

'We arrested a young man, Coudoyer, lover of the servant Rosalie, this morning,' he finished. 'We found in his pockets very little money, but in his box at the inn where he is employed, an old-fashioned watch which belonged to the dead woman, and which he said had been given to him long ago by the servant Rosalie, who had it as a present from Madame Bertaux. It's all pretty plain.'

He went into more details about M. Jacob, the owner of the house, Madame Bertaux, and so forth, till Henri cut him short.

'Did you find any finger-marks?' asked Henri.

'No,' said the Chief.

'And this young man, Coudoyer, what is he like?'

'Oh, quite a simple person,' the Chief answered him. 'Just a waiter, and with a good record, the last person in the world you'd suspect of doing a thing like this.'

'There were no finger-marks, which shows an expert was at work,' said Henri, 'and you have arrested Coudoyer?'

'On suspicion,' said the other, 'and on finding that watch in his trunk.'

'Yes,' said the Paris man; 'but the thing you didn't find was finger-marks, yet a woman had been murdered and furniture handled by the murderer. Your judgment must be wrong about Coudoyer; he must be no simple person, but an expert criminal; either that, or you have arrested the wrong man.'

That seemed pretty conclusive, but the Monaco man didn't get enthusiastic over it; he seemed rather to resent Henri's deductions, which cast a shadow on his own intelligence.

'We must go by what we find,' said he. 'We searched very thoroughly for finger-marks on all surfaces possible, even to the table legs, even to a ten-franc Casino counter lying on the floor by the bureau. We may not be equal in intelligence to Paris, but we are thorough.'

That was a hit at Henri, for it was after the botching of the Jondret affair in Paris, which, however, wasn't Henri's doing; however, the little man took it up and swelled out his chest. You've never seen Henri? Well, he's a little man with a pointed beard, and when he gets in a temper he puffs himself out—like that...

'Yes, you seem to be thorough,' said he. 'You actually find a ten-franc Casino counter on the floor, and then you arrest a resident of Monte Carlo, or at least an employee, for you know well that employees are not allowed in the Casino. Now, tell me,' said Henri, 'didn't it hit you at once that the ten-franc counter must have been dropped by the murderer and no one else?'

'How do you mean?' said the other.

'This way. It wasn't the old lady's if your statement about her is correct, for she never went out; it isn't Rosalie's, and it isn't Coudoyer's, for they are employees and can't use the Casino; it isn't M. Jacob's, because he is, as you said, a resident engaged in business, and can't use the Casino. It must evidently have belonged to a person who was neither of these people, who was neither Madame Bertaux nor M. Jacob nor Rosalie nor Coudoyer, some person other than any of these people who are known to have used Madame Bertaux's room or been connected with it; it most evidently belonged to a stranger, a fifth person, and a person, moreover, who has or had the entry to the Casino.'

'A moment,' said the Chief. 'That argument seems tempting; but suppose Coudoyer had that counter in his possession at the time of the murder and dropped it by accident? It is not impossible for a waiter to acquire a Casino counter; it might have been given to him, it might have been picked up by him, it might have come into his possession in several different ways.'

'Just so,' said M. Henri; 'but the most probable way for it to come into his possession would be through the Casino. In these cases we must move in the direction pointed out by the finger of Probability; in our work there is no certainty, otherwise there would be little work for us to do. I take it, then, the probability is that a person who had been playing at the Casino, and who had a counter left over, forgotten in his or her pocket—a thing that often happens, I assure you—paid a visit to the rooms of

Madame Bertaux, and through accident dropped and left behind the counter.

'Now, what does that prove? Very little, you will say, yet to me it seems that here is evidence not without value.

'We can say, to begin with, that it is highly probable the counter was dropped neither by Coudoyer nor Rosalie nor M. Jacob, none of whom have the *entrée* to the Casino, nor Madame Bertaux, who was an invalid, but by someone else. Madame Bertaux had no friends. I understand from you that neither M. Jacob nor Rosalie knew of any visitors. Therefore the counter must have been dropped by a visitor who came in secret, or at least in a manner which drew the attention of no one in the house.

'A curious thing for anyone to pay a visit like that. Now, when we come across anything strange or curious in this world, time or common sense will often put in our hands a solution quite simple.

'There would be something curious in the secret conduct of this stranger if he came for a good and not for an evil purpose. We, in fact, find the old lady murdered, and we say to ourselves: "Here is the fruit of the purpose that inspired our stranger—there is nothing curious in the matter at all. He came in secret to murder her."

'"There is nothing curious in the matter at all." That is the motto that every detective ought to take; every baffling crime seems at first sight to have something curious in its texture or make-up; but that is not so; in nearly every case the seeming strangeness is an illusion due to scanty or muddled evidence.'

'Well,' said the Chief of Police, 'what you say seems just, and if we could find the man who owned the counter your argument would bear heavily against him. We fancy we have found him in Coudoyer. Well, seeing you have taken an interest in this

business, why not give us the benefit of your experience? Come
and examine the chief parties in the affair for yourself, and look
at the room.'

'I will do that with pleasure,' said M. Henri.

We left the hotel and went straight to the Rue Paradis. The
body had been removed, but the room was in just the same state
as when the tragedy was discovered. It was a pleasant, sunlit room
on the first floor, with a window opening upon a small balcony.
M. Henri went first to the balcony and inspected the drain-pipe
by which the assassin had climbed; then he returned and stood
with his hands behind his back looking at the room. Opposite the
window there was a sofa, and by the window was the armchair in
which the invalid had been sitting when she was attacked.

Small objects of furniture stood about, including a fragile table
bearing a vase of flowers; on another table stood the jewel-box,
empty.

M. Henri, having inspected all these things individually, asked
that Rosalie, the maid, should be called. The girl, when she came
into the room, did not strike me very favourably. She was pretty,
but pert-looking, shallow, just the tool one might fancy a scoundrel
would easily handle. I confess, when I saw her, my belief in the
innocence of Coudoyer was not increased.

'Tell me,' said M. Henri, 'what were you doing last night at
nine o'clock?'

'I have already told Monsieur the Inspector,' replied she. 'I was
with a friend.'

'She was with Coudoyer,' put in the Chief. 'Several people saw
them together at twenty minutes to nine; after that no one saw
them together. Her story is that they walked about together. She
returned at half-past nine, after the crime had been discovered.'

'That will do,' said M. Henri, and he dismissed Rosalie. Then he turned to the Chief. 'Give me the girl's story,' said he, 'as she told it to you.'

'There was very little more,' replied the other. 'She parted, so she said, with Coudoyer at the corner of the Rue Marcell at twenty minutes past nine. He went for a walk by himself and returned home at ten.'

'And the murder was committed at nine?'

'Yes.'

'Who discovered the body?'

'M. Jacob. He was seated downstairs, reading, at nine o'clock, when he fancied he heard a cry. He thought it was from the rooms above, and then he fancied it was from the street. He went on reading, but felt, somehow, uneasy, went upstairs and knocked at the old lady's door, got no answer, and opened the door. Then he telephoned for the police.'

'Tell me,' said M. Henri, 'why haven't you arrested that girl as well as Coudoyer?'

'She's as good as arrested,' replied the other; 'she can't escape, and we are just letting her play about for a few days. Coudoyer had accomplices. None of the jewellery has been recovered, with the exception of that old watch which he swore was given him by Rosalie, who had it as a present from the old lady.'

'Let's have a talk with M. Jacob,' said Henri.

We went to the flat below, and found M. Jacob in. A middle-sized, prosperous-looking, elderly person, greatly disturbed by the tragedy of the night before. He told us all he knew. He had never heard of the gift of the watch to Rosalie, though, indeed, as he pointed out, it was little likely that he should have heard of it, for though he was on good terms with the old lady and often went up to have a chat with her, a little affair of that sort would scarcely be mentioned between them.

'You never saw or heard of a Casino counter in her possession?' asked Henri.

M. Jacob was greatly astonished at the question: the police had not told him of the finding of the counter. No, he had never seen one in the possession of the old lady, it was the most unlikely thing for her to have, and no one else in the house would possess such a thing. Then we took our departure, to visit Coudoyer, who was held at the police department under arrest.

He was a pale-faced individual, with restless, shifty eyes. He did not impress me favourably; but, still, I would never judge a man by his appearance.

He told a tale substantially the same as that given by the servant Rosalie. He protested that his character was good, that his employers could speak well of him, that he was engaged to be married to Rosalie—and would a man about to marry commit a crime like that?

He said that he had never been even on the steps of the Casino.

He admitted that it was possible to pick up a counter dropped by some gambler in the café where he served, or in the street, but stated emphatically that he had not done so.

Yes, the watch, that was the only thing they had against him, but it had been given him by the girl; he could not prove this, because Madame Bertaux was dead, but it was a fact. Then, half unwillingly, but evidently speaking the truth, he said that he believed, or had strong suspicion, that Rosalie was not faithful to him; that she had a 'young man' other than himself. But he could give no name; the thing was a suspicion based on something she had mentioned.

That was what he had to say both on his own account and in answer to questions. When he was removed, the Chief turned to M. Henri.

'Now,' said he, 'you have seen all the important people in connection with this case, and here is a diagram showing the position in which the body was when found. What's your opinion?'

'I haven't any fixed opinion just yet,' said M. Henri, 'but from what I have seen I believe that man will be convicted. Monte Carlo never guillotines, so he will not pay the extreme penalty, and after a while it is possible he may regain his freedom.' A strange sort of speech, to which the Chief listened with a half-smile.

'And what about Rosalie?' he asked.

'I can't say anything about her,' replied Henri. 'I'm only telling the fortune of Coudoyer.'

'You would make your fortune as a fortune-teller,' said the Chief; 'you speak so convincingly.'

'I believe I could make money at that business,' replied the other; 'and legitimately, for my fortune-telling would be based on circumstance and character. I say Coudoyer may regain his freedom, for the simple reason that in my belief Coudoyer is innocent. Mind you, that is only a belief.'

'And you base it—?'

'On the ten-franc counter, and on Rosalie's "young man," the existence of whom I half believe in.'

'That eternal counter!'

'Yes, that eternal counter—and other things that it seems to have revealed to me.'

'What are they?'

'I cannot tell you; you would say, "Oh, this is nonsense!" and besides, to let daylight in on half-formed ideas tends to shrivel them; and besides, to talk is fatal in a case like this: walls have ears, ideas have wings. I believe the murderer is now walking about Monte Carlo; I believe this climber of drain-pipes and assassin of old ladies fancies himself secure, but that, at a whisper, a breath of air, he would take measures which would prevent him ever from being caught. But this I will do if you like: I will lend you Malmaison, of the Paris *Sûreté*; he is not in very good health, and a change to the sunny South will do him good. He will come here, of course, as a private individual; nobody knows him here; and if he is successful the credit will go to you, for he is not longing after notoriety.'

You may be sure the Chief did not hesitate to accept this offer; it was all to the good and nothing to pay, for Paris and Monte Carlo are very necessary to one another and often lend mutual assistance without the exchange of a franc.

So it was settled.

After that and for a long time I heard nothing more. My business took me to Vienna and Rome. I heard, indeed, that Coudoyer and the girl had been condemned, both to imprisonment, and for life. Henri had prophesied truly, though he had not included the girl in his forecast. Then one day, and in pursuit of my business, I returned to Monte Carlo, only to find that the man on whose tracks I had been travelling had doubled back and been arrested at Milan. I was pretty much disgusted. I had committed a fault; he had got wind of me, and my reputation would suffer.

Being what you call at a loose end that evening, I went to the Casino. I don't care for music or plays, but people always interest me, especially the Casino crowd, and there I went; and scarcely had I made the tour of the rooms when whom should I find but Malmaison.

He was dressed to represent the part of a well-to-do business man, but I could not mistake him. I must tell you about Malmaison—that he is the most self-obliterating person in the world. In Paris he adopts a disguise; his name is unknown, never published in the papers; that is why he is so deadly. Here in Monte Carlo his best disguise was to be his real self.

I knew him, but then I am in the inner circle. Our eyes met, and I saw at once that I was not to speak. Then he turned from the table, and as he turned I saw the hand which was behind his back close twice.

I followed him slowly as he walked away, followed him through the room, stopping occasionally to look at the play, followed him outside, past Ciro's, and along a road leading to the Rue Paradis. Here he stopped, and we spoke to each other. Henri must have told him of my knowledge of the Bertaux affair, for he began to speak of it at once.

'And it is fortunate I met you to-night,' said he, 'for things have come to a crisis. I believe I have got my man; indeed, I could have pointed him out to you in the room where he was playing. He did not see me, I only got a glimpse of him, but to-night I expect he will re-visit the house where the murder took place and where I have taken rooms.'

'Taken rooms?' said I.

'Yes,' he said. 'Madame Bertaux's flat was to let; people weren't anxious to rent it just after the crime, so M. Jacob, who owns the place and lives below, let it to me. I have been there a good while watching the Casino and the strangers who have come to Monte Carlo. I had to wait a good while, but I found my man—and my woman.'

'Who was the woman?'

'Rosalie—she was justly condemned.'

'And the man—?'

'Was her young man, a rival to Coudoyer.'

'And to-night,' I said, 'you expect him to re-visit the scene of the crime. What bait have you put out for him?'

'You'll see,' said Malmaison.

We had reached the door, and he opened it with a latch-key. The door of M. Jacob's flat was closed.

'You haven't told M. Jacob?' said I.

'Not a word,' he replied. 'I believe in Henri's motto, which is "Be dumb." He believes I am just a prosperous rentier, and as I pay my rent in advance he doesn't bother about anything else. Why should I tell him?'

He led the way up, and I found myself again in Madame Bertaux's room; but very different it looked now, with cigar and cigarette boxes about and glasses and other signs of good cheer.

Malmaison made me take the arm-chair, then he opened the window and left it standing half open.

'You expect him to come through the window?' said I.

'Let us expect nothing,' said he. 'I believe in Henri's idea that not only ought one to be dumb, but that, given a true theory, too many brains in the know may set up ether vibrations warning the criminal. However, a sketch of how the case stands up to a certain point will do no harm.'

He offered me a cigar and went on:

'I came here on seemingly an impossible task, but M. Henri had given me an idea of how to set to work. It was only during the last few days, however, that the truth became quite evident. The criminal is first of all and above everything else a gambler; the crime was committed to recoup his gambling losses. He has a cousin who runs an hotel here. A very shady man, this cousin. He it was, I suspect, who turned the stolen jewellery into money; a worse man, perhaps, than the actual murderer, who was urged by Play and the Devil to commit his crime.'

As Malmaison talked and as I looked at him, noticing his good clothes, his large watch-chain and the rings on his fingers, the idea came to me that the bait he had put down to catch the assassin was himself, and it gave me a very queer sensation, the thought that through that open window the tiger might suddenly appear. However, I said nothing, and he went on:

'The criminal has two addresses here. One is the hotel owned by his cousin. He doesn't stay there; he has a house of his own, a pleasant little house which he picked up cheap and where he lives free of taxes, the only drawback being that when he wants to play at the Casino he can't, owing to the fact that he's a resident employed in a bank. He is also a man with a certain power over women, and so it came about that Rosalie fell under his spell.

'Now you will see how things conspired to bring this man to his undoing. He has a brother very like himself who travels in wine for Meyer and Capablanca, of Bordeaux.

'This brother, when he visits Monte Carlo, stops at the cousin's hotel and plays at the Casino, and one fine day it occurred to the criminal, who was then only a bank cashier, to drop into the Casino under the brother's name and giving the address the brother had always given. The chief difference between the two men was the fact that the brother wore glasses. So you see it was quite an easy matter to buy a pair of glasses, and, handing the brother's card over the counter, gain admittance—or use his ticket for the season.

'Well, there you are: a man well-to-do and comfortable, yet sucked by the whirlpool of the tables—drawn into the net. Most likely the first time he went in under the guise of his brother he thought it would be the last; he just went in to see the play and have a flutter. Then the passion grew. Or it may be that he was a gambler at heart with a passion full grown to be satisfied—who knows? One can only say that the tables took him and turned him into a murderer, and that Henri jumped to the fact that the man who dropped that ten-franc counter might be a resident who played at the Casino *under disguise.*'

Malmaison rose and held up a finger.

'Here he is,' said he.

I could hear a far-away step in the silent street outside.

Malmaison closed the window.

'Why do you close the window?' I asked.

'I only left it open to let in a footstep,' said he. 'Come, this gentleman will enter boldly by the front door, if I am not mistaken. Quick!'

I took my hat and followed him downstairs to the hall, where we stood waiting while the footsteps paused outside. The hall light was on. We heard the noise of the key in the latch; the door opened, and a man entered. It was only M. Jacob.

I pitied Malmaison. I felt like a man watching a play which has suddenly broken down, a hunter who hears the footsteps of a tiger and finds them to be the footsteps of a lamb.

'Good evening, monsieur,' said Jacob when he saw Malmaison.

'Good evening,' replied the other. 'I was just going to show my friend out. How fortunate we have met, for my friend wished to ask you some questions concerning real estate in Monte Carlo.'

'Come into my room,' said M. Jacob, 'and we can talk.'

He opened the door of his flat and we entered the sitting-room, where he put on the light and offered us cigarettes, which Malmaison refused.

'Monsieur Jacob,' said he whilst we took seats, 'excuse my asking, but how much money did you make playing at the Casino to-night?'

The murderer rose to his feet at this terrible question, the full weight of which he had not quite realised. He knew he was caught, but not how seriously.

'Ah!' said he—'a spy of the bank!'

'No,' said Malmaison, 'I have nothing to do with the bank of which you are cashier. I am a police officer in search of a certain ten-franc counter which was dropped—'

He did not finish the sentence. Jacob had made a dash for the door.

The struggle did not last a minute.

It wasn't much, for I had managed, seeing the truth, to seize Jacob from behind. We found the glasses in his pocket and a large number of banknotes which he had won that night. At the Bureau of Police, where we brought him, he was told that his cousin, the hotelkeeper, had confessed to the whole business; this was an untruth, but it served, for in his anger he rounded on the cousin and told how he had disposed of the jewels. Both men received life sentences. He rounded on Rosalie, the girl who had begun by stealing the antique watch as a present for Coudoyer and ended by assisting M. Jacob in his plans, the girl who had not given him away simply because she would have had to give herself away too, and who took her condemnation and sentence without a word, knowing she would do herself no good through freeing Coudoyer; feeling perhaps jealous that Coudoyer should escape whilst she had to suffer. Women are strange things.

I have told you the story for two reasons. First of all, it is interesting as it shows the methods of M. Henri. He seized directly on the really essential thing, the counter. When he mentioned the counter to M. Jacob he saw at once what I did not see, that Jacob was the man who had dropped it, saw it by some subtle signal in the man's manner. Also, it seemed to him that the drain-pipe by which the assassin was supposed to have climbed was too fragile to support a grown man, and that the marks on it were 'artificial.'

When he sent Malmaison to Monte Carlo he told him to watch Jacob and, if possible, to secure the rooms left vacant by the death of Madame Bertaux.

Now, if Jacob had been a really clever man he would never have gone to the Casino again after the finding of that counter by the police, but, lulled to security by the conviction of Coudoyer and the girl, and little dreaming how that counter had talked to Henri, instead of destroying those fatal glasses he put them on and walked into the trap.

It was the finding of those glasses on him that really broke him down and saved a long trial by inducing him to confess.

The other reason for my telling you this story is to show you the pull of the tables and exhibit to you the men who run them as what they are, men who for the sake of profit sacrifice men to the Demon of Play.

The Demon kills a man every day on an average at Monte Carlo, kills him by his own hand and sends his soul to perdition. And what shall we say of the men who do not commit suicide yet are ruined; of their wives and children?

I am no priest; my business in life is the taking of criminals—criminals—criminals, but what shall we say of the men who are licensed by society to kill for gain?

Are they so much better than M. Jacob?

He crossed and put another cigarette-end on the pile in the ash-tray.

I did not answer his question. I was looking through the open window and the balmy night at the jewelled necklace of Monte Carlo, and the far-off light of Cap Ferrat winking across the sea.

# HAVE YOU GOT EVERYTHING YOU WANT?

## Agatha Christie

Agatha Christie (1890–1976), the most popular detective novelist who has ever lived, is often thought of as a quintessentially English woman who produced quintessentially English stories. The stereotype does her less than justice. Christie, whose father was American, was a cosmopolitan figure who was as happy travelling on the Orient Express, or working on an archaeological dig in the Middle East as she was enjoying the views of the River Dart from Greenway, her house in Devon.

It is sometimes suggested that her mystery fiction was almost always set in cosy English villages (for which the crime writer Colin Watson coined the generic term 'Mayhem Parva'), but this is simply not true. Even Jane Marple, the spinster-sleuth from the village of St Mary Mead, travelled as far as the Caribbean in one novel, while *Death Comes as the End* (1945) is a whodunit set in Ancient Egypt. Several of her short stories also benefit from overseas settings, notably 'Triangle at Rhodes', a splendidly plotted Hercule Poirot mystery. This story features one of her less famous recurrent characters. After making an initial appearance in a magazine in 1933, it was included the following year in the collection *Parker Pyne Investigates*.

'*P*AR ICI, MADAME.'

A tall woman in a mink coat followed her heavily encumbered porter along the platform of the Gare de Lyon.

She wore a dark-brown knitted hat pulled down over one eye and ear. The other side revealed a charming tip-tilted profile and little golden curls clustering over a shell-like ear. Typically an American, she was altogether a very charming-looking creature and more than one man turned to look at her as she walked past the high carriages of the waiting train.

Large plates were stuck in holders on the sides of the carriages.

PARIS-ATHENES. PARIS-BUCHAREST.
PARIS-STAMBOUL.

At the last named the porter came to an abrupt halt. He undid the strap which held the suitcases together and they slipped heavily to the ground. '*Voici, Madame.*'

The *wagon-lit* conductor was standing beside the steps. He came forward, remarking, '*Bonsoir, Madame,*' with an *empressement* perhaps due to the richness and perfection of the mink coat.

The woman handed him her sleeping-car ticket of flimsy paper. 'Number Six,' he said. 'This way.'

He sprang nimbly into the train, the woman following him. As she hurried down the corridor after him, she nearly collided with a portly gentleman who was emerging from the compartment next to hers. She had a momentary glimpse of a large bland face with benevolent eyes.

'*Voici, Madame.*'

The conductor displayed the compartment. He threw up the window and signalled to the porter. The lesser employee took in the baggage and put it up on the racks. The woman sat down.

Beside her on the seat she had placed a small scarlet case and her handbag. The carriage was hot, but it did not seem to occur to her to take off her coat. She stared out of the window with unseeing eyes. People were hurrying up and down the platform. There were sellers of newspapers, of pillows, of chocolate, of fruit, of mineral waters. They held up their wares to her, but her eyes looked blankly through them. The Gare de Lyon had faded from her sight. On her face were sadness and anxiety.

'If Madame will give me her passport?'

The words made no impression on her. The conductor, standing in the doorway, repeated them. Elsie Jeffries roused herself with a start.

'I beg your pardon?'

'Your passport, Madame.'

She opened her bag, took out the passport and gave it to him.

'That will be all right, Madame, I will attend to everything.' A slight significant pause. 'I shall be going with Madame as far as Stamboul.'

Elsie drew out a fifty-franc note and handed it to him. He accepted it in a business-like manner, and inquired when she would like her bed made up and whether she was taking dinner.

These matters settled, he withdrew and almost immediately the restaurant man came rushing down the corridor ringing his little bell frantically, and bawling out, '*Premier service. Premier service.*'

Elsie rose, divested herself of the heavy fur coat, took a brief glance at herself in the little mirror, and picking up her handbag and jewel case stepped out into the corridor. She had gone only a few steps when the restaurant man came rushing along on his return journey. To avoid him, Elsie stepped back for a moment into the doorway of the adjoining compartment, which was now empty. As the man passed and she prepared to continue her journey to the dining car, her glance fell idly on the label of a suitcase which was lying on the seat

It was a stout pigskin case, somewhat worn. On the label were the words: 'J. Parker Pyne, passenger to Stamboul.' The suitcase itself bore the initials 'P.P.'

A startled expression came over the girl's face. She hesitated a moment in the corridor, then going back to her own compartment she picked up a copy of *The Times* which she had laid down on the table with some magazines and books.

She ran her eye down the advertisement columns on the front page, but what she was looking for was not there. A slight frown on her face, she made her way to the restaurant car.

The attendant allotted her a seat at a small table already tenanted by one person—the man with whom she had nearly collided in the corridor. In fact, the owner of the pigskin suitcase.

Elsie looked at him without appearing to do so. He seemed very bland, very benevolent, and in some way impossible to explain, delightfully reassuring. He behaved in reserved British fashion, and it was not until the fruit was on the table that he spoke.

'They keep these places terribly hot,' he said.

'I know,' said Elsie. 'I wish one could have the window open.'

He gave a rueful smile. 'Impossible! Every person present except ourselves would protest.'

She gave an answering smile. Neither said any more.

Coffee was brought and the usual indecipherable bill. Having laid some notes upon it, Elsie suddenly took her courage in both hands.

'Excuse me,' she murmured. 'I saw your name upon your suit-case—Parker Pyne. Are you—are you, by any chance—?'

She hesitated and he came quickly to her rescue.

'I believe I am. That is'—he quoted from the advertisement which Elsie had noticed more than once in *The Times*, and for which she had searched vainly just now: '"Are you happy? If not, consult Mr Parker Pyne." Yes, I'm that one, all right.'

'I see,' said Elsie. 'How—how extraordinary!'

He shook his head. 'Not really. Extraordinary from your point of view, but not from mine.' He smiled reassuringly, then leaned forward. Most of the other diners had left the car. 'So you are unhappy?' he said.

'I—' began Elsie, and stopped.

'You would not have said "How extraordinary" otherwise,' he pointed out.

Elsie was silent for a minute. She felt strangely soothed by the mere presence of Mr Parker Pyne. 'Ye—es,' she admitted at last. 'I am—unhappy. At least, I am worried.'

He nodded sympathetically.

'You see,' she continued, 'a very curious thing has happened—and I don't know the least what to make of it.'

'Suppose you tell me about it,' suggested Mr Pyne.

Elsie thought of the advertisement. She and Edward had often commented on it and laughed. She had never thought that she… perhaps she had better not… if Mr Parker Pyne were a charlatan… but he looked—nice!

Elsie made her decision. Anything to get this worry off her mind.

'I'll tell you. I'm going to Constantinople to join my husband. He does a lot of Oriental business, and this year he found it necessary to go there. He went a fortnight ago. He was to get things ready for me to join him. I've been very excited at the thought of it. You see, I've never been abroad before. We've been in England six months.'

'You and your husband are both American?'

'Yes.'

'And you have not, perhaps, been married very long?'

'We've been married a year and a half.'

'Happily?'

'Oh, yes! Edward's a perfect angel.' She hesitated. 'Not, perhaps, very much go to him. Just a little—well, I'd call it straightlaced. Lot of puritan ancestry and all that. But he's a *dear*,' she added hastily.

Mr Parker Pyne looked at her thoughtfully for a moment or two, then he said, 'Go on.'

'It was about a week after Edward had started. I was writing a letter in his study, and I noticed that the blotting paper was all new and clean, except for a few lines of writing across it. I'd just been reading a detective story with a clue in the blotter and so, just for fun, I held it up to a mirror. It really *was* just fun, Mr Pyne—I mean, he's such a mild lamb one wouldn't dream of anything of that kind.'

'Yes, yes; I quite understand.'

'The thing was quite easy to read. First there was the word "wife" then "Simplon Express", and lower down, "just before Venice would be the best time".' She stopped.

'Curious,' said Mr Pyne. 'Distinctly curious. It was your husband's handwriting?'

'Oh, yes. But I've cudgelled my brains and I cannot see under what circumstances he would write a letter with just those words in it.'

'"Just before Venice would be the best time",' repeated Mr Parker Pyne. 'Distinctly curious.'

Mrs Jeffries was leaning forward looking at him with a flattering hopefulness. 'What shall I do?' she asked simply.

'I am afraid,' said Mr Parker Pyne, 'that we shall have to wait until before Venice.' He took up a folder from the table. 'Here is the schedule time of our train. It arrives at Venice at two twenty-seven to-morrow afternoon.'

They looked at each other.

'Leave it to me,' said Parker Pyne.

II

It was five minutes past two. The Simplon Express was eleven minutes late. It had passed Mestre about a quarter of an hour before.

Mr Parker Pyne was sitting with Mrs Jeffries in her compartment. So far the journey had been pleasant and uneventful. But now the moment had arrived when, if anything was going to happen, it presumably would happen. Mr Parker Pyne and Elsie faced each other. Her heart was beating fast, and her eyes sought him in a kind of anguished appeal for reassurance.

'Keep perfectly calm,' he said. 'You are quite safe. I am here.'

Suddenly a scream broke out from the corridor.

'Oh, look—look! The train is on fire!'

With a bound Elsie and Mr Parker Pyne were in the corridor. An agitated woman with a Slav countenance was pointing a dramatic finger. Out of one of the front compartments smoke was pouring in a cloud. Mr Parker Pyne and Elsie ran along the corridor. Others joined them. The compartment in question was full of smoke. The first comers drew back, coughing. The conductor appeared.

'The compartment is empty!' he cried. 'Do not alarm yourselves, *messieurs et dames. Le feu*, it will be controlled.'

A dozen excited questions and answers broke out. The train was running over the bridge that joins Venice to the mainland.

Suddenly Mr Parker Pyne turned, forced his way through the little pack of people behind him and hurried down the corridor to Elsie's compartment. The lady with the Slav face was seated in it, drawing deep breaths from the open window.

'Excuse me, Madame,' said Parker Pyne. 'But this is not your compartment.'

'I know. I know,' said the Slav lady. '*Pardon*. It is the shock, the emotion—my heart.' She sank back on the seat and indicated the open window. She drew in her breath in great gasps.

Mr Parker Pyne stood in the doorway. His voice was fatherly and reassuring. 'You must not be afraid,' he said. 'I do not think for a moment the fire is serious.'

'Not? Ah, what a mercy! I feel restored.' She half-rose. 'I will return to my compartment.'

'Not just yet.' Mr Parker Pyne's hand pressed her gently back. 'I will ask you to wait a moment, Madame.'

'Monsieur, this is an outrage!'

'Madame, you will remain.'

His voice rang out coldly. The woman sat still looking at him. Elsie joined them.

'It seems it was a smoke bomb,' she said breathlessly. 'Some ridiculous practical joke. The conductor is furious. He is asking everybody—' She broke off, staring at the second occupant of the carriage.

'Mrs Jeffries,' said Mr Parker Pyne, 'what do you carry in your little scarlet case?'

'My jewellery.'

'Perhaps you would be so kind as to look and see that everything is there.'

There was immediately a torrent of words from the Slav lady. She broke into French, the better to do justice to her feelings.

In the meantime Elsie had picked up the jewel case. 'Oh!' she cried. 'It's unlocked.'

'*Et je porterai plainte à la Compagnie des Wagons-Lits,*' finished the Slav lady.

'They're gone!' cried Elsie. 'Everything! My diamond bracelet. And the necklace Pop gave me. And the emerald and ruby rings. And some lovely diamond brooches. Thank goodness I was wearing my pearls. Oh, Mr Pyne, what shall we do?'

'If you will fetch the conductor,' said Mr Parker Pyne, 'I will see that this woman does not leave this compartment till he comes.'

'*Scélérat! Monstre!*' shrieked the Slav lady. She went on to further insults. The train drew in to Venice.

The events of the next half-hour may be briefly summarised. Mr Parker Pyne dealt with several different officials in several different languages—and suffered defeat. The suspected lady consented to be searched—and emerged without a stain on her character. The jewels were not on her.

Between Venice and Trieste Mr Parker Pyne and Elsie discussed the case.

'When was the last time you actually saw your jewels?'

'This morning. I put away some sapphire earrings I was wearing yesterday and took out a pair of plain pearl ones.'

'And all the jewellery was there intact?'

'Well, I didn't go through it all, naturally. But it looked the same as usual. A ring or something like that might have been missing, but no more.'

Mr Parker Pyne nodded. 'Now, when the conductor made up the compartment this morning?'

'I had the case with me—in the restaurant car. I always take it with me. I've never left it except when I ran out just now.'

'Therefore,' said Mr Parker Pyne, 'that injured innocent, Madame Subayska, or whatever she calls herself, *must* have been the thief. But what the devil did she do with the things? She was only in here a minute and a half—just time to open the case with a duplicate key and take out the stuff—yes, but what next?'

'Could she have handed them to anyone else?'

'Hardly. I had turned back and was forcing my way along the corridor. If anyone had come out of this compartment I should have seen them.'

'Perhaps she threw them out of the window to someone.'

'An excellent suggestion; only, as it happens, we were passing over the sea at that moment. We were on the bridge.'

'Then she must have hidden them actually in the carriage.'

'Let's hunt for them.'

With true transatlantic energy Elsie began to look about. Mr Parker Pyne participated in the search in a somewhat absent fashion. Reproached for not trying, he excused himself.

'I'm thinking that I must send a rather important telegram at Trieste,' he explained.

Elsie received the explanation coldly. Mr Parker Pyne had fallen heavily in her estimation.

'I'm afraid you're annoyed with me, Mrs Jeffries,' he said meekly.

'Well, you've not been very successful,' she retorted.

'But, my dear lady, you must remember I am not a detective. Theft and crime are not in my line at all. The human heart is my province.'

'Well, I was a bit unhappy when I got on this train,' said Elsie, 'but nothing to what I am now! I could just cry buckets. My lovely, lovely bracelet—and the emerald ring Edward gave me when we were engaged.'

'But surely you are insured against theft?' Mr Parker Pyne interpolated.

'Am I? I don't know. Yes, I suppose I am. But it's the *sentiment* of the thing, Mr Pyne.'

The train slackened speed. Mr Parker Pyne peered out of the window. 'Trieste,' he said. 'I must send my telegram.'

III

'Edward!' Elsie's face lighted up as she saw her husband hurrying to meet her on the platform at Stamboul. For the moment even the loss of her jewellery faded from her mind. She forgot the curious words she had found on the blotter. She forgot everything except that it was a fortnight since she had seen her husband last, and that in spite of being sober and straightlaced he was really a most attractive person.

They were just leaving the station when Elsie felt a friendly tap on the shoulder and turned to see Mr Parker Pyne. His bland face was beaming good-naturedly.

'Mrs Jeffries,' he said, 'will you come to see me at the Hotel Tokatlian in half an hour? I think I may have some good news for you.'

Elsie looked uncertainly at Edward. Then she made the introduction. 'This—er—is my husband—Mr Parker Pyne.'

'As I believe your wife wired you, her jewels have been stolen,' said Mr Parker Pyne. 'I have been doing what I can to help her recover them. I think I may have news for her in about half an hour.'

Elsie looked enquiringly at Edward. He replied promptly: 'You'd better go, dear. The Tokatlian, you said, Mr Pyne? Right; I'll see she makes it.'

IV

It was just a half an hour later that Elsie was shown into Mr Parker Pyne's private sitting room. He rose to receive her.

'You've been disappointed in me, Mrs Jeffries,' he said. 'Now, don't deny it. Well, I don't pretend to be a magician but I do what I can. Take a look inside here.'

He passed along the table a small stout cardboard box. Elsie opened it. Rings, brooches, bracelets, necklace—they were all there.

'Mr Pyne, how marvellous! How—how too wonderful!'

Mr Parker Pyne smiled modestly. 'I am glad not to have failed you, my dear young lady.'

'Oh, Mr Pyne, you make me feel just mean! Ever since Trieste I've been horrid to you. And now—this. But how did you get hold of them? When? Where?'

Mr Parker Pyne shook his head thoughtfully. 'It's a long story,' he said. 'You may hear it one day. In fact, you may hear it quite soon.'

'Why can't I hear it now?'

'There are reasons,' said Mr Parker Pyne.

And Elsie had to depart with her curiosity unsatisfied.

When she had gone, Mr Parker Pyne took up his hat and stick and went out into the streets of Pera. He walked along smiling to himself, coming at last to a little café, deserted at the moment, which overlooked the Golden Horn. On the other side, the mosques of Stamboul showed slender minarets against the afternoon sky. It was very beautiful. Mr Pyne sat down and ordered two coffees. They came thick and sweet. He had just begun to sip his when a man slipped into the seat opposite. It was Edward Jeffries.

'I have ordered some coffee for you,' said Mr Parker Pyne, indicating the little cup.

Edward pushed the coffee aside. He leaned forward across the table. 'How did you know?' he asked.

Mr Parker Pyne sipped his coffee dreamily. 'Your wife will have told you about her discovery on the blotter? No? Oh, but she will tell you; it has slipped her mind for the moment.'

He mentioned Elsie's discovery.

'Very well; that linked up perfectly with the curious incident that happened just before Venice. For some reason or other you were engineering the theft of your wife's jewels. But why the phrase "just before Venice would be the best time"? There seemed nonsense in that. Why did you not leave it to your—agent—to choose her own time and place?

'And then, suddenly, I saw the point. *Your wife's jewels were stolen before you yourself left London and were replaced by paste duplicates.* But that solution did not satisfy you. You were a high-minded, conscientious young man. You have a horror of some servant or other innocent person being suspected. A theft must actually occur—at a place and in a manner which will leave no suspicion attached to anybody of your acquaintance or household.

'Your accomplice is provided with a key to the jewel box and a smoke bomb. At the correct moment she gives the alarm, darts into your wife's compartment, unlocks the jewel case and flings the paste duplicates into the sea. She may be suspected and searched, but nothing can be proved against her, since the jewels are not in her possession.

'And now the significance of the place chosen becomes apparent. If the jewels had merely been thrown out by the side of the line, they might have been found. Hence the importance of the one moment when the train is passing over the sea.

'In the meantime, you make your arrangements for selling the jewellery here. You have only to hand over the stones when the robbery has actually taken place. My wire, however, reached you in time. You obeyed my instructions and deposited the box of jewellery at the Tokatlian to await my arrival, knowing that otherwise I should keep my threat of placing the matter in the hands of the police. You also obeyed my instructions in joining me here.'

Edward Jeffries looked at Mr Parker Pyne appealingly. He was a good-looking young man, tall and fair, with a round chin and very round eyes. 'How can I make you understand?' he said hopelessly. 'To you I must seem just a common thief.'

'Not at all,' said Mr Parker Pyne. 'On the contrary, I should say you are almost painfully honest. I am accustomed to the classification of types. You, my dear sir, fall naturally into the category of victims. Now, tell me the whole story.'

'I can tell you in one word—blackmail.'

'Yes?'

'You've seen my wife: you realise what a pure, innocent creature she is—without knowledge or thought of evil.'

'Yes, yes.'

'She has the most marvellously pure ideals. If she were to find out about—about anything I had done, she would leave me.'

'I wonder. But that is not the point. What *have* you done, my young friend? I presume there is some affair with a woman?'

Edward Jeffries nodded.

'Since your marriage—or before?'

'Before—oh, before.'

'Well, well, what happened?'

'Nothing, nothing at all. This is just the cruel part of it. It was at a hotel in the West Indies. There was a very attractive woman—a Mrs Rossiter—staying there. Her husband was a violent man; he had the most savage fits of temper. One night he threatened her with a revolver. She escaped from him and came to my room. She was half-crazy with terror. She—she asked me to let her stay there till morning. I—what else could I do?'

Mr Parker Pyne gazed at the young man, and the young man gazed back with conscious rectitude. Mr Parker Pyne sighed. 'In other words, to put it plainly, you were had for a mug, Mr Jeffries.'

'Really—'

'Yes, yes. A very old trick—but it often comes off successfully with quixotic young men. I suppose, when your approaching marriage was announced, the screw was turned?'

'Yes. I received a letter. If I did not send a certain sum of money, everything would be disclosed to my prospective father-in-law. How I had—had alienated this young woman's affection from her husband; how she had been seen coming to my room. The husband would bring a suit for divorce. Really, Mr Pyne, the whole thing made me out the most utter blackguard.' He wiped his brow in a harassed manner.

'Yes, yes, I know. And so you paid. And from time to time the screw has been put on again.'

'Yes. This was the last straw. Our business has been badly hit by the slump. I simply could not lay my hands on any ready money. I hit upon this plan.' He picked up his cup of cold coffee, looked at it absently, and drank it. 'What am I to do now?' he demanded pathetically. 'What *am* I to do, Mr Pyne?'

'You will be guided by me,' said Parker Pyne firmly. 'I will deal with your tormentors. As to your wife, you will go straight back to her and tell her the truth—or at least a portion of it. The only point where you will deviate from the truth is concerning the actual facts in the West Indies. You must conceal from her the fact that you were—well, had for a mug, as I said before.'

'But—'

'My dear Mr Jeffries, you do not understand women. If a woman has to choose between a mug and a Don Juan, she will choose Don Juan every time. Your wife, Mr Jeffries, is a charming, innocent, high-minded girl, and the only way she is going to get any kick out of her life with you is to believe that she has reformed a rake.'

Edward Jeffries was staring at him, open-mouthed.

'I mean what I say,' said Mr Parker Pyne. 'At the present moment your wife is in love with you, but I see signs that she may not remain so if you continue to present to her a picture of such goodness and rectitude that it is almost synonymous with dullness.'

'Go to her, my boy,' said Mr Parker Pyne kindly. 'Confess everything—that is, as many things as you can think of. Then explain that from the moment you met her you gave up all this life. You even stole so that it might not come to her ears. She will forgive you enthusiastically.'

'But when there's nothing really to forgive—'

'What is truth?' said Mr Parker Pyne. 'In my experience it is usually the thing that upsets the apple cart! It is a fundamental axiom of married life that you *must* lie to a woman. She likes it! Go and be forgiven, my boy. And live happily ever afterwards. I dare say your wife will keep a wary eye on you in future whenever a pretty woman comes along—some men would mind that, but I don't think you will.'

'I never want to look at any other woman but Elsie,' said Mr Jeffries simply.

'Splendid, my boy,' said Mr Parker Pyne. 'But I shouldn't let her know that if I were you. No woman likes to feel she's taken on too soft a job.'

Edward Jeffries rose. 'You really think—?'

'I *know*,' said Mr Parker Pyne, with force.

# THE LONG DINNER

## *H.C. Bailey*

Henry Christopher Bailey (1878–1961) served an apprenticeship as a novelist writing historical romances before the First World War, before becoming a leading exponent of Golden Age detective fiction. His principal series character, Reggie Fortune, first appeared in the short stories collected in *Call Mr Fortune* (1920); six more volumes of tales appeared before he featured in a novel, *Shadow on the Wall* (1934). Bailey continued to write about Fortune until the late Forties, although by then his rather mannered style of writing had begun to seem outmoded. His best work does, however, have a powerful and distinctive moral sense.

Bailey, a *Daily Telegraph* journalist by profession, enjoyed taking his wife and daughter on holiday to the Swiss and Austrian Alps, where they went on walking tours. When he retired, the family moved to a house perched on the mountainside above the small resort of Llanfairfechan in North Wales, in part because the local views reminded them of their favourite Alpine scenes. He set several of his short stories, as well as scenes in his novels, in continental Europe. 'The Long Dinner', which was included in *Mr Fortune Objects* (1935), is one of Reggie Fortune's most memorable cases.

'I DISLIKE YOU,' SAID MR FORTUNE. 'SOME OF THE DIRTIEST linen I've seen.' He gazed morosely at the Chief of the Criminal Investigation Department.

'Quite,' Lomas agreed. 'Dirty fellow. What about those stains?'

'Oh, my dear chap!' Mr Fortune mourned. 'Paint. All sorts of paint. Also food and drink and assorted filth. Why worry me? What did you expect? Human gore?'

'I had no expectations,' said Lomas sweetly.

A certain intensity came into Mr Fortune's blue eyes. 'Yes. I hate you,' he murmured. 'Anything else you wanted to know?'

'A lot of things,' Lomas said. 'You're not useful, Reginald. I want to know what sort of fellow he was, and what's become of him.'

'He was an artist of dark complexion. He painted both in oils and water-colours. He lived a coarse and dissolute life, and had expensive tastes. What's become of him, I haven't the slightest idea. I should say he was on the way to the devil. What's it all about? Why this interest in the debauched artist?'

'Because the fellow's vanished,' said Lomas. 'He is a painter of sorts, as you say. Name—Derry Farquhar. He had a talent and a bit of a success years ago, and he's gone downhill ever since. Not altogether unknown to the police—money under false pretences and that sort of thing—but never any clear case. Ten days ago a woman turned up to give information that Mr Derry Farquhar was missing. He had some money out of her—a matter of fifty pounds—three months ago. She don't complain of that. She was used to handing him donations—that kind of woman and that kind of man. What worries her is that, since this particular fifty pounds, he's faded out. And it is a queer case. He's lived these ten years in a rat-hole of a flat in Bloomsbury. He's not been seen there for months. That's unlike him. He's never been long away before. A regular London loafer. And his own money—he's got a little income from a trust—has piled up in the bank. August and September dividends untouched. That's absolutely unlike him. Besides that: one night about a fortnight ago—we can't fix the date—somebody was heard in the flat making a good deal of noise. When Bell went to have a look at things, he found the place in a devil of a mess, and a heap of foul linen. So we sent that to you.'

'Hoping for proof of bloodshed,' Reggie murmured. 'Hopeful fellow. Shirts extremely foul, but affordin' no evidence of foul play. Blood is absent. Almost the only substance that is.'

'So you don't believe there's anything in the case?'

'My dear chap! Oh, my dear chap,' Reggie opened large, plaintive eyes. 'Belief is a serious operation. I believe you haven't found anything. That's all. I should say you didn't look.'

'Thank you,' said Lomas acidly. 'Bell raked it all over.' He spoke into the telephone, and Superintendent Bell arrived with a fat folder.

'Mr Fortune thinks you've missed something, Bell,' Lomas smiled.

'If there was anything any use, I have,' Bell said heavily. 'I'll be glad to hear what it is. Here's some photographs of the place, sir. And an inventory.'

'You might pick up a bargain, Reginald,' said Lomas, while Reggie, with a decent solemnity, perused the inventory and contemplated the photographs.

'Four oil paintings, fifteen water-colours. Unframed,' he read, and lifted a gaze of innocent enquiry to Bell.

'I'd call 'em clever, myself,' said Bell. 'Not nice, you know, but very bright and showy. Nudes of ladies, and that sort of thing. I should have thought he could have made a tidy living out of them. But a picture dealer that's seen 'em priced 'em at half a dollar each. Slick rubbish, he called 'em. I'm no hand at art. Anyway—it don't tell us anything.'

'I wouldn't say that. No,' Reggie murmured. 'Builds up the character of Mr Farquhar for us. Person of no honour, even in his pot-boilin' art. However. Nothing else in the flat?'

'Some letters—mostly bills and duns. Nothing to show what he was up to. Nothing to work on.'

Reggie turned over the correspondence quickly. 'Yes. As you say.' He stopped at a crumpled, stained card. 'Where was this?'

'In a pocket of a dirty old sports coat,' Bell said. 'It's only a menu. I don't know why he kept it. Some faces drawn on the back. Perhaps he fancied 'em. No accounting for taste. Looks like drawing devils to me.'

'Rather diabolical, yes,' Reggie murmured. 'Conventional devil. Mephistopheles in a flick.' The faces were sketched, in pencil, with a few accomplished strokes, but had no distinction: the same face in variations of grin and scowl and leer: a face of black brows, moustache, and pointed beard. 'Clever craftsman. Only clever.' He turned the card to the menu written on the front. 'My only aunt!' he moaned, and, in a hushed voice of awe, read out:

DÎNER

*Artichauts à l'Huile*

*Pommes de Terre à l'Huile*

*Porc frais froid aux Cornichons*
*Langouste Mayonnaise*
*Canard aux Navets*
*Omelette Rognons*
*Filet garni*
*Fromage à la Crème*
*Fruits, Biscuits.*

'Good Gad! Some dinner,' Lomas chuckled.

'I don't say I get it all,' Bell frowned. 'But what's it come to? He did himself well some time.'

'Well!' Reggie groaned. 'Oh, my dear chap! Artichokes in oil, cold pork, lobster, duck and turnips—and a kidney omelette and roast beef and trimmings.'

'I've got to own it wants a stomach,' said Bell gloomily. 'What then?'

'Died of indigestion,' said Lomas. 'Or committed suicide in the pangs. Very natural. Very just. There you are, Bell. Mr Fortune has solved the case.'

'I was taking it seriously myself,' Bell glowered at them.

'Oh, my Bell!' Reggie sighed. 'So was I.' He turned on Lomas. 'Incurably flippant mind, your mind. This is the essential fact. Look for Mr Farquhar in Brittany.'

Bell breathed hard. 'How do you get to that, sir?'

'No place but a Brittany inn ever served such a dinner.'

Bell rubbed his chin. 'I see. I don't know Brittany myself, I'm glad to say. I got to own I never met a dinner like it.' He looked at Lomas. 'That means putting it back on the French.'

'Quite,' Lomas smiled. 'Brilliant thought, Reginald. Would you be surprised to hear that Paris is asking us to look for Mr Derry Farquhar in England?'

'Well, well,' Reggie surveyed him with patient contempt. 'Another relevant fact which you didn't mention. Also indicatin' an association of your Mr Farquhar with France.'

'If you like,' Lomas shrugged. 'But the point is they are sure he's here. Dubois is coming over to-day. I'm taking him to dine at the club. You'd better join us.'

'Oh, no. No,' Reggie said quickly. 'Dubois will dine with me. You bring him along. Your club dinner would destroy his faith in the English intelligence. If any. And I like Dubois. Pleasant to discuss the case with a serious mind. Good-bye. Half past eight.'...

With a superior English smile, Lomas sat back and watched Reggie and Dubois consume that fantasia on pancakes, Crêpes Joan, which Reggie invented as an expression of the way of his wife with her husband...

Dubois wiped his flowing moustaches. 'My homage,' he said reverently.

By way of a devilled biscuit, they came to another claret. Dubois looked and smelt and tasted, and his eyes returned thanks. 'Try it with a medlar,' Reggie purred.

'You are right. There is no fruit better with wine.'

They engaged upon a ritual of ecstasy while Lomas gave himself a glass of port and lit a cigarette. At that, Reggie gave a reproachful stare. 'My only aunt! Forgive him, Dubois. He's mere modern English.'

'I pity profoundly,' Dubois sighed. 'A bleak life. This is a great wine, my friend. Of Pauillac, I think, eh? Of the last century?'

'Quite good, yes,' Reggie purred. 'Mouton Rothschild 1900.'

Dubois's large face beamed. 'Aha. Not so bad for poor old Dubois.'

They proceeded to a duet on claret...

Lomas became restive. 'This unanimity is touching. Now you've embraced each other all over, we might come to business and see if you can keep it up.'

Dubois turned to him with a gesture of deprecation. 'Pardon, my friend. Have no fear. We agree always. But I will not delay you. The affair is, after all, very simple.'

'Quite,' Lomas smiled. 'Tell Fortune. He has his own ideas about it.'

'Aha,' Dubois's eyebrows went up. 'I shall be grateful. Well, I begin, then, with Max Weber. He is what you call a profiteer, but, after all, a good fellow. It is a year ago he married a pretty lady. She was by courtesy an actress, the beautiful Clotilde. One has nothing else against her. They live together very happily in an apartment of luxury. Two weeks ago, they find that some of her jewels, which she had in her bedroom, are gone. Not all that Weber had given her, the most valuable are at the bank, but diamonds worth five hundred thousand francs. Weber comes to the Sûreté and makes a complaint. What do we find? The servants, they have been with Weber many years, they are spoilt, they are careless; but dishonest— I think not. There is no sign of a burglary. But the day before the jewels were missed a man came to the Weber apartment who asked for Madame Weber and was told she was not at home. That was true in fact, but, also, Weber's man did not like his look. A *gouape* of the finest water—that is the description. What you call a blackguard, is it not? The man was shabby but showy; he resembled exactly a loafer in the Quartier Latin, an artist *décavé*—how do you say that.'

'On his uppers. Yes. Still more interesting. But not an identification, Dubois.'

'Be patient still. You see—here is a type which might well have known *la belle* Clotilde before she was Madame Weber. Very well.

This gentleman, when he was refused at the Weber door, he did not go far away. We have a *concierge* who saw him loitering till the afternoon at least. In the afternoon the Weber servants take their ease. The man went to a café—he admits it—one woman calls on a friend here, another there. What more easy than for the blackguard artist to enter, to take the jewel case, to hop it, as you say.'

'We do. Yes.'

'Well, then, I begin from a description of Monsieur the Blackguard. It is not so bad. A man who is plump and dark, with little dark whiskers, who has front teeth which stand out, who walks like a bird running, with short steps that go pit pat. He speaks French well enough, but not like a Frenchman. He wears clothes of orange colour, cut very loose, and a soft black hat of wide brim. Then I find that a man like this got into the night train from the Gare St Lazare for Dieppe—that is, you see, to come back to England by the cheap way. Very well. We have worked in the Quartier Latin, we find that a man like this was seen a day or two in some of the cafés. They remember him well, because they knew him ten years ago when he was a student. They are like that, these old folks of the Quartier—it pays. Then his name was Farquhar, Derek Farquhar, an Englishman.' Dubois twirled his moustaches. 'So you see, my friend, I dare to trouble Mr Lomas to find me in England this Farquhar.'

'Yes. Method quite sound,' Reggie mumbled. 'As a method.'

'My poor Reginald,' Lomas laughed. 'What a mournful, reluctant confession! You've hurt him, Dubois. He was quite sure Mr Farquhar was traversing the wilds of Brittany.'

'Aha,' Dubois put up his eyebrows, and made a gesture of respect to Reggie. 'My dear friend, never I consult you but I find you see farther than I. Tell me then.'

'Oh, no. No. Don't see it all,' Reggie mumbled, and told him of the menu of the long dinner.

'Without doubt that dinner was served in Brittany,' Dubois nodded. 'I agree, it is probable he had been there not so long ago. But what of that? He was a painter, he had studied in France, and Brittany is always full of painters.'

'Yes. You're neglectin' part of the evidence. Faces on the back of the menu.' He took out his pocket-book, and sketched the black-browed, black-bearded countenance. 'Like that.'

'The devil,' said Dubois.

'As you say. Devil of opera and fancy ball. The ordinary Mephistopheles. Associated by your Mr Farquhar with Brittany.'

'My dear Fortune!' Dubois's big face twisted into a quizzical smile. 'You are very subtle. Me, I find this is to make too much of little things. After all, drawing devils, it is common sport—you find devils all over our comic papers—a devil and a pretty lady—and he drew pretty ladies often, you say, this Farquhar—and this is a very common devil.'

'Yes, rational criticism,' Reggie murmured, looking at him with dreamy eyes. 'You're very rational, Dubois. However. Any association of the Webers with Brittany?'

'Oh, my friend!' Dubois smiled indulgently. 'None at all. And when they go out of Paris, it is to Monte Carlo, to Aix, not to rough it in Brittany, you may be sure. No. You shall forgive me, but I find nothing in your menu to change my mind. I must look for my Farquhar here.' He shook his head sadly at Reggie. 'I am desolated that you do not agree.' He turned to Lomas. 'But this is the only way, *hein*?'

'Absolutely. There's no other line at all,' said Lomas, with satisfaction. 'Don't let Fortune worry you. He lives to see what isn't there. Wonderful imagination.'

'My only aunt!' Reggie moaned. 'Not me, no. No imagination at all. Only simple faith in facts. You people ignore 'em when they're not rational. Unscientific and superstitious. However. Let's pretend and see what we get. Go your own way.'

'One does as one can,' Dubois shrugged.

'Quite. Fortune is never content with the possible. We must work it out here. I've put things in train for you. We have a copy of Farquhar's photograph. That's been circulated with description, and there's a general warning out for him and the jewels. We're combing out all his friends and his usual haunts.'

'"So runs my dream, but what am I?"' Reggie murmured. '"An infant cryin' in the night. An infant cryin' for the light—" Well, well. Are we down-hearted? Yes. A little Armagnac would be grateful and comfortin'.' He turned the conversation imperatively to the qualities of that liqueur, and Dubois was quick with respectful responses. Lomas relapsed upon Olympian disdain and whisky and soda.

When he took Dubois away, 'Fantastic fellow, Fortune, isn't he?' Lomas smiled. 'Mind of the first order, but never content to use it.'

'An artist, my friend,' said Dubois. 'A great artist. He feels life. We think about it.'

'Damme, you don't believe he's right about this Brittany guess?'

'What do I know?' Dubois shrugged. 'It means nothing. Therefore it is nothing for us. However, one must confess, he is disconcerting, your Mr Fortune. He makes one always doubt.'

This, when he heard of it, Reggie considered the greatest compliment which he ever had, except from his wife. He also thinks it deserved...

Some days later he was engaged upon the production in his marionette theatre of the tragedy of *Don Fuan*, lyrics by Lord

Byron, prose and music by Mr Fortune, when the telephone called him from a poignant passage on the rejection of his hero by hell.

'Yes, Fortune speaking. "Between two worlds life hovers like a star." Perhaps you didn't know that, Lomas. "How little do we know that which we are." Discovery of the late Lord Byron. I'm settin' it to music. Departmental ditty for the Criminal Investigation Department. I—'

'Could you listen for a moment?' said Lomas sweetly. 'You might be interested.'

'Not likely, no. However. What's worryin' you?'

'Nothing, except sympathy for you, Reginald. I'm afraid you'll suffer. To break it gently, we've traced Farquhar. But not in Brittany, Reginald.'

Reggie remained calm. 'No. Of course not,' he moaned. 'You weren't trying. I don't want to hear what you've missed. Takes too long.'

A sound of mockery came over the wire. 'Are you ever wrong, Reginald? No. It's always the other fellow. But the awkward fact is, Farquhar hadn't gone to Brittany, he'd gone to Westshire. So that was the only place we could find him. We have our limitations.'

'You have. Yes. *C'est brutal, mais ça marche.* You're clumsy, but you move—sometimes—like the early cars. What has he got to say for himself?'

'I don't know. We haven't put our hands on him yet. We—what?'

'Pardon me. It was only emotion. A sob of reverence. Oh, my Lomas. You found the only place you could find him, so you haven't found him. The perfect official. No results, but always the superior person.'

'Results quite satisfactory,' Lomas snapped. 'We had a clear identification. He's been staying at Lyncombe. He's bolted again. No doubt found we were on his track. But we shall get him. They're combing out the district. Bell's gone down with Dubois.'

'Splendid. Always shut the stable door when the horse has been removed. I'll go too. I like watching that operation. Raises my confidence in the police force.'...

As the moon rose over the sea, Reggie's car drove into Lyncombe. It is a holiday town of some luxury. The affronts to nature of its blocks of hotel and twisting roads of villas for the opulent retired have not yet been able to spoil all the beauty of cliff and cove.

When Reggie saw it, the banal buildings and the headlands were mingled in moonlight to make a dreamland, and the sea was a black mystery with a glittering path on it.

He went to the newest hotel, he bathed well and dined badly, and, as he sat smoking his consolatory pipe on a balcony where the soft air smelt of chrysanthemums and the sea, Dubois came to him with Bell.

'Aha.' Dubois spoke. 'You have not gone to Brittany then, my friend?'

'No. No. Followin' the higher intelligence. I have a humble mind. And where have you got to?'

'We have got to the tracks of Farquhar, there is no doubt of that. What is remarkable, he had registered in his own name at the hotel, and the people there they recognise his photograph—they are sure of it. In fact, it is a face to be sure of, a rabbit face.'

'The identification's all right,' Bell grunted. 'The devil of it is, he's gone again, Mr Fortune. He went in a hurry too. Left all his traps behind, such as they were. The hotel people think he was just bilking them. He'd been a matter of ten days and not paid anything,

and his baggage is worth about nothing—a battered old suitcase
and some duds fit for the dust-bin.'

'Oh, Peter!' Reggie moaned. 'No, Bell, no. I haven't got to look
at his shirts again?'

'I'm not asking you, sir. There's no sort of reason to think there
was anything done to him. He just went out and didn't come back.
Three days ago. I don't see any light at all. What he was doing here,
beats me. You can say he was hiding with the swag he got in Paris.
But then, why did he register in his own name? Say he was just a
silly ass—you do get that kind of amateur thief. But what has he
bolted for? He couldn't have had any suspicions we were on to him.
We weren't, at the time he faded out.'

'But, my friend, you go too fast,' said Dubois. 'From you, no,
he could not have had any alarm. But there is the other end—Paris.
It is very possible that a friend in Paris warned him the police were
searching for him.'

'All right,' Bell grunted. 'I give you that. Why would he make
the hotel people notice him by bolting without paying his bill?
Silly again. Sheer silly. He'd got a pot of money, if he did have the
jewels, like you say. Going off without paying 'em just sent them
to inform the police quick.'

'That is well argued. You have an insight, a power of mind,
my friend.' Dubois's voice was silky. 'But what have we then? It is
quite natural that Farquhar should disappear again, it is not natural
that he should disappear like this. For me, I confess I do not find
myself able to form an idea of Farquhar. That he is the type to rob
such a woman as Clotilde, there is evidence enough—he had the
knowledge, he had the opportunity. So far, there are a thousand
cases like it. But that he should then retire to such a paradise of the
bourgeois, that is not like his type at all.'

'That's right,' said Bell. 'No sense in it anyway.'

'No. As you say,' Reggie murmured. 'That struck me. Happy to agree with everybody. We don't know anything about anything.'

'*Bigre!* You go a little strong,' Dubois rumbled. 'Come, there is at least a connection with Clotilde, and her jewels are gone. Be sure of that. Weber is an honest man—except in business. And what, now, is your hypothesis? You said look for him in Brittany. This at least is certain—he had not gone there. What the devil should he have to do with this so correct Lyncombe? As much as with our rough Brittany.'

'Yes. Quite obscure. I haven't the slightest idea what he's been doing. However. Are we down-hearted? No. We're in touch with the fundamental problem now. Why does Mr Farquhar deal with Brittany and Clotilde and Lyncombe? First method of solution clearly indicated. Find out what he did do in Lyncombe. That ought to be an easy one, Bell. He must have been noticed. He'd be conspicuous in this correct place. Good night.'

The next day he sat upon the same balcony, spreading the first scone of his tea with clotted cream and blackberry jelly, when the two returned.

'What! Have you not moved since last night?' Dubois made a grimace at him.

'My dear chap! Just walked all along one of the bays. And back. Great big bay. Exercise demanded by impatient and fretful brain. Rest is better. Have a splitter. They're too heavy. But the cream is sound.'

Dubois shuddered. 'Brr! You are a wonderful animal. Me, I am only human. But Bell has news for you. Tell him, old fellow.'

'It's like this,' Bell explained. 'About a week ago—that's three or four days before he disappeared, we can't fix the date nearer—Farquhar went to call at one of the big houses here. There's no doubt about that. It's rather like the Paris case. He was seen loafing round before and after—as you said, he's the sort of chap to get noticed. The house he went to belongs to an old gentle-man—Mr Lane Hudson. Lived here for years. Very rich, they say. Made his money in South Wales, and came here when he retired. Well, he's eighty or more; he's half paralysed—only gets about his house and grounds in a wheeled chair. I've seen him; I've had a talk with him. His mind's all right. He looks like a mummy, only a bit plumped out. Sort of yellow, leathery face that don't change or move. Sits in his chair looking at nothing, and talks soft and thick. He tells me he never heard of Farquhar: didn't so much as know Farquhar had been to his house: that's quite in order, it's his rule that the servants tell anybody not known he's not well enough to see people, and I don't blame him. I wouldn't want strangers to come and look at me if I was like he is. I gave him an idea of the sort of fellow Farquhar was, and watched him pretty close, but he didn't turn a hair. He just said again he had no knowledge of any such person, and I believe him. He wasn't interested. He told me the fellow had no doubt come begging for money; he was much exposed to that sort of thing—we ought to stop it—and good day Mr Superintendent. Anyhow, it's certain Farquhar didn't see him. The old butler and the nurse bear that out, and they never heard of Farquhar before. The butler saw him and turned him away—had a spot of bother over it, but didn't worry. Like the old man, he says they do have impudent beggars now and then. So here's another nice old dead end.'

'Yes. As you say. Rather weird isn't it? The flamboyant debauched Farquhar knockin' at the door—to get to a paralysed old rich man who never heard of him. I wonder. Curious selection of people to call on by our Mr Farquhar. A pretty lady of Paris who's married money and settled down on it; a rich old Welshman who's helpless on the edge of the grave. And neither of 'em sees Mr Farquhar—accordin' to the evidence—neither will admit to knowin' anything about him. Very odd. Yes.' Reggie turned large, melancholy eyes on Dubois. 'Takes your fancy, what? The blackguard artist knockin', knockin', and, upstairs, a mummy of a man helpless in his chair.'

'Name of a name!' Dubois rumbled. 'It is fantasy pure. One sees such things in dreams. This has no more meaning.'

'No. Not to us. But it happened. Therefore it had a cause. Mr Lane Hudson lives all alone, what—except for servants?'

'That's right, sir,' Bell nodded. 'He's been a widower this long time. Only one child—daughter—and there's a grandson, quite a kid. Daughter's been married twice—first to a chap called Tracy, now to a Mr Bernal—son by the first marriage, no other children.'

'You have taken pains, Bell,' Reggie smiled.

'Well, I got everything I could think of,' said Bell, with gloomy satisfaction. 'Not knowing what I wanted. And there's nothing I do want in what I've got. The Bernals come here fairly regular—Mr and Mrs Bernal, not the child—they've been staying with the old man just now. Usual autumn visit. They were there when Farquhar called, and after—didn't go away till last Wednesday; that's before Farquhar disappeared, you see, the day before. Farquhar didn't ask for the Bernals, and they didn't see him at all, the servants say. So there you are. The Bernals don't link up any way. That peters out, like everything else.'

'Yes. Taken a lot of pains,' Reggie murmured.

'What would you have?' Dubois shrugged. 'To amass useless knowledge—it is our only method; one is condemned to it. Ours is a slow trade, my friend. We gather facts and facts and facts, and so, if we are lucky, eliminate ninety-nine of the hundred and use, at last, one.'

'Yes. As you say,' Reggie mumbled. 'Where do the Bernals live, Bell?'

'In France, sir,' said Bell, and Reggie opened his eyes.

'Aha!' Dubois made a grimace, and pointed a broad finger at him. 'There, my friend. The one grand fact, is it not? In France! And Brittany is in France! But alas, my dear Fortune, they do not live in Brittany! Far from it. They live in the south, near Cannes; they have lived there—what do I know?—since they were married, *hein*?' he turned to Bell.

'That's right,' Bell grunted. 'Lady set up house there with her first husband. He had to live in the south of France—gassed in the war.'

'You see?' Dubois smiled. 'It is still the useless knowledge. And your vision of Brittany, my friend, it has no substance still.'

'I wonder,' Reggie mumbled, and sank deep in his chair...

He is, even without hope, conscientious. That night he examined another set of Farquhar's dirty linen, but neither in that nor the rest of the worthless luggage found any information. Prodded by him, Bell enquired of the Hudson household where the Bernals were to be found, but could obtain only the address of their Cannes villa, for they were reported to be going back by car. Dubois was persuaded to telegraph Cannes and received the reply that the Bernal villa was shut up; monsieur and madame were away motoring, and their boy at school—what school nobody knew.

'Then what?' Dubois summed up. 'Nothing to do.'

'Not to-night, no,' Reggie yawned. 'I'm going to bed.'

'To dream of Brittany, *hein*?'

'I never dream,' said Reggie, with indignation...

But he was waked in the night. He rubbed his eyes and looked up to see Dubois's large face above him.

'Oh, my hat,' he moaned. 'What is it? Why won't it wait?'

'Courage, my friend. They have found him. At least, they think so. Some fishermen, going out yesterday evening, they found a body on the rocks at what they call Granny's Cove. Come. The brave Bell wants you to see.'

'Bless him,' Reggie groaned, and rolled out of bed. 'What is life that one should seek it? I ask you.' And, slipping clothes on him, swiftly he crooned, '"Three fishers went sailin' out into the west, out into the west, as the sun went down"—and incredibly caught the incredible Farquhar.'

'You are right,' Dubois nodded. 'Nothing clear, nothing sure. The more it changes, the more it is the same, this accursed case. It has no shape; there is no reason in it.'

'Structure not yet determined. No,' Reggie mumbled, parting his hair, for he will always be neat. 'We're not bein' very clever. Ought to be able to describe the whole thing from available evidence of its existence. Same like inferrin' the age of reptiles from a fossil or two—"dragons of the prime, tearin' each other in the slime, were mellow music unto him." Yes. The struggle for life of the reptiles might be mellow music compared to the diversions of Mr Farquhar and friends. Progressive world, Dubois.'

'Name of a dog!' Dubois exclaimed. 'When you are philosophic, my stomach turns over. What is in your mind?'

'Feelin' of impotence. Very uncomfortable,' Reggie moaned, and muffled himself to the chin and made haste out.

In the mortuary Bell introduced them to a body covered by a sheet. 'Here you are, sir.' He stepped aside. 'The clothes seem to be

Farquhar's clothes all right. Sort of orange tweed and green flannel trousers. But I don't know about the man.'

Reggie drew back the sheet from what was left of a face.

'*Saprelotte!*' Dubois rumbled. 'The fish have bitten.'

'Well, I leave it to you,' said Bell thickly…

Under a sunlit breeze the sea was dancing bright, the mists flying inland from the valleys to the dim bank of the moor, when Reggie came out again.

He drove back to his hotel, and shaved and bathed and rang up the police station. Bell and Dubois arrived to find him in his room, eating with appetite grilled ham and buttered eggs.

'My envy; all my envy,' Dubois pulled a face. 'This is greatness. The English genius at the highest.'

'Oh, no. No,' Reggie protested. 'Natural man. Well. The corpse is that of Mr Farquhar as per invoice. Prominent teeth not impaired by activities of the lobsters. Some other contours still visible. The marmalade—thanks. Yes. Hair, colourin', size and so forth agree. Mr Farquhar's been in the sea three or four days. Correspondin' with date of disappearance. Cause of death, drowning. Severe contusions on head and body, inflicted before death. Possibly by blows, possibly by fall. Might have fallen from cliff; might have been dashed on rocks by sea. No certainty to be obtained. That's the medical evidence.'

'You are talking!' Dubois exclaimed. '*Flute!* There we are again. Whatever arrives, it will mean nothing for us. Here is murder, suicide, accident—what you please.'

'I wonder.' Reggie began to peel an apple. 'Anything in his pockets, Bell?'

'A lot of money, sir. Nothing else. The notes are all sodden, but it's a good wad, and some are fifties. Might be five or six hundred pounds. So he wasn't robbed.'

'And then?' said Dubois. 'It is not enough for all the jewels of Clotilde, but it is something in hand. Will you tell me what the devil he was doing at the door of this paralysed millionaire? It means nothing, none of it.'

'No. Still amassin' useless knowledge, as you were sayin'.' Reggie gazed at Dubois with dreamy eyes. 'I should say that's what we came here for. Don't seem the right place, does it? However. As we are here, let's try and get a little more before departure. Usin' the local talent. Bell—your fishermen—have they got any ideas where a fellow would tumble into the sea to be washed up into Granny's Cove?'

'Ah.' Bell was pleased. 'I have been asking about that, sir. Supposing he got in from the land, they think it would be somewhere round by Shag Nose. That's a bit o' cliff west o' the town. I'm having men search round and enquire. But the scent's pretty cold by now.'

'Yes. As you say,' Reggie sighed. His eyes grew large and melancholy. 'Is it far?' he said, in a voice of fear.

'Matter of a mile or two.'

'Oh, my Bell.' Reggie groaned. He pushed back his chair. He rose stiffly. 'Come on.'

Shag Nose is a headland from which dark cliffs fall sheer. Below them stretches seaward a ridge of rocks, which stand bare some way out at low tide, and in the flood make a turmoil of eddies and broken water.

The top of the headland is a flat of springy turf, in which are many tufts of thrift and cushions of stunted gorse.

'Brr. It is bleak,' Dubois complained. 'Will you tell me why Farquhar should come here? He was not—how do you say?—a man for the great open spaces.'

'Know the answer, don't you?' Reggie mumbled.

'Perfectly. He came to meet somebody in secret who desired to make an end of him. Very well. But who then? Not the paralysed one. Not the son-in-law either. It is in evidence that the son-in-law was gone before Farquhar disappeared.'

'That's right. I verified that,' Bell grunted. 'Bernal and his wife left the night before.'

'There we are again,' Dubois shrugged. 'Nothing means anything. For certain, it is not a perfect alibi. They went by car; they could come back and not be seen. But it is an alibi that will stand unless you have luck, which you have not yet, my dear Bell, God knows.'

'Not an easy case. No,' Reggie murmured. 'However. Possibilities not yet examined. Lyncombe's on the coast. Had you noticed that? I wonder if any little boat from France came in while Farquhar was still alive.'

Dubois laughed. Dubois clapped him on the shoulder. 'Magnificent! How you are resolute, my friend. Always the great idea! A boat from Brittany, *hein*? That would solve everything. The good Farquhar was so kind as to come here and meet it and be killed by the brave Bretons. And the paralysed millionaire, he was merely a diversion to pass the time.'

'Yes. We are not amused,' Reggie moaned. 'You're in such a hurry. Bell—what's the local talent say about the tide? When was high water on the night Farquhar disappeared?'

'Not till the early morning, sir. Tide was going out from about three in the afternoon onwards.'

'I see. At dusk and after, that reef o' rocks would be comin' out of the water. Assumin' he went over the cliff in the dark or twilight, he'd fall on the rocks.'

'That's right. Of course he might bounce into the sea. But I've got a man or two down there searching the shore and the cliff-side.'

'Good man.' Reggie smiled, and wandered away to the cliff edge.

'Yes. It is most correct,' Dubois shrugged. 'I should do it, I avow. But also I should expect nothing, nothing. After all, we are late. We arrive late at everything.'

Reggie turned and stared at him. 'I know. That's what I'm afraid of,' he mumbled.

He wandered to and fro about the ground near the cliff edge, and found nothing which satisfied him, and at last lay down on his stomach where a jutting of the headland gave him a view of the cliffs on either side.

Two men scrambled about over the rocks below, scanning the cliff face, prying into every crevice they could reach... one of them vanished under an overhanging ledge, appeared again, working round it, was lost in a cleft... when he came out he had something in his hand.

'Name of a pipe!' Dubois rumbled. 'Is it possible we have luck at last?'

'No.' Reggie stood up. 'Won't be luck, whatever it is. Reward of virtue. Bell's infinite capacity for takin' pains.'...

A breathless policeman reached the top of the cliff, and held out a sodden book. 'That's the only perishing thing there is down there, sir,' he panted. 'Not a trace of nothing else.'

Bell gave it to Reggie. It was a sketch-book of the size to slide into a man's pocket. The first leaf bore, in a flamboyant scrawl, the name Derek Farquhar.

'Ah. That fixes it, then,' said Bell. 'He did go over this cliff, and his sketch-book came out of his pocket as he bounced on the ledges.'

'Very well,' Dubois shrugged. 'We know now as much as we guessed. Which means nothing.'

Reggie sat down and began to separate the book's wet pages.

Farquhar had drawn, in pencil, notes rather than sketches at first, scraps of face and figure and scene which took his unholy fancy, a drunken girl, a nasty stage dance, variations of impropriety. Then came some parades of men and women bathing, not less unpleasant, but more studied. 'Aha! Here is something seen at least,' said Dubois.

'Yes, I think so,' Reggie murmured, and turned the page.

The next sketch showed children dancing—small boys and girls. Some touch of cruelty was in the drawing—they were made to look ungainly—but it had power; it gave them an intensity of frail life which was at once pathetic and grotesque. They danced round a giant statue—a block in which the shape of a woman was burlesqued, hideously fat and thin, with a flat, foolish face. There were no clothes on it, but rough lines which might be girdle and necklace.

'What the devil!' Dubois exclaimed. 'This is an oddity. He discovers he had a talent, the animal.'

Reggie did not answer. For a moment more he gazed at the children and the statue, and he shivered, then he turned the other pages of the book. There were some notes of faces, then several satires on the respectability of Lyncombe—the sea front, with nymphs in Bath chairs propelled by satyrs and satyrs propelled by nymphs. He turned back to the dancing children and the giant female statue, and stared at it, and his round face was pale. 'Yes. Farquhar had talent,' he said. 'Played the devil with it all his life. And yet it works on the other side. What's the quickest way to Brittany? London and then Paris by air. Come on.'

Dubois swore by a paper bag and caught him up. 'What, then? How do you find your Brittany again in this?'

'The statue,' Reggie snapped. 'Sort of statue you see in Brittany. Nowhere else. He didn't invent that out of his dirty mind. He'd seen it. It meant something to him. I should say he'd seen the children too.'

'You go beyond me,' said Dubois. 'Well, it is not the first time. A statue of Brittany, eh? You mean the old things they have among the standing stones and the menhirs and dolmens. A primitive goddess. The devil! I do not see our Farquhar interested in antiquities. But it is the more striking that he studied her. I give you that. And the children? I will swear he was not a lover of children.'

'No. He wasn't. That came out in the drawing. Not a nice man. It pleased him to think of children dancin' round the barbarous female.'

'I believe you,' said Dubois. 'The devil was in that drawing.'

'Yes. Devilish feelin'. Yes. And yet it's going to help. Because the degenerate fellow had talent. Not wholly a bad world.'

'Optimist. Be it so. But what can you make the drawing mean, then?'

'I haven't the slightest idea,' Reggie mumbled. 'Place of child life in the career of the late Farquhar very obscure. Only trace yet discovered, the Bernals have a child. No inference justified. I'm going to Brittany. I'm goin' to look for traces round that statue. And meanwhile—Bell has to find out if a French boat has been in to Lyncombe—you'd better set your people findin' the Bernals—with child. Have the Webers got a child?'

'Ah, no.' Dubois laughed. 'The beautiful Clotilde, she is not that type.'

'Pity. However. You might let me have a look at the Webers as I go through Paris.'

'With all my heart,' said Dubois. 'You understand, my friend, you command me. I see nothing, nothing at all, but I put myself in your hand.' He made a grimace. 'In fact there is nothing else to do. It is an affair for inspiration. I never had any.'

'Nor me, no,' Reggie was indignant. 'My only aunt! Inspired! I am not! I believe in evidence. That's all. You experts are so superior...'

Next morning they sat in the *salon* of the Webers. It was over-whelming with the worst magnificence of the Second Empire—mirrors and gilding, marble and malachite and lapis lazuli. But the Webers, entering affectionately arm in arm, were only magnificent in their opulent proportions. Clotilde, a dark full-blown creature, had nothing more than powder on her face, no jewels but a string of pearls, and the exuberance of her shape was modified by a simple black dress. Weber's clumsy bulk was all in black too.

They welcomed Dubois with open arms; they talked together. What had he to tell them? They had heard that the cursed Farquhar had been discovered dead in England—it was staggering; had any-thing been found of the jewels?

Nothing, in effect, Dubois told them. Only, Farquhar had more money than such an animal ought to have. It was a pity.

Clotilde threw up her hands. Weber scolded.

Dubois regretted—but what to do? They must admit one had been quick, very quick, to trace Farquhar. They would certainly compliment his *confrère* from England—that produced perfunctory bows. What the English police asked—and they were right—it was could one learn anything of who had worked with Farquhar, why had he come to the apartment Weber?

The Webers were contemptuous. What use to ask such a ques-tion? One had not an acquaintance with thieves. As to why he came, why he picked out them to rob—a thief must go where there was something to steal—and they—well, one was known a little. Weber smirked at his wife, and she smiled at him.

'For sure. Everyone knows monsieur—and madame.' Dubois bowed. 'But I seek something more.'

They stormed. It was not to be supposed they should know anything of such a down-at-heel.

'Oh, no. No,' said Reggie quickly. 'But in the world of business'—he looked at Weber—'in the world of the theatre'—he looked at Clotilde—'the fellow might have crossed your path, what?'

That was soothing. They agreed the thing was possible. How could one tell? They chattered of the detrimentals they remembered—to no purpose.

Under plaintive looks from Reggie, Dubois broke that off with a brusque departure. When they were outside—'Well, you have met them!' Dubois shrugged. 'And if they are anything which is not ordinary I did not see it.'

Reggie gazed at him with round reproachful eyes. 'They were in mourning,' he moaned. 'You never told me that. Were they in mourning when you saw 'em before?'

'But yes,' Dubois frowned. 'Yes, certainly. What is the matter? Did you think they had put on mourning for the animal Farquhar?'

'My dear chap! Oh, my dear chap,' Reggie sighed. 'Find out why they are in mourning. Quietly, quite quietly. Good-bye. Meet you at the station.'...

The night express to Nantes and Quimper drew out of Paris. They ate a grim and taciturn dinner. They went back to the sleeping car and shut themselves in Reggie's compartment. 'Well, I have done my work,' said Dubois. 'The Webers are in mourning for their nephew. A child of ten, whom Weber would have made his heir—his sister's son.'

'A child,' Reggie murmured. 'How did he die?'

'It was not in Brittany, my friend,' Dubois grinned. 'Besides it is not mysterious. He died at Fontainebleau, in August, of diphtheria. They had the best doctors of Paris. There you are again. It means nothing.'

'I wonder,' Reggie mumbled. 'Any news of the Bernals?'

'It appears they have passed through Touraine. If it is they, there was no child with them. Have no fear, they are watched for. One does not disappear in France.'

'You think not? Well, well. Remains the Bernal child. Not yet known to be dead. Of diphtheria or otherwise! I did a job o' work too. Talked to old Huet at the Institut. You know—the prehistoric man. He says Farquhar's goddess is the Woman of Sarn. Recognised her at once. She stands on about the last western hill in France. Weird sort o' place, Huet says. And he can't imagine why Farquhar thought of children dancin' round her. The people are taught she's of the devil.'

'But you go on to see her?' Dubois made a grimace. 'The fixed idea.'

'No. Rational inference. Farquhar thought of her with children. And there's a child dead—and another child we can't find—belongin' to the people linked with Farquhar. I go on.'

'To the land's end—to the end of the world—and beyond. For your faith in yourself. My dear Fortune, you are sublime. Well, I follow you. Poor old Dubois. Sancho Panza to your Don Quixote, *hein*?'...

They came out of the train to a morning of soft sunshine and mellow ocean air. The twin spires of Quimper rose bright among their minarets, its sister rivers gleamed, and the wooded hill beyond glowed bronze. Dubois bustled away from breakfast to see officials. 'Don Quixote is a law to himself, but Sancho had better be correct, my friend.'

'Yes, rather,' Reggie mumbled, from a mouth full of honey. 'Conciliate the authorities. Liable to want 'em.'

'Always the optimist, my Quixote.'

'No. No. Only careful. Don't tell 'em anything.'

'Name of a name!' Dubois exploded. 'That is necessary, that warning. I have so much to tell!'

In an hour, they were driving away from Quimper, up over high moorland of heather and gorse and down again to a golden bay and a fishing village of many boats, then on westward, with glimpses of sea on either hand. There was never a tree, only, about the stone walls which divided the waves of bare land into a draught-board of little fields, thick growth of bramble and gorse. Beyond the next village, with its deep inlet of a harbour, the fields merged into moor again, and here and there rose giant stones, in line, in circle, and solitary.

'Brrr,' Dubois rumbled. 'Tombs or temples, what you please, it was a gaunt religion which put them up here on this windy end of the earth.'

The car stopped, the driver turned in his seat and pointed, and said he could drive no nearer, but that was the Woman of Sarn. 'She is lonely,' Dubois shrugged. 'There is no village near, my lad?'

'There is Sarn.' The driver pointed towards the southern sea. 'But it is nothing.'

Reggie plodded away through the heather. 'Well, this is hopeful, is it not?' Dubois caught him up. 'When we find her, what have we found? An idol in the desert. But you will go on to the end, my Quixote. Forward, then.'

They came to the statue, and stood, for its crude head rose high above theirs, looking up at it. 'And we have found it, one must avow,' Dubois shrugged. 'This is the lady Farquhar drew, devil a doubt. But, *saperlipopette*, she is worse here than on paper. She is real; she is a brute—all that there is of the beast in woman, emerging from the shapeless earth.'

'Inhuman and horrid human, yes,' Reggie murmured. 'Cruelty of life. Yes. He knew about that, the fellow who made her, poor beggar. So did Farquhar.'

'I believe it! But do you ask me to believe little children come and dance round this horror. Ah, no!'

'Oh, no. No. That never happened. Not in our time. Point of interest is, Farquhar thought it fittin' they should. Very interestin' point.' Reggie gave another look at the statue, and walked on towards the highest point of the moor.

From that he could see the tiny village of Sarn, huddled in a cove, the line of dark cliff, a long rampart against the Atlantic. Below the cliff top he made out a white house, of some size, which seemed to stand alone.

His face had a dreamy placidity as he came back to Dubois. 'Well, well. Not altogether desert,' he murmured. 'Something quite residential over there. Let's wander.'

They struck southward towards the sea. As they approached the white house, they saw that it was of modern pattern—concrete, in simple proportions, with more window than wall. Its site was well chosen, in a little hollow beneath the highest of the cliff, sheltered, yet high enough for a far prospect, taking all the southern sun.

'Of the new ugliness, eh?' said Dubois, whose taste is for elaboration in all things. 'All the last fads. It should be a sanatorium, not a house.'

'One of the possibilities, yes.' Reggie went on fast.

They came close above the house. It stood in a large walled enclosure, within which was a trim garden, but most of the space was taken by a paved yard with a roofed platform like a bandstand in the middle. Reggie stood still and surveyed it. Not a creature was to be seen. The acreage of window blazed blank and curtainless.

'The band is not playing.' Dubois made a grimace. 'It is not the season.'

Reggie did not answer. His eyes puckered to stare at a window within which the sun glinted on something of brass. He made a little inarticulate sound, and walked on, keeping above the house. But they saw no one, no sign of life, till they were close to the cliff edge.

Then a cove opened below them in a gleaming stretch of white shell sand, and on the sand children were playing: some of them at a happy-go-lucky game of rounders, some building castles, some tumbling over each other like puppies. On a rock sat, in placid guard over them, a man who had the black pointed beard, the heavy black brows, which Farquhar had sketched on his menu. But these Mephistophelean decorations did not display the leer and sneer of Farquhar's drawing. The owner watched the children with a grave and kindly attention which seemed to be interested in everyone. He called to them cheerily, and had gay answers. He laughed jovial satisfaction at their laughter.

Reggie took Dubois's arm and walked him away. 'Ah, my poor friend!' Dubois rumbled chuckles. 'There we are at last. We arrive. We have the brute goddess, we have the children, we have even the devil of our Farquhar. And behold! he is a genial paternal soul, and all the children love him. Oh, my poor friend!'

'Yes. Funny isn't it?' Reggie snapped. 'Dam' funny. Did you say the end? Then God forgive us. Which He wouldn't. He would not!'

Dubois gave him a queer look—something of derision, some-thing of awe, and a good deal of doubt. 'When you talk like that'—a shrug, a wave of the hands—'it is outside reason, is it not? An inspiration of faith.'

'Faith that the world is reasonable. That's all,' Reggie snarled. 'Come on.'

'And where?'

'Down to this village.'

The huddled cottages of Sarn were already in sight. Then odours, a complex of stale fish and the filth of beast and man, could be smelt. Women clattered in sabots and laboured. Men lounged against the wall above the mess of the beach. A few small and ancient boats lay at anchor in the cove, and one of a larger size, and better condition, which had a motor engine.

They found a dirty *estaminet* and obtained from the landlord a bottle of nameless red wine. He said it was old, it was marvellous, but, being urged to share it, preferred a glass of the apple spirit, Calvados. 'Marvellous, it is the word,' Dubois grinned. 'You are altogether right. Calvados for us also, my friend. It is more humane.'

The landlord was slow of speech, and a pessimist. Even with several little glasses of Calvados inside him he would talk only of the hardness of life and the poverty of Sarn and the curse upon the modern sardine. Reggie agreed that life was dear and life was difficult, but, after all, they had still their good boats at Sarn—motor-boats indeed. The landlord denied it with gloomy vehemence: motors—not one—only in the *Badebec*, and that was no fishing-boat, that one. It was M. David's.

'Is it so?' Reggie yawned, and lit his pipe. He gazed dreamily down the village street to the hideous little church. From that—under a patched umbrella, to keep off the wind, which was high, or the sun, which was grown faint—came a fat and shabby *curé*. 'Well, better luck my friend,' Reggie murmured, left Dubois to pay the bill, and wandered away.

He met the *curé* by the church gate. Was it permitted to visit that interesting church? Certainly, it was permitted, but monsieur would find nothing of interest—it was new; it was, alas! a poor place.

The *curé* was right—it was new; it was garish, it was mean. He showed it to Reggie with an affecting simplicity of diffident pride, and Reggie was attentive. Reggie praised the care with which it was kept. 'You are kind, sir,' the *curé* beamed. 'You are just. In fact they are admirably pious, my poor people, but poor—poor.'

'You will permit the stranger—' Reggie slipped a note into his hand.

'Ah, monsieur! You are generous. It will be rewarded, please God.'

'It is nothing,' said Reggie quickly. 'Do not think of it.' They passed out of the church. 'I suppose this is almost the last place in France?'

'Sometimes I think we are forgotten,' the *curé* agreed. 'Yes, almost the last. Certainly we are all poor folk. There is only M. David, who is sometimes good to us.'

'A visitor?' Reggie said.

'Ah, no. He lives here. The Maison des Iles, you know. No? It is a school for young children—a school of luxury. He is a good man, M. David. Sometimes he will take, for almost a nothing, children who are weakly, and in a little while he has them as strong as the best; I have seen miracles. To be sure it is the best air in the world, here at Sarn. But he is a very good man. He calls his school "of the islands" because of the islands out there'—the *curé* pointed to what looked like a reef of rocks. 'My poor people call them the islands of the blessed. It is not good religion, but they used to think the souls of the innocent went there. Yes, the Maison des Iles, his school is. But you should see it, sir. The children are charming.'

'If I had time—' said Reggie, and said good-bye.

Dubois was at the gate. Dubois took his arm and marched him off. 'My friend, almost thou persuadest me—' He spoke into Reggie's ear. 'Guess what I have found, will you? That motor-yacht, the yacht of M. David, she was away a week ten days ago. And M. David on board. You see? It is possible she went over to England. A guess, yes, a chance, but one must avow it fits devilish well, if one can make it fit. A connection with all your fantasy—M. David over in England when Farquhar was drowned. Is it possible we arrive at last?'

'Yes, it could be. Guess what I've heard. M. David keeps school. That wasn't a bandstand. Open-air class-room. M. David is a very good man, and he uses his beautiful school to cure the children of the poor. He does miracles. The old *curé* has seen 'em.'

'The devil!' said Dubois. 'That does not fit at all. But a priest would see miracles. It is his trade.'

'Oh, no. No. Not unless they happen,' Reggie murmured.

'My friend, you believe more than any man I ever knew,' Dubois rumbled. 'Come, I must know more of this David. The sooner we were back at Quimper the better.'

'Yes. That is indicated. Quimper and telephone.' He checked a moment, and gazed anguish at Dubois. 'Oh, my hat, how I hate telephones.'

Dubois has not that old-fashioned weakness. Dubois, it is beyond doubt, enjoyed the last hours of that afternoon, shut into privacy at the post office with its best telephone, stirring up London and Paris and half France till sweat dripped from his big face and the veins of his brow dilated into knotted cords.

When he came into Reggie's room at the hotel it was already past dinner-time. Reggie lay on his bed, languid from a bath. 'My dear old thing,' he moaned sympathy. 'What a battle! You must have lost pounds.'

'So much the better,' Dubois chuckled. 'And also I have results. Listen. First. I praise the good Bell. He has it that a French boat—cutter rig with motor—was seen by fishermen in the bay off Lyncombe last week. They watched her, because they had suspicions she was poaching their lobsters and crabs, which they unaccountably believe is the habit of our honest French fishermen. She was lying in the bay the night of Tuesday—you see, the night that Farquhar disappeared. In the morning she was gone. They are not sure of the name, but they thought it was *Badboy*. That is near enough to Badebec, *hein*? In fact, myself, I do not understand the name Badebec.'

'Lady in Rabelais,' Reggie murmured. 'Rather interestin'. Shows the breadth of M. David's taste.'

'Aha. Very well. Here is a good deal for M. David to explain. Second, M. David himself. He is known; there is nothing against him. In fact he is like you, a man of science, a biologist, a doctor. He was brilliant as a student, which was about the same time that Farquhar studied art—and other things—in the Quartier Latin. David had no money. He served in hospitals for children; he set up his school here—a school for delicate children—four years ago. Its record is very good. He has medical inspection by a doctor from Quimper each month. But, third, Weber's nephew was at this school till July. He went home to Paris, they went out to Fontainebleau, and—piff!' Dubois snapped his fingers. 'He is dead like that. There is no doubt it was diphtheria. Do you say fulminating diphtheria? Yes, that is it.'

'I'd like a medical report,' Reggie murmured.

'I have asked for it. However—the doctors are above suspicion, my friend. And now, fourth—the Bernals are found. They are at Dijon. They have been asked what has become of their dear little boy, and, they reply, he is at school in Brittany. At the school of M. David, Maison des Iles, Quimper.'

'Yes. He would be. I see.'

'Name of a name! I think you have always seen everything.'

'Oh, no. No. Don't see it now,' Reggie mumbled. 'However. We're workin' it out. You've done wonderfully.'

'Not so bad.' Dubois smiled. 'My genius is for action.'

'Yes. Splendid. Yes. Mine isn't. I just went and had a look at the museum.'

'My dear friend,' Dubois condescended. 'Why not? After all, the affair is now for me.'

'Thanks, yes. Interestin' museum. Found a good man on the local legends there. Told me the Woman of Sarn used to have children sacrificed to her. That'll be what Farquhar had in his nice head. Though M. David is so good to children.'

'Aha. It explains, and it does not explain,' Dubois said. 'In spite of you, M. David remains an enigma. Let poor old Dubois try. I have all these people under observation—the Webers, the Bernals—they cannot escape me now. And there are good men gone out to watch over M. David in his Maison des Iles. To-morrow we will go and talk to him, *hein?*'

'Pleasure,' Reggie murmured. 'You'd better go and have a bath now. You want it. And I want my dinner.'…

When they drove out to Sarn in the morning a second car followed them. In a blaze of hot sunshine they started, but they had not gone far before a mist of rain spread in from the sea, and by the time they reached the Maison des Iles they seemed to be in the clouds.

'An omen, *hein*?' Dubois made a grimace. 'At least it may be inconvenient—if he is alarmed; if he wishes to play tricks. We have no luck in this affair. But courage, my friend. Poor old Dubois, he is not without resource.'

Their car entered the walled enclosure of the Maison des Iles, the second stopped outside. When Dubois sent in his card to M. David, they were shown to a pleasant waiting-room, and had not long to wait.

David was dressed with a careless neatness. He was well groomed and perfectly at ease. His full red lips smiled; his dark eyes quizzed them. 'What a misery of a morning you have found, gentlemen. I apologise for my ocean. M. Dubois?' he made a bow.

'Of the Sûreté.' Dubois bowed. 'And M. Fortune, my distinguished *confrère* from England.'

David was enchanted. And what could he do for them?

'We make some little enquiries. First, you have here a boy— Tracy, the son of Mme Bernal. He is in good health?'

'Of the best.' David lifted his black brows. 'You will permit me to know why you ask.'

'Because another boy who was here is dead. The little nephew of M. Weber. You remember him?'

'Very well. He was a charming child. I regret infinitely. But you are without doubt aware that he fell ill on the holidays. It was a tragedy for his family. But the cause is not here. We have had no illness, no infection at all. I recommend you to Dr Lannion, at Quimper. He is our medical inspector.'

'Yes. So I've heard,' Reggie murmured. 'Have you had other cases of children who went home for the holidays and died?'

'It is an atrocious question!' David cried.

'But you are not quite sure of the answer?' said Dubois.

'If that is an insinuation, I protest,' David frowned. 'I have nothing to conceal, sir. It is impossible, that must be clear, I should know what has become of every child who has left my school. But, I tell you frankly, I do not recall any death but that of the little nephew of Weber, poor child.'

'Very well. Then you can have no objection that my assistant should examine your records,' said Dubois. He opened the window, and whistled and lifted a hand.

'Not the least in the world. I am at your orders.' David bowed. 'Permit me, I will go and get out the books,' and he went briskly.

'Now if we had luck he would try to run away,' Dubois rumbled. 'But do not expect it.'

'I didn't,' Reggie moaned.

And David did not run away. He came back and took them to his office, and there Dubois's man was set down to work at registers. 'You wish to assist?' David asked.

'No, thanks. No,' Reggie murmured. 'I'd like to look at your school.'

'An inspection!' Dubois smiled. 'I shall be delighted. I dare to hope for the approval of a man of science so eminent.'

They inspected dormitories and dining-room and kitchen, classrooms and workshop and laboratory. M. David was expansive and enthusiastic, yet modest. Either he was an accomplished actor, or he had a deep interest in school hygiene, and his arrangements were beyond suspicion. In the laboratory Reggie lingered. 'It is elementary,' David apologised. 'But what would you have? Some general science, that is all they can do, my little ones: botany for the most part; as you see, a trifle of chemistry to amuse them.'

'Yes. Quite sound. Yes. I'd like to see the other laboratory.'

'What?' David stared. 'There is only this.'

'Oh, no. Another one with a big microscope,' Reggie murmured. 'North side of the house.'

'Oh, la, la,' David laughed. 'You have paid some attention to my poor house. I am flattered. You mean my own den, where I play with marine biology still. Certainly you shall see it. But a little moment. I must get the key. You will understand. One must keep one's good microscope locked up. These imps, they play everywhere.' He hurried out.

'*Bigre!* How the devil did you know there was another laboratory?' said Dubois.

'Saw the microscope yesterday,' Reggie mumbled.

'Name of a dog! Is there anything you do not see?' Dubois complained. 'Well, if we have any luck he has run away this time.'

They waited some long while, and Dubois's face was flattened against the window to peer through the rain at the man on watch. But David had not run away, he came back at last, and apologised for some delay with a fool of a master, heaven give him patience! He took them briskly to the other laboratory, his den.

It was not pretentious. There were some shelves of bottles, and a bench with a sink, and a glass cupboard which stood open and empty. On the broad table in the window was a microscope of high power, and some odds and ends.

Reggie glanced at the bottles of chemicals and came to the microscope. 'I play at what I worked at. That is middle age,' David smiled. 'Here is something a little interesting.' He slipped a slide into the microscope and invited Reggie to look.

'Oh, yes. One of the diatoms. Pretty one,' Reggie murmured, and was shown some more. 'Thanks very much.' A glance set

Dubois in a hurry to go. David was affably disappointed. He had hoped they would lunch with him. The gentleman with the registers could hardly have finished his investigations. He desired an investigation the most complete.

'I will leave him here,' Dubois snapped, and they got away. 'Nothing, my friend?' Dubois muttered.

'No. That was the point,' Reggie said. '"When they got there the cupboard was bare."'

As their car passed the gate, a man signalled to them out of the rain. They stopped just beyond sight of the house, and he joined them. 'Bouvier has held someone,' he panted. 'A man with a sack.' They got out of the car and Dubois waved him on.

Through the blinding rain-clouds they came to the back of the house, and, on the way up to the cliffs, found Bouvier with his hand on the collar of a sullen, stupefied Breton. A sack lay on the ground at their feet.

'He says it is only rubbish,' Bouvier said, 'and he was taking it to throw into the sea, where they throw their waste. But I kept him.'

'Good. Let us see.' Dubois pulled the sack open. 'The devil, it is nothing but broken glass!'

Reggie grasped the hand that was going to turn it over. 'No, you mustn't do that,' he said sharply. 'Risky.'

'Why? What then? It is broken glass and bits of jelly.'

'Yes. As you say. Broken glass and bits of jelly. However.' Over Reggie's wet face came a slow benign smile. 'Just what we wanted. Contents of cupboard which was bare. I'll have to do some work on this. I'm going to the hospital. You'd better collect David—in the other car. Good-bye.'…

Twenty-four hours later, he came into a grim room of the *gendarmerie* at Quimper. There Dubois and David sat with a table between them, and neither man was a pleasant sight. David's florid colour was gone, he had become untidy, he sagged in his chair, unable to hide fatigue and pain. Dubois also was dishevelled, and his eyes had sunk and grown small, but the big face wore a look of hungry cruelty. He turned to Reggie. 'Aha. Here you are at last. And what do you tell M. David?'

'Well, we'll have a little demonstration.' Reggie set down a box on the table and took from it a microscope. 'Not such a fine instrument as yours, M. David, but it will do.' He adjusted a slide. 'You showed me some beautiful marine diatoms in your laboratory. Let me show you this. Also from your laboratory. From the sackful of stuff you tried to throw into the sea.'

David dragged himself up and looked, and stared at him, and dropped back in his chair.

'Oh, that's not all, no.' Reggie changed the slide. 'Try this one.'

Again, and more wearily, David looked. He sat down again. His full lips curled back to show his teeth in a grin. 'And then?' he said.

'What have you?' Dubois came to the microscope. 'Little chains of dots, eh?' Reggie put back the first slide. 'And rods with dots at the end.'

'Not bad for a layman, is it, M. David?' Reggie murmured. 'Streptococcus pyogenes, and the diphtheria bacillus. I've got some more.'

'Indeed?' David sneered.

'Oh, yes. But these will do. Pyogenes was found in poor little Weber: accountin' for the virulence of the diphtheria. Very efficient and scientific murder.'

'And the others?' Dubois thundered. 'The other children who went home for their holidays and died. Two, three, four, is it, David?'

David laughed. 'What does it matter? Yes, there are others who have gone to the isles of the blessed. But, also, there are many who have been made well and strong. I mock at you.'

'You have cause, Herod,' Dubois cried. 'You have grown rich on the murder of children. But it is we who laugh last. We deliver you to justice now.'

'Justice! Ah, yes, you believe that.' David laughed again. 'You are primitive, you are barbarous. Me, I am rational, I am a man of science. I sacrifice one life that a dozen may live well and happy. These who stand in the way of the rich, their deaths are paid for, and with the money I heal many. What, if life is valuable, is not this wisdom and justice? Let one die to save many—it is in all the religions, that. But no one believes his religions now. I—I believe in man. Well, I am before my time. But some day the world will be all Davids. With me it is finished.'

'Not yet, name of God!' Dubois growled.

'Oh yes, my friend. I am sick to death already. I have made sure of that.' He waved his hand at Reggie. 'You will not save me—no, not even you, my clever *confrère*. Good night! Go chase the Weber and the Bernal and the rest. David, he is gone into the infinite.' He fell back, a hand to his head.

Reggie went to him, and looked close and felt at him. 'Better take him away,' he pronounced. 'Hospital, under observation.'

Dubois gave the orders… 'Play-acting, my friend,' he shrugged.

'Oh, no. No. That kind of man. Logical and drastic. He's ill all right. There was the diplococcus of meningitis in his collection. Might be that.' And it was…

Ten days afterwards Dubois came to London with Reggie and gave Lomas a lecture on the case. 'I am desolated that I cannot offer you anyone to hang, my friend. But what can one do? The wretched Farquhar—I have no doubt he was murdered between David and Bernal. But there is no evidence. And, after all, David, he is dead, and we have Bernal for conspiracy to murder his stepson. That will do. It was, in fact, a case profoundly simple, like all the great crimes. To make a trade of arranging the deaths of unwanted children, that is very old. The distinction of David was to organise it scientifically, that is all. The child who was an heir to fortune, with a greedy one waiting to succeed, that was the child for him. Weber's nephew stood in the way of the beautiful Clotilde to Weber's fortune. Mrs Bernal's little boy was in the way of her second husband to the fortune of her father, the old millionaire. And the others! Well here is a beautiful modern school for delicate children, nine out of ten of them thrive marvellously. But, for the tenth, there is David's bacteriological laboratory, and a killing disease to take home with him when he goes for his holidays. Always at home, they die; always a disease of infection they could pick up anywhere. *Bigre!* It was a work of genius. And it would have gone on for ever but that this worthless Farquhar blunders into Brittany upon it, and begins to blackmail the beautiful Clotilde, the Bernal. Clotilde pays with her jewels, and has to pretend a robbery. Bernal will not pay—cannot, perhaps. Farquhar approaches the old grandfather, and Bernal calls in David, and the blackmailer is killed. The oldest story in the world. Rascals fall out, justice comes in. There is your angel of justice.' He bowed to Reggie. 'Dear master. You have shown me the way. Well, I am content to serve. Does he serve badly, poor old Dubois?'

'Oh, no. No. Brilliant,' Reggie murmured. 'Queer case, though. I believe David myself. He wanted to be a god. Make lives to his desire. And he did. Cured more than he killed. Far more. Then this fellow, who never wanted to be anything but a beast, blows in and beats him. Queer world. And David might have been a kindly, human fellow, if he hadn't had power. Dangerous stuff, science. Lots of us not fit for it.'

# THE PACKET-BOAT MURDER

## Josephine Bell

Doris Bell Collier (1897–1987) wrote her first crime novel, *Corpse at the Mill*, at the age of 32, after training to be a doctor. Although it failed to find a publisher, she had better luck with her next attempt, *Murder in Hospital*, which was published in 1937 under the name Josephine Bell. Hiding her identity behind a pen-name (Bell was her grandmother's maiden name, and Joseph her father's first name) was unavoidable, because the rules governing medical practitioners forbade any form of advertising. Before long, Bell established herself as a prolific writer of traditional mysteries, some of which made good use of her medical expertise; her first series character, David Wintringham, was a doctor.

After the Second World War, Bell was elected to membership of the Detection Club, and also joined the fledgling Crime Writers' Association, founded in 1953. Together with Michael Gilbert and Julian Symons she co-edited the CWA's first anthology of short stories, *Butcher's Dozen* (1956), and her own work in the short form was characteristically professional. She served as Chair of the CWA in 1959–60. This story first appeared in the *Evening Standard*, and was collected in *The Evening Standard Detective Book: Second Series* (1951).

'COME ACROSS, STEVE,' SAID DAVID WINTRINGHAM, POURING his guest a generous brandy, while Jill handed him a cup of coffee. 'Something is bothering you. Let's have it.'

'As long as it doesn't involve David in another case,' said Jill.

'It can't do that,' answered Superintendent Mitchell gloomily. 'The case is over. The chap was guillotined this morning.'

'He was *what*?' two voices cried incredulously.

The superintendent nodded.

'Extradition case. They put me on to it. You must have seen it in the papers. Frank Hayward. French girl he picked up on holiday.'

'I remember vaguely,' said David. 'Something to do with a cross-channel steamer. Tell it us straight, Steve.'

'O.K., I will. Frank Hayward and his wife did a little motor tour of northern France this August. At one of the hotels they stayed at the proprietor's daughter took a fancy to Frank and he to her.

'Mrs Hayward didn't suspect anything, but she played into their hands by falling in love in her turn—with the town where the hotel was. So they stayed there over a week, and visited it again for three days before setting off for their return to England.

'These last days must have made Frank aware that he had taken on more than he could manage. He was careful, though. He never wrote the girl a line, and she only got his address through her father, who had kept the letter Hayward wrote him, asking for a room for the second visit. He had written this letter on notepaper headed with his English address.

'The next thing we know for certain is what happened at Dieppe during the embarkation of passengers for Newhaven.

'Hayward drove his car to the quayside, saw Mrs Hayward on board, where he had booked a cabin for her, as she was a bad sailor, and then walked along the quay to watch the car going into the hold. I forgot to tell you they were going by the night boat.'

David nodded.

'They have old-fashioned steam cranes on the quay at Dieppe: very picturesque at night with the fires and the wisps of smoke floating back across the road lamps. Well, as Hayward watched the grappling-irons being put on his car he was joined by the girl. She was seen talking to him. She must have told him she was coming with him, could not live without him, something of that sort. The French are highly emotional, you know.'

'They can take love very seriously,' said David.

'I wouldn't know,' said Mitchell with a disapproving glance. 'The next thing we have for certain is that Hayward argued with the girl at the foot of the gangway for some time, according to the sailor in charge of it, and then he went on board. He gave up his ticket at the purser's office, got a landing ticket, and stayed in the corridor near the office for a considerable time.

'The girl must have come on board, and he must have intercepted her before she could see the purser. A little while after this she left him to go to the ladies' room, but she joined him again afterwards.

'They went on to the upper deck and through the door at the forward end of it on the side overlooking the harbour.

'There was a drizzle of rain that night. It must have been both misty and dark out there. Aft of the door the rain-screens of canvas had been let down over the rails, cutting off any view of

the harbour. There is always a lot of noise on the quayside near a
boat about to leave. I don't suppose anyone heard them out there.
No passengers took seats on deck that night, so probably no one
came near them at all.

'At some point in their talk Hayward must have attacked the
girl and she must have slumped across the rails of the foredeck. He
must then have pitched her overboard into the harbour.

'Directly afterwards he went back through the door to the other
part of the deck, making his way down to his wife's cabin.

'On the way to the cabin he took off his mackintosh, which
he had worn up till then, folded it inwards and carried it into the
cabin over his arm.'

'Why did he do that?'

'Because he had discovered when he got to the lighted part of
the deck that there were fresh white-paint stains on it. The rails of
the foredeck were covered with fresh paint. If there was a notice
they can't have seen it, but in any case no one was expected to go
out there in such weather.'

'Then the girl's clothes must have had paint on, too,' said Jill.

'They did. He must have known that, and he hoped to conceal
his mackintosh. But he had been away from that cabin too long;
his wife was annoyed with him, and in the close air, of course, she
detected the smell of paint at once.

'She had a look at the stains after the ship started. Hayward told
her he got them on the quay when he was watching the car go on
board. He could not stop her taking the mac to a cleaner when they
got home, which clinched that bit of evidence.'

'Now for the discovery,' said David.

'The girl's body was picked up next morning early, floating in
the harbour, only a few hours after her death. The post-mortem

showed her lungs to be full of water, and it also showed her neck was broken.'

'Did she hit anything on the way down the ship's side or in the water?'

'There was no wound of any kind on her face or head.'

'Mr Hayward must have knocked her unconscious and overdid it,' said Jill. 'He would want to stop any chance of her resisting being pushed overboard, screaming or holding on to the rail.'

'I doubt if anyone would have heard her. But, yes, the paint stains on the front of her costume suggested that she had slithered down the rail. There was no paint on her hands, though.'

'How was Hayward incriminated?' asked David.

'She had a handbag on a strap over one shoulder and hanging under the other arm. It had not come away from the body. In it were found a slip of paper with Hayward's name and English address still visible, two traveller's cheques, no currency either French or English, no ticket for the journey.'

'Queer she had no ready money.'

'It might have been in coins in her pocket and fallen out. She had the traveller's cheques.'

'But no ticket. Apart from the paint, which is not conclusive, how do we know she was really on board? Or if on board, that she did not commit suicide in the harbour?'

'Because in the right-hand pocket of her jacket she had a landing ticket.'

'Oh, but,' said David, 'you said she never got to the purser's office!'

'She got to the ladies'-room,' said Jill. 'That's why you knew she must have gone there, isn't it? Because the stewardess takes your boat ticket and gives you a landing ticket, a yellow one—the others are brown or white.'

'Quite right,' said Mitchell approvingly. 'And Hayward didn't know that, or he would have taken more trouble. The fact that she had no railway ticket on from Newhaven suggests she intended to go with Hayward in the car or take a ticket when she knew exactly where he was going.

'She didn't trust him, obviously. But her having a landing ticket and traveller's cheques point against suicide very strongly. Everyone was agreed on that. Besides, a girl with a broken neck can't very well jump off a ship, can she?

'I was in charge of this end of it, and we got the mackintosh business straight, so there was nothing for it but to extradite Hayward when the French asked for it.

'There was a lot of excitement at the trial. The prosecution brought in a maid from the hotel who had been a confidante of the girl's—the mother was dead—and not a very sensible adviser. She saw it all as a first-class romance and at the same time, with French hard-headedness, as a source of future profitable blackmail. For all that the judge was obviously on her side. They found him guilty, naturally, and I hardly blame them. Unpleasant type. It was a bit hard on him having the guillotine, though. Nasty old-fashioned method, the knife.'

'Quite,' said David. 'It was really very bad luck, since it was not he, after all, who killed the girl.'

'David!' cried Jill. 'What *do* you mean?'

'I was afraid of this,' said Mitchell, 'when I started talking.'

'Like the cranes at Dieppe and the execution method,' said David, 'the inquest must have been a bit old-fashioned, too, and in more than one sense of the word. Anyone who has their lungs full of water and a broken neck as well must have got them in that order, and no other.'

'Oh!' breathed Jill.

'Who picked her up out of the water, and finished her off, and why?' David asked sternly.

'The assistant who came over there with me,' said Mitchell with a sigh, 'was a man who had been in the Commando raid on Dieppe. He was left behind severely wounded on that occasion, and for eight months he was looked after by the Maquis.

'He was hidden in the house of a longshoreman of about his own age who had been invalided out of the French Army for TB at the start of the war and had kept out of the German conscripted labour force for the same reason.

'My assistant and I both thought the way you did about the girl's death, and as he speaks the lingo and wanted to look up his old friends anyhow, I gave him a free hand. I don't know if it was this actual man or another, but my chap told me the one who did it was desperately poor, as most of them are except the racketeers; his family of young children was practically starving.

'He was in his boat in the harbour that night; they go scavenging for anything saleable to exchange for food. He saw the girl thrown over. He picked her up and found she was not breathing, though her heart was still going.

'She had money; four thousand francs and a couple of English pounds. He took it. Then she showed signs of coming round, so he thought it would be kinder to finish her off quickly than to put her back in the water to go on drowning.'

'Your assistant refused to name this man?'

'Absolutely. They had saved his life, and, besides, he felt a bit responsible. You see, he spent some of his eight months after he recovered teaching them Commando ways of killing.

'If the French doctor had been a bit more up to date at the

inquest he would have recognised the method used in breaking the girl's neck. But he didn't. It worries me, though, when I think of Hayward's end, and that the girl might have been saved.'

'Don't let it,' said Jill soothingly. 'Hayward meant to kill her, so he *was* a murderer, by intention.'

'She was asking for it, too,' said David. 'The French often take love too seriously.'

# VILLA ALMIRANTE

## *Michael Gilbert*

Michael Gilbert (1912–2006) was a busy man. Not only was he a full-time solicitor who achieved considerable distinction in the profession, rising to become a senior partner in a leading firm of Lincoln's Inn lawyers, he was also one of the finest British crime writers of his generation. Throughout his career, he demonstrated an admirable commitment to providing his readers with a varied diet; as well as whodunits following the classic template, short stories and novels about police officers, lawyers, adventurers and spies poured from his pen.

His settings were as diverse as his plot material. *Death in Captivity* (1952) is an ingenious 'impossible crime' mystery with a superbly realised and highly original setting in an Italian POW camp. Gilbert's personal experience of life as a prisoner of war in Italy gave the story an extra dimension of authenticity, and it was successfully filmed by Don Chaffey as *Danger Within*. The main background in *Be Shot for Sixpence* (1956) is the area around the Austro-Hungarian border, *After the Fine Weather* (1963) is set in the Austrian Tyrol, and *The Etruscan Net* (1969) in Italy. This little-known short story, first published in *Argosy* in 1959, is a reminder of his fascination with the country which played such a significant part in his life.

L UCIFERO, LIEUTENANT OF CARABINIERI IN CHARGE OF POLICE
work in the district of Lerici, paused for a moment at the head
of the flight of steps which spiralled down to the Villa Almirante.

Where he stood, his heels were at chimney top level. All the
villas along the coast road were like that, set each on its own ledge
in the steep, dusty hillside; the garden, a narrow sleeve of olive and
orange tree and arbutus, resting one end on the road and the other
three hundred feet below where the wine-dark sea complained and
hissed over the rocks.

Dusk had fallen. The only sign of life was a chink of light from
the kitchen quarters, a separate building to the left of the villa,
where the Italian cook-housekeeper, Signora—Signora—Lucifero
frowned. It was his boast that he knew all his own people by name.

Signora Telli. Of course. The Signora Telli was a war widow who
ran the house for its English owner, helped by her son, the burly
Umberto, and a local girl called—well, really, there were so many
girls, one could not remember all of them—probably called Maria.

A loud gust of laughter sounded from the terrace on the seaward
side of the villa. The house-party was in good form. Interesting
people, thought Lucifero, one of whose tasks—one of whose
pleasures—it was to get to know the English visitors who came,
year by year in spring and autumn, to escape their own fog and mist
and drizzle and bask in the warm sunshine of the Ligurian coast.

Lucifero knew those fogs and mists only too well. He had spent
an eternity of two years in London in the wine shipper's office of

his uncle; two years of cold and wet and flat beer and rock-like food fried into hard indigestible lumps; two miserable years, as far as anyone could be miserable who was twenty and healthy—and handsome.

The lieutenant passed a leather-gloved finger lightly across the top of his mouth, and smiled to himself in the gathering dark-ness. Perhaps it had not been so bad, after all. There had been consolations.

There had been Anna. There had been Geraldine, a graduate of Oxford University, but not too proud to be seen about with a young wine shipper's clerk. And his exile had paid one quite unforeseen dividend.

When Italy entered the war—most ill-advisedly Lucifero had thought even at the time—against the Allies, his quick and fluent grasp of English had stood as a barrier between him and the more unpleasant forms of national service. Rapid qualification as an interpreter had been followed by posts in the officer prisoner-of-war camps at Chieti, at Sulmona, and finally at Garvi, where he had proved so sympathetic to his charges that he had narrowly escaped being carried with them into Germany at the time of the Armistice.

To have joined the exclusive Carabinieri, and to have reached the rank of lieutenant in the short time since the war, was itself no mean achievement. But modesty was not among Lucifero's failings. He knew that it had been well earned. There had been no element of favour in his promotion. Hard work, attention to detail, and a facility for psychology had made him a successful policeman. The psychology, in particular, of women.

Few men, thought Lucifero, understood women as he did.

There was a second burst of laughter from the terrace on the seaward side of the villa. At that hour of the evening the party would be sitting out over their drinks as they waited for dinner to be served. Four of them had arrived ten days before. There was Lord Keaough, their host, the owner of the villa in which he spent two months of every year, an austere and craggy nobleman, and precisely Lucifero's idea of what an English peer should be, even to his baffling name. With him had come Mr Colin Sampson, the publisher; Mr Ralph Marley, the poet; and Miss Natalie Merrow.

His hand actually on the brass knocker, Lucifero paused, as a connoisseur will pause in front of a fine but puzzling painting; a gourmet before an intriguing wine. He had observed Miss Natalie for three seasons now. He had been certain, at first, that she was Lord Keaough's mistress. But that idea had died. She was of the Left Bank; cosmopolitan, bohemian. Knowledgeable about love, yes. But as yet disinterested in it.

Lucifero visualised her as he had seen her three evenings before for a few seconds in the Albergo Maritime, her skin browned by the sun to a colour which would have looked vulgar in a blonde but was perfect under her dark, carefully and carelessly arranged mop of black hair. Lucifero corrected himself. Not black. Peasant women had black hair. This was the colour of very old, dark chestnut. Altogether an interesting specimen to a psychologist; a little tightly wrapped up in herself at present. One day she would fall apart deliciously in some lucky man's hands.

It had been a curious scene at the albergo. The four of them at their table with their drinks. At one side Lord Keaough, immobile, cut from a single piece of well-tanned leather. At the other the girl, between the publisher—with his chubby face and horn-rimmed glasses, boyish and bookish—and the poet, dark-haired, bright-eyed, Byronic, and indubitably drunk.

Lucifero had thought for a moment that they were going to do what English people of their class never did in public: that they were going to quarrel. Words had floated from Ralph Marley, high-pitched, emphatic, tumbling over themselves in bitter, eager spite. And Colin Sampson, normally, Lucifero surmised, a man of peace, had said something so sharp that even Lord Keaough had opened his sleepy eyes.

Lucifero had been sitting six tables away, unable to distinguish a word that was spoken but acutely aware of what was happening. He had half expected to see a glass emptied in someone's face. In his native Calabria knives would have been out long since.

Then Ralph Marley had climbed to his feet, turned his back on the party, and walked away. The others had watched him in silence.

The poet, pushing his way between the tables, had passed within a few feet of Lucifero, and Lucifero had observed his face, an odd mixture of petulance and passion. Now, standing with one hand actually on the brass dolphin knocker of the villa, he tried to picture it. He tried to bring it back into his mind, past the very different picture of Ralph Marley that was presently occupying his thoughts.

It was Umberto who answered the knock. He was only eighteen, but as heavy and as chunky as marble from the quarries of Carrara.

'Tenente?'

'Good evening, Umberto. You are well? And your mother, I hope.'

'Very well indeed.' He seemed almost to be standing guard in the hallway. 'Do you wish me to tell—the Lordship—that you are here?'

Lucifero smiled to himself at this evasion. He was aware, none more so, of the difficulties which attended the pronunciation of Lord Keaough's name in any language, but above all in the Italian tongue which tries so conscientiously to separate every vowel from its neighbour.

'Be good enough,' he said, 'to inform Lord Kuff that I would appreciate a word with him, alone, on a matter of importance.'

'They are on the terrace.' Umberto considered. 'The doors to the salon are open. There is no privacy there. Perhaps the dining-room?'

'The dining-room should do well. But warn your mother that her excellent meal may have to wait a little. What we have to discuss will not be done within five minutes.'

Lucifero was standing in front of the empty fireplace in the dining-room when the door opened and Lord Keaough came in.

'Good evening, Tenente. Lucifero, is it not? I seem to remember that you speak excellent English, so I shall not have to inflict my terrible Italian on you. Do sit down.'

'Your Lordship speaks excellent Italian,' said Lucifero, but he made no attempt to move back into his native tongue. Nor did he sit. 'What I have to tell you will not take a great deal of time. I have to start with a question. How long is it since anyone here has seen Signor Ralph Marley?'

He wished that the lighting was better. The single economical central bulb hid more of Lord Keaough's face than it revealed.

'Ralph? Let me think. To-day is Friday. It was some time on Wednesday afternoon when he walked out on us.'

'Walked *out*? You imply—?'

'He stood not upon the order of his going. He said no good-byes. He took no luggage. He went.'

'Yes,' said Lucifero. Curious how much a single word could imply. To walk was one thing. To walk out was another. He must remember the difference. 'Can you tell me any more?'

'All that I know, and that's precious little. But perhaps you will tell me something first. Has he got into trouble?'

'Why do you ask?'

'In most countries,' said Lord Keaough, 'police mean trouble.'

Lucifero showed white teeth under a hairline of black moustache. 'Signor Marley is in no trouble now,' he said. 'He is dead.'

Lord Keaough leaned forward, bending from the waist in a gentle, courteous gesture of interrogation. 'Dead?' he said.

Lucifero stared at him, opened his mouth to speak, and closed it again in resignation. 'Yes. His body was taken from the sea by a fisherman this morning, a half-mile out from Portovenere.'

Lord Keaough stood, looking out through the window, as if he could see the hidden lines of the bay and estimate the currents as they set between the towering headlands.

'If,' agreed Lucifero, reading his thoughts, 'he had entered the sea just here, in twenty-four or thirty-six hours he would have been carried to Portovenere.'

'Yes,' said Lord Keaough. 'I'm afraid that's it. Shall I tell the others, or would you prefer to tell them yourself?'

Lucifero had given thought to this. Two factors influenced him. The first, that the lights in the salon would probably be better; the second that the other two, younger members of the party would hardly have the same unnatural control over their feelings as was being exhibited by this impossible aristocrat.

'Let us go to the salon,' he said. 'Perhaps you will permit *me* to tell your guests the news.'

'Of course, of course.'

Lord Keaough led the way down the short passage and into a large bright, pleasant room.

Natalie Merrow was sitting, upright, on one end of the sofa, an unopened book beside her, and Colin Sampson was standing behind her, talking to her or at her. He stopped in mid sentence when the door opened.

'This is Lieutenant Lucifero, of the Police,' said Lord Keaough. 'He has some bad news for us.'

'Ralph!' said Natalie.

'What's happened to him?' said Colin.

If it was acting—and the possibility had always to be borne in mind—it was very fine acting. Not an amateur or bungled effort. Precisely the right intonation, exactly the correct proportions of realisation, shock, and pity.

'I have to tell you,' he said. 'I have already told his Lordship, the body was recovered from the sea, near Portovenere, early this morning. By a fishing boat returning to harbour.'

'Yes,' said Colin. It was as if he was confirming something which had been hinted at before. A possibility had turned into a probability. That was all.

'You will, I hope, excuse the observation,' said Lucifero. 'But, in some way, this news seems not to surprise you greatly.'

The other two looked at Lord Keaough, who said, 'Ralph was a poet, and a great admirer of Lord Byron.'

'I see,' said Lucifero. 'He had the same idea? To swim across the gulf?'

'Yes. We attempted to dissuade him, of course.'

'Why?'

'Ralph was neither as good a poet as Byron,' said Colin, 'nor as good a swimmer.' Then he blushed, as if conscious that he had been guilty of some impropriety.

Lucifero said, 'The indications are that Mr Marley started his ill-fated swim in the late afternoon of Wednesday. I say late afternoon because he would hardly contemplate such a feat in the dark. This coincides also with what his Lordship has told me. That you last saw Mr Marley on Wednesday afternoon.'

They looked at him warily.

'Yes?' said Lord Keaough.

'If that is so, why was his absence not reported before?'

'Because,' said Lord Keaough, 'we did not know that he had been drowned.'

'But you realised that he was missing.'

'If we brought in the police every time Ralph walked out,' said Mr Sampson, an edge once more perceptible in his voice, 'we should keep you gentlemen pretty busy.'

'Mr Marley,' explained Lord Keaough, 'was a poet.'

'Temperamental?'

'You could call it that,' said Mr Sampson.

'Really, Colin,' said Natalie. 'Ralph is hardly twenty-four hours dead. I think we might refrain from speaking ill of him. Just until he is buried, perhaps?'

Lucifero looked at them curiously. There was something that he did not understand. Something to be docketed for future reference.

'I'm afraid,' said Lord Keaough, 'that Mr Marley had cried "wolf" too often. Last year he walked out on us in Rome, after a little difference of opinion, and reappeared in Venice. In Venice early one morning, for no reason at all, he decided to go to Scotland—'

'He said, afterwards, that he preferred grouse to pigeons,' observed Natalie.

'And on that occasion, too, he took no luggage. Not even a toothbrush. It was—a sort of—affectation.'

'A poet must be free,' recited Mr Sampson. 'Untrammelled by any bonds. Unrestrained by any conventions.'

'And on this occasion, you assumed that he had walked out on you—' Lucifero managed this newly-acquired idiom quite smoothly— 'on account of—what? Some recent difference of opinion?'

'We had a sort of quarrel on Tuesday evening,' said Lord Keaough. 'It started at dinner, and went on over our drinks at the Albergo Maritime. As no doubt you observed, since you were seated a few tables away.'

'Yes,' said Lucifero. 'I did, I think, observe something.' But Lord Keaough, he could have sworn, had sat with his back to him throughout the incident. 'If you feel at liberty to tell me what it was about—?'

'It's not a secret,' said Mr Sampson. 'My firm, Blakelock & Sampson, that is, had decided that we could not publish his latest book of verse. We had lost money heavily on the other three. Besides, we are not really publishers of poetry—'

'Messrs. Blakelock and Sampson,' said Natalie, 'make all their real money out of detective stories.'

Mr Sampson flushed again. Really, thought Lucifero, for a man in his middle thirties he was extraordinarily susceptible. And was the girl teasing him because she liked him or because she hated him? Time would no doubt give him the answer.

'There was the usual talk,' said Mr Sampson. 'That all publishers are philistines who batten on the genius of the artist and squeeze him to death for their own profit.'

'His eminent prototype, Lord Byron, also made many uncomplimentary references to publishers,' observed Lucifero. 'Could any of you tell me more precisely when you last observed Mr Marley on Wednesday?'

'We pretty well live our own lives here,' said Lord Keaough. 'Get up when we like. Do what we like. We usually meet in the evening for a drink, and have dinner together. On Wednesday, actually, we all four of us had luncheon together. Ralph seemed to have got over his sulks, though he didn't eat much. In the afternoon I retired to my room for my siesta.'

'I painted,' said Natalie.

'I went for a walk, towards Tolaro,' said Mr Sampson.

'We three met for our drink—at about six?' The others agreed. 'At about six. There was no sign of Ralph then or later.'

'You painted, where?' asked Lucifero.

'On the hillside, overlooking Carrara. An hour's walk there. Three-quarters of an hour back, downhill. I was here by six.'

'And you awoke from your siesta—?'

'I call it a siesta,' said Lord Keaough. 'I don't really sleep. I lie on my bed, and read a little, and then do some writing. I came down at half past five.'

'And you heard and saw nothing?'

'I heard Signora Telli calling out once to Maria in the garden. Maria was, I think, putting out the laundry. Or more likely, at that hour, getting it in.'

'I must question the servants afterwards,' agreed Lucifero.

'Is it important?' said Lord Keaough.

Lucifero's head came round slowly. 'Important?' he said.

'I mean, we are agreed what happened. The late afternoon was Ralph's time for bathing. He had often told us that he would try this particular swim. If it was an accident—'

'But it was *not* an accident,' said Lucifero. 'Mr Marley was taken from the sea fully dressed. And there is no seawater in his lungs. His head was crushed. He was dead before he entered the sea.'

Three faces turned towards him. Three pairs of eyes centred on his. The hard lines which fenced Lord Keaough's nose and mouth seemed a little more marked, but he remained implacably impassive. There was a puzzled frown behind Natalie's eyes, and her lips were parted, showing her small white teeth. Mr Sampson was blushing again.

The servants told him little about the dead man, but quite a lot about their patron and his guests; and, without realising it, a good deal about themselves, too.

'Signor Marley was a man of moods, Tenente,' said Signora Telli. 'A great poet, so we were told. But for me, I judge a man by the way he lives not by what he writes. And it is my opinion, and I say it with the proper reserve due when a man has been called unexpectedly to his Maker, that that young man did not live well. He had not a good name. We hear about such things more than you would imagine. Two years ago, there was an Austrian girl who threatened to kill herself—you heard?'

Lucifero had heard. But he was not greatly interested in what had happened two years before. 'On the Wednesday afternoon,' he said, 'did you yourself see Mr Marley?'

'Not in the afternoon at all. I was busy in my kitchen. Umberto was at the market. Maria might have seen him. She was in the garden part of the time, and may have seen him if he went to bathe.'

Maria was summoned. She was seventeen, a dark girl with a pert, peasant face and a budding beauty. She was also, clearly, very nervous. Lucifero thought it better to question her in Signora Telli's presence.

She had been in the garden on three—or perhaps four—occasions. First to collect some of the firewood which Umberto had chopped and left. Then to pick radishes and lettuce for the evening meal. Twice to bring in washing. She had *not* seen Signor Marley.

She was positive she had not seen him. If she had seen him, she would have said so. What reason would there be to lie? She had *not* seen him.

'Understood,' said Lucifero dryly. 'Are you affianced to Umberto?'

Both women seemed to be struck dumb by this question. Signora Telli said at last, 'There is nothing finally arranged. It is an understanding. But Umberto is only just eighteen.'

'He is a good boy,' said Lucifero. 'And old for his age. I was affianced before I was eighteen.'

'He is the best of sons,' agreed the Signora. 'And Maria will be a good wife to him—when the time is proper.' She smiled suddenly at the girl, who smiled back. 'You wish to question Umberto?'

'But if he was at the market,' said Lucifero, 'what could he tell me?'

Signora Telli dismissed Maria with a jerk of her head. When the door had closed behind her, she said, 'I have something to tell *you*. It concerns his Lordship.'

'Yes,' said Lucifero.

'What I have to say has, you must understand, nothing to do with the drowning of Signor Marley.'

'Of that I must be the judge.'

'It is something which I have long felt should be said—to someone in authority. He is a kind patron, generous and easy to work for.' She seemed suddenly unsure of herself. 'But—'

'But?'

'I think he is a spy.'

Lucifero prided himself that he was difficult to surprise, but for a moment he felt his mouth falling open. Then he recovered himself.

'It does not seem very likely,' he observed mildly. 'We are not at war.'

'If he is not a spy, why does he sit for hours and hours on the terrace, with a great pair of glasses—' she demonstrated with her hands—'staring out at the ships?'

'Perhaps it is the birds he watches. Not the ships.'

She looked at him doubtfully, to see if he was laughing at her. He pinched her arm and said, 'Do not worry. If he is a spy, you have discharged your duty by telling me of your suspicions.'

Nevertheless, before he left for the night he walked back to the house to have a further word with Lord Keaough.

'There is much to do,' he said, 'but it cannot be done until morning. We shall have to examine the private beach at the foot of your garden, and the rocks about it. And there is a fuller autopsy to be made.'

'I've been thinking,' said Lord Keaough. 'What seems most probable is that Ralph went down for his swim, tried the short cut to the beach down through the rocks—it is dangerous, but he had done it before—and slipped, hitting his head as he went into the sea. There is only one difficulty. If that was so, he would have dropped his bathing costume, and we should have found it. Unless it fell and floated out to sea with him.'

Lucifero said, 'When found, Signor Marley was wearing an open shirt and linen trousers. Under the trousers, he was wearing bathing shorts.'

'I see,' said Lord Keaough. 'Then my theory may well be correct.'

'Very likely. Meanwhile, I must ask you and your friends to be patient.'

'We are none of us planning to leave,' said Lord Keaough. 'We are at your disposal. I have no doubt you will soon discover the truth.'

'Speriamo,' said Lucifero, and took his leave.

In police work things did not often happen quickly. It was time and hard work that solved most problems. Some facts, a very few facts, emerged. A painstaking, inch-by-inch search of the grassy plateau which crowned the knoll—a hidden place, open only towards the sea, and much used by the inhabitants of the villa for sunbathing—brought to light two hairpins, the lid of a tin of face-cream, a number of old matchsticks, and a 1930 five-lire piece. There were two routes down to the beach: the one cut from the smooth rock, serpentine but safe; the alternative descent over the sheer rocks, a mountaineer's route. Nothing of significance was discovered on either. Nor was this strange.

'If he went to the beach by the path,' said Lucifero to Lord Keaough, 'he would leave no mark. If he fell from here, he would strike one of those rocks. It has been washed too well by the sea to leave clues for us.'

'Has the autopsy been helpful? Or perhaps you are not allowed to tell us?'

'Certainly I can tell you. It shows two things. That Mr Marley entered the sea with little in his stomach—'

'Which agrees with late afternoon.'

'Yes. And that his head was broken by impact on the rocks. A considerable impact, one would say. There are tiny fragments of rock splinter still embedded in the bone.'

'All of which—' began Lord Keaough.

'All of which,' agreed Lucifero, 'points to your solution being the right one.'

That had been on the Saturday. By Wednesday, routine and order and a surface calm had returned to the Villa Almirante. Lucifero had kept his distance. He spent long hours on the hillside above and to one side of the villa with an excellent pair of glasses. He could see the terrace where Lord Keaough sat, similarly equipped. He studied Lord Keaough. Lord Keaough studied—what? He could see most of the steeply-sloped garden, although the knoll and the beach were both hidden, one by trees, the other by the steep, overhanging bluff. They were days of intense heat. The sun emerged coyly from its veil of early morning mist, swung through a cloudless sky, and retired at last in sulky, crimson splendour behind the hills of the Cinque Terre. Lucifero was content to wait. Given such people, in just such a situation, it was inevitable that something would happen. It *must* happen. If it did not he would make it happen.

Three times already he had sent for Maria, and each time his questions had been shrewder and Maria's protest more voluble. On the final occasion, the young Umberto had escorted her to the police station, and had waited in the outer room, glowering and unapproachable...

On the late afternoon of that Wednesday, Lucifero, from his vantage point, watched Colin and Natalie walk down the garden together. They disappeared into the trees. Curse the trees, thought Lucifero. They hid too much. No trees, no problems.

The minutes ticked by. The heat-waves danced and shimmered off the rocks. Something moved at the top of the garden slope, a flash of white. Lucifero steadied his binoculars in his sweating hands. It was Umberto, moving with quiet but purposeful delibera-tion, keeping behind the shelter of the olive trees, making for the knoll. A peeping Tom? Lucifero thought it possible, but unlikely. Umberto's interest in girls, and in Maria in particular, was much too simple and much too direct for him to have to stimulate his passion by spying on others.

Lucifero contained his soul in patience. A flash of colour among the trees. Natalie appeared, walking quickly for such a hot afternoon. It was too far away to read expressions, but Lucifero deduced from her walk that she was angry.

He shut up his glasses, jumped to his feet, and ran down the hill.

Outside the villa, Natalie passed him. Her face was flushed, but that might have been exercise. She said, 'Good afternoon, Lieutenant,' but made no attempt to stop or talk. She had recovered whatever poise she might have lost.

Lucifero saluted gravely, then ran quickly down the steps, and entered the Villa Almirante without knocking.

Lord Keaough was sitting on the balcony in a wicker chair, his glasses to his eyes. He said without looking up, 'You've come in at the right moment, Tenente. Is that chance, or have you been watching, too?'

'I have been watching, too,' said Lucifero.

It had, of course, occurred to him that if the truth was apparent to him, it might well be apparent also to as shrewd an observer as Lord Keaough.

'I would suggest,' Lucifero said, 'that you walk down by the main path, taking your time; I will go by the side path. It is possible, by the exercise of agility, to work across from it to the path above the bathing beach. Try to keep in sight, and do not interfere until I give the signal. Whatever happens.'

He paused and added again, 'Whatever happens.' Lord Keaough nodded, and walked down the steps into the garden.

Colin Sampson lay flat on his back, his eyes tightly shut. The strong sun beat down through the trees, and penetrated his screwed-up eyelids. If I was twenty years younger, he thought, I should be crying. This seemed such an odd thought that he sat up abruptly. He had just asked Natalie to marry him. And she had refused. Being totally inexperienced, he had misread this refusal as coyness and had tried to grab hold of her. And he had had his face smacked.

And now he was quite ready to argue himself back into a mood of self-respect. Natalie, he had come to the conclusion, had been more upset by Ralph's death than any of them had suspected. This was a two-edged thought. It meant that she had been fond of Ralph. No. Fond was the wrong word. It meant that she had been emotionally involved with him. But it meant also that if he approached her again, when she was more herself...

At this point, he found himself staring into the anger-crazed face of Umberto; a face which was, unnervingly, only a few inches above the ground. Umberto had been snaking forward towards Mr Sampson on his elbows and knees. Now, having been discovered, he scrambled to his feet, and it could be seen that he was holding in the hand a wicked-looking malacca stick, an inch thick; a sort of Penang Lawyer which some guest had left behind him.

Mr Sampson got up awkwardly, and was just in time to avoid the first blow which came hissing down and grazed his left arm.

'Stop,' he said. 'Stop it, I say. There is some mistake.'

The next blow cut him about the shoulders with a cracking force which threatened his collar-bone. He flung an arm round Umberto in a frenzied grapple. But the thirty-five-year-old publisher was no match for the eighteen-year-old peasant boy. Umberto tore himself away with contemptuous ease and raised the stick again. Mr Sampson abandoned any shreds of dignity and began to shout.

A shot exploded out of the bushes below the knoll. Lucifero, sweating with haste and exertion, had drawn his police gun from his holster and fired—into the air.

For an instant all movement ceased. Then Umberto twisted about, and ran for the path which led up to the house. He found Lord Keaough blocking it. He hesitated before that frail but indomitable figure, and was lost. Lucifero had reached level ground, and was walking towards him.

'That will be enough,' he said. 'More than enough.' He had returned his gun to its holster. He knew that he would have no cause to use it. The situation was under control.

'Murdering swine,' said Mr Sampson.

'Enough,' said Lucifero again. 'We will go up to the house. All of us.'

When they reached the small paved courtyard which lay between the villa and the servant's annexe, Lucifero called a halt. He said to Mr Sampson, 'Be kind enough to telephone the Carabinieri post and ask for Sergeant Malagodi.'

And to Umberto, 'I shall charge you, formally, with the murder of your English guest, Mr Ralph Marley. For the moment, you may go into the kitchen. If you try to leave it without my permission, you do so at your own peril.'

He said this in a high clear voice, in which Lord Keaough thought he detected an undercurrent of distinct satisfaction.

Half an hour later Lucifero, Lord Keaough, Mr Sampson, and Natalie were seated in the salon, discussing the unexpected events of the morning. Sergeant Malagodi, a dour Sicilian, had arrived, and was in the kitchen, sitting over Umberto, who had so far said nothing at all.

'I've been trying to work things out,' said Mr Sampson. 'Umberto is terrifically jealous. Almost unhinged. If he imagined that Ralph had been—paying attentions—to Maria, that would account for his attacking him, and toppling him into the sea.'

'And his attack on you?'

'Well—I suppose—he might have had the same idea about me.' He was aware that Natalie's eyes were on him.

'If I may be forgiven the observation,' said Lucifero. 'In Mr Marley's case, there might be grounds for such suspicion. In yours, they would be—well—far fetched. So much so, that unless someone had sowed the seed in his mind…' He paused.

Lord Keaough gave a dry chuckle. 'He means you're not a ladies' man, Colin,' he said. 'Not yet.'

Natalie said sharply, 'And I'm glad he's not. As the only lady present, I can assure you there is no more stomach-turning description—'

She was interrupted by a loud scream.

The three English jumped to their feet. Lucifero sat still, swinging one jackbooted leg over the other.

A second scream. Loud, shrill protests. The clatter of feet, and Maria was there, a Maria with wild, hurt face and dishevelled clothes. A Maria beyond all fear and past all shame.

'Arrest me,' she cried. 'Arrest me, and let Umberto go. I am a wicked girl. Take me away. Put me in your prison cell.'

Signora Telli appeared behind her, ducked nervously to the company, and put a hand on Maria's arm. Maria shook it off.

'I will confess all,' she said.

'Excellent,' said Lucifero. 'No doubt a confession will make much plain.'

His cool voice had its effect. Maria stopped trembling. She said rapidly but clearly, 'Signor Marley professed himself much attracted to me. I was in the garden when he came down to bathe. We went together to the knoll. He—I—I cannot tell you, but we struggled. As I broke away from him he stepped back, and fell. It was a long time before I even dared to look. When I did so, he was most evidently dead. The sea was already carrying him away.'

'Silly girl,' said Lucifero. 'It has, of course, been plain all along that that is what happened. It only needed that you should speak out and speak the truth. Why, instead, did you tell lies to Umberto about poor Signor Sampson here?'

'It was all those questions you asked me, Tenente. Umberto was suspicious. I had to tell him something. So I told him lies— about Signor Sampson, to lead him away from the truth. I was a bad girl.'

'You are a liar,' said Lucifero. 'Like most girls of your age. But you are not a murderess. That is quite evident. The truth is always evident—when people bother to tell it. Mr Marley's death was, as to the larger part, accident, as to a very small part, self-defence. You will have to give evidence at the Inquest to-morrow. That is all. And I hope by that time you will have recovered your self-possession. Take her away now, Signora, and tell Umberto I wish to see him.'

As he left the villa, Lucifero was content. All had come out surprisingly well. Mr Sampson had decided not to prefer any charge against Umberto. Indeed, for the publisher, the auguries were good. His plight had stirred a motherly interest in Natalie, and Lucifero judged that her first refusal of him might be by no means final.

Maria had, of course, behaved stupidly. But as well desire the world to stop in its course, as desire girls of seventeen to behave sensibly. Umberto, as soon as he got her alone, would beat her for lying to him, and would then marry her. Many a successful marriage has been founded on a good beating.

As for Mr Marley—poor Ralph Marley. That twentieth-century Byron, dreaming of who knew what? What conquests, what

triumphs, what Isles of Greece? Stumbling to his death, pushed
by a serving-maid.

Lucifero had reached the top of the steps. As he opened the
gate, he remembered some lines of Byron's which seemed a suit-
able epitaph for his successor:

> With more capacity for love than earth
> Bestows on most of mortal mould and birth,
> His early dreams of good outstripp'd the truth,
> And troubled manhood followed baffled youth.

Only one question remained unanswered. Was Lord Keaough a spy?